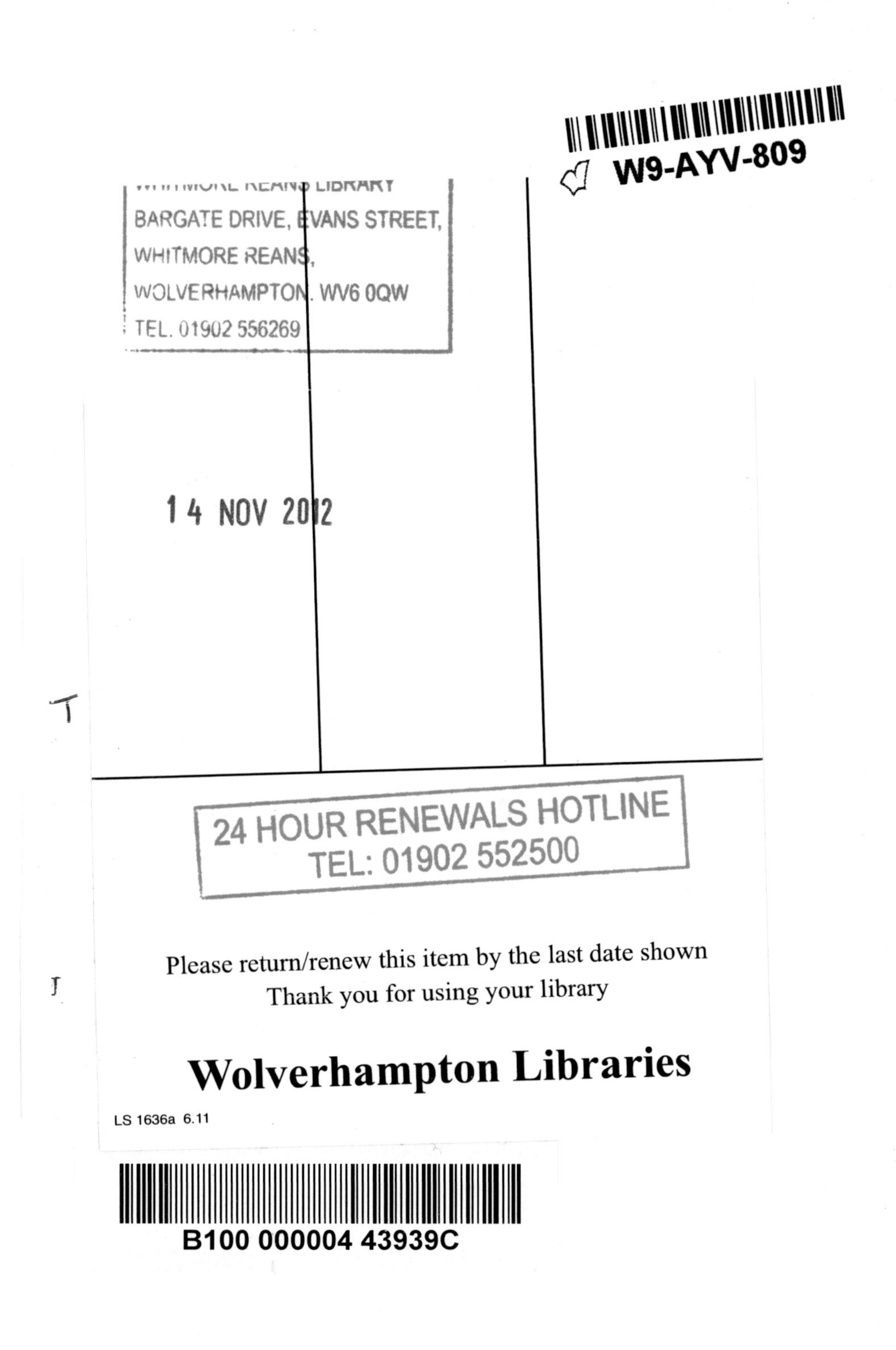

LOVE ALL

ALSO BY ELIZABETH JANE HOWARD

The Beautiful Visit
The Long View
The Sea Change
After Julius
Odd Girl Out
Something in Disguise
Getting It Right
Mr Wrong
Falling

The Cazalet Chronicle

The Light Years
Marking Time
Confusion
Casting Off

The Lover's Companion
Green Shades
Slipstream

LOVE ALL

Elizabeth Jane Howard

MACMILLAN

First published 2008 by Macmillan
an imprint of Pan Macmillan Ltd
Pan Macmillan, 20 New Wharf Road, London N1 9RR
Basingstoke and Oxford
Associated companies throughout the world
www.panmacmillan.com

ISBN 978-1-4050-4161-4 HB
ISBN 978-0-230-71143-3 TPB

1 3 5 7 9 8 6 4 2

A CIP catalogue record for this book is available from the British Library.

Typeset by SetSystems Ltd, Saffron Walden, Essex
Printed and bound in the UK by
CPI Mackays, Chatham ME5 8TD

For Frances and Sargy Mann

Before

PERCY

He looked at what he could see of her face – half turned away from him but unmistakably downcast – and tried another tack.

'It isn't that I don't love you. It's – all the other things.'

'Them. They've always been there.'

'Of course they have. But, unfortunately, they change.'

There was a short silence, after which she muttered reluctantly, 'How do you mean – exactly?'

'Don't sulk, Percy. This isn't easy for me, you know.'

She did look at him then, and he wished she hadn't.

'The children,' he began, 'are growing up. They're beginning to notice I'm hardly ever at home. They need a stable, affectionate family life. They need both parents . . .' He elaborated at length on this and felt better. Nobody, he thought, could have put the situation more clearly and responsibly.

'So you're not going on your location hunt. You're going to stay at home and sail boats on the Round Pond and take them to the zoo – things like that?'

'I have to go to Los Angeles. That was scheduled months ago. I told you. I just thought that as I was going away it would be better to tell you before I went. I could have just written, but I thought you'd rather be told face to face.'

'I see.'

'You do begin to, don't you, Perce? You do realize it has nothing to do with what I feel for you?'

'Yes. At last I do.' She pushed away the coffee cup and folded her hands on the table. 'We fancied each other for a while and now you've changed your mind. That's all. It's not your fault. I was pretending as much as you were.'

His eyes, which had been fixed on her, flickered, but he said breezily, 'What on earth do you mean *pretending*?'

'That we loved each other.' She decided it would be safe now to light a cigarette without her hands trembling too noticeably.

'But, darling, you've missed the point completely. We do love each other. Well, I know I do. I was just trying to explain why one can't always have what one wants. However hard it may be—'

'I haven't missed the point. Love doesn't come into it. That's not too hard, is it?'

There was a pause, and then she added, 'I mean if you really loved somebody—'

He got up from the table.

'I'm sorry. I'm not up to your notions of love.' He said it in the tone men she had known employed when they told her how afraid they were that they hadn't got time for reading novels.

'Poor you.'

She watched his look of startled exasperation. Without the beard, she thought, he'd have a weak face. Unexpected pain rose in her gorge and she swallowed it. The thing to do was to get out. I can stand, she thought. She felt distinctly shaky.

He was holding out his hand to her. 'Darling. Don't let's spoil our last weekend together. We've got the whole of today – and tonight. Lynne is staying with her mother for Sunday lunch so we've got until about four tomorrow.'

His tone now was indulgent. He was offering her a special treat. She'd fallen for these spasmodic goodies for nearly two years now.

On her feet, but holding the table with one hand to be on the safe side, she looked at him directly as she said, 'I'm sorry.

I'm not up to your notions of lust.' And then, to be fair, she added, 'Poor me.'

And that was it. She'd gone quickly to the bedroom, collected her things and left.

She'd walked through streets lined with dark red blocks of mansion flats to the 74 bus stop on Old Brompton Road and waited for a bus that boasted an appearance every twenty minutes, standing for what seemed like hours in the dank, still air. It was one of those colourless, windless days people pretended was the beginning of spring. The bus, when it came, was almost empty, and she went upstairs and found a seat at the front. Here, with warm tears sliding down her cold face, she went over the whole scene again.

It had been a shock. People cry from shock. But it wasn't really, because from the moment they'd met that afternoon – as usual at Earl's Court station – she'd sensed something was wrong. Usually when they met he'd give her a meaningful, casual kiss on the cheek and take her hand, leading her through the streets to the gloomy little ground-floor flat that was lent to him by a friend for these occasions. Today he'd been waiting for her. Usually she waited for him. And there was no kiss. Instead he presented her with a small bunch of pink and white striped tulips. She had started to thank him, but he was already striding ahead. They stopped at the pâtisserie for croissants and a packet of coffee – they always began their weekends with breakfast.

When they finally reached the flat, the first few minutes were spent switching on lamps – daylight penetrated enough to navigate the room without bumping into furniture, but no more – putting on the kettle, so encrusted with scale that it took an age to boil, making the bed with their linen kept in a cardboard box for the purpose, and lighting the gas fire in the sitting room. They usually breakfasted in the tiny kitchen that contained, besides minimal cooking equipment, a small, rickety table and two chairs with tubular steel legs that were arranged at an angle almost designed to trip one up. She'd put the tulips in a large jar that had once been full of pickled onions. During all this they'd hardly spoken. She reflected now that she hadn't even missed their customary hug, when he would enfold her in his arms. She did ask how his week had been and he'd replied, 'Awful. Just utterly frustrating and awful.' He didn't ask about hers.

When the coffee was made and they were drinking it, she'd told him about giving in her notice.

'Why? Why did you do that?'

'I just got rather sick of it. It wasn't leading to anything.' Even then she'd not been honest.

'So what will you do? Get a job with another publisher?'

She'd taken the plunge. 'Well, I thought – yes, I expect I shall eventually – but I thought that perhaps I might take a holiday first.' And when he didn't react, she added, 'I thought perhaps I might go out to Los Angeles with you. I mean, nobody need know.'

And that was when he told her. He simply couldn't go on as they were. It was tearing him to pieces, sapping his energy, making Lynne unhappy, and was just the wrong thing to do. He was unable to concentrate on his work – was starting a new series, and as the ratings hadn't been great for the last lot he knew this was his last chance. And he hadn't written a word of his second novel for months now, and felt terribly guilty. Altogether, it was time to make a break.

There had been a silence during which she could neither speak nor look at him. Then, when he started all that awful rubbish about loving and went on to even worse stuff about 'stable, affectionate family life', it was as though he was ripping apart the cosy, candle-lit veil that had enshrouded them and exposing all the romance, the secrecy, the excitement to such a harsh light it seemed to her their entire affair dwindled, became as pallid as a fire in full sunlight. He'd just wanted a bit on the side: love had never had anything to do with it. She tried to envisage a stable, affectionate family life, and failed. It was something that had never come her way.

But I went along with it – with all of it, she thought, as the small flurries of hatred for him changed course and she recognized herself as every whit as dishonest as he, full of craven pretence. She hadn't even wanted him very much. She'd wanted other things she'd thought could be exchanged for sex, and long after it was clear she wouldn't get them, she continued to play the part of the romantic second string, prepared to accept any crumbs of time and attention he could bestow. So, really, she had been just as much out for herself as he, but her hopes were far more unrealistic and high-flown. He'd simply wanted a jovial extra-marital affair, while she wanted – what? A great love? A romance of heroic proportions? So I picked up, or let myself be picked up by an overworked married man with two children and a wife with post-natal depression. I pretended he was a great writer because he wrote a novel I couldn't understand, though ever since I've known him he's done nothing but write the Inspector Starkey stuff for television.

But even as such acrid thoughts occurred, she remembered snatches of their earliest times together – their first dinner at Ciccio's in Church Street when she'd discovered how difficult it was to eat spaghetti if you never took your eyes off the other person's face. In the taxi afterwards, he'd asked if he might come home with her, but she'd said no, she lived with her aunt. And before he even said anything, she realized how stuffy it sounded.

'It must be rather restrictive,' he'd said eventually. 'I mean, aunts don't really go with the swinging sixties.'

He'd dropped her outside the house in Maida Vale, told the cab to wait and taken her arm. 'Adelaide Villa,' he read. It was painted in black on the glass fanlight. 'Is that your aunt's name?'

'No, she's called Florence.'

'Nearly as good. An aunt called Adelaide or Florence living in Maida Vale is pretty good, I must say.'

It was probably the first of what she now recognized as a number of crass notes he'd struck. 'Maida was a battle.' But he turned her chin, kissed her, caressed her cheek with two fingers, and made her incapable of thought.

'I'll ring you at your office,' he'd said. 'Sleep well, Persephone.'

But she hadn't slept much that night. She'd locked the front door and crept quietly upstairs. Her aunt's bedroom door – ajar, the light on – couldn't be ignored.

'Shall I come in and say good night to you?'

'Why not?'

Floy was sitting up in bed wearing her navy roll-necked jersey – the room was freezing – and her scarlet mittens, the bed littered with seed catalogues, which she marked up. She was smoking as usual, a very small cigar. Marvell, her large black cat, lay stretched on his side across her legs. 'Marvell was delighted you didn't come home to dinner. He's rather partial to haddock,' she'd said after her cheek, as cold as an apple, had been kissed.

'I hope you ate your share.'

'Enough. Food is only a hobby with me; with Marvell it's a profession.' She patted the bed. 'Sit down, dear one, and tell me.'

'What?'

'What did they say when you told them?'

'Oh – that.' For a second she'd been aware of a sharp glance over her aunt's half-spectacles. She moved some catalogues to sit down. Marvell instantly got to his feet and plodded about over the papers. It took him a long time to find anywhere as comfortable as he had left.

'They didn't seem to mind much. But I wasn't doing anything interesting. Anyone could do it.'

'And so?'

'I thought I'd try for a job in publishing.'

'Good idea. But have a holiday first. Once you get a job you'll have to work for months before you get another.'

'Floy. A holiday at this time of year? I loathe snow and everywhere else would be too expensive.'

There had been a short silence, and then Floy, as she had known she would, said, 'You could go and stay with your father.'

'I could, I suppose.' Then she'd remembered earlier times when she had, and said, 'I couldn't really. I know you don't believe me, but he doesn't want me around, honestly.'

'He always says he does – when he writes to me, anyway.'

'I know, but it doesn't mean anything. He's being dutiful. I'm just another duty. And I really hate diplomatic life. I don't know which I hate most, the sitting-down parties or the standing-up ones. The only time I feel sorry for my mother is when I think of her putting up with all that.'

'She didn't put up with it for very long.' Floy, who had never married, disapproved of others taking marriage lightly. Then, as though she'd felt she had been harsh, she'd said, 'You could, of course, pay your mother a visit.'

'I don't even know where she is. The last I heard of her she rang me from the airport to say she'd met a wonderful man and was going to India to *help* him in his *work*.' The emphasis denoted her bitter incredulity at such an idea. 'She doesn't care about me either. She's too Greek about me not being a boy. But I'll think about it,' she'd finished untruthfully, as she got up from the bed and met Marvell's implacable gaze.

'Well,' said Floy, having been kissed for the second time, 'I want you to know I shall only relinquish you with a low growl to the absolutely right person.'

Tears had rushed to her eyes, and she'd left the room quickly.

She remembered now, as the bus trundled through a park,

that she'd lain awake for hours, wondering whether perhaps she had met the right man.

At their next meeting, she'd gathered he was married. He didn't actually say so, but the implication was there, and when she asked him outright, he gave the impression he'd told her already.

It seemed to her now that the whole relationship had been sustained by her wilful dreams: she wanted to belong to somebody, to be first for them, wanted somebody to admire and appreciate her – he'd certainly done that when they were in bed. His marriage and all it entailed should have warned her, but she'd translated it into a mythological – as it now seemed – love in which she was totally and selflessly immersed. The hundreds of hours of suppressed unhappiness and bleak uncertainty had exploded at his complacent remark about her notions of love. It was absolutely true: he wasn't up to it – never had been. She was crying again, and furious with herself for it. It wasn't simply that she'd been taken in but that she'd been determined to be taken in.

So now, she conceded, she was pretty well back where she'd started two years ago, having resigned from the publishers, just as she'd left the BBC. The only difference now was that she wasn't going to some party vaguely connected with work – like the party where she'd met Denis – she was going home to Maida Vale and her aunt. Floy would know, at once, that something was wrong, but she never asked questions. When she'd told Floy the previous evening she was going to quit her job, yet again, and might be going on a holiday for a bit, Floy had simply said, 'Good. You haven't had a decent holiday for years.'

Marble Arch. Time to change buses for the one that went up Edgware Road.

She'd left the house so early that morning the post hadn't arrived; a postcard and a letter were waiting for her. Marvell was sitting on them, but he rose to his feet at the sight of her and jumped off the table with a heavy, papery thud that made the letter and card skid off the table. As she bent to pick them up, he head-butted and uttered high-pitched offended remarks that she knew were almost certainly about food. His saucer, placed just outside the little room to the right of the front door, was empty. Floy must be out.

'You'll have to wait.'

The postcard was from a girl in the office who had recently married, and was honeymooning in Saint-Tropez. The letter was from her father.

As she wandered through the hall into the sitting room, the Morris willow-pattern paper gave way to the grander honeysuckle one – grander, but not cleaner. Floy had put up the wallpapers years ago when she bought the house before the Second World War and they had become foggy with dirt – except one small noticeably cleaner square to the right of the fireplace where she had rubbed the paper clean with bread. The experiment had been unexpectedly successful but, with rationing, she refused to continue as she said people, or even birds, needed the bread more and to use it on the wall was rather Marie Antoinette-ish. The rest of the room was much of a piece, in a state of gentle decay, curtains faded where the sun had caught them and the upholstery worn and heavily scarred by a succession of cats. The lampshades were of parchment darkened by the smoke of cigars and hand-stitched at the edges with what looked like bootlaces. There was a beautiful, slightly foxed landscape mirror over the fireplace and pictures on the walls, mostly bought by Floy's grandparents, with the exception of an enchanting Gwen John drawing of a cat cleaning itself, and an incandescent Italian landscape by Edward Lear, both of which Floy had acquired. The carpets were hazardous, with huge rents ineffectively cobbled together at intervals. The room was far too cold to settle in without a fire, and she opened the door that led into the conservatory.

This large octagonal room had been the reason Floy bought the house, and over the years she'd had it double-glazed and installed a large factory gas-heater, which made it the warmest place in the house. The air was kept damp by a humidifier, and the warm chlorophyllic air, when she went in, was both exotic and comforting. Floy had also acquired a black-and-white marble floor: 'Happened to be passing over Primrose Hill when they were demolishing some nice old houses to make room for some dwarfish monstrosities for very rich and, I imagine, very small people to live in. The builders said I could have the marble if I removed it pronto. It took seventy-two trips in the Austin but, my word, it was worth it.'

She'd then found – come upon – two ex art students who were interested in laying a marble floor. 'Why?' she'd asked; it didn't seem to have much to do with art. 'Never done it before,' they'd replied. 'I thought that was such a good reason, I let them get on with it. Beautifully laid to a fall so that all the water drains away. It cost me sixty pounds and a packet of cigars for the whole job.' Floy loved telling people about her floor. There were zinc trays on stilts all around that enabled her to tend seedlings at waist height. Percy couldn't remember a time when Floy hadn't been acutely rheumatic. The trays were filled with peat or gravel into which pots and seed boxes were plunged. An unusually large old stephanotis meandered up the wall, which was painted white, its waxy flowers adding their scent to the green air. She sat down in one of the two basket chairs beside the small round iron table to read her post.

Then I'll get out of my mistress clothes and make some coffee. I might even have another bath, she thought. The clothes were simply not wearable at home. Thin black stockings, no vest – far too unromantic – a tight black skirt that showed her knees, fortunately elegant, like her mother's, and a tight but thin scarlet polo-neck sweater that Denis had bought for her. Her feet hurt. He liked high heels but she didn't have the pointed Gothic toes required. She kicked off the shoes. It's amazing what we put up with, she thought, all the clothes we're expected to wear, from school uniforms to bridesmaids' dresses. A mistress's outfit was just another. She thought of Jackie in her bright white satin and garland of improbable rosebuds over her veil, and turned over the glossy postcard, all turquoise and green and glaring sand. There were nine exclamation marks in the short message, which suggested Jackie was having a super time and had a sense of humour about the drawbacks. 'Stephen's sunburned! And an insect bite in an awkward place!'

Percy felt she'd leapfrogged from bridesmaid to mistress without a second glance at the altar. But her next move seemed utterly uncertain. It was her fault. She could have stayed with the publishers, copy-editing, graduating in time to actually being an editor. But it had been a lonely job, not much better than typing at the BBC. Worse than doing something boring was not knowing what else to do. She recognized then that, without even giving internal voice to it, she had secretly set her heart on the clandestine trip to Los Angeles with Denis. She hadn't stopped for a minute to think whether he'd agree to it. She'd just assumed that if she made herself free, and paid for herself, he'd be delighted to take her along. It was only going to be three weeks, but it had seemed like a turning point beyond which there had been no need to look. Now here she was on the brink of everlasting uncertainty – people of twenty-three were known for lasting nearly three times as long.

It was appalling to have got this far and discovered no special gift or vocation, no serious love. She was drifting, which she remembered her father saying her mother had always done. Was it Greek to drift? Would she end up like her mother after the war – a kind of emotional gypsy travelling from one man to another, one country to another? Very unlikely, she thought. I don't have the looks for it. All she'd inherited from her mother was pale olive skin and black hair. The lustrous velvet eyes, the rich mouth, the figure that, over the years, could only be described as voluptuous, the riveting profile she remembered being transfixed by as she once sat beside her mother in an aeroplane, all this had passed her by. Instead, she'd inherited her father's long, narrow nose, his wide mouth with lips that had never seemed a pair, the upper one thin, turned up at the corners, resting on a slightly fuller, less shapely, cushion. She knew all this because, in her painting phase, she'd tried to make portraits of him, mostly from photographs. She remembered describing his eyes – when she was struggling with them – as lying-down diamonds. Like hers, they were a pale grey-green, and had a wary expression, as though at any moment they might see something unexpected. The pictures she'd tried to make of him had been as much an exploration of the idea of a father as it had been about wanting to paint. It hadn't lasted long.

The one thing her parents had in common was their lack of enthusiasm, expressed in different ways, about being parents. Her childhood, spent everywhere but never anywhere for long, had shown her this, slowly, painfully, but ultimately with great clarity. They had surges of guilt, of course, when they moved her to a school nearer to wherever one of them looked like staying for a time; quite early on, she had boarded, which, she thought, made their whereabouts irrelevant since visits from either were rare. So, after the disastrous term at the Anglo-American School in Athens, living with her grandparents in their claustrophobic little flat, she'd been sent to England, when she was nearly twelve, to 'a school called Cheltenham in a part of England called Gloucestershire'. That's what she told the air hostess who had been deputed to look after her on the plane. Her aunt was meeting her, she'd answered when asked, and the hostess, who had yellow hair and blue eyelids, had said that would be nice, wouldn't it?, and she'd replied that she didn't know. But she did. Nothing was nice. She was always in the way or, like now, being put out of it. No doubt she'd shortly be in her aunt's way, and that would continue until she was old enough to fend for herself.

It hadn't turned out like that at all. She had come through Customs – nothing to declare, of course – and a small woman, who looked like a pirate and wore dungarees, gum-boots and a red woolly hat, had stepped towards her. 'Persephone, isn't it?' she'd said. She pronounced her name in a funny way. 'Perse*phone*,' she'd answered. It was a Greek name. Her grandparents, of course, said it correctly. Her father called her Percy, and her mother Treasure.

'Well, I'm your aunt Florence, but you may call me Floy.'

She sat beside her aunt in her dirty little van, the back of which contained sacks full of something mysterious and three trees. She was silent, listless and wary. Though there was nothing to look forward to, there was always the chance of things getting worse.

'Are you taking me straight to school?' she'd asked, after a while.

'Certainly not. We're going to my house. You don't have to go to school for a week. That's good, isn't it?'

'I expect it is.' She made an effort. 'Why do you have trees in the back of your car?'

'I'm a gardener. But I shan't be working much this week because I want to make the most of you – Perse*phone*.'

'*Ef karistó*,' she'd answered automatically. Her grandmother had always impressed upon her the need to be grateful and polite.

'How is your father?'

'He's in Caracas.'

'And your mother?'

'I don't know. She wasn't in Athens. I was with my Dimitriou grandparents. My grandmother has something wrong with her heart, so I couldn't stay.'

'Oh dear. Is it sad to leave Athens?'

'Not particularly,' she had answered stiffly. Either everything or nothing was sad. It was difficult to explain to a stranger.

'Well, I'm glad you've come to me.'

'Just for a week.'

'Well, the holidays too, I hope. At least, whenever your parents can't have you.'

She hadn't replied to this. This aunt obviously subscribed to the notion that her parents wanted her, which was only a small step away from wanting to be rid of her.

When, eventually, they'd arrived at the house, which was set back off a wide road down which lorries and buses and much other traffic thundered, she read – as Denis had that first night he brought her home – that the low double-fronted house was called Adelaide Villa. It looked very large, which it was, compared to her grandparents' flat, and she wondered briefly whether, like her father's various houses, it would be full of secretaries and servants, though nobody came out to greet them and carry her suitcase, which she had now humped up the steps to the front door.

'Darling. Let me take your case. Is it very heavy?'

'Not particularly.' She flinched at the endearment, but the case wasn't heavy. She was, by now, used to leaving things behind, usually with little choice of what they were. Grown-ups' view of what was necessary to pack never coincided with hers, and the consequences had often been hard. She no longer argued, insisting only upon three possessions: a much-battered sheep with boot-button eyes, a leather writing case that zipped up and had her initial on it, and her set of Jane Austen, six volumes in red leather, embossed with gold, that she had been given, she now remembered, two years earlier by this same aunt. Before Austen, it had been *The Secret Garden*, *The Brown Fairy Book* and *Black Beauty*. But after these necessities, she allowed whoever was currently in charge of her to pack what they pleased.

Her aunt unlocked the door and they stood in the hall, which had a lot of doors and a staircase on the right-hand side. A large marmalade cat sat on the hall table beside a bowl of cyclamen. He rose politely to his feet when he saw them.

'Do you like cats?'

'I do, quite. Shall I take my case up to the spare room?'

'We'll go up together.'

It was a small room, looking on to the roof of a large glass greenhouse and thence to the back garden. It had wallpaper with wild roses on it and a dark red carpet.

'This isn't the spare room. It's your room. The spare room is for guests. You are family.'

This had confused her. Her aunt sounded kind and she feared kindness. When she gets sick of me it'll be another story. She didn't want to have something to lose. She's just saying that because people say these things without meaning them. Anyway, she was being packed off to boarding-school in a week, so what was the point of a room of her own?

'I usually stay in spare rooms,' she said, and turned to stare out of the window.

But even during that first week, she realized that Floy, as she learned to call her, was different from other people. The discovery had been both exciting and painful. It was as though, she thought now, her fingers were frozen and somebody had held them up to the fire of Floy's attention, and while they ached, she couldn't resist being scorched by it. She also tested it on the mornings they spent buying the horrible school uniform and the evenings sewing on the nametapes Floy had thoughtfully ordered. To begin with she'd felt passively unconcerned about what she had to wear, but as she noticed Floy was anxious that she should, as far as possible, have what she wanted, her attitude became offensively indifferent. She shrugged and sulked and didn't answer when Floy asked her if something was comfortable or fitted. Later, during a silent cab ride back to Adelaide Villa,

Floy said that perhaps they should have one more sortie 'to buy you something pretty that has nothing to do with school'.

'There's no point—' she'd begun, and found she was crying.

Floy gave her a handkerchief and talked about how frightening it must be going off to a new school and how she understood homesickness. Percy stopped crying at once to stare at her aunt. 'Homesickness? How can I possibly have that? Why on earth do you think I would?'

'I just thought you might. Never mind.' And the rest of the journey passed in silence.

Back at the house, she had stomped upstairs to her room without a word. 'Tea will be ready in ten minutes,' Floy called after her.

She decided to stay in her room and wait for Floy to come and fetch her. When she finally – through hunger – descended, tea had disappeared. Floy wasn't in the kitchen or in the sitting room. She found her in the conservatory watering her plants.

'You didn't tell me tea was over.'

'I told you when it would be. I thought you didn't want any.'

'I do.'

'Oh dear. Well, supper will be in an hour or two.' And her aunt turned back to the plants.

It had felt as though it was all getting away from her again, as though she was losing Floy's attention and care, which, she grasped vaguely, were important to her. Floy asked her, quite calmly, to move, so she could refill her can. 'Anyway, I'll be gone in seventy-two hours,' Percy blurted out. There was a silence. As a last throw, she said, 'I am homesick. I mean, I will be – at school.'

It wasn't true, but it worked. Floy put down the watering-can and hugged her. It was the hug that made her cry, not homesickness, but how could Floy have known that? She clung to her aunt and cried.

Much later, when they had had dinner, and played three games of bezique – a card game Floy had taught her – and had looked in the evening papers for a film she might like to see before she left, and after she had gone upstairs and had her bath and Floy had come to say good night to her in bed and she was finally alone, she had understood at last that she would be homesick after all. She didn't want to leave Floy or this house or this room – which had already begun to feel like *her* room – and go to yet another new place.

At the end of the week Floy had taken her to Paddington station and seen her on to the school train. Terror at the prospect before her and fear that she would break down in front of a crowd of strangers had reduced her to Arctic silence. Floy, having found the mistress responsible for the journey, and having introduced her as 'Perse*phone* Plover, my niece', gave her a quick kiss, saying, 'I think it's probably better if I go now. Unless you want me to stay?'

She said she didn't mind and managed not to look at Floy while saying it. Her aunt turned away and walked back down the platform; she'd watched until Floy was through the barrier and had merged into the crowds beyond it. Behind her the mistress, Miss Burton, said, 'Persephone, this is Joanna Harcourt. She's another new girl,' and she turned to see a small girl with fair hair, freckles so thick they were like pollen and eyes red-rimmed from recent crying. When they boarded the train, Miss Burton told them to sit together, and throughout the journey she'd listened to Joanna's account of what she had left behind: her pony, her brothers, her cat and the wonderful dolls' house her father had actually made her.

She didn't stay at the school for long – stuck it for five weeks – and had then run away. That, when she looked back on it now, seemed ridiculously difficult. The school was at least five miles from the station. She remembered telling Floy she had planned her escape carefully. In fact, she had merely chosen a

Sunday afternoon when fewer staff were around, during the free time between lunch and supper. She had already kept back half of the money Floy had given her and just slipped out after lunch, walked down beside the long drive so nobody saw her and into Cheltenham, then asked her way to the station. At Paddington, she showed a taxi driver all the money she had left – a little over three shillings – and asked if he would take her to Maida Vale. Luckily Floy was there.

She had stormed past Floy, once more, into the hall, and said, 'I've come back. I hate it so much there. I hope you won't mind,' and burst into tears, an uncontrollable flood.

Remembering it now made her cry once more and she laid her head on her arms and abandoned herself so completely she didn't hear Floy come in.

'Zephie darling. Zephie.'

So she told Floy about Denis.

'And now you have no job, no lover and no holiday. My poor Zephie, it all sounds most disappointing.'

She wanted to say it was far more than that, but really it wasn't – disappointing perfectly described it – or, rather, what it had turned out to be. She started to apologize for being so secretive, but Floy would have none of it. 'Nonsense. You're grown-up now. You have a perfect right to a private life. I'm only sorry it wasn't a nicer one.'

Later in the day she said, 'I've been thinking. I have rather a big piece of work in the West Country, and I could do with some help. Would you like to come and assist me for a week or two? A change is always good and it would give you some time to work out what you want to do.'

She thought she would. 'Where is it?'

'A house near a small town called Melton. A house with a very large garden, apparently, that is in a marked state of desuetude. My client wants advice and probably some drawings. You'll find yourself at the other end of a tape measure, and caring for Marvell. We're to stay in the house, so we don't have to struggle with hotels that don't understand travelling cats. And it's beautiful country – time you saw a bit more of that.'

She said, 'Yes, it is. I'd love to come.' She reflected gratefully that it was really the bracing affection of Floy, plus the incessant demands of Marvell for food and attention, that would take her mind off anything else.

FRANCIS

The council chamber, an extremely small room crowded by a long rectangular table, a heavily pargeted ceiling where younger spiders learned their craft, and four narrow, Gothic windows with thickly leaded diamond panes, only one of which could be opened, seemed to be full of ancient and much-used air. In winter it was extremely cold, since its only radiator was usually out of order. In summer it was hot and incurably stuffy. Some years ago a councillor had procured ten plastic chairs – designed for the most ingenious discomfort – so they would stack when not in use, but the narrowness of the room and the size of the table precluded this. The décor hadn't changed in living memory: ochre walls decorated by framed photographs of past town clerks above an olive green dado. Strip-lighting had been installed to supplant the three ceiling lights with green-glass shades.

Meetings were seldom attended by the full council, and on this fine April morning there were only seven present. The agenda looked mercifully short, Francis thought. He was one of the new members proposed – surprisingly, he thought – by Jack Curtis, a businessman who commuted to London most weekdays, and apparently never missed a council meeting. They had already got through 'Apologies for Absence', the position and size of a new car park, the present state of litigation about a much-disputed right of way, the preliminary plans for a new one-way street, and had reached 'Any Other Business'. Mrs

Quantock, folding her agenda as she spoke, clearly expected a comforting silence. Francis could feel Jack Curtis staring expectantly at him. He knew what he was supposed to say but couldn't find the words or, rather, he felt anything that might come to mind was certain to provoke uncontrollable laughter – his own probably – since the notion now seemed so unlikely to find the slightest interest or favour in a body devoted largely to car parks, street-lighting and rights of way.

'You mentioned rather an interesting idea to me the other day.' Jack was looking at him beadily and Francis realized that everyone else was now looking at him too.

'A festival,' he muttered. 'That's what I thought.'

'Oh, we already have one. In June. The flower festival has always been in June.'

'I don't think Francis was thinking of flowers, Mrs Quantock. You were thinking of something rather more inclusive, weren't you? At least, that's the impression I got.'

Why don't you tell them? It was you who were so keen on the idea, thought Francis. Aloud, he said, 'Actually, I was thinking of the arts. A festival about them.'

Margaret Steadwell, the assistant headmistress at St Anne's School for Girls, said, 'And what kind of art had you in mind?' She had heard he was an artist, and had no time for recently produced paintings, but her tone was carefully broad-minded.

'I really don't think we need another festival. To begin with, our finances wouldn't run to a further outlay.'

'Ah. But it need not result merely in expenditure, Mrs Quantock. There's no reason why a festival shouldn't be a remunerative business.' Jack Curtis was at last taking over, Francis thought with relief. He sat back, surreptitiously scratching his gnat bites and listened, unaware of how much Mrs Quantock and Jack disliked one another.

Festivals, Jack began, were proving an enormous tourist attraction. Look at Edinburgh, Cheltenham and Aldeburgh.

From being relatively small ventures just after the war, they had become of international interest, bringing revenue to the places in which they were held and providing events of great educational value – here he looked at Margaret Steadwell. A festival would put the town of Melton on the map, as it were. There would be employment for the young. Hotels, restaurants, pubs and B-and-Bs would all benefit. And he, for one, would do his best to promote such a scheme despite his rather over-full schedule.

When, interminable minutes later, the meeting closed, with the proviso that everyone consider the festival idea for discussion at the next council meeting, Francis managed to evade Jack by rushing past him down the first flight of stairs to the gents', into which he locked himself until he could hear no further sounds of the committee leaving the building.

HATTY AND MARY

Everybody went on and on about time and not being late and hurrying up, but none of them did it themselves. They stood or sat around not quite finishing their breakfast and talked about being quick and getting on and things like that.

'If you've finished, Hatty, put your mug and bowl in the sink and pop up and clean your teeth or we'll be late.'

Aunt Mary usually dropped her off at her school before she went off to shop in Melton, or sometimes went to the other school where she taught cookery. The staircase was straight out of the kitchen, and she'd trailed up half of it when Dad called, 'Have you fed Sonia?'

'Yes. No. I didn't need to. She still had a lot from last night.'

'Rabbits don't like nasty old wilted greens, as you well know.'

What did 'well know' mean? Either you knew or you didn't.

'Harriet, I said put your breakfast things away.'

She slid back down the banisters, picked her stuff up off the table and dumped it in the sink, which was full of last night's supper plates anyway. Poor Mrs Peabody would have to take everything out to run the hot water. A lot of things they told you to do were stupid.

Back on the stairs she met Francis coming down. 'Hello, hello, hello,' he said, and bent down to kiss her. He hadn't shaved for about three days now, but she didn't mind. He was her uncle, but he told her to call him Francis. He was her mother's brother, and the nearest link to Mama, who was dead from a car accident ages ago. Sometimes she would put him into a wig and lipstick and a long skirt and make him shave, of course, and higher up his voice to see if he reminded her of Mama, and sometimes she'd pretend he did, but mostly she couldn't remember anything. We don't talk about Mama much. She thought, probably, they did but didn't want her to hear. Sometimes she'd creep out of bed and sit on the stairs for ages when they were all in the kitchen and listen. But it was boring stuff about pigs or tomatoes.

Aunt Mary was calling her. She had such a kind voice that her telling you to do things didn't count as bossy. It was Dad who was the tyrant. 'Hatty, come on now, chop-chop,' whatever that meant.

Oh, well, if they didn't want her teeth cleaned properly that was that. It was 'curtains' as the old man who sometimes helped Dad always said at the end of everything. He told her 'chop-chop' was Chinese for 'Be quick'. Why not just say, 'Be quick'? You wouldn't catch her saying 'Chop-chop'. Honestly, they treated her like she was child.

They were shouting again. If you thought of a year, being five minutes late was nothing. If you thought of your whole life, five minutes was like an atom.

'I forgot Sonia,' she said in the car.

'It's all right, darling. I popped out and fed her.'

'The trouble is I don't really like her. She hasn't become a pet. And she kicks me.'

'Well, you did say you wanted her, and we said if you had her, you had to look after her.'

'I only said I wanted her because I wanted a cat. I don't want someone in a cage, I want someone free. And friendly,' she added.

'I know, sweetie. It's my fault. I can't help being allergic to cats, though.'

'What happens to you?' She'd had an idea.

'Oh, my face swells up like a balloon and my eyes get itchy and I feel as though I'm getting flu.'

'Oh.' She'd had the idea of being allergic to Sonia, but the balloon part would be difficult.

Aunt Mary said, 'Of course, people react in different ways. You know, if you really don't like Sonia, it would be better for her if we found her another home.'

She blushed and felt found out. Aunt Mary was quite right. She ought to see it from the rabbit's point of view. She hadn't thought about it. She felt tears coming to her eyes at her cruelty. 'It's awful, not loving someone, isn't it?'

'Don't cry, sweetheart. It happens to everyone sometimes.'

She blew her nose. 'It would be awful if it was everybody all the time.'

'Unspeakably awful.' They had arrived at the white gates of the school. 'Better run. See you at four.'

'I quite love her fur.' She was out of the car.

'Well, that's something. Off you go.'

Mary watched her trotting up the drive, waited until she'd turned to wave and waved back, before she put the car in gear. She did this every time. For five years now, ever since poor Celia had died, she had tried to do at least some of the things Celia might have done for her daughter. Originally she'd come to see Thomas through the funeral and help him find a nanny for three-year-old Hatty. They'd gone through two in less than six months, neither of them able to cope with the frequent awe-inspiring tantrums, Hatty's refusal to eat anything she hadn't chosen herself, the orgies of destruction, the bedwetting, and the bleak determination to do nothing she was asked or told to do.

The only person she would respond to was her father, but Thomas – shocked and shattered by his wife's sudden death – was in no state to do anything about his daughter. When he started drinking, he'd confided to his sister that Harriet reminded him endlessly of Celia, that he felt besieged by indifference, or something worse, and guilt.

And so, in the end, and after much soul-searching, she had sold her flat in London, resigned her job at Claridge's, and had a difficult farewell dinner with Adrian. With hindsight, she could see that that last meal was one of regret tempered by courtesy. 'You know,' he'd said, truth submerged by his uneasy goodwill, 'that you can always count on me. I'll always be here.' She had colluded: 'Of course.' It was five years now since he'd kissed her cheek before seeing her into a taxi. Since then, there had been one Christmas card and an invitation to his wedding to which she hadn't gone.

She'd kept her books, a few family pictures, sent some furniture down to the farm, and the morning after dinner with Adrian, she had driven down to be with Thomas and to set about bringing up this almost doubly orphaned little girl.

She arrived at a household disabled by grief. Thomas was barely speaking to the wretched nanny and was already drinking heavily to try to sleep at nights. Hatty was enduring her own hell of frenzied misery. The girl who cleaned for them had already left because of tension with the nanny. The house was a tip. Food rotted in the larder and fridge, and piles of laundry lay round the washing-machine. 'It really isn't my place to wash clothes other than the little one's things, Miss Musgrove.' And the beautiful pammet tiles on the kitchen floor hadn't been cleaned for weeks. Any movement in the house agitated small forays of dust that rose and resettled gracefully.

The nanny went within the week. Mary had fortunately already managed to find and employ a Mrs Peabody, the widow of one of the gardeners from their former family home up the hill who had babysat for Celia sometimes.

The extreme good fortune of this was made plain after the

nanny left for she soon discovered what little else could be done while looking after a three-year-old – let alone Hatty, in her state. She knew her priority must be Hatty, whatever the state of the house, however exhausting the tantrums. She spent every minute of Hatty's day with her and gradually they began to have conversations.

'Mummy's got dead,' she said one evening, in her bath, allowing Mary to soap her back for the first time. Her skin was as smooth as a pale brown egg.

'I know. It's very sad.'

'No. It isn't. It's very, very naughty, Miss Mary.' Echoes of a nanny.

'Is it?'

'No. I don't think things are naughty. I think they're bad.'

Mary lifted her out of the bath and enveloped her in a towel on her lap. Hatty wriggled and, looking her in the eye, said, 'How long will she be dead?'

The directness of this question, the confusion it implied, was momentarily confounding. She was stroking the damp curls from Hatty's forehead. Keeping her hand there she said, 'Darling, Mummy won't be coming back. When people die they don't come back.' She was still subjected to the grave, searching gaze. It was information that was wanted, the truth – no matter what. The least, the most, she could do was to give it.

'My mama died when I was twelve, a bit older than you, but I knew she wouldn't come back. She couldn't, because she was dead. It's sad for you, because of course she loved you, and she didn't want to leave you. She just had a horrible accident.'

'I know. In a car.' She said it wearily as though often repeated.

'I'm afraid that now you'll have to make do with me.'

'You're just Daddy's sister. He told me. Aunt Mary, he said.'

'Yes. But you can call me Mary, if you like.'

'I won't call you anything.' And she escaped from the towel

and lay naked on the floor, looking up at her aunt with challenging hostility. Mary picked up the towel, folded it, and left the bathroom.

A dozen times a day she'd been forced into these small psychological gambles. Sometimes they paid off, sometimes they made things worse. By the time Hatty was settled for the night, she was usually exhausted.

Then there was Thomas, her brother, someone she'd known – but not entirely – all her life. Their very early years were spent at Melton, in the decaying family house of that name. Thomas was two years older and she was in awe of him. By the time she was four she'd already begun to accept that his glamorous looks – curling auburn hair, large blue eyes and creamy, freckle-free complexion – had a marked and usually favourable effect on every grown-up, even, if only briefly, their mother. Her own appearance, at its best, attracted little maternal attention. Her hair was brown and straight, her eyes an indeterminate hazel and she was quite without the power to engage any interest at all, except from her brother. Thomas relied upon her whenever they were alone: she was the patient when they played doctors, the prisoner when he was a pirate, the humble subject when he was a king. She didn't mind: it was enough that he played with her, needed her and provided her with scraps of careless praise. He went away to school when she was seven, just as the war had turned, which caused her inexpressible anguish. She spent hours tending his ferret and the fat old pony they shared, and slept with his threadbare monkey clasped in her arms.

For the rest, she went as a day girl to a local school where, largely because she was shy and therefore lonely, she took to reading, a pleasure dependent upon nobody but herself. Her parents had sold Melton and moved to Kenya – to escape the privations of war – when she was six. She and Thomas had been sent to live with an aunt who inhabited the dower house on the estate and could not be ousted from it during her lifetime. The subsequent isolation drew Thomas closer than ever to Mary.

But holidays came round with comforting regularity. She learned to bowl to Thomas, to help him with his stamp collection and the rickety tree-house he made one summer and, later, to rehearse him when he was learning his part as Lady Macbeth in the Christmas play at school, to which their aunt took her.

They would go for long, cold, rainy walks together purely to get out of the house and, she remembered, he would discuss his future with her endlessly. A racing driver? Medicine? One of the services, perhaps. Or maybe an explorer, a diplomat, a tycoon. What sort of tycoon?

'I'll think of something.'

'Of course you will.'

In all the time she lived in that house, Mary thought now, her relationship with Aunt Gertrude had remained unremittingly impersonal, and, as she grew older, it became clear to her that, while taking her nephew and niece into her house was her duty, it had nothing of love or companionship in it for any of them. Aunt Gertrude lived entirely for herself, cocooned by the gratification of her small, but exacting requirements.

She only sent for Mary if family news demanded it. 'I'm sorry to tell you that your parents have died in Nyeri. A car accident.' Mary wondered now whether it was the fact that it had been Nyeri for which her aunt had apologized. It was the day of the Normandy landings, but she hadn't felt very much. Grief at being abandoned had long since congealed to resentment.

On a particular day, she remembered, the last before Thomas went back to school, they'd paid a ritual visit to their old home – to the exterior. The old man who had bought it was an irritable recluse and their one attempt to call on him had resulted in ignominious flight, pursued by a pack of yapping Jack Russells. They had wandered round the park, the glasshouses and lodge already crumbling. It was an evening in early September and she had sat in a glasshouse on a stand that had once contained tomatoes, while Thomas, on a precariously rotting ladder, collected wizened bunches of grapes from the enormous old vine that, unpruned and unchecked for years, had so invaded the place that any sunlight had been quelled to an aqueous dusk, and the brick floor was ankle deep in several autumns' worth of dead vine leaves that crushed to dust as she trod on them.

All those last evenings before his return to school were memorable to her. The next day always loomed and stained the present with premonitions of what would happen tomorrow: the last lunch stiffened by the presence of Aunt Gertrude, who always noticed and rebuked her for not eating, and the waiting in the hall for the taxi. 'Do you hate it?' she'd asked the year before. 'Not any more.' The taxi. His luggage. She would stand on the steps outside the house as he ran down to the cab and hopped nimbly in, too old to kiss her now. She would stand there until the taxi had cleared the bend in the drive and was out of sight before she crept back into the silent house and up to his room where all the effort of the day, to be calm and matter-of-fact, collapsed and grief invaded her heart. There was nobody to tell. Often, then, she would start writing him a letter with jokes or funny remarks.

There was a young lady from Ryde,
Who ate too many apples and died.
The apples fermented
Inside the lamented,
And made cider inside her inside.

But this particular evening was different because it was the first time her future was mentioned or, at least, the first time she had thought to mention it. A friend of his at school had a father who was a cabinet minister, and he had wondered whether politics might be the career for him, and after she had agreed this might be an interesting life, she had said, 'And me? What will become of me?'

'I expect you'll marry someone. Girls usually do.'

'But you told me you don't see the point of marriage.'

'For me, I don't. Catch.' A large bunch of grapes landed on her lap. It had three good ones in it.

'Well, why would it be good for me?'

'Girls seem to want love and all that – that's what Galbraith says and he knows a lot about girls, for various reasons. Don't ask me.'

'I wouldn't marry anyone unless I loved them. And there might not be anyone.'

'Well, you could always come and live with me.' He'd climbed down the ladder with the stalk of another bunch of grapes in his teeth and sat beside her picking out the good ones. 'I'll tell you a secret if you like. Only you mustn't ever tell anyone else.'

Silent with joy, she crossed her heart and hoped to die.

'My great plan is to make an awful lot of money, and then I'll buy back our house and we'll live in it for ever.'

Not only was her future decided in the best way she could imagine but, on top of that, in the house, their home – only it would be a hundred times better because they would be grown-ups in it.

'Mary, it's a bit girlish to cry because you're pleased about something. Good thing you don't go to my school.'

Hastily, she wiped her face with the hem of her skirt. 'I was just surprised, that's all.'

She had been nearly thirteen then, and Thomas was at public school. But nothing was ever as bad as it had been after that. She had a future now. She was going to live with Thomas. She had to prepare for it properly.

Aunt Gertrude, who was both greedy and demanding, had a

cook whose disposition was divided equally between her temper and her skill. She did not like children in her kitchen, so Mary wrote a note that she put under Mrs Fitch's bedroom door on her half-day.

Dear Mrs Fitch,

I know that you know everything about cooking, so please would you teach me some things about it? I will be very good and do everything you say and nothing that you do not.

Yours sincerely,

Mary Musgrove

PS I can only learn when I am not at school so I would have to learn after 5 p.m., excepting for the weekends.

Nothing happened. After three days it occurred to her that Mrs Fitch was not, perhaps, much of a letter-writer, and she braved the kitchen. Mrs Fitch was a very large person, with a rather surprising waist. She gave an insincere cry of alarm at Mary's approach. 'You'll give people a turn if you creep about like that.'

She wore a whitish apron and was mixing something in a basin.

'I'm sorry. I've come about my letter.'

'So I can see.'

There was a silence. Mrs Fitch took her fat white hands out of the basin and rubbed them together until most of what looked like sticky flour fell off.

'Well, what do you think?'

'What do I *think*? Haven't you anything better to do?'

'No.'

Mrs Fitch looked at her.

'Well, could I just watch?'

'You can *watch*. I can't stop you watching, can I?'

And that was the beginning of many hours in the kitchen.

She graduated from being onlooker to 'helper', fetching things, peeling and chopping, separating eggs, making a roux. Eventually she was allowed her own basin in which she learned to rub flour and butter together to make shortcrust pastry. Mrs Fitch seldom barked at her – teaching softened her amazingly. She even sympathized with Mary when things went wrong, as it did with her first attempt at chocolate éclairs. 'You've beaten the mixture too long after you put the flour into the hot water; the minute it's shiny, you stop. Drat it. Never mind. Do as little as you can, that's my motto.' She never used cookery books, but possessed one of her own: a black clothbound one, of the kind Mary used at school, in which she wrote recipes of which she approved in a spidery hand with very black ink. Once she discovered Mary wanted to cook properly to look after her brother, nothing was too much trouble. She had a very soft spot for Thomas, and always made him chocolate cake when he came home from school. By the time she was fifteen, she had become experienced enough to experiment.

She was seventeen when Aunt Gertrude began to die, which she did as she had lived: in slow motion. Thomas was by now at university in Bristol. Months of baked custards and beef tea ensued, and a series of nurses who inflamed Mrs Fitch's temper. If the nurses tried to help they were interfering; if they kept to their profession they were stuck-up. When Aunt Gertrude eventually died Thomas and Mary – as 'my only living relatives' – were each left five thousand pounds immediately, with another twenty thousand each when they reached the age of twenty-one. Their parents had left them nothing.

'Where are we going to live?' wondered Mary aloud, one day shortly after the funeral.

'I'll be in Bristol. Only in term times, though.'

'But where shall I be?'

'You'll have a nice little flat in London and I'll come and stay with you in the holidays.'

And so, some three months later, she had taken possession of the keys to a flat in Bayswater that consisted of two large rooms, a small bathroom and a smaller kitchen. It was on the first floor of an immense stucco house. The owner had included some carpet, a divan bed, a gas stove with a hole in the oven door, and two ancient gas fires. She had kept some of her aunt's linen and kitchen equipment, and these things, plus three pieces of furniture that Thomas had chosen – a walnut bureau, a round rosewood dining-table and four chairs – arrived that first day. The men had trudged up and down the stone stairs, asking where she wanted the furniture and six tea-chests, and when she'd said – foolishly, as it turned out – the front room, had stood about, clearly waiting for something. She found a ten-shilling note, which the older man pocketed with no sign of gratitude and they tramped away. She'd waited until she heard the front door on to the street slam, shut her own front door and leaned against it.

She remembered now how it had felt for that hardly imagined completely unknown future to be suddenly the present. She had her own place. She was, from now on, totally responsible for herself. But the flat was dirty and she had nothing to clean it with. And she had no food and would eventually be hungry. She was alone. It was late afternoon in March, already dusk, and she had no idea where the nearest shops might be.

All that first week, she struggled with the flat. The cleaning took for ever because she had to boil a kettle whenever she wanted hot water: the squat little boiler in a cupboard refused to light. She marched from the flat to the shops several times a day, returning with the endless pieces of equipment for ordinary domestic life. She lived on sandwiches, fruit and cups of tea, and fell into bed at night, asleep before she'd begun to make a mental list of things for the next day. But her exhaustion was tempered by increasing excitement. Thomas was seven, six, five days away, and the mere thought of his arrival – four days, three days – was so exhilarating that tiredness became almost enjoyable. This was what she had always wanted: to make a home for herself and Thomas. She stuck some thick brown paper to the hole in the cooker door. She bought furniture – a fridge and a sofa, both secondhand – and, the day before he was to arrive, a bunch of anemones, some candles and a bottle of wine.

That evening she'd managed to wash her hair in the kitchen sink and afterwards lay in front of the gas fire reading *Agnes Grey*, but the light was bad and her hair had dripped on to the pages. She repeatedly scanned the room, trying to imagine what Thomas would see when he first came in. She had unpacked the tea chests, and pushed the round table in front of the large window overlooking the street. She had taken the loose covers off the sofa and had them cleaned. There were no bookshelves, so she'd arranged her books against a wall adjoining Thomas's walnut bureau. The anemones glowed from their jug on the round table, but the walls were dingy and needed new paint; the carpet – once probably a biscuity colour, encrusted with cigarette burns and spills of an indeterminate but indelible nature – was uncontrollably dirty. Her attempts at cleaning it had made no difference. Thomas will do things, she thought. We'll do it together. Together they could do anything. She'd gone to sleep that night happier than she'd ever been in her life.

And it was lovely when he came. He was nice about the flat, was impressed by their first dinner in it – stewed rabbit and chocolate mousse – and when she started talking about her plans, was full of ideas, quite frightening ones, that would cost far more than they could afford. The carpet must go. They must paint the walls . . . yellow, he thought, and then they would have a party.

She had gazed at him, entranced, and agreed to all his schemes without a murmur. He'd grown his hair, which had become a darker shade of auburn with a lock that he kept pushing out of his eyes. His clothes were new and unfamiliar – a bright blue flannel shirt, open to expose his astonishingly white neck, randomly patched jeans, and what looked like extremely expensive chestnut brown boots. She asked him about Bristol, and he said it had taken him rather a long time to find his way around, but it was fine, a hundred times better than either of his grisly schools. There were lots of societies to join, and he'd made two friends, Vikram and Max. Max knew an enormous amount about French Impressionist painting and Vikram was going to be a film director so they went to the cinema a lot. What about work? He was reading archaeology. It was all right, but not exactly catching his imagination. 'I might change courses, but I can't do that till the end of the year.'

'I'll ask them to our party,' he said later, 'and they'll bring some girls. We'll have to get this place done up first.'

She'd been so happy to be with him, doing things with him, cooking for him, that it was over a week before it dawned on her he had no idea about money. He'd gone out 'foraging', as he put it, one afternoon, and later the front-door bell rang and she went down to find him propping up an enormous mirror. 'Look what I've found. Need your help to get it upstairs.' It was rectangular with a rounded top, the frame gilded with worn patches of red. 'It was dirt cheap, and we've got far too many bare walls.'

'How much was it?'

'Incredibly cheap – I can't quite remember. I bought a few other things I'll have to go back and fetch. A huge kilim rug to cover that awful carpet, some candlesticks and a chest of drawers. Don't know how I'll get that back. Suppose I could put it in a cab. It all came to a hundred and something.'

'How did you pay for it?'

'I wrote a cheque. You'll have to pay me back, though, because I'm madly overdrawn and the cheque will bounce.'

He'd spent nearly a hundred and fifty pounds. 'At the first shop,' he said, 'but I got a few things at another one. There's a fantastic street full of antiques and junk. I'm surprised you didn't find it.'

She had been painting all morning, finishing the ceiling, for Thomas had hired a ladder that was to be returned at the end of the week. Her neck was stiff, and it occurred to her, abruptly, that she would have liked to choose these things with him, and that if she'd been there he might not have spent so much. New to having a bank account, and naturally frugal, she had kept a careful record of all her money.

'I'm afraid you'll have to write a cheque for the other shop. He wouldn't let me take anything until he had one. It's on a piece of paper somewhere.' He searched and found it. 'To sundry goods,' it said, 'fifty pounds. Cheque made payable to T. Boatswain.'

She went to fetch her chequebook. Thomas overdrawn and not in the least worried. She had visions of him being taken away, arrested for debt and, at this rate, herself as well. Anger followed panic. He was older than her, he really shouldn't go spending her money without even asking, without giving her a chance to say, no, she didn't like that carpet or mirror. But she was more afraid of having a row with him, far more than any anxieties about debt or money for her Pitman's course.

'Have you found it?' He'd followed her to the bedroom.

She put the chequebook on the upturned tea-chest she used as a dressing-table and wrote out the cheque to him for two hundred pounds.

'What about the other man?'

'Thomas, we can't afford any more.'

'But you've got thousands.'

'I've got to pay for my Pitman's course and live on the rest of that money until I get a job. I've already spent a lot getting the flat straight. Anyway, you can't just buy things without asking me. When do you get your next allowance?'

'I don't know. Beginning of next term, I expect.'

'So you've got no money for the next four weeks.'

'I have. You've just given me two hundred pounds. Thanks.'

'Thomas, that's to pay off your overdraft. It's not spending money.'

'Are you seriously suggesting I should cart this bloody mirror all the way back to Portobello Road?'

The argument had escalated. She was mean, bourgeois and petty, and didn't care about his feelings. He was irresponsible, spendthrift, selfish and unprepared to face reality. It blew over as suddenly as it had flared up, and he remarked that they were behaving like an old married couple.

'What on earth do you mean?'

'Like people too used to each other. For better, for worse, as they say in films and things.'

'And this is for worse?'

'For all I know it may be for better. Anyway. We're having a pointless row because we're different. It always comes as a surprise to married couples too.'

'So, what do we do about it?'

'Compromise? Money's more important to you than it is to me, is how I see it. And you think I'm irresponsible. Of course, we'll probably go on trying to change each other. I just wanted to make your flat beautiful for you.'

'It's our flat, Thomas. It's your home just as much as mine. We've got nowhere else. I'm just afraid of losing it. I don't know when I'll finish the course at Pitman's. And I don't know what sort of job I might get when I do. At least you know your time at Bristol will be paid for.'

'Don't forget, we get twenty thousand when we're twenty-one. We could go round the world. Get a boat – have our own boat.'

'Thomas. You said we were going to try to buy back Melton with that money, mend the roof and take over the farm.'

'We could do both. Go round the world and then get the house. It can't possibly cost more than thirty-five thousand pounds, and I'll farm the farm. There's a place you can go to in Gloucestershire to learn all about farming and estates. I'll go there.'

His enthusiasm – his shining eyes, his certainty – infected her. Everything seemed possible. In the end, she agreed to keep the mirror and to inspect the kilim on the understanding that they bought no more. In the middle of shaking hands on it, he hugged her.

'You smell of ginger biscuits.'

'I ate a packet when I was out. Another ghastly extravagance. Where will it all end, I wonder?'

Not at all where either of them had expected, she thought, as reminiscence was cut short by her arrival at Abbey Court, the Edwardian pile where she taught cookery and the rudiments of domestic science to girls whose parents had enough money to pay for such establishments in return for keeping their daughters safely out of the way until the worst years of adolescence were over.

No, it hadn't turned out at all as she, and particularly Thomas – in charge, in those distant days, of their rosy futures – had envisaged. It was true they now lived on the estate, in the principal farmhouse, but as tenants, not owners. The family house, Melton, was now owned by a self-made millionaire who had recently bought it. There had been months of vans and lorries carting full and empty skips; builders, plumbers, electricians, decorators had ground up the lane that led from the lodge gates of the main house to the farm where they lived. Mrs Peabody had been complaining that the ruts were so deep she could hardly get her bicycle past them.

The owner was reputed to have moved in but so far nobody had seen him.

HUGO

'I'm sorry, darling, but it's not on. If I'd known that's what you were after, I could have told you ages ago.'

'Could you? Seems to me you've rather led me on.'

'Have I? *What* have I led you on to?'

'To thinking you liked me.'

'Of course I like you. Wouldn't have gone out with you if I didn't.'

'Well, more than like, then. Fancied me.'

'I do quite fancy you. Quite.'

'Well, then.'

'Oh, Hugo, don't be so dim. Fancying doesn't mean I want to spend the rest of my life with you. Spend the rest of my life in that horrible house with your mother. It's not even yours. I loathe the country anyway.'

'We could have a flat in London.'

'My flat, you mean. You couldn't afford one. You haven't got a penny. You may have a fixed address, but you've got no job, let alone a profession.' Before he could think of a response, she took his chin between two cool fingers and turned his face towards hers. 'Do you know what I think, sweetie? I think you were after my money. You're what they used to call a fortune-hunter. Well, that might have been OK in the eighteenth century, but not any more, it isn't.'

'Oh, Lord. Rumbled again.' He hoped she'd laugh, but she didn't. A sense of humour had never been her strong point.

'You can be poor and love someone. Perhaps that hadn't occurred to you.'

'It occurred to me, among other things. Where do you want to go? I've got to get back. I have a hair appointment at four thirty.'

'I don't know. Paddington, I suppose.'

'Right.'

But before they got to the first set of red lights, he realized he was in for more humiliation. Lunch had cleaned him out – in fact, he hadn't even had enough for the tip. She'd paid it. Now, like a fool, he had no return ticket. He'd expected to be staying in London much longer – at least until he'd patched things up with her. Just then he remembered he'd left his things at her flat, but when he mentioned it, she said, 'I thought of that. I got Marie to pack them. They're in the boot.'

Nothing for it, he had to ask her for the cash for a ticket and a taxi at the other end. What was more, he had to ask her now before they got to Paddington in case she didn't have enough on her. 'I'll pay you back as soon as I get home.'

'Don't bother, darling. By the way, I should tell you it was Angela Shannon who warned me about you last week. I don't think fortune-hunting in London is going to work. I should give it up. And if you really want to turn your house into a health farm or a hotel or something, you should go on a training course or work in one or it won't have a hope in hell.'

She burrowed in her bag and produced a five-pound note. 'There you are, darling. Have a good journey.'

'Why aren't you furious with me if that's what you think of me?'

'Oh. Because I'm familiar with the situation – it's happened before. One of the little hazards of being rich. And because I just don't care enough about you to mind.'

She leaned towards him and gave him a quick – extremely careless, he felt – kiss. ''Bye now. Your bag's in the boot.'

In the train he sat back, eyes shut, so he'd appear asleep. She didn't understand him. Of course he knew he'd have to go somewhere to learn how to run a health farm or hotel or whatever, but he didn't have the cash to pay for it. She must have known. All he'd wanted her to do was to come in on the enterprise with him, back it and him up. She knew all the right people, the ones who might put some capital his way, and he did love her. It wasn't just that she had money. She was extremely attractive, intermittently beautiful, even. She'd read economics at the LSE and had been in several jobs – a bank in the City, a travel firm and a glossy magazine. Hadn't stayed in them. Got bored, she said. But that was the point: she didn't *have* to stay in them. She had all the right connections. She could have been his business partner, as he'd suggested, but she had laughed. She's heartless, basically, that's the trouble, and having always had money, she doesn't in the least understand how crippling it is to be without.

He had more or less dropped her or the idea of being in love with her after Swindon – he rather admired his strength of character for that – but the question now was what next? He couldn't pay for a course, and while he'd considered the idea of starting at the bottom and working his way up, he'd dismissed it quickly. The idea of collecting shoes from outside guests' doors and returning them clean in the early hours, or at a kitchen sink washing up, or being shouted at by chefs pretty much ruled it out. Besides, what would it teach him? To clean shoes and wash up, for God's sake. He didn't even have to do that at home. He now retreated mentally into what the now absent Patsy called SSS or 'Second Son Syndrome'. It's pretty unfair, he thought, that Ashley should be Lord Yoxford when he spends his time on the other side of the world making pots of money with no interest in the house or estate. If he had inherited the title it would have been an entirely different matter. Ashley had inherited quite a bit of lolly too. If he'd got it, he would have turned the house into a paying proposition – converted the coach house for his mother, set to on the house, installed at least ten bathrooms, central heating, a swimming-pool for guests, a resident masseur and a few gym instructors. He could have made tons of money, had his pick of well-heeled women, widowed or divorced or even contemplating the latter, handmade shirts from Jermyn Street, shoes by Lobb, be a member of at least two London clubs, holidays aboard incredibly rich people's yachts, a villa in Tuscany. These fantasies were like a double brandy. They bucked him up for a bit, but euphoria soon dissolved into infinitely depressing reality. He wasn't Lord Yoxford, nor likely to be. Naturally he didn't wish his brother dead, just wished he'd pull his domestic weight more.

He spent the rest of the journey making notes for a letter to Ashley, outlining the problems and suggesting two courses open to him: to either come home and deal with the roof and the wet rot or send adequate funds to deal with them. Their mother, he could add, should also be regarded as a joint financial responsibility as she was virtually penniless. He hoped Ashley would see the situation was at crisis point and, knowing his brother, was fairly sure it would at least produce a no doubt inadequate injection of funds. Their mother missed him dreadfully, he'd put at the end. This wasn't true. She made no secret of the fact that she was slightly afraid of him. It was he – Hugo – whom she cared for and, naturally, she made him a pitifully small allowance, but no need to mention that.

As he got out of the train and carried his luggage over the bridge to the station yard, wondering whether anyone at home would have the cash to pay for his taxi, he saw a chauffeur-driven Bentley draw up to the spot where it said 'No Parking'. The chauffeur leaped out and a man brushed past him. He wore a charcoal cashmere overcoat and carried a slim briefcase, which hit Hugo's knee.

'I'm so— Aren't you Hugo Carson?'

'Yes.'

'Got a car coming?'

'No.'

'Let me give you a lift.'

The station was about five miles from Melton. Hugo was slightly in awe of him from their one previous encounter at Admiral Connaught's Easter cocktail party. There was a good deal of local gossip about this – brilliant, *nouveau riche*, apparently – tycoon. Hugo wondered uneasily what they would talk about. But it was easy. Jack Curtis asked if he'd heard about the festival of the arts in Melton and, on hearing he hadn't, proceeded to outline his numerous ideas for it. By the time the car had negotiated the rutted, weed-infested drive and drawn up in front of his home, Hugo had promised to be on the committee, get his mother and sister involved and use all his 'local contacts' to further the scheme, to help raise funds – how on earth? – and to write a piece for the local paper. Gosh! He thanked Jack, who insisted on first-name terms now, for the lift, and virtually staggered into the house stuffed with alarming, undigested ideas – alarming because he knew nothing about the arts, and undigested because no one had ever expected so much of him.

He lay in his bath before dinner – Betts had beaten him to it and the water was uninvitingly temperate – with fantasies of the citizens of Melton folk-dancing in the town square while he entertained several of the more famous artists who had arrived from London, even Paris or New York, or amused a jazz musician or television personality who might have opened the festival, or gave self-deprecating radio interviews that cunningly implied he was indispensable, or possibly – one must be realistic – met a talented, famous and wealthy artist who'd fall for him and be so impressed by the house she'd spend thousands restoring it.

Despite there being no vodka, a dinner of rabbit rissoles and stewed rhubarb, and the boring string of lies about his London adventures with which he regaled his mother and Betts, he felt more cheerful than he had ever felt on a first evening home.

ADMIRAL CONNAUGHT

It took Admiral Connaught a few painful minutes to get down the stairs from the council chamber. He had considered a stop at the gents' to be on the safe side, but some silly bugger had forgotten to unlock it so he padded across the car park to his old Vauxhall. The air outside was refreshing, little surges of breeze, south-south-west, that sent the white clouds scudding across a sky that had plenty of blue in it. A real April day with the trees about to break, and people's gardens bright with daffodils and forsythia. He lived three miles outside Melton in the village – it wasn't much more than a hamlet, really – of Bockhampton. Why on earth, considering how much they bored him, did he continue to sit on committees? Because they kept asking him, he supposed. They all seemed to think that a rear admiral added gravitas. And he kept agreeing to the parish council, the local Conservative Association, a couple of charities that weren't even local, and so on. It all came from a sense of duty – something he'd been afraid to shrug off when he retired – entrenched in the view that one did not do as one pleased until one had done everything possible that one thought right. But, really, he was getting a bit old for this sort of thing and perhaps at seventy he might be allowed to say so. He had loathed the idea of retirement, as much as he'd loathed his sea days ending and becoming chairborne in the Admiralty, but, of course, he had got used to both. A good deal of life consisted of getting used to things. He began to count up what he had got used to: living in a poky cottage with a thatched roof, rising damp and no headroom; Letty getting ill and never really recovering again, their travel plans and walking holidays in the Lake District going for a burton. When they went away – if they went away – it had to be in hotels, but not even nice ones because they were too expensive. Real walks were out. Instead he wheeled Letty about in countless chairs along innumerable sea fronts because, she said, the sea air was good for her and she knew how he loved the sea.

But that wasn't how he loved the sea at all – looking at its futile coming and going against a dull shore: he wanted it all round him, to have no horizon but the sky, to live with this illimitable quantity of water, whose beauty and power, whose moods – which could change so suddenly from tranquillity to ferocity – had entranced him from the first time he went to sea. It had been love from the beginning, not with the ships he'd served in and eventually commanded but the element in which they swam. Navigation was his strong suit and led, he supposed, inevitably, to his steady elevation. By the end of the Second World War he was a captain, but from there on the seafaring part of his profession had slowly declined. He taught, he sat in offices filled with paper, committees and other men like himself; inspections, courts martial, interminable arguments with the Admiralty, civil servants and others became his lot.

In fact the last time he'd gone to sea he'd been a kind of superior guest. He'd asked their lordships to allow him to board an aircraft-carrier on exercises. He'd known then it would be the last time. They were on the point of retiring him with the courtesy rank of rear admiral.

That was eight years ago, and since then Christopher had been killed in Cyprus, Letty had contracted rheumatic fever and the girl had married that frightful sod who, thank God, she was now divorcing. Providing her with somewhere for her and the baby to live and the expenses of nursing Letty had required the move from the Hampshire rectory to a smaller and cheaper house; hence Pear Cottage. He'd got used to most of this – no choice, really – but nothing he said or thought got him used to Christopher's death.

An ambush. They'd said the jeep he'd been travelling in had been blown up, killing all four occupants. There had been a brief bulletin about it on the six o'clock evening news, and by lunch time the next day he'd been told one of them was Christopher. His life was now divided into two parts: before Christopher and after Christopher. Curiously it was the BC part of it that caused him most grief. He hadn't realized how deeply, entirely, he had loved his son. He had never been a demonstrative man, didn't touch people easily or express his feelings, and for most of Christopher's early childhood he'd been away at sea. They'd met at various intervals as strangers. Each time he would find Christopher had grown or changed in different, mysterious ways: walking and talking, leaving for boarding-school and shocking homesickness, spending a school holiday with a friend in Ireland and upsetting his mother by doing so. Each time he came home confused by how much more he wanted to see the boy than his sister or – though he never dared to voice it internally – their mother. There was this increasingly lanky stranger, broken-voiced, acned, hands and feet more or less out of control, a stranger around whom, each time, he felt a dreadful paralysing shyness, and to whom he could hear himself talking in awkward clichés, and the ensuing silence until Christopher would escape.

He had tried to reassure Christopher that his choice to join the army was fine as far as he was concerned, but he also acknowledged he'd had secret hopes that his son would adopt his own service and give them something in common, something they could talk about. His regiment was sent to Cyprus as part of the Joint Truce Force, and on his last leave he had brought a girl home to lunch. She had come from London and Christopher had fetched her from the station. Letty had got Mrs Hayes in to roast a chicken and made a blackberry fool herself for the occasion. They'd waited and waited gently arguing about why he was bringing the girl. Letty said it must be serious or he wouldn't have asked her, and he'd said nonsense, Christopher could bring anyone home whenever he liked, it was a perfectly natural thing to do. Yes, of course it was natural, but it must mean something – and they had reached the point of acrimony. They decided the train must be late – or perhaps not, Letty had suddenly suggested. Perhaps Christopher had an accident?

The train had been late. A signal failure had held it up for nearly half an hour. Nobody's fault, but he remembered the girl couldn't stop apologizing. She had sandy hair with a fringe that nearly covered her eyes and a nervous laugh that seemed to have nothing to do with amusement. Christopher introduced her as Suzanne, then fell to a solicitous silence, helping her to food and drink, and otherwise gazing at her with a blend of encouragement and anxiety.

After lunch, Christopher had taken Suzanne for a walk, and he had washed up the lunch things with Letty.

'What did you think of her?'

'It doesn't matter what we think. It's Christopher's life and we have no right to interfere.'

He knew that.

'I can't see why asking you what you think of her is interfering.'

'I mean that whatever we think of her – those extraordinary clothes and arriving so late, that definitely off-white accent and rushing off after lunch – it's nothing to do with us.'

'No.'

'After all, it may not come to anything.' She'd begun laying a tray for tea.

'Darling, I'll do that. You have your rest.'

She protested – they might come back at any moment: she

didn't want Christopher to think she was inhospitable. But he took the cups from her and led her gently into the sitting room where he tucked her up under the old car rug on the sofa.

The funny thing was that, afterwards, he couldn't remember what on earth he'd done during that long last afternoon. He must have done the tea tray because he stopped Letty doing it and she'd wanted it done. He must have done something. Worry, perhaps? They were gone a long time. Christopher still had two more days' leave. There was plenty of time to see him. Perhaps he would have driven him somewhere where they could have a good walk and a talk together. Savernake, that would have been the ticket, take a few sandwiches with them if Letty didn't mind. But it was good Christopher had asked a girl home – natural he'd want to be alone with her. He could remember that thought recurring.

Anyway, they had eventually returned, just before six o'clock, giving Letty plenty of time to wake from her rest and start worrying about why they were so long.

It was during tea that Christopher announced he thought he'd go up to London, take the train with Suzanne, if they didn't mind too much. There was a show he wanted to see, and Suzanne had tickets for it. It seemed a shame to let her down.

Of course he must go. 'We shall miss you,' Letty had said. He hadn't said anything. Christopher had been with them for eight of the ten days. He had every right to spend the last two as he wanted.

He'd driven them to the station, waited to see them off, and after Suzanne had thanked him and got on to the train, he had, without thinking, made a clumsy lunge at his son and they'd cracked their heads together, knocking Christopher's hat askew. 'Keep in touch,' he'd managed to say, and Christopher – he would remember this for ever – had squeezed the top of his left shoulder. That was it. Christopher waved and the girl did the same. The train left.

Afterwards, after the news came, he fretted endlessly about that unspent afternoon, the time he might have had with his son, the last two days, which Christopher would probably have spent at home if it hadn't been for Suzanne. Poor girl, he was eventually able to think, she must be grieving – but he knew nothing about her, neither her full name nor where she lived, and she hadn't got in touch. So that was that.

JACK

Jack Curtis was eating a breakfast that his cook, Miss Pomfret, had arranged for him on a Regency supper table in his study. Since his divorce from Linda – finalized just before he bought Melton House – he had eaten most of his meals alone. The alternative, Mrs Fanshawe, was irksome. She was a perfectly good secretary, but she agreed with everything he said and her irritating little whinny of a laugh got on his nerves. Anyway, that maddeningly evasive interior decorator still hadn't finished the dining room. Weeks, he'd spent, searching for 'just the right' table. So Jack continued to eat in his study.

This room now had dark green damask walls, an off-white carpet and curtains so tasselled and swagged they reminded him of an opera house. There were built-in bookcases at each side of the splendid marble chimneypiece, which he was steadily filling with first editions of twentieth-century novels sent monthly by Hatchards. He intended to work his way through them, hoping thereby to improve his insight into human relations – an aspect of life his ex-wife said he knew nothing of. He read novels as others read about travels in Borneo, the antics of the characters as foreign to him as anything in Sarawak. Naturally, he had no more agreed with Linda about this than he had about almost everything else. He knew how to get people to do what he wanted and, what was more, usually without them realizing. While that implied insight – quite a lot of it, if you asked him – he knew something was missing. And for the last twenty years he'd worked so prodigiously hard he'd had no time to discover what it was.

He'd come a long way. His foster-parents, though not poor, were constantly short of money. Life in the semi-detached on Western Avenue had been frugal, routine and dull, and he had known relatively early that he couldn't settle for a normal nine-to-five office job. Practically all significant family conversations were about money or, more often, the lack of it. The boys at school frequently boasted about their father's cars, their pocket money, and holidays they'd been on. The poorer ones kept quiet, and he was among them. He made no friends because he couldn't bear the idea of them coming to his house. So perhaps it was logical that when he left home to make a very different life for himself, he saw it entirely in terms of making money. Money meant choice and glamour, power and glory: he just had to make some.

It took him more than twenty years to graduate from a spotted seventeen-year-old, fired after six weeks in his first job for a distinctly 'lacklustre department-store vacuum-cleaning demonstration' – the manager's phrase – through nearly six years in the RAF to working for an estate agent where he soon discovered he could sell property, however unprepossessing, and moved into a bed-sit, which he owned.

His initial ambitions had been modest: a decent job and his own place. But his social life was virtually non-existent. He went to the cinema and the local pub sometimes with one of the girls from the office. He also tried picking up a couple of girls randomly. One was looking for a companion to join her on a scuba-diving course at the YMCA – terrifying, and he couldn't afford it – and the other was on the game. He went to bed with her once: expensive and not worth it. He ought to get himself a car, a work colleague had said kindly; he'd stand a much better chance of finding girls if he had one.

Thereafter he'd set himself goals and achieved them: a car,

promotion to junior partner, a better car, a proper flat with a nice large room where he could give parties. The only party he ever actually gave there was for his foster-parents, Norman and Dora, when his foster-father had retired and they were moving to Bexhill-on-Sea. He'd seen as little of them as the relationship would allow. They had raised him and relinquished him without effort, and he was relieved they required no more of him. He'd felt, however, that the occasion needed to be marked and, during the phone call when they announced their news, had invited them to see his new flat the next Saturday, with the perhaps slightly less worthy secondary motive of showing them how he'd got on. They'd accepted, and at once panic set in.

Parties, during his childhood with them, had been few: once a year a few neighbours and one or two people from Norman's office and their wives came for drinks to 'Glencoe': gin and lime or sherry for the ladies and whisky for the men. Dora would make sausage rolls, shrimp-paste sandwiches and cheese biscuits, and all the furniture in the front room would be removed or rearranged. Everybody was punctual and conversation was minimal while Norman took the drinks orders and stumped to and from the kitchen with glasses, Dora pressed food on the guests and the women remarked on how Jack had grown. Nearly everyone laughed at nearly everything. He couldn't see the point, really, except that afterwards he'd get the leftovers for supper. The only parties he'd been to since he'd left home had been a stag night he hadn't enjoyed – his first hangover put him off whisky for life – and one or two half-hearted pub crawls, again with people from work, and one truly terrible evening an elderly client invited him to her hotel for what turned out not to be a party at all. The only people he could invite to his gathering were staff from Gore & Clinton: Humphrey, whom he'd succeeded, Tim, who'd been taken on to fill his place, and Amelia, the secretary he shared.

Amelia, a short, thin girl with earnest eyes and hair scraped back into a tight bun, turned up trumps. After he'd asked her if she could come for drinks and she'd refused because she was out that night, he'd had a moment of total despair and, noticing, she'd said, 'If you don't mind me bringing my friend, perhaps I could come.' He didn't mind at all. Would she help him? Together they went to the off-licence. Champagne, he thought, would impress. Amelia suggested sherry as well, in case. She bought very small fried pastry envelopes from an Indian shop she knew, olives, lumpfish roe to put on small biscuits and a bunch of yellow tulips, then went with him to the flat in the afternoon to arrange things.

'Who is your friend?' he'd asked, hoping it wouldn't be a drab secretary, but prepared to be nice to whoever it was since he was so grateful to Amelia.

'He's called Wystan Blunt. He's training to be an architect. I let him down last week so I couldn't again.'

At the time, he'd thought the party had gone off really rather well – in spite of Dora refusing the champagne: 'I've never been one for fizzy drinks. Surely you remember?' And Norman seriously advising Jack he wouldn't get the wear out of the new car that he would have from a Morris. They both commented about the flat in studiedly offhand voices – 'Very nice' – as though not terribly impressed, but he knew it wasn't so.

Days later, it occurred to him it had been very like their parties, which he'd thought so pointless – except for one thing. Amelia had become a friend, and because of her Wystan came into his life. Wystan was a small, wiry man, not much taller than Amelia, with ginger hair and dark brown eyes behind giant horn-rimmed specs. But he exuded friendliness on a scale Jack had never before encountered or even imagined. At first he didn't trust him, nobody could be so enquiringly and affectionately curious without some grim motive, but as the months went by and Wystan regularly sought him out, he looked forward more and more to their cosy suppers – sometimes with

Amelia, sometimes just the two of them. Wystan introduced him to French and Italian films, to the Proms and, even before qualifying as an architect, showed a talent for spotting the practical possibilities of any property on which Jack needed advice. When he qualified he married Amelia, who left the firm to help him.

By then Jack had set up his own business. It did well. He'd realized people buying property needed repairs and alterations and had gradually built up a small band of workmen: a plumber, an electrician, a plasterer, a joiner and a brickie, who worked for him under clients' directions. Soon their work was of such a high standard that it was easy to persuade wealthier clients to employ him. Costs were high, but with house prices rising and builders heavily in demand, he was well on the way to becoming rich. He'd got hold of even better workmen and paid them a third more than the going rate. He borrowed money to buy a site with planning permission for eight luxury flats, and bought a warehouse on the river, then converted it into offices with a luxurious penthouse flat and roof garden.

It was Wystan who found someone to design that roof garden. Jack interviewed everyone he employed, so he'd arranged to meet a Mr Plover on site. Only it wasn't a Mr Plover, it was a Miss – a funny old bird in her sixties, maybe, in a woolly hat and breeches with thick woollen stockings and highly polished brogues. She was extremely businesslike. She asked if he had anything particular in mind for the garden and, when he said he hadn't, observed that people usually said they wanted something natural and wild when they actually preferred something spectacular with low maintenance so she would recommend the latter. He agreed, and she whipped out a large steel tape and a small ivory compass from the baggy pockets of her tweed jacket and asked him if he would be so good as to hold one end of the tape.

'We have the measurements in the office.'

'I never rely on any measurements excepting those I make myself.'

She finished by drawing a rough map of the terrace in a small red-leather notebook with the points of the compass marked upon it. 'Perhaps I should make it clear that I like to plant the gardens I design. And to oversee the installation, of course, water, brickwork, paving and so on.'

'As long as you give me a price and stick to it, you can do as you please.' He liked her. She was professional and could, he'd sensed then, be trusted.

'Good, Mr Curtis. I promise not to take you for a ride.'

She'd made a first-class job. In fact, when he inspected it he could almost see the point of gardens. When he told her this, her small craggy face – the colour of a Rich Tea biscuit – lit up for a split second with a smile, and she'd responded demurely, 'We aim to please. I'm glad you like it.'

That had been a few years ago, and at intervals he had either employed or simply recommended her, and she had never changed. Once, he offered her a place in his set-up – a handsome retainer to work exclusively for him. She'd refused. He upped his offer and she'd still refused.

'I have a surfeit of clients whom I look after. I'm more than happy to work for you when it suits.'

And now she was coming to look at the formidably large and derelict gardens at Melton, a house he'd seen in *Country Life*, a mansion with a park 'in need of some renovation'. 'Not half,' Wystan had said when he saw it. They had toured the house, all three floors, and sat on the shallow, lichen-streaked steps looking out on to the hayfield that had been a park.

'What do you think?'

'A bottomless pit. It's a fine house,' he added, 'but it's been seriously neglected. Are you sure you want to live here? I mean, there are other grades of housing between this and Dolphin Square.'

He did want to live there. It epitomized his success – such a contrast to the Paddington bedsit – and, of course, he wanted to impress people and particularly himself. Also, the extensive works on a twelve-bedroom house would take his mind off his only recent failure – his ex-wife, Linda, whose defection had been a real shock.

During this bitter divorce, he'd progressed from righteous rage, resentment and weary malice to a drab world-weariness, a sort of melancholy awareness that all women were probably like her. It was when he met Christobel that he came to the uneasy probability that he'd been partly responsible. It was unsettling. He couldn't really work out what he'd done wrong. It wasn't as if he'd spent too much time with her; he hadn't refused to go to parties with her or to let her have parties, though they bored him totally. He'd put up with it all and still she wasn't satisfied, told him he was anti-social, had no interests, no understanding of people or the inclination to do so.

Linda got the house, and he moved into a service flat and concentrated upon making more money. His interests had broadened. He now had a stockbroker to deal with his investments. He opened two new branches of his estate agency, and began buying further pieces of land with building permission. Most evenings, back then, he was knackered, just about able to eat a solitary meal in a restaurant, slope up to the impersonal little box where his bed would have been made, his coffee pot and cup washed up and his bathroom left immaculate. It was efficient and it depressed him. At weekends he'd go to the cinema or a concert, usually with one or both of the Blunts, then out with them for dinner. He looked forward to those evenings particularly, though he wasn't up to initiating them. Neither of them ever said anything about Linda, but he knew they hadn't liked her. After the divorce they had a regular weekly date, the thought of which was enormously comforting. On one of these evenings, Amelia had finally said, 'Jack, isn't it time you brought someone along to join us?'

He caught himself smiling awkwardly, remembering the conversation.

She'd told him he was an attractive man, and lots of women would go out with him if he only asked, wouldn't they, Wystan? And Wystan had grinned uncertainly and said of course they would.

He'd gone back to the flat that night and looked at himself in the bathroom mirror. His hair – dark, with no grey – was receding noticeably from either side of his pronounced peak, and lines ran down from his angular nose to the corners of his uneven, but full lips. His eyes were of no determinate colour. He surveyed himself with a kind of dull anxiety, a shrewd petulance. Whatever he looked like he couldn't carry on like this, boxed up and alone.

It wasn't that he didn't meet people. He met them all the time. If a client wanted something unusual, he'd always see them, preferably where they lived, so he could interpret what they meant when they said 'spacious' or 'period'. Sometimes what they were after just wasn't available on the market at their price and he'd show them something else and usually persuade them it was better than what they had originally wanted. So it wasn't that he didn't meet people. He just didn't get to spend much time with them.

That was why, when Tom, a business associate, invited him to a small drinking club – 'It's quite select. You can't get in unless you're a member' – he'd accepted and found himself sitting in a basement in Soho. He had never been anywhere like it before, yet it seemed bizarrely familiar, just as he'd always imagined such places to be: the muted, rather orange lighting, the desultory strains of jazz played by a pianist on a battered upright piano in a far corner; the ceiling covered with something like red baize; the cluster of tables, like the one he sat at, huddled around a small rectangle of polished wood; the stumpy little table lamps with their fake art-deco shades of coloured plastic; the blue haze of tobacco smoke settling just below the ceiling. He was surprised by how quiet it was. There must have been at least thirty people in the room. People talked, but very softly, so the occasional outbreak of laughter sounded out of place.

The penny dropped fully just before Tom returned with their drinks. The company was mixed. There were girls – not so many of them, half a dozen or so, perhaps. The second he realized he hadn't thought 'women' – he knew.

Some hours later, after the pounds – a good many – had dropped, he'd wondered how on earth he'd done it. He'd gone along with all of it: impassively negotiating what was on offer and what it would cost; allowing her to manipulate him to some urgency when, at first, he couldn't get it up; the way his vanity had responded to her pretty run-of-the-mill clichés – 'You're a bit of a dark horse, aren't you?' All lies, of course, so why had he enjoyed hearing them? 'Come back, love, won't you? I'm Chris, just ask for me.'

He'd had no intention of returning, but he did – and asked for her. He went back about a dozen times. Though he didn't choose to accept it at the time, she massaged his ego, restored his sense of himself as a powerful man who could do what he liked. Then something happened that put an end to his connection with her. He'd ask her about herself from time to time, more out of courtesy than interest. Her name was Christobel, but Chris seemed more sensible in her profession. She'd been married. Divorced? No, he died, in the Suez crisis – he'd been in the marines. By now he'd told her about Linda and she'd usually listen with her customary sympathy to everything he said. It was during one of those sessions, as he listed his grievances, that it dawned on him unexpectedly that she wasn't really listening. She looked sad and nodded professionally, but there was no sincerity. He'd caught sight of himself too – the whole dreary cavalcade of self-pity he had poured forth to her, not just this once but several times. God, how many men had told her their wives didn't understand them? Of course, that – as much as anything else – was what she was paid for but—

'Of course, I'm sure she'd tell you a different story.' Even that sounded unkind. 'What I mean is she can't have been entirely to blame.'

'Oh, well, it takes two to tango, doesn't it, love?' she said equably.

'Sorry to have gone on about it. You must be sick of men telling you this sort of thing. Disappointments and so on.'

'Most of us don't get what we want.' She got up and went to the dressing-table where her kimono lay on the back of the chair, put it over her shoulders and began to comb her black hair.

'Why don't we – get what we want?'

'I suppose most of us don't know what it is. Or what to do with it when it happens.'

He thought now of all the things he'd wanted and got. He couldn't think of a single thing that had eluded him. 'You simply have to work at it. I know that.'

'You'll be all right, then.'

She had lit the lamp by her dressing-table and was putting lipstick on, making her lips larger. It was part of the ritual, her way of saying, 'Time's up.' He'd got off the bed and dressed. He had become used to putting cash on her dressing-table. She used to count it, but she didn't any more. 'Not with my regulars,' she'd said, when he asked why.

She made him feel special, he noticed, yet kept their relationship strictly professional. He once tried to kiss her mouth. Absolutely no-go. On the other hand, any other part of her was no holds barred; a sort of abandonment without intimacy.

She had taken a cigarette out of the pack on her table, and he went up to her to light it. As she'd tilted her head to catch the flame, her face was momentarily illuminated. He glimpsed a different version of her then: the enlarged pores round her nose beneath the heavy makeup; the shade of her skin below the eyes, pasted with a lighter colour, was like grey ash; her mouth turned down and puckered underneath the glossy false lips. Her eyes – much smaller than they appeared and imprisoned behind the barbed wire of her false eyelashes – were glazed with fatigue; the roots of her hair had a tidemark of an unremarkable palish brown. He had never, in his life, seen so much – a split second of total comprehension, like a close-up in a film. For better or worse, he sensed he had just met her.

She'd drawn deeply on her cigarette and turned off the lamp. The room resumed its seedy glow.

'You're lovely, darling, but you'll have to get off. I've got a customer waiting, and I've got to tidy up.'

At the door he'd turned because he couldn't help it and said, 'Why do you do it?'

'Why do you think?'

'Money – but I don't see—'

'I *need* the money.' She'd got up and straightened the bed. 'No drugs, nothing like that. I've got a kid, see, and she's not getting the rotten education I had. Nosy, aren't you? For Pete's sake, lose yourself or I'll be in trouble.'

He left. He never saw her again. He thought sometimes of trying to do something – send her some flowers and a note saying he'd gone abroad on business, or buy something for the kid, but he had no idea what age it was. So he did nothing.

MRS QUANTOCK

'No, dear. Put your right arm in first. That's your bad arm, don't you remember? Bad arm first.'

'I don't know which—'

Mrs Quantock thrust her mother-in-law's arm into the flannel sleeve and pulled the rest of the nightdress over her head. There was a muffled squawk of protest, but eventually the other arm was thrust into the appropriate sleeve and Mrs Quantock Senior's head emerged, her hair like tufts of wire-wool, below which her angry little eyes, pale grey and red-rimmed, glared beadily at her daughter-in-law. 'I do wish, Beryl, that you wouldn't be so bossy. And rough,' she added. 'My poor foot. You never think of that.'

'It's Elsie, not Beryl.' My foot, your poor foot, she thought.

'Where's Beryl?'

'Beryl's in Bournemouth, Mother.'

'Whatever is she doing there?'

'She lives there. Now, you get into bed and I'll make your Horlicks.'

She'd had a very trying day, and though she hardly ever snapped at Mother, she did have nasty thoughts about her, which she knew were wrong. Fred never did a thing for her, but she knew she couldn't really expect him to. He was a man, after all. He went off to work every morning, came home for his tea, read the newspaper while he ate it, then settled down to the television. Occasionally, he read out some piece of the newspaper to her, always something he was angry about. 'Shocking,' she'd say, or 'Some people.'

There wasn't much, really, to be said for her life here at home where her various duties as wife, mother and daughter-in-law had turned out to be disconcerting, arduous and unrewarding. When she was younger her notions of life – well, from thirteen on – had been nourished by the cinema and romantic novels passed from hand to hand at school. Some day, she'd thought back then, her prince would come – on horseback, or in evening clothes like John Barrymore – and single her out to walk down the aisle in a beautiful white satin dress, carrying a simple bouquet of white roses and lily-of-the-valley, which she'd throw to her best friend Violet. She'd never really thought beyond those superb moments.

Then she'd met Fred, when she was working at the White Stag and he was in the ticket office at the station before the war. She was seventeen, and she and Violet had stopped talking about Rex Harrison and Clark Gable and substituted various unspecified local men with whom they were urgently determined to fall in love and marry.

Marriage was the thing. They discussed it interminably, how many children they would have and their names. They talked about their weddings, the bridesmaids' dresses, their trousseaux and, once, what the honeymoon would be like, but that reduced them both to nervous giggles.

Elsie had surmised that Violet knew more about 'it' – sex – than she did, but wasn't about to enlighten her. Violet had been the proud subject of a French kiss, which she had said made her feel funny inside. Further questioning reduced her to another fit of giggling.

So, the next time he asked her Elsie had agreed to go for a walk with Fred. He was very fond of trains so he talked about them until they reached the path by the river, which was nice and quiet with no one in sight. It was an early-summer evening and the sun was dropping swiftly over the edge of the trees on the opposite bank so that some of the river was gold and some of it black. They found a seat, a wooden bench that had a metal plaque: 'In memory of Councillor Davis'. Fred suggested they sit and she was glad to because she had her best shoes on and they weren't worn in.

They'd sat for a while and then he'd asked if she was cold. She said no, and then, because she thought he wanted her to be, she said, well, a bit. He put his arm round her and said, 'I think the world of you,' and then he was kissing her – on the mouth – and she was enveloped in the aroma of tobacco and Wright's coal tar soap.

He stopped kissing her after a bit, but only to move her so she was almost lying sideways across the bench with a screw from the plaque digging into her neck. Then, after the second, far longer, kiss when she was almost breathless, he withdrew, gazed at her. 'I got money saved.' His blue eyes seemed to be searching her face but she didn't know what for until he said, 'I knew, soon as I saw you behind the bar in the public, you were the one for me. Knew it.' He repeated himself. There were beads of sweat on his forehead, and below his anxious eyes he was blushing. He put out his hand and stroked her hair. This unexpected gesture – his gentleness – did it. She was overwhelmed by all sorts of feelings and a sensation she'd never had before. It could only be love.

'Elsie?'

She was loved. She was wanted.

They were married that autumn, but she never again had that amazing sensation of something coming to life in her body.

Now, nearly thirty-two years later, after the war, after two children, grown-up and leading their own lives, after Fred's father's death and his mother coming to live with them, after the baby that had died, after years of housework, washing, shopping, preparing food and clearing up, she had begun to make some sort of life for herself.

It started after she'd lost the baby and the doctor gave her those pills to make her feel better. He'd asked her where she was going for her holiday and she said they weren't having one this year because of the mother-in-law living with them. She didn't feel the need to tell him they hadn't had a holiday in years, that Fred didn't like them. They'd been to Hastings once when Rhoda and Kevin were thirteen and fourteen respectively. It rained nearly every day and the landlady obviously wanted them out of the house, except at mealtimes, and the beach – when it was actually fine enough to go on it – was all stones, and Fred said every time they went on the pier it cost a fortune.

She came to with a start as she remembered the conversation with the doctor all those years before.

'Sorry?'

'It was just a suggestion. My wife would be pleased to tell you about it. She's this year's president.' 'It' turned out to be the Women's Institute and, looking back, she could honestly say it was the beginning of her having a life of her own.

It was amazing, at first, just to have her skills appreciated – to notice on Thursday mornings that her chocolate sponges sold out in the first hour, to have her opinion asked about administrative matters. She went to flower-arranging classes and lectures about first aid. She actually started the annual flower show and in the end spent one heady year as president. And she made friends, began to know all kinds of people whose faces she had only ever seen in shops or at the surgery. She became known as somebody whose common sense and powers of administration were valued. In the end, she became a councillor, and that was the moment she realized Fred was proud of her.

'Elsie!'

But Mrs Quantock Senior was something of a spanner in the

works. She intensely resented her daughter-in-law spending any time not devoted to her welfare and contrived all kinds of 'little accidents' that wouldn't have happened 'if only you'd been at hand'.

Generally Elsie took this in her stride – after all, for twenty years she had allowed the feeding, nursing, protecting and clearing up after the whole Quantock family to govern her life, but no more. Now, Melton, the town, its problems, its future, its campaigns, its well-being generally had taken over. By the time she reached the town council, the battle for the bypass had been won, but many other pressing concerns had to be resolved. The Melton cinema, for instance, that had fallen into disuse when television had begun to exert its vice-like grip. Since then it had been used as a warehouse, a venue for the amateur dramatic society, twice for the annual Christmas bazaar, by the Scouts for gymnastic ploys and even, for one season, as a cinema club, with films so highbrow, foreign and incomprehensible that its audience disappeared in a matter of months.

Funny, she thought, what a lot of thoughts you can get through just making a cup of Horlicks. She'd only skimmed the surface, really, but she could have stopped anywhere, like a film, and spent hours thinking about one short minute, like Fred stroking her hair, or Brian's weak little howling that she'd never been able to calm and her feeling that he wanted to die – to *not* be with her – because she'd failed him. She mustn't dwell on it, though, not because everyone told her not to but because she couldn't bear it.

He didn't even live long enough to smile; they were strangers, except he'd had nobody but her. She thought that if he'd died alone, it must have been her fault somehow. If you know you've done something wrong you can be sorry for it – it's just when you have no idea—

THOMAS

'You spoil that child.'

'Nonsense.' His sister stood up from the rabbits' hutch. 'If she did it now, she'd be late for school.'

'She can't have an animal if she doesn't look after it.'

'Yes, Thomas, darling, I know.'

Mary got into the car and sounded the horn just as Hatty came running out of the house.

He watched her scramble into her seat and waved as they drove off. Mary, hand out of the window, waved back. He couldn't see Hatty's side of the car so she might have waved as well.

Before they were out of sight he turned back to the house. Hatty had left the back door open. The kitchen looked out on to what had been the old farmyard, a rectangle flanked by stables on one side and cowsheds on the other. Facing the house were the remains of a small glasshouse and a couple of sheds, one used for fodder and the other for chickens. He and Mary kept their cars in the stables as well as various sacks of potting mixture, compost, sharp sand, dehydrated manure and grit. The wooden gate to the lane was always kept open.

The yard was in its usual spring disarray of churned-up mud, except for the oval patch in the middle where Mary had tried to make a small garden. Luckily, visitors to the nursery saw none of this. They approached it from the front of the house where they could park their cars in the corner of a field that was otherwise pretty well covered by the long plastic tents under which the growing stock was kept. He'd invested in a small wooden shed where people paid their money. The place was practical without being attractive. He wished he had old-fashioned glasshouses like those at Melton House, even if they were in a parlous state and would cost a fortune to renovate. He wondered, briefly, whether the new owner would go in for that sort of thing, stirring up old ambivalent feelings. The idea that it might be seriously restored was reassuring, but it made him envious and he despised himself for it.

After opening the ends of the plastic tents to allow the fresh, cool air to penetrate, he spent the rest of the morning potting up the seedling geraniums. He'd left it rather late for them to flower by the end of May when customers would come looking for them. It was a monotonous job. Francis was out on a painting commission, but had promised to help in the afternoon. Really, he needed a full-time paid helper, but couldn't afford it. If he did find someone – he enjoyed fantasies and often indulged them – he could enlarge his tree nursery, much more interesting than, as he put it, fodder for hanging baskets and pots. Trees and shrubs were more his line, or would be, but that sort of stock took time to develop, and you needed to build a reputation to get the customers who wanted them.

Two years ago he'd decided to go in for box and yew, sturdy little things from the start; rabbits didn't eat them and they weren't vulnerable to pests. He had upwards of a thousand now, large enough to be sold to gardeners patient enough to wait for them to grow, good for hedging or parterre, but not yet large enough to prune. He also had some beech, several varieties of oak and a few prunus. Mary always urged him to consider the smaller trees, since so many gardens were too small for the larger ones – Mary, what a tower of strength. What would he have done without her? She cooked, shopped and managed the house; she looked after Hatty; she did a part-time job to bring in extra money; and at weekends she helped in the nursery. She did everything Celia would have done. Except, of course, she wasn't Celia.

The familiar feeling – a kind of surging black avalanche – descended, burying the fragments of ordinary life that from day to day he doggedly built up, leaving him with nothing but the numbness of her eternal absence. She was dead.

Before he had known anything about it, she was dying in an ambulance and dead before he'd got to her in the hospital. No farewell. Nothing. That terrible night he'd stared down at her smooth, incredibly young white face while somebody asked him if she was his wife. They left him alone with her, tactful, kind, before he'd even asked. He'd run his fingers gently through her hair as he used to when he woke her in the mornings, but this time was different. She was still. When he took his hand away, there was blood on two of his fingers. When he raised one of her hands to caress it and let it go, it fell back abruptly on her breast. He leaned over to kiss her. Her mouth was icy dry, and when he stood up, he saw his tears on her face.

Outside, they offered him a cup of sugary tea – idiotic, really, but he drank it. They drove him home. Hatty was still sleeping. The policewoman, who'd stayed with her, asked if he had a friend or relative who could come. He would ring his sister, he'd said. They left him then, and he rang Mary in London.

She had arrived at three in the morning. It seemed an age before she came, but it was only two and a half hours. During that time, he existed in a kind of limbo – could not keep still but wandered about the house, picking things up, putting them down, trying to believe what had happened, but unable to keep his mind on anything long enough to be sure. He kept seeing her on the white hospital bed, and he couldn't bear it. Once he thought he was simply having a nightmare – a momentary triumph at that solution – and had even gone upstairs to look in his bed and check. Signs of her were everywhere. He picked up the brush from her dressing-table and pulled out one of the long, burnished hairs. She'd left very early that morning for a shoot in London, leaving Mrs Peabody in charge of Hatty. 'I'll be back for supper and Mrs P will put the shepherd's pie in the oven.' He had gone out with her to the car. 'I wish you didn't feel you had to do this.'

'It's OK, lovey,' she'd said. 'It is, really. As long as I don't have to do it all the time, it's fine. I like to do my bit.' She hadn't added – she never said – she *had* to do it. She earned more money in a day than the farm did in a month. Just before she got into the car, she turned to him. 'I love my life – our life.' She put an arm round him. A quick kiss. She tasted of toothpaste. 'Don't wait for me – it's too cold.'

But he *had* watched her disappear through the gate and round the curve in the lane, listening until he could no longer hear the sound of her engine.

She rang around six in the evening to say they'd just finished and she'd be late, was Hatty all right, and leave her some pie. 'Hatty needs a story,' she'd added. He could hear she was tired.

'Why don't you stay the night with Francis and come down first thing?' But she said no, she really wanted to get home.

At some point during those dreadful hours he went to Hatty's bedroom. From the light in the passage he could see she was deeply asleep. Her bear and the white monkey Celia had bought her for her third birthday lay at each side of her. The thought of her without Celia terrified him. Guilt followed fear. How could he tell her? How would he treat her? He had never loved anyone before Celia, and now, faced with bringing up their child – a baby, really – he wasn't sure he had the love for it.

When Mary arrived, he was sitting at the kitchen table that had been laid by Mrs Peabody for the supper that had been meant for himself and Celia.

FRANCIS

With Thomas off to his plants, and Mary with Hatty, Francis could have a nice quiet breakfast by himself. He tried, most mornings, to be late enough to avoid the fuss of getting Hatty off to school, but early enough to avoid Mrs Peabody who usually arrived at nine to clear up the kitchen which, by that time in the morning, was distinctly lived-in. Not surprising, really, he thought, as he put the kettle on for coffee and inserted two pieces of bread into the malevolent toaster, for in spite of a large sitting room, Thomas's small study and, upstairs, three bedrooms, the kitchen was where they lived. It was a long, rectangular room with a low, beamed ceiling, a flagged floor, and must, originally, have been rather dark, but a series of oblong windows cut high in the long wall, and the pair of casements each side of the back door usually gave enough light. In winter and a good deal of the spring, the Rayburn kept them warm.

As they all spent so much time there, it had become claustrophobically cluttered. Apart from all the kitchen stuff, their outdoor clothes hung from a series of pegs so overburdened that the jackets and coats slipped to the floor, knocking over ranks of gum-boots, Hatty's bicycle, and various sticks and umbrellas bunched precariously in a stand too shallow for them. Thomas left piles of seed catalogues and newspapers in tottering heaps. Hatty had abandoned half-done jigsaws, her dolls' pram – hardly ever used – packs of cards and school books. He'd stored his easel and other painting gear there and also installed his hi-fi system. One shelf was crammed with his records. A jam-pot filled with drooping wildflowers Hatty had picked or a beautiful ceramic bowl Celia had brought from the flat she and Francis had shared in London when she'd married usually sat on the kitchen table.

He'd bought it for her birthday when he'd sold his first picture. It was round and shallow, glazed a rich blue and decorated with creamy, irregularly shaped stars. They usually piled it with fruit, but today it contained everyday rubbish, elastic bands, pencils that needed sharpening, shopping lists, a tube of hand cream, a torch, a box of matches and some drawing-pins. One day, he thought – as he frequently thought – he'd clear it up and fill it with lemons, avocados and large, freckled pears. As his sister would have done if she was still with them.

Black smoke was rising from the toaster, which, as was its wont, had clung to its prey. Using two knives he prised the pieces from its clutches and scraped them over the sink, made a mug of instant coffee, shifted earlier breakfast crumbs elsewhere on the table, shoved some quince jelly on to the toast – now the consistency of hardboard – and got on with his meal. Usually, on Fridays, he had the day off for painting, but today was pretty well mucked up. Thomas was so behind with his potting up Francis felt bound to help him for at least half of it, and this morning he had promised to finish the commission, taken on weeks ago, to paint Easton Hall. The old lady who kept a gallery in Melton had got him the job, and as she was the only person who ever sold any of his pictures, it would be mad to turn it down. He had started with enthusiasm, but after several rejected attempts, it was made clear to him that what was wanted was a watercolour, every detail depicted with a boring clarity that could be turned into a postcard, letter-heading or even a Christmas card. Lord Yoxford lived in Hong Kong while the rest of the family subsisted in a state of almost flamboyant poverty. Betsy, his lordship's sister, ran a small livery stable kept precariously afloat by teaching girls from local boarding-schools. Hugo, between attacks of entrepreneurial delusion, speedily spent his small allowance on clothes and his deeply secondhand Porsche with a view to impressing a floating heiress, and Lady Yoxford – as she had done all of her life – did absolutely nothing. It was Lord Yoxford who had commanded the painting, but it was Betsy who had trapped him into sparse, nasty lunches after a morning's work. He really should be stronger and extricate himself.

Most of his life, he reflected, as he dismounted his bike to push it up the steep, winding lane that led to the back drive of Easton Hall, ever since he could remember, had been spent getting out of things. So many people seemed to know what he should be doing. When he was a child, he had assumed it was just part of the awful helplessness of that condition. He'd struggled through prep school and run away quite a lot – once quite successfully until he was penniless. At school, to evade the worst of games, he had pretended he had to wear glasses. To steer clear of his ghastly godmother, he'd claimed her Persian cat gave him asthma. He'd missed the war, as he was too young. He shunned golf with his father, bridge with his mother, and university by not passing the exams. He'd even sidestepped learning to dance with his sister, Celia. But he *did* know the answer to the repetitive irascible questions about what the hell he was going to do with himself.

'An art school? I meant how are you intending to earn your living, boy? I'm not asking you what you would like to do.'

His mother came into the room with a ten-pound note while he was packing. 'I'm sorry it isn't more, darling, but it's all I've got. Oh, and this. She'd thrust a small packet of black tissue paper into his breast pocket. 'Its one of those horrid little diamond dog brooches Daddy keeps remembering our anniversaries with. Cash it in, dear. He doesn't mean it, you know.'

'Oh, yes, he does.'

'Oh dear. He thinks you should go into the family business but, no, he's not really casting you off or anything like that.'

'I'd quite like to be cast off. By him,' he added, anticipating his mother's face – wrongly, as it turned out, for when he looked up from his suitcase, she was smiling.

'I'll drive you to the station,' she said.

'Give my love to Celia,' she said in the station yard. She didn't leave the car. 'I don't want to see you off, darling. If you don't mind.'

He walked round and they kissed awkwardly through the open car window.

'Thank you so very much for the loot.'

In the train, he suppressed a surge of irritation at her for assuming he'd go straight to Celia, and then, for the first time probably, he'd wondered how it would be for her now, both children gone, left with that tyrannical old bore. Perhaps, at her age, she didn't mind so much. Of course he *was* going straight to Celia.

He'd rung the bell of her flat several times, but there was no answer. It was Sunday evening, early autumn, and the street in Maida Vale was very quiet. Leaves from the plane trees drifted silently on to the pavement. It began to rain. There were five other bells besides Celia's. What had once been a tall, capacious family house was now converted into flats, and looking up, he could see lights in some of the windows. He was just starting to wonder whether it would be worth ringing any of the other bells when he heard the welcome sound of a taxi.

He waited till she'd come through the gate and up the path to the steps before he stood up. 'It's all right. It's only me.'

'So I see.' She'd smiled delightedly, and he'd felt the familiar frisson of pure pleasure – the sight of her filled him with a kind rapture. Now she wasn't here, he reflected, he could only remember fragments – her serious eyes, the gold-red glint of her hair, her voice when she teased him, her irrepressible giggle when he made her laugh, the perfect line from cheekbone to chin, her beautiful mouth.

'You don't get any plainer,' he'd said, when they had hugged.

'I've got a few years left.'

'You don't want to go on modelling for ever, do you?'

'Of course not. Open this, darling, while I go and change.'

He'd opened the wine and collected glasses from the skeletal kitchenette, wedged into a corner of the sitting room; it spoiled the faded elegance of the egg-and-dart plasterwork, the ceiling rose, no longer in use, the two large Victorian sash windows and the marble fireplace fitted with a gas fire. The marble was discoloured, and the tiles on the hearth were cracked. Celia had put a charcoal grey carpet on the floor, but the boards beneath it creaked. The walls were yellow-white and the only two paintings were his, one of oasthouses by a hopfield, and one of fishing-boats in Hastings. They were the sort of paintings he ignored now. He'd thrown himself on to the battered old sofa and had found himself at eye level with a large jug of elegant lilies. It was a modest milieu for someone whose face so regularly appeared on the front cover of fashion magazines.

She returned so quietly that her hand on the back of his neck gave him a shock. 'Darling France. Didn't mean to frighten you. Make with the wine.' Her feet were bare, and she was wearing old black culottes he'd seen many times before and a man's collarless shirt, too big for her. Her hair was scraped back from her face and tied with a piece of olive green chiffon. 'I suppose you've had a row at home.'

'Yep. Pretty well walked out. Told Reggie I definitely won't be gracing his office and, no, I won't go to university. I want to go to art school. Who did I think was going to pay for that? I told him I'd applied for a scholarship. He doesn't seem to realize I won't get one because he's too well off. So, there we go.' He'd looked at her curled in the armchair opposite and tried to smile.

'Cheers.' He didn't feel at all cheerful.

'Let's talk about you. Is your life very glamorous? Are you making masses of money? Are dozens of men in love with you?'

She held out her glass for wine. 'I'll tell you all that when we're having dinner. There's a nice place round the corner.'

In the street, she took his arm with a confiding intimacy that somehow touched him, made him feel wanted. When they reached the restaurant, he noticed how she seemed to enhance the place just by walking in. The *patron* beamed; the waiter hovered to take their coats with reverential care. The other diners, who had at first casually glanced at them, looked again more pointedly. They were led to the only corner table in the room that wasn't by a window.

'I didn't know you were so famous.'

'I'm not. Well, people in the business know me, but that's it.'

It's just your beauty, he'd thought, like the sun coming out on a grey day. He didn't say it because her chief charm was her unassuming awareness. She was used to it – used to being herself. She had no idea what it was like to be the rest of us.

She leaned forward and took his hand.

'Darling France. You're not to worry. I earn pots of money. This is my supper and you can stay in the flat as long as you like.'

He did stay – for the winter months and on into the spring. When she'd said she wanted to live somewhere larger, he found her a maisonette, the top half of one of the larger houses in Belsize Avenue, vacated by an old couple who had done nothing to it since the thirties when they'd moved in.

'I can see it could be beautiful, but, honestly, darling, I don't have the time. Builders, estimates and the rest of it . . .'

'I'll do all that. I'll love it. It's something I know I can do, the drawings and all that, and I can do the decorating. Give me a chance to pay you back – don't be mean.'

And he tried, all that winter, to do just that. He did the

housework for her, and even learned to cook so she ate some meals at home. He took her clothes to be cleaned, accompanied her to airports when she was off on foreign shoots, picked her up on her return, went as her chaperone to parties, did anything she asked, but nothing he could do equalled her total generosity to him.

She bought him a sofa-bed, paid for him to have life-drawing classes at a private art school while he was applying for the larger ones and, hopefully, a scholarship. Above all, she took seriously his desire to paint. She even effected a reconciliation, of sorts, with their father, who agreed to support Francis partially if he got into an art school.

'And when are you going to make me a grandfather?' Reggie, as usual, changed the subject genially and carelessly, and Francis sensed her apprehension.

'I don't know.' She implied it was out of her hands.

'Not still going round with that motor-racing chap, are you?'

She shook her head. 'That was in Rome. Ages ago.'

'Glad to hear it. Those chaps are not a good bet. Always crashing and, when they do it once too often, leave you a widow with a brood on your hands.'

And so on. This scenario, with imaginative variations, had applied to a submariner, a war correspondent, an actor with a string of divorces behind him, and an MP, whom he had described simply as being on the wrong side. Actually, Francis thought now, he'd have objected to almost any candidate while still urging her to get on with having a family. 'And whatever you do, don't marry a photographer,' he usually ended, and Celia usually retorted she'd no intention of marrying anybody.

'Not for ages.'

'Badgering away at you.'

'We're not called Brock for nothing.'

She was driving them back to London in her new drophead MG.

'You do drive with terrifically due care, not unlike an old nanny.' He was longing to drive it himself.

'All right. We'll change over when we get to Sevenoaks.'

At supper they played a game imagining all the men of whom their father would not approve her marrying – extra points if you outlined the terrible consequences.

'A bishop.'

'Good God, no. Dad's so broad-minded about religions.'

'Actually, he just doesn't care about them.'

'Point to you. I've often noticed that liberality equates with ignorance.'

'How often?'

'Oh, don't discourage me from philosophizing. How about a conjuror?'

'Think of the rabbit maintenance. And all that travelling, not to mention being sawn in half by mistake.'

'You know, I don't think you can saw the whole of somebody in half by mistake.'

They moved into the new flat in May. He remembered those months, that winter, spring and summer, as perhaps the happiest in his life. He'd been accepted by Camberwell School of Art. When not at his drawing class, he was organizing and painting the new flat. In between he took any odd job that was going, but whatever he was doing, it seemed to be with or for Celia. Often she was away.

'Maybe we should just get married? That would set the cat among the pigeons.'

'No, it wouldn't. I want a husband *and* a brother. Besides, I don't feel in the least lustful towards you. Or soppy,' she added, after thinking about it.

'You'd say if you wanted me to go, wouldn't you?'

'Of course I would.'

But she didn't.

MRS QUANTOCK

The next council meeting, held two weeks earlier than usual and convened by 'general request', had an unusually high attendance. Elsie knew the 'request' had come from Jack Curtis and suspected he'd taken considerable trouble to pack the meeting with people favourable to the festival idea. There was an air of wary bonhomie that she had every reason to distrust. It was noticeable in nearly everyone. None of them caught her eye as they divested themselves of raincoats and greeted one another with broad-minded remarks about the rain.

The meeting had been mustered so suddenly that there was no agenda. The one hastily rustled up – 'to discuss the desirability of a festival of the arts to be held in the town the following autumn' – had, at one point, contained only the one item. Elsie, determined to hold her own, had added a question concerning the renovation of the public lavatories in view of complaints during previous summers and a further price rise for entry to the forthcoming flower festival. But this proposed agenda, plus the sinister fact that many, if not all, the committee members arrived together, gave her the uneasy feeling she was in an acute minority – was even, possibly, isolated. In fact, she had the idea there had already been a meeting at which all kinds of decisions had probably been made behind her back. 'Keep your dignity,' she told herself. She was slightly consoled by the late appearance of the Admiral, who'd had trouble starting his car, and Miss Steadwell, who always struck her as a nice, reliable lady. Francis

Brock was also late, but as he'd started the thing it hardly mattered.

She thought, afterwards, that the whole business went exactly and as disastrously as had been planned. They raced through the first two items. Of course the lavatories should be renovated, high time, said those who had neither used nor inspected them. The matter of the entry fee for the flower festival should naturally be left to Mrs Quantock's discretion. After all, if it weren't for her, there would be no flower festival and many thanks were due to her in this respect.

Then they were on to *the* festival, not even 'of the arts' any more, just *the* festival. Elsie had never had the slightest use for any of 'the arts'. She thought them vaguely similar to cocktail parties and nightclubs or the behaviour of film stars she'd read about as a girl. A collection of puzzling, often apparently pointless activities, usually at terrible expense, indulged in by people who had nothing better to do. Of course she'd had 'art' class at school and 'composition' in English, and she sang in church and, when she was older, she had danced occasionally in the town hall – a winter chance to mingle with the opposite sex. She'd read dozens of novels by Denise Robins and Barbara Cartland to occupy herself between leaving school and starting work. Boys read about football and girls read about love. 'Art', whatever that was, had nothing to do with it. Pictures in museums were 'art'. That was fine. They didn't get in the way. They were there for those who fancied that sort of thing, but you didn't have to get involved if you didn't want to. She knew that in the days before cameras people had had to make do with what they could knock up for themselves, but times had changed. She used to listen to music on the radio, but nowadays they only played silly songs with no tune, or just a racket that made her head ache.

It occurred to her that maybe the whole 'art' business was a class thing and she looked covertly down and round the table. Almost at once her eye fell on Admiral Connaught, a gentleman if ever there was one. She wouldn't have thought he'd have any time for 'art' – sports, in his day, no doubt, but nothing airy-fairy. On the other hand young Francis Brock was an 'artist', and spoke as if he'd been to a public school, but that might just be an unlucky fluke. George Chance, though – while he wasn't local, he'd been in Melton for years; a cocky young man he'd been apparently – had settled down as editor of the local paper, which probably meant he was keen on a festival for anything as long as it was a good story. Mr Southern with his antiques and Derek Mainwaring with his theatre would definitely side with Curtis. Miss Steadwell, a teacher, probably thought 'the arts' were educational.

People were looking at her to start proceedings. She coughed, and they fell silent. *Que sera, sera*, she thought and somehow it being in a foreign language made it strangely less disconcerting.

★

Of course they'd had a private meeting before they came. A meeting at which, it was clear to her, everything had been decided. There was to be a festival and the council – she, the Admiral and possibly George Chance were the only ones who hadn't been – were forewarned. The rest of them had come up, thick and fast, with all kinds of motley notions: doing a Greek play in Greek, morris dancing in the market square, a jazz concert in the meadow by the river; something called chamber music in the community centre; morning lectures on art and literature in the cinema, and so on.

She listened and said nothing. She knew most of them had no idea what they were talking about and almost nobody mentioned the cost – thousands of pounds, in her opinion. Actually, the Admiral did, but was shouted down by Mr Curtis and Lady Yoxford's son – smoothly inserted to the meeting without proper procedure – in an animated discussion about sponsorship, both of them showing off, she thought, with no experience. Finally, it was proposed, again by Mr Curtis, that there should be a festival committee comprised of Mr Curtis, Hugo Carson, Derek Mainwaring, George Chance, Francis Brock and Margaret Steadwell. The Admiral was asked but refused, saying he didn't feel he had anything to contribute though he wished the committee well, and Mr Southern, the antiques dealer, who did not feel he could give adequate time to such a large venture. That left Elsie. Everybody turned to her questioningly.

Her first thought was to resign. But she didn't.

PERCY

Floy always played the Third Programme on the radio in the car on long journeys and today it was Bach. Good, thought Percy. Conversation's difficult when the van rattles so much. It was also good because she couldn't stop thinking about Denis, and she couldn't face talking about him. As they passed Heathrow, she imagined him on the plane, though it wouldn't be for another ten days. All the same, the signs to the airport reminded her of what might have been. She'd written him a note. Well, six notes, actually, the first three quite long. She'd only sent the last – short and dignified – better if they didn't meet again stuff. He hadn't answered. If only she had been giving up the love of her life to save his marriage, she could feel a bit noble . . . But it was him. Perhaps he'd found someone else. It was possible. Actually it was more than likely – probably taking her to Los Angeles.

'Facing up to things makes me so angry,' she said aloud.

'Better than making you frightened,' Floy replied, as though she'd heard everything.

She changed the subject. 'What's this man we're going to work for like?'

'I don't know much more about him than you will, really, once you meet him. I've done quite a few projects with him. He's made a lot of money. He mentioned recently he was divorced. He's always been very straight to deal with – bills paid and doesn't change his mind halfway through a job as so many of them do, particularly the rich ones. I don't think he's very . . . used to people. I'm rather surprised he's bought a country house. He's always seemed to me essentially an urban creature. How's Marvell?'

'Asleep. Half asleep,' she amended, as he raised his head and yawned very slowly at her. He had a cosy basket in the back of the van, but chose to lie on Floy's suitcase.

They left the A4. It was late afternoon and the country was dressed for summer – hawthorn foaming in the hedges, primroses nestling in rich, verdant grass on the banks, the oaks rosy, the beeches tender green, fields of cows and elderly lambs. Above it all and beyond, a blue sky crowded with banks of white cloud and a fitful sun casting shadows on the land below. Percy, who wasn't used to country landscape, or at least not of the English variety, felt as though she was seeing it for the first time.

They came to a crossroads, and a sign to the right said 'Melton 3 Miles'. Floy turned into a steep-banked lane topped with hedges. They passed an open gate and another sign that said 'Melton Nursery Garden 1 Mile', and after another half-mile they passed a derelict-looking lodge at the entrance to a drive that ran between a well-established avenue of beeches. The house that came into view was faced with stone the colour of dark honey. It had a portico that framed the wide front door and was flanked by rows of rectangular windows. At each end of the façade was a single-storey wing with archways. While the drive and sweep before the house were encrusted with weeds, its paintwork gleamed from recent care.

'Front or back?' Floy said aloud. 'I think front to start with.'

They had just emerged from the van when a figure dressed in an emerald green trouser suit appeared and descended the steps that led up to the house.

'You must be Mrs Plover. Hello. I'm Mrs Fanshawe. As Mr Curtis is still in town, he has asked me to greet you. Welcome to Melton.'

'Thank you. I'm *Miss* Plover, actually, and this is my niece, Persephone Plover.'

'Pleased to meet you. Don't bother with your bags. Hou-arn will carry them for you. Hou-arn!'

An extremely small man in tight, shiny black trousers and a fairly white cotton jacket came scurrying down the steps.

'*Porter les bagages*,' Mrs Fanshawe commanded, as he stared dejectedly at her. '*Les bagages. Porter.*' She pointed to the modest assortment of bags and waved her arms vaguely towards the steps, whereupon he pounced on them, slung one piece over his shoulder, picked up two more and staggered into the house. 'His English is non-existent, so I have to use my French.' She rolled her eyes in a liberal manner.

'Is he French?' Percy asked. He didn't look it.

'He came from an agency. I haven't the faintest what he is.'

They trooped up the shallow stone steps into a square hall, and Percy noticed that Mrs Fanshawe's glistening blonde hair sprang from darker origins. The hall had a marble floor in an intricate pattern of black, white, and unusual streaked brown – as if someone was in the middle of making fudge, she thought. The walls were upholstered in chestnut hessian on which were hung a collection of oil portraits of gloomy, prosperous-looking men. She had time to observe this because they had come to a halt. Mrs Fanshawe was clearly uncertain what they should do next.

'Tea will be served in the morning room, but perhaps you would care to wash your hands first? If you'd be so kind as to indicate which bags belong to you personally, I'll see that Hou-arn gets it right.'

As they climbed the stone staircase – it had a beautiful balustrade, Percy noticed – something else occurred to Mrs Fanshawe. 'Miss Plover, I do hope you won't take this amiss, but Mr Curtis doesn't care for vehicles being parked at the front.

If you would give Hou-arn the keys, he'll move it into the courtyard to the rear of the house.'

'Thank you, but my niece can perfectly well take it if you tell us where to go.'

'I'm sure Mr Curtis wouldn't like you to go to the trouble—'

'My van is rather difficult to start. What time do you expect Mr Curtis to be back?'

'His ETA is always rather uncertain. Borage is fetching him from Heathrow and the plane is due at six. He expects to be here in time for dinner, which is usually at eight.'

'In that case there's plenty of time for us to park the van after tea,' Floy said, so firmly that Mrs Fanshawe could only give a dissatisfied sigh of assent.

Their rooms proved to be opposite each other at the end of a passage. 'I've put you in the Lilac, facing the park and your niece in the Berry, which looks out on the courtyard. Hou-arn will bring your luggage shortly. The morning room is on the left of the front door as you descend the stairs.'

She left them, followed by Hou-arn. Percy went immediately to Floy's room and found her standing in the middle of a lilac carpet.

'Goodness.'

'Yes, indeed. It couldn't be called anything else, could it?'

There were chintz curtains covered with lilac blossom, a bedspread to match, and a purple headboard patterned with small heads of white lilac. A bowl of mixed branches of the same shrub stood on a round table in the window. There were prints of it on the mauve silk wallpaper, and an open door to the *en-suite* bathroom revealed tiles, towels and even soap to match.

'It's like being in a very grand hotel,' Percy said. 'My room has berries everywhere. It was good you stopped "Hou-arn" parking the van. He wouldn't have kept quiet about Marvell, though if he really can't understand much, I suppose telling people anything might be worse. Does Mr Curtis live here by himself?'

'Well, he clearly has staff.'

'No, I mean, family – friends.'

'I don't think he has many friends.'

After a dainty and rather uneasy tea in the morning room – all pale Prussian blue and mirrors with tortuous gilded frames – Floy said she and Percy would park the van and perhaps have a little walk before dinner.

Marvell was torn between gladness to see them and crossness for waiting so long. They gave him a snack and set out for their walk with him. He leaped with theatrical clumsiness, Percy thought, on to Floy's shoulder, his paws slipping on her waxed jacket until he had clawed his way, via her muffler, to her neck. Floy, apparently unmoved, took out her pad and a pencil from behind her ear and started drawing. At the back of the house they were confronted by a pair of lodges at each corner of the courtyard, facing each other, with small paved approaches to their front doors. Between them was a large pair of gates, one of which hung drunkenly on broken hinges. Walking through they came upon a derelict pleached-lime alley, and further on, through a tall wooden gate, into an immense walled garden with glasshouses at the far end that ran to its entire width. The paths bordering the beds had been hedged with box, now ragged and in many parts dead. Espalier fruit trees on the walls had been abandoned, and slack branches hung aimlessly. Willowherb, dandelions, nettles, chickweed and ground elder flourished. Reaching the glasshouses, they found most of the glazing broken and scattered on the ground. The pot stands and seed trays had rotted away and shards of broken terracotta lay everywhere. The only sturdy and solid objects were two iron water tanks that had once collected run-off rain from the glazed roofs and still brimmed with black, still water. A vine that had run riot unchecked – and had ironically kept some of the roof intact – had shed years of leaves, now fragile as brown ash, deep on the floor.

Marvell had given up Floy's shoulder, and was walking ahead, behind and between them, occasionally springing on to the stands so that he could be more easily stroked and admired.

Beyond the glasshouses, a gate in the wall led to what must once have been an elaborate water garden set in a parterre of box, its boundaries hedged with yew and a pergola along one side, richly embroidered with wisteria. The fountain at the centre was not working. The large square basin into which the water had once fallen was dry and cracked, with weeds growing through it, and the ancient remains of two shrews nestled among them. The long narrow canals that formed a cross with the fountain at its centre were also dry and studded with empty, disintegrating tubs that had once contained water plants.

Percy, who had remained respectfully silent while her aunt made copious notes, now said, 'It must have taken an enormous number of people to keep all this going.'

'Yes. It's a sorry sight. All right, my darling, come up.'

Marvell had been making it plain he was tired of walking, so Floy lifted him and deposited him in the sling she wore for his comfort.

'Look. I don't need you for measuring. Why don't you explore the park? The other side of the house,' she added, as Percy looked blank. 'But don't forget that dinner is at eight,' she called, as Percy turned away.

Dinner? she thought, as she struggled with the idea that Floy didn't want her. Dinner was about as far in the future as she dared – no, felt like considering. What's after that? She really had no idea. Why did she suddenly feel so awful? She'd avoided thinking of Denis for nearly a whole day, which was good. He wasn't worth it. Nor am I worth thinking about, but that's never stopped me.

She reached the front of the house and set off down the avenue of beeches, which were coming into full leaf. Primroses and tiny purple violets grew in the wide gaps between them, and when she looked up through the leaves at the patchwork of blue and vivid yellowy green, veined by the high slender branches, she felt . . . not exactly happier, rather that there was less of her and more of the world.

She reached the end of the drive and the apparently uninhabited lodge. She was just wondering which way to go down the road when two things happened. The sky had been gradually darkening to a charcoal grey as large drops of rain began to fall, and an extremely muddy sports car turned into the drive so suddenly and fast it nearly ran her over. It screeched to a halt within a foot of her. She put out her hands and touched the bonnet.

'God. I didn't see you. I'm so sorry.'

'You didn't look.' He was quite a young man – in his early thirties, she thought.

He'd got out of the car and was opening the passenger door. 'Get in, before you're soaked.' His blond hair was already streaked with rain.

Shocked and angry, she got into the car. The rain was drumming on the roof and she was shivering.

'I wish I had some brandy to give you.'

'You might have killed me.' She was aware unexpectedly of feeling quite grateful to him. If he hadn't nearly killed her, she wouldn't have realized how much she didn't want to be dead.

'I do know. What can I say? I mean, I've said I'm sorry – what else can I do?'

'Nothing, I should think.'

'At least let me give you a lift to wherever you are going. I was just popping into Melton House. This is the drive – private property, actually. The owner can be quite tricky about that sort of thing apparently. My name's Hugo Carson, by the way.'

'You could take me back to the house.'

'Are you staying there?' He started the engine.

'Yes.'

'You a new secretary or something?'

'Nothing like that. My aunt's designing Mr Curtis's gardens for him.'

'Oh. That's it.'

She sensed he was uneasily impressed, and was glad now he had grasped that her relationship with the owner of Melton was strictly business. He parked the car in front of the main door.

'Thanks for the lift.'

'What time is your dinner?'

'I've no idea. Soon, I should think.' She hoped this might discourage him, but it didn't. As they reached the hall, Juan emerged through a baize door, scuttled up to an enormous gong slung from a lion's mouth and began to beat it. A small print fell off the wall, and just as Percy had decided to escape upstairs, Mrs Fanshawe, in an electric blue trouser suit, appeared as if by magic, tapped Juan on the shoulder to stop the gong and told him to fetch a dustpan and brush to sweep up the broken glass. 'Only the dressing gong,' she called reassuringly to Percy. 'You have half an hour.'

Dressing gongs implied black ties and long dresses. She only had one evening dress and hadn't brought it. She put on her Mary Quant tunic over a silk shirt, both bought in the winter sale, and hoped she'd get by.

Drinks were in the library, which was dark green and white but had, she noticed at once, a comforting array of books. Floy, sitting upright in a chair embroidered with unicorns, was wearing her blue kaftan with its tarnished silver braid encrusted with small pieces of mirror glass.

'And you must be Persephone.'

'I am.'

'I'm Jack Curtis. How do you do? Champagne?'

'Thank you, Mr Curtis.' She loved champagne.

He wore evening trousers and a velvet jacket of midnight blue. He was about the same age as Denis, she thought, but while Denis had something boyish about him, this man might be younger than he appeared.

'Now,' he said, 'I've asked the young man who apparently rescued you from a cloudburst to dine with us. Mrs Fanshawe took him off to wash and brush up. He comes from the other large house round here, Easton Park. Let me top you up.' He looked across the room at Floy, drinking her whisky, who indicated no more was needed.

A silence descended and Jack Curtis looked at his watch – a jolly expensive one, Percy thought – and she gazed with interest at the rows of novels in their paper jackets. They were untouched, as though still in the bookshop. The silence was broken by all three simultaneously:

'I wonder whether I could borrow—'

'I noticed you have a nursery garden very—'

'I believe Mr Carson has some scheme he—'

At this point the washed and brushed-up guest, accompanied by an anxious Mrs Fanshawe, entered the room. 'Dinner is served, Mr Curtis.'

'Right. Let's go and eat.'

It was a very good dinner: gulls' eggs, a roast saddle of lamb, various cheeses and a cherry tart.

Conversation, what there was of it, was dominated by their host, who seemed to feel the need to shoulder entire responsibility for it, but his method – purposeful cross-examination of each person in turn – stifled any lively discourse. Hugo was the only one who tried, but as Jack took no notice of him, until it was his turn, this made no difference.

Jack began with Floy, whom he still called Miss Plover, asking her for her reaction to the grounds, which he knew she'd already inspected. She replied that she'd only just begun to make rough drawings, but certainly felt they needed a preliminary private talk together about his priorities and intentions for the upkeep.

Here Hugo broke in: 'You should see the awful old pile where my family live, Miss Plover. Easton Park's been neglected for as long as I can remember. You wouldn't believe it to look at it now, but Edward VII stayed there with my grandfather, the notorious second Lord Yoxford, who originally bought it.'

Jack took no notice of this and continued to question Floy, so Hugo pretended he'd been talking to Percy, who, keeping her eyes on her plate, said, 'How grand – to have a grandfather who was lord.'

Hugo, she already appreciated, was someone who wanted to impress others into admiring silence. Mockery inspired silence of quite another kind.

When Floy made it clear she needed more time to look over his grounds, Jack turned his attention briefly to Mrs Fanshawe – she sat next to Floy and he was a methodical man – and asked her whether he was free tomorrow morning. She behaved as though he'd ambushed her, dropping her fork and napkin and burrowing in her bag for her notebook. 'You have a phone call from New York at eleven fifteen, Mr Curtis, but I don't think there's anything—'

'Cancel it. Or delay it until five o'clock.'

It was Percy's turn soon and she wondered what he'd ask her.

'Persephone. Percy, if I may – as your aunt calls you that – have you always acted as her assistant?'

'No. I used to work for a publisher, but I do help my aunt out quite often. It's very kind of you to put me up, though, Mr Curtis,' she added.

'No, no. Not at all.' But she sensed that he was pleased – wasn't used to being thanked.

'And what will your next permanent job be?'

'I don't know. I'm sort of having a break before I decide.'

'Do you have secretarial skills?'

'Well, yes, up to a point. I can type and do a bit of shorthand. But mostly I was editing. Or, rather, reading manuscripts to see if they were publishable.'

'Do you mean to say people write books without knowing whether they'll be published?'

'Oh, yes. Hundreds of them. Thousands, probably.'

'How extraordinary. What on earth makes them do that?' He turned his attention to Hugo. 'And how is our assistant honorary treasurer getting along? Hugo has the key task of raising money for Melton's first festival of the arts,' he explained to the rest of them, and everybody looked at Hugo, except Mrs Fanshawe, who stared rather hard at her plate.

'Haven't had an awful lot of luck, I'm afraid.'

'Did you write to all the people on that list I gave you?'

'Yes. I mean – well – not all of them.'

Jack leaned back in his chair while Juan removed his plate. 'How many?'

Hugo screwed up his face to denote intense concentration. 'Something in the neighbourhood of, er, about eight, I think.'

'My dear Hugo, I gave you that list nearly a week ago.' Hugo said nothing. 'And what's been the response?'

'So far, there hasn't been much.'

'Much. Any?'

'Well, a firm wrote back and said they'd take it to their board meeting. We'd just missed one so we couldn't expect to hear anything before the end of May.'

By now there was a general feeling of unease round the table. Floy rose – if Jack would excuse her, she'd like to write up her notes and collect some of her reference books from the van – indicating, with a nod to Percy, that she was to be included. Mrs Fanshawe, murmuring something about phone calls, also escaped.

'Poor man. His head is well and truly in the lion's mouth.'

'Pity it doesn't have a gong hanging from it,' said Percy, as they crossed the hall and made for the front doors. 'He's rather a ghastly tyrant, isn't he?'

'He does like to be in control. But anyone who is unsure of themselves likes that.'

'The "reference books" are Marvell, aren't they?'

'Tomorrow I'll ask our host if we can have him in my room.' They found him irrecoverably asleep on Floy's old car rug. 'He hasn't touched his supper.'

'I was afraid of that. He never likes tinned food two meals running.' Percy bent to stroke him. He opened his eyes – the colour of cloudy lime juice – long enough to convey complete lack of interest in either of them.

'Darling, I'm afraid this means that one of us must pop into Melton first thing tomorrow to get some food for him.'

'Of course I'll go. But I would just point out he *is* a tyrant and not in the least unsure of himself.'

'An exception to the rule,' Floy said fondly.

'Coley?'

'He's off coley. Some cooked chicken, perhaps, and a spot of raw liver. You'll have to take him with you. Don't let him escape.'

The next day she remembered to turn right at the bottom of the drive and passed a second entrance to the estate, its gates locked, and immediately beyond them a track, at the end of which was what looked like a farm. She noted it because of a handwritten sign that said, 'Melton Nursery Gardens'. Handy for Floy, she thought.

How different this was from her – she called it normal – life. About now she'd usually be sitting in her stifling half-partitioned office, her bright brown tepid tea already drunk, with a huge typescript she was marking up for a typesetter, and at least three more hours before she could legitimately eat her sandwich. Now here she was driving with Marvell to an unknown place. The sun was out, gilding the fresh greens of the hedges and the verge, decorated with primroses and celandines, and the blue sky was studded with small transparent clouds. It was impossible not to feel caught by the ordinary beauty that touched everything in sight. And then the astonishing house and its – what was he? pompous? tyrannical? neurotic? probably a bit of all three – owner. There must be some mysterious, startling streak in him because, despite being terrible in company, he was clearly tremendously rich.

MARY

'Apparently she simply said she was tired – they'd had the Carters to lunch – and she'd lie down for a bit. When he went to wake her, she was dead.'

'What a terrible shock for him, poor man.'

'I know, but before you get too sorry for him, you'd better read this.' He handed a bright blue wad of paper to her.

'Thomas! It's addressed to Francis.'

'He gave it to me. Read it.'

She read it. 'Goodness.'

'Isn't it just? Francis wants us to have a family conference this evening.'

'Hatty—'

'Oh, get her to stay overnight with that schoolfriend of hers – Margaret Snow, isn't she?'

'Meg Frost.'

'Her.'

This wasn't the moment, she thought, to tell her brother it would be nice for Hatty if he could take the trouble to remember her friends' names. And surely they could talk about the whole sad business after Hatty had gone to bed. But she foresaw the doom-laden supper, with Thomas in his usual moody state, Hatty repeatedly asking him what was the matter, and Francis, hands shaking, eyes unnaturally bright, trying to deal with his mother's death and the prospect of his father. She stopped clearing lunch and went to ring Mrs Frost.

It was her afternoon off from the school and the day she changed the sheets and loaded the machine for a series of washes. Thomas was digging up and packing an order for a beech hedge, and Francis had taken some watercolours to be framed. She had time to think quietly and without interruption about their predicament.

Anne Brock's sudden death was, of course, a dreadful shock for poor Reggie. It was also a different kind of shock for Francis. Even if his father's disapproval had tainted their relationship, she was still his mother. Thomas had never liked his father-in-law, but had in the past made considerable and repeated efforts for Celia's sake. Now Anne was gone, his love for Celia would probably affect his judgement: if Reggie wanted to come and live with them, Thomas would no doubt accept him.

For that was the main tenor of the letter. After the terrible news, and details of the funeral this coming Friday, Reggie had made his position, or rather the lack of it, clear. He was no longer young – mid-sixties, Mary thought – and had never dealt with the petty domestic side of life. He even mentioned the proverbial boiled egg. Anne had left her money to Celia, and after Celia's death to Hatty. Without that money he had to sell the house, as he couldn't afford a housekeeper. He was in a mess, what with Anne's death, and finding a laundry for his shirts, and money, and needing to keep his little car because of his gammy leg and so on. The final, obvious solution was to give up his independence and throw in his lot with all that remained of his family. He wouldn't be a financial burden and could put a proportion of his pittance into the pot. And he was sure this was the solution both poor Celia and her mother would have wished for. 'As for the little differences that have arisen between us, Francis, I'm more than prepared to let bygones be bygones, and in any case they pale in comparison to my heavy burden of grief. Your ever affectionate, Father.'

Her first thought was for Francis. Actually, as the day wore on her only thought was for him. There was no outbuilding on the farm that could be converted to give the old brute private quarters, and even if they could, there was no guarantee he would stay in them. He revelled, according to Thomas and Francis, in cutting the ground from under people's feet, which naturally required nearby relatives or a steady stream of more casual encounters. Maybe his reputation was exaggerated. Maybe he was just a *bit* of an old bore. But then she recalled the Francis she'd first got to know, when he'd come to them after Celia died – his timid uncertainty about himself, his painting and his worth, his instinctive conviction that he was no good and, above all, his grief—

She'd only met him very briefly, twice, before he'd come down, some months after the funeral – to see Hatty and Thomas, he'd said. She'd fetched him from the station on a cold spring evening. On the platform, she knew instinctively he hadn't recognized her until she walked up to him. He was standing vacantly at the spot where he had descended from the train, two bags beside him.

'Francis? I'm Thomas's sister, Mary.'

'I know you are. Kind of you to meet me.' He picked up his bags and followed her to the car.

The silence on the drive back was uncomfortable. Then, just as she was about to break the ice, he'd said, 'How are things? How are they?'

'Better, I think. Better than they were, anyway.'

'That's because of you.'

She could never forget the small flush of pleasure that the – probably merely courteous – remark had given her.

'The nannies weren't working out at all. They were no match for Hatty, and no company for Thomas. Something had to change.'

'So you gave up your life in London, your career, everything to be an aunt.'

'It wasn't much of a career, more of a job.' After a pause, she said, 'I suppose I'd better warn you that while Hatty *is* settling, she's still quite disturbed. Thomas finds it difficult. They haven't really found a way to comfort each other. She reminds him of Celia all the time, and she wants to be his baby.'

He'd started to say, well, she was, wasn't she? But she interrupted: 'I don't mean his child. She's nearly four, but she wants to be about two. She clings to him and is furious with him. Anyway,' she finished more cheerfully, 'it's lovely you've come.'

That first time he'd stayed a fortnight, weathering the difficult and unpredictable climate of the family struggling with their shock. She watched Francis's cautious, tender approach to his brother-in-law and the child with gratitude. Thomas was surly, not to say hostile, for the first week and Hatty intensified her wretched antics to engage her father. It came to a head at the end of that first week. At supper time – a meal they had early so Mary could get the child to sleep at a reasonable time – Hatty, wanting her father to feed her, had pushed her spoon into his hand and knocked over his beer.

'Stop it! Now look what you've done. You're old enough to feed yourself, anyway.'

Before Mary could get a cloth, Hatty started slapping her palms in the puddle, splashing the beer. Thomas grabbed her hand roughly and slapped it. Hatty screamed, stood on her chair, threw mashed potato at her father, then shrieked in tearless rage, 'I hate you, you pig, pig, horrible pig.'

Without a word Thomas picked her up from her chair, and carried her upstairs. Hatty, silenced a moment with shock, began screaming again as he plodded up the staircase.

'Oh dear.' She remembered Francis looking at her, appalled.

'He shouldn't—' he began.

'I know.' She was clearing up the mess. 'It's grief,' she said.

A door slammed, and a moment later Thomas walked heavily down into the kitchen. The screams continued.

'Sorry about that. I've put her into her cot. She can't get out of that, can she? God. I could do with another beer.'

Francis looked as though he was about to say something, glanced at Mary and was silent. Nobody ate much dinner. By the time they had got to the baked apples, the screams had changed to bitter sobbing.

'She'll stop soon,' Thomas said. He said it to Francis – a kind of apology.

Mary murmured something and slipped out of her chair.

'Where are you off to?'

'To see if she's all right.'

'Sorry about that. I'm afraid we've been having a lot of trouble with Harriet lately – tantrums, scenes. Always wanting to be the centre of attention. Mary's wonderful with her, except she spoils her, to my mind. She's not a baby any more, after all.'

'I should have thought someone of three and a half was not far off being one.'

Later she'd asked Francis what they'd talked about when she went up: she'd been afraid of them starting a row. When she came down again, she settled Hatty on her lap and wiped her nose with a tissue. 'Lovely apple. Mary's going to share it with you. One spoon for you and one for me.' She shot a warning glance at her brother. 'Less said the better.'

Thomas, who had poured himself a large whisky, muttered something about an apology. 'She'll never learn if you don't make her—'

'Thomas. Shut – up.'

Hatty, her mouth full of apple, said, 'Thomas. Shut – up.'

Thomas stood up suddenly, appraised them for a moment, then took his glass and the bottle to the far end of the kitchen and the door that led to his small dark study.

She watched Francis gazing at Hatty, whose face was swollen and sticky with mucus and tears, and wished for a mad moment he was the father. She said, 'It isn't always this bad. Now, darling, Mary's going to put you to bed with Slinky because he won't go to sleep without you hugging him. Do you want to give Uncle Francis a kiss?' At the foot of the stairs, Hatty's eyes assessed him for a moment and Francis received an unexpectedly juicy kiss. He kissed her back. 'Kiss,' she said, with evident satisfaction.

From that evening Francis began to pay more attention to Thomas. He helped him in the yard with his pigs. He discussed farm issues, helped sort out the tortuous paperwork and, in the end, he dared mourn with him. They spent long evenings in the study after supper, eventually talking about Celia. Sometimes Mary heard Thomas sobbing and felt huge relief he'd at last found someone who, he'd accepted, acknowledged his misery.

'Francis has been very hard hit, you know, by Celia's death. I'd no idea how much she meant to him. Did you?'

'I know how I'd feel if you died.'

'Oh, well, that wouldn't be at all the same thing.'

She nearly said nothing was the same thing, but thought better of it.

'Nice chap. Much more to him than I thought.'

The first evening after Francis left, Hatty was full of questions. Why had he gone? When was he coming back? 'He should live here,' she concluded, having received, from her point of view, thoroughly unsatisfactory answers.

'I miss him too, Hatty,' her father had said.

'I miss him most. He tells me about Greeny Hopper.'

Thomas said, rather diffidently, 'I could read about him to you, if you like.'

'He's not in a book. He's a real, unordinary frog that only Francis knows about. He has ventures all the time, but he only tells Francis. It's very dangerous being him, but he doesn't care cos he's so awfully brave. Probably the bravest frog in the world, Francis said.'

It was the longest exchange they'd had together for months, she reflected, and when Thomas went out to feed the pigs, he asked Hatty to go with him. She missed Francis, she realized, as she cleared away lunch. She was surprised by how much.

Some time after that – after he'd paid them a couple more, brief, visits, after the swine fever, when Thomas was agonizing about what to do and had got very drunk one evening worrying – she'd got in touch with Francis and asked him to come down, and he did. For the summer, he'd said.

By then Hatty was at nursery school, and Mary had found herself a part-time job teaching domestic science at a local girls' school. Money was tight, and it was a relief to get out, to have work and be paid for it. Growing and selling vegetables was Thomas's new plan and Francis supplied support and enthusiasm. He had come, ostensibly, to paint, but when it rained or the light was dull, he made himself useful. He helped Thomas rig his polythene tents, he painted the kitchen a sunny yellow and Hatty's room 'the colour of Slinky's nose' or Elastoplast pink. He taught her to swim, and helped her to read. He once took Mary to the cinema in Melton. And Greeny Hopper resumed his dangerous life.

But while the tomatoes cropped heavily, Thomas could find nowhere to sell them. It was clearly no-go, and Mary was torn between relief that Thomas had arrived at this conclusion quickly and anxiety about his subsequent depression.

She remembered now the evening when Francis had come in from painting and, cleaning his brushes at the sink, had dropped his bombshell.

'I ought to get back to town. The person I rented my flat to will be on his way to America next week.'

'Oh, no. Oh, Francis – don't.' To her dismay, her eyes had suddenly filled with tears.

He put down his brushes and turned to look at her. 'Mary. Mary, dear, what is it?' He reached for her and put his arms round her, as one humiliating sob escaped. She drew in a deep breath to stop such nonsense.

'I'll be back, you know.'

'Thomas,' she eventually managed to say, 'I don't know how – I can't think what— He'll go out of his mind if we can't think of something else. It's only that.' She was scrabbling for her handkerchief, her dignity.

He pulled a piece of paint rag out of his pocket. 'It was once a handkerchief. A bit retired now. Not much use, I'm afraid.'

'I'm so sorry. Ridiculous of me.'

'No, no. It isn't ridiculous.'

There was a comforting silence, during which she was able to mop her face.

'Would you like a cup of tea? Or Nescafé – or anything?'

She shook her head.

'A drink, perhaps? Wine or gin, something like that?'

'No, Francis, I'm fine.'

But he still looked concerned.

'Why do you think I need a drink?'

'When women weep they usually need a glass or cup of something, don't they?'

She smiled. 'Do you think it might be a good idea for Thomas to have a partner – for work, I mean?'

He'd resumed wiping the brushes, she the ironing.

'It would be marvellous, but who?'

'I'll have to think about it,' she said, not knowing at all how to.

He went the next day, and both Thomas and Hatty said how much they missed him. She said nothing.

Three weeks later he turned up in a small white van. It was afternoon, and she'd been helping Thomas pick out seeds from a catalogue. He'd decided to try for winter vegetables. She heard the noise of an engine approach, stop, and a car door slam.

'Are we expecting anyone?'

'No. I'd better go and see.'

By the time she reached the yard, he was walking towards the kitchen door. Francis.

'Francis?' He was wearing a rather dirty roll-neck Aran sweater and his olive corduroys. 'I thought it was someone delivering something,' she said, after a family hug.

'It's me delivering me. I thought about it and then I decided it was easier just to turn up.'

It was not quite what he said to Thomas. 'I've had to give up my flat so no fixed address, and the teaching job I thought I'd landed fell through, so I'm unemployed.'

He said it lightly as he accepted a mug of tea, but she noticed he looked exhausted, cheekbones white between the shadows under his eyes and the darker shadows of a distant shave.

Thomas was clearly delighted he'd come. 'Stay as long as you like.' After tea, he took Francis off to see what he was doing in the polythene tent and when they returned was already suggesting Francis should help him.

Hatty flung herself at him, and furnished him with an endless account of everything that had happened to her at school that day.

Mary could see Thomas was getting restive and suggested Hatty should help Francis with the unloading of his van. 'It's full of my worldly goods,' he'd said earlier.

'Is Greeny Hopper in it?'

'Certainly not. He never goes in anything as boring as a van.'

'What's he coming in?'

'A balloon. Very late at night. You won't hear him.'

It was several days before it dawned on Mary that he was

there for good. He'd come in from the yard and sat opposite her at the kitchen table where she was stringing beans. 'If it seems to work out,' he said, 'if you and Thomas feel OK about it. I can pay my share of rent and stuff, and I thought if I helped Thomas half time, I could get some sort of teaching job, if there is one in these parts.'

'What about your painting?'

'What indeed?' After a pause, he said, 'I have a sneaking feeling I'm no good. That my father's right. I'm wasting my time. I had to go and see him before coming here. I told him and my mother a pack of half-truths – that I was sick of London and working for an advertising agency. He had a real go at me . . .'

Taking a chance, she said, 'What would your whole truths have been?'

He looked at her and she was shocked.

'Oh. I couldn't bear living in that flat without Celia. It was OK when I knew she was happy with Thomas. She'd often pop in when she was on a modelling job, but after she . . . died, it wasn't the same. I simply couldn't – it was full of her presence – or perhaps full of her absence—' His voice had become almost inaudible.

Without looking at him, she put out a hand to his on the table and held it.

'Kind Mary,' he said. 'Goodness, you are kind. Do you think Thomas will agree to me staying – for a trial run anyway? I could always bugger off if it didn't work.'

'I think he'll be very glad to have you. And so will Hatty.'

'And you? You won't mind? I promise I'll pull my weight. It won't just be more shirts to iron and more beans to string.'

'Of course not. It won't be. It will be lovely to have you here.'

She knew, saying it, how true that was.

And now their much happier family life was to be infiltrated.

At least, that was the most likely outcome. Both Thomas and Francis would agree. Neither of them would want it, but each would feel the other thought it right. And she, with no direct connection to Celia, wouldn't count – not really.

FLOY AND JACK

Jack had been closeted with Floy since lunch time. The drawings she'd made for the gardens lay all over his immense desk, and Floy now sat opposite him. They had been skirting round a disagreement for some time now, and Jack was beginning to admire her implacable common sense.

'But, surely, the best thing would be to get everything shipshape first. I like your plans, I really do, but I can't see the point of drawing the whole thing out for years.'

'Then you will have to decide now how many staff you're prepared to employ for the upkeep.'

'And how many do you estimate that to be?'

'If you restore the whole place – walled garden, borders, hedging and so on, and the glasshouses, paths and forestry – I reckon that with a good head gardener, three under-gardeners and perhaps a gardener's boy, the place could be kept up. There would be the initial cost of a great deal of planting and replanting, of course.'

There was a short silence. Then he said, 'Your idea would be to do the whole thing in stages. Where would you start?'

'With the trees and the hedging, because they take longest. The avenue needs a good deal of attention, and so do many of the trees in the park. You could employ a couple of tree specialists for that. Then I would reinstate the walled garden, and one of the glasshouses. I doubt you'll need as many as three. The garden would need to be ploughed and picked over to get rid of the pernicious weeds. Most of the yew can be saved, but the box is only good for cuttings. Most of it will have to be cleared. And you'll need builders to repair the glasshouse if, indeed, it's not past repair.'

'Can you give me a rough idea of the cost?'

She pushed a piece of paper across the desk to him. 'Of course, this is approximate. It has to be. We would need estimates from builders and the tree people. If you do it my way, I reckon you could manage with a good head gardener, an assistant and, if you could find him, a gardener's boy of about sixteen or seventeen. Those are my estimates for salaries.'

'That's a lot of money for a gardener, isn't it?'

'Not for someone who knows his or her job. They don't come cheap, but if they're good, they'll make all the difference.'

'I suppose you wouldn't . . .'

'No, Jack, I'm too old for one thing. And, more important, I wouldn't want to do it. I'll interview or vet anyone who applies for the job, if you like, have a talk with them and see if they're keen enough to make a good thing of it. And, if you like, I'm prepared to keep an eye on the initial work. It's potentially a marvellous place. I could oversee the tree people, builders and so forth, if you like. I should have to be paid for that, of course.'

He made a gesture of petulant assent, and looked at his watch. 'Friends,' he began. 'I assumed, perhaps wrongly, that after all these years . . .'

'Friends can also be businesslike. I like to keep things clear between us. You have been extraordinarily generous in allowing me to bring my niece—'

'Oh, yes, Percy. Not really your assistant, is she? She doesn't seem to know much about gardening.'

'No, I must confess I wanted her to come for other reasons.'

'Love trouble? Needed a break to get over it?'

There was a pause, and then she said briskly, 'She lives with me, and is between jobs. If it's all right with you, I'd be grateful if she could stay here while I sort out the tenders for estimates. Then, when you've decided which plan to adopt, we'll go back to London.'

'Oh dear. Whatever shall I do without you?'

She sensed that although this remark was meant to be flippant, he didn't like the prospect. 'I shall be back.'

'I'll pay you five hundred a month to stay.'

She smiled. He liked the way her weatherbeaten nut of a face broke into a welter of friendly wrinkles when she did that.

'Smiling means no?'

'I'm flattered to be bribed.'

There was a knock on the door and Mrs Fanshawe appeared. She murmured something inaudible.

'I can't hear you.'

'The meeting—' She tried to go on, and collapsed into a snuffling cough.

'Is everybody there?'

She shook her head, then whispered, 'Three of them.'

'You'd better go to bed, Mrs Fanshawe, before you give whatever you've got to the rest of us.'

'The minutes, Mr Curtis?'

'I'll sort something out. Off you go.' She went.

'Could your niece take the minutes?'

'I should think so.'

'Would you ask her?'

Percy, who'd been rather disconsolately reading *Country Life*, was delighted by the idea. 'I'd feel as though I was earning a bit of my keep. Only you'll have to feed Marvell. He's in your room, on your bed.' He had been promoted to living in the house, although not given the run of it – a situation he intensely resented, making mad dashes to escape from either of their rooms whenever they went to see him.

MRS FANSHAWE

She'd done her best. After Mrs Quantock's arrival, she had successively greeted five more members of the festival committee, each time enduring a blast of piercingly cold air when Hou-arn opened the door, conducted them to the morning room, and apologized for keeping them waiting. She'd done her best to get Mr Curtis to stop going on and on about the gardens with the elder Miss Plover. Now she was being told she wasn't wanted to take the minutes. Though she felt awful, voice practically gone, head throbbing and feverish, she couldn't help noticing the slight. She'd worked so hard to become indispensable. Not a kind word, she thought bitterly, as she almost bumped into the girl, Percy, on the main staircase. Not one single kind word.

'Oh, Mrs Fanshawe, I've been asked to take the minutes for the festival meeting. Have you got the papers and other things?'

'They're all in the morning room, Miss Plover.' She had to repeat herself, which brought on another fit of coughing.

'You do sound in a bad way. After the meeting, would you like me to come and see if there's anything you want? Which is your room?'

She made a gesture of dissent with the hand not holding her bag. 'But thank you.'

By the time she'd climbed the far steeper flight of stairs, she was shivering so violently she could hardly stand and collapsed on to her bed without even removing the counterpane, which was covered with bunches of roses that matched the wallpaper.

Random miserable thoughts flared up like a rash. What had her mother said when Keith left her? That was it: 'You're no spring chicken.' No spring chicken. Well, now she was going to miss her appointment to get her roots done at the hair salon in Melton. Honestly. He'd behaved as if her minute-taking was pointless. As though anybody could do her job. Actually, almost as if he didn't need her at all. Never a word to say she was invaluable. Not a word.

Scraps of all the conversations she'd dreamed up between herself and her employer – that, for months now, had bolstered her shaky self-confidence – fluttered into her mind.

'Will that be all, Mr Curtis?'

'No, it damn well won't.' He used what she called manly language. Then, in an entirely different tone, 'Danielle, surely you know what I'm going to say to you?' From here the main stream divided, multiplied into a dozen delightful rivulets.

'You're such a surprising person.'

'You know, of course, I love you?'

'All my life I've been looking for the right girl – no, woman.'

'I can't go on rattling about in this house alone . . .'

'You need someone to look after you, for a change. Will you let me do that?'

'You mustn't despair,' she told herself a while later. She was sitting at her dressing-table taking off her face, which was in an awful state, what with her nose running so and the crying – mascara all smudged, and her foundation caked in little ridges round her nose and mouth. 'Of course you're not looking your best.' At the moment, she found it difficult to recall what her best was.

'Looks aren't everything,' she said, surprisingly, aloud, but she was too tired even to consider what 'everything' might be.

PERCY AND JACK

After a week or so of luxury in this extraordinary house, with little to do but hold measuring tapes for her aunt and housekeeping for Marvell, Percy was really grateful to have something more professional to do. A festival of arts sounded exciting. She had accompanied some authors to literary festivals, but had been restricted to their events only. Now she'd be involved, a little anyway, with the launch of a festival in a bigger way.

The morning room had been cleared to accommodate the committee round the drum table that normally stood in one of its bay windows. The atmosphere was that of a group who had been waiting too long for something to happen that they didn't particularly want to happen. Percy introduced herself, explained she'd been asked to take the minutes, and sat in the only remaining gilt chair next to the large one clearly meant for Jack, as he'd asked her to call him. The only person she recognized was Hugo, who winked at her with unconvincing bravado.

Otherwise there were four men. One looked rather like a fox in a blue suit; his hair, cut so that it rose vertically from his head, was bright red. Another, much older man, whom it would have been difficult not to call bald, rested his paunch uneasily on the table's edge. Another, his hair like a girl's, wore a bright yellow flannel shirt open at the neck with a crimson silk scarf so loosely tied he kept adjusting it. The fourth, a man in a fisherman's jersey, looked younger than the others. He had a high white forehead surmounted by dark curly hair. He gave her a tentative smile.

There were two women, one— Here Jack entered the room and swooped down beside her with perfunctory apology for the delay.

He opened the meeting briskly.

*

'I don't know about you, but I could do with a drink.' He strode ahead of her, across the hall and into the library. Percy followed him. The heavy white curtains had been drawn, and a fire lit, which was sorely in need of attention. 'Shall I put some wood on the fire?'

'Thanks. Or you could ring the bell for Juan.'

'No need.' When she'd done her best, she sat back on her heels to watch it, to make sure it was really going.

'Champagne?'

'Lovely. Thank you.'

'What did you think of them all?'

'Well,' she began carefully, 'they don't seem to know much about festivals.'

'Nor do I. Not a thing.'

'Why are you so keen on having one, then?'

'Several reasons, I suppose. I'm living here now, more or less, and it gives me something to do – here, I mean.'

'What else?'

'It's quite amusing to try to get a collection of people to do something they don't, or they hadn't thought they might, want to do.'

'You can't be doing it just for that.'

'Oh, but I can.'

'But what if they don't really want to go in for all the work and fuss entailed?'

'You'll see. Already they've reached the point where they've accepted the general idea.' He was sitting on a sofa opposite her and now he reached over to take her glass for a refill. 'By the next meeting they'll have come up with ideas and will start disagreeing with each other. They'll all have little axes to grind.'

'Sounds awfully patronizing to me.'

'Oh, it is. But very little gets done without patronage of one sort or another. It's the end result that matters, and *that* I'm keen on.'

'So, really, you're going to run it.'

'No. I'm going to be its patron. Actually, I had an idea. It occurred to me during the meeting, when you started talking about authors and all that. You made so much more sense than the others. The most obvious person present to run it is you.'

This shook her. 'What? I – I can't possibly do that. I don't even live here. I mean, it's very—'

'There's nothing to stop you doing it, is there?'

'Yes, of course there is. I have to get a new job – in London.'

'But you haven't actually got one, have you?'

'I mean,' she said, with embarrassment, 'I *have* to earn my living.'

'Of course you do. I'm offering you free board and lodging plus twenty-five pounds a week.'

'How can you? From the meeting we've just had it's pretty clear there isn't any money in the festival yet.' She met his maddeningly cool gaze defiantly.

There was a pause. Then he said, 'That won't be a problem because I shall be paying you.'

'Oh. So I just do everything you want?'

'Not at all. I know nothing about any of the arts. Started to read a bit, but the rest of it is Greek to me. I shall be available purely for practical advice about administration. There. Don't say yes or no. Think about it. '

'Does my aunt know about this?'

'Of course not. The idea only occurred to me during the meeting. Consult her. But please don't talk to anyone else about this until you've made up your mind.'

'All right. But please don't mention it to Floy at dinner. I want to talk to her by myself.'

At that moment Floy entered the room dressed in her old red housecoat, worn always for evenings when the company did not change. 'I gather Mrs Fanshawe is not well and has retired to bed. Perhaps, Zephie, you might go up and see if there's anything she needs?' This, though said to her niece, was aimed at Jack.

'Don't bother. I'll get Miss Pomfret to make a tray for her and Juan can take it up.'

Percy got to her feet. 'I did say I'd go and see how she was.' And she was out of the room before Jack could reply, colliding with Juan, who announced dinner was served in the morning room.

But Mrs Fanshawe – having feverishly completed an entire dream white wedding was now lying on fantastically white sand under a palm tree beside Mr Curtis, as she so teasingly still called him – merely muttered that she didn't want anything, thank you ever so much. She sounded quite grumpy, Percy thought.

Three hours later she was sitting in Floy's lilac-encrusted room with Marvell on her lap, waiting for Floy to get into bed and listen to her.

'You sound as though you've decided against the idea already.'

'I haven't – completely. It came out of the blue. I wanted to know what you thought first.'

'I think it sounds interesting. After all, it won't go on for ever, and it could be a most rewarding experience. You always say you don't like working in an office by yourself, and this would mean working with all kinds of people. And you already know about the literature side of it.'

'But I don't know much about music – I mean, how to get musicians to come. And I haven't the slightest idea how to get an art exhibition together. And if the chap who owns the theatre decides to put on an awful play, how can I stop him?'

'My dear Zephie, I hope at least some part of your lengthy education has fitted you to deal with any ignorance you encounter. You will find people who do know, and you can listen to them.'

'Here?'

'Wherever.'

'But I worry he – Mr Curtis – Jack will just boss me about all the time. I'll be a stooge. And then I'll sulk and quarrel.'

'That's up to you. In my experience, he's good to work for. He's direct, clear about what he expects, and perfectly prepared to leave the authority to people who know what they're talking about.'

'Or who don't. Look at this house.'

'He's done wonders to it. He's given it a new roof, damp-proofed it, got rid of the dry rot, and rebuilt the sash windows on the southern front. He's rewired, replumbed, and repaired the ceiling plaster in the hall, installed six new bathrooms and rebuilt the kitchen. If it hadn't been for him the whole thing would have decayed beyond repair. A few hundred yards of chintz is neither here nor there.'

'How do you know?'

'Darling, when we weren't out measuring things, I've spent hours poring over the contracts he had with builders of every description – what they've done and what it cost. I was researching the right people to do the preliminary work outside, the demolishing and the digging, that sort of thing.' There was a pause while Marvell landed on her lap and she helped him settle down. Then she said, 'He asked me to work for him, as a matter of fact. A permanent job. Said he'd convert the coach house for me. The second time I turned him down.'

'But why don't you? Are you absolutely sure you won't?' Percy had a sudden vision of them living in the coach house, a cosy, safe prospect, and letting the house in London, but keeping a bit for visits. It would be fun to do the festival if Floy was at hand to consult.

'No, darling. I'm not cut out to be a head gardener. I'm more like a flying doctor. And I have all my old clients to consider. And Marvell, who much prefers London.'

'What about me?'

'Persephone. Grow up. The job you've been offered is finite – a year at the very most, I should imagine. And I've agreed to pop down regularly to oversee the basic changes and planting. A new occupation will do you good.'

A moment later, she bent over the bed to kiss her aunt who said, 'You can always come home when it's over. You surely know that by now.'

She did know.

'Regard it as a challenge,' her aunt called, as she shut the bedroom door.

She decided to think properly about it in bed. She had a choice to make, after all. Choice is an adult luxury, she'd always thought. Everything was just arranged for you until you were grown-up, whether you liked it or not. As a child she hadn't liked it at all. Now, filled with the comfortable and happy certainty of reciprocated love and a decision to make, she acknowledged that freedom to choose wasn't necessarily the universal remedy she'd imagined. Maybe her childhood wasn't so terrible. She hadn't chosen to come to England to live with Floy, for instance. Actually, *had* she been asked to choose, she would have refused, as she had anything her parents suggested. How wrong she would have been. Floy had changed her life. From the first, Floy had loved her unconditionally. Perhaps that was the definition of love? But she'd still bleated on to others about her deprived childhood – notably to Denis. How untrue, if she really thought about it.

She had never returned to Greece, which made her feel guilty. They'd made such efforts to provide her with a home during the holidays. Each summer, for three years, her grandparents had taken her to Spetses, where they had a small summer house, for three weeks. When it was hot, which it usually was, she'd been allowed to sleep in the small garden under the fig tree surrounded by jasmine that was mysteriously sweeter in the dark. Mornings she spent in the sea while Grandfather – after a brief, powerful swim – has sat on the beach with his newspapers, wearing his Panama hat and smoking. At noon he would take her to a café where he drank ouzo and she had a Fanta, and at two they went home to Grandmother and lunch – of tiny fried fish, tomato salad and honey-soaked pastry, which Eleni bought at the shop, or macaroni stewed with aubergines, peppers and onion and a bowl of figs and grapes – on the terrace. In the heat of the day the air smelled of thyme and the sea. Her grandmother would make her wash the salt out of her hair before a nap in the little darkened room. Silence would seem to be everywhere. Sometimes she'd open her shutters a chink so there was a streak of glittering light that let her read, but usually she fell into a dreamless stupor.

When she woke and opened the shutters, the profound silence would be over. She could hear Eleni banging about with pots in the kitchen, or the murmur of voices on the terrace where her grandmother was dispensing tea to friends. Then she would slip out of the house and run down the narrow stone path to the beach and into warm but cool water and float on her back and watch the sky change as the sun began its descent into the distant sea. Before it set, when the fishing-boats were still dark, but the hill behind her had begun to blossom with weak yellow lights, she would leave the water and walk back up the path to the house, the air like warm velvet, scented with the jasmine and charcoal, and the sky, as it darkened, was adorned with trembling stars. She could remember thinking this was what pictures were for – to make a moment last for ever. The last evening she spent there, when she was twelve, she had sat on a rock beside the path and waited until she felt so full of the scene it would become indelible.

And it did. It was something she could recall at will. Not always, of course, but sometimes.

She *had* been extremely happy during those summers. The 'poor little Percy' routine was flawed. Her Dimitriou grandparents had given her a routine of peaceful pleasure she knew many children had never had.

She had lied to Floy, once, about her homework, and Floy, her Pirate Aunt, said nothing. She had confessed the next evening, having felt awful the whole day at school about it. 'I can't bear to tell you lies.'

Floy had said, 'Good. I don't like you telling them.' And after a pause she'd said: 'Actually, it is the lies one tells oneself that are the most dangerous. They go unchallenged and become ingrained. But I expect you've noticed that.'

The remark stuck in her mind, though she hadn't really understood it. Not until that awful spring evening with Denis in the flat when it struck her how much she'd lied to herself about him. It had shifted her idea of herself, her image; an uncomfortable and stark dislocation.

And now here she was again. So neither of her parents had been much good, but her grandparents and, above all, Floy had more than made up for it. Here she was with a perfectly good choice: go back to London or stay and take a risk running a festival. When she had made up her mind, she fell asleep.

★

Jack stayed up after the others had gone to bed. He was used to being alone, and the evening had given him a good deal to think about. It had been obvious from the committee meeting that – as in most meetings – none of its members possessed the driving force required to get the festival off the ground. Of course he had it but was hampered by his ignorance of the arts, so complete he couldn't influence the material suggested. He had seen, of course, that some of the ideas discussed were non-starters. Local amateurs wouldn't generate publicity or money – someone had to sketch out a viable programme to generate funding; he could raise money once that existed. But even before that they needed to explore all the possible venues. He got out his scarlet Smythson leather note-book, unscrewed his Cartier pen and wrote, 'Venues. How many, and what size?' That calmed him. He always liked making lists. 'Possible programme director'. Well. On impulse he'd asked the girl. She'd contributed most to the meeting, obviously understood books, and for all he knew she might have some experience with music and so forth. Even if she didn't, she looked like she might have friends who did. He'd made the offer, and hadn't allowed her to turn it down as her aunt had done with the gardening job earlier. Though with Floy he'd been pretty sure of a refusal, but it was a successful tactic to secure her services in overseeing the gardens. No – on the whole, he didn't think Percy would refuse him. If she did, he might have to raise the offer. That worked in a surprising number of cases.

As he finished his last drop of Macallan's, he thought of her. She wasn't particularly attractive, certainly not his type – no figure for a start. He'd never gone for dark hair – blonde or redhead was more to his taste – and green eyes had always seemed a bit . . . Well, he preferred blue – Linda. But then, as Linda had painfully shown, looks weren't everything. Kindness – he thought of Amelia – counted for a lot. You don't just want sex. You want affection – or something like it, though he couldn't say exactly what.

Well, she was intelligent, and she had secretarial experience and she was Floy Plover's niece. That was a pretty good start. He turned out the lights in the library, and as he walked up the stairs to his palatial bedroom, he thought it would also be nice to have somebody other than Mrs Fanshawe or the staff living in the house.

MARY

This can't go on, she thought, unable to think how it could not. Reggie, as he'd told her to call him, had been installed for little more than a week, and already it felt like a month – no, a timeless age. It was August, a cloudless summer morning with a golden shaft of hot sunlight invading the kitchen through the open door, and checkering the floor through the windows. A wasp was fitfully inspecting streaks of marmalade and honey on the breakfast plates. Mrs Peabody wasn't due for another hour. Thomas was at work in the nursery and Hatty on the first week of her fortnight in Cornwall with a schoolfriend whose parents had a house near Truro. Francis had offered to do the weekly shop and Major Reggie Brock had chugged off in his car to play golf. Thank God for golf, she thought, something she could never before have imagined she might think.

Once the decision had been made – Thomas and Francis assuming her consent – they had all worked together to find the best way of accommodating him. Converting an outhouse was far too expensive, unless he contributed, and as he hadn't yet sold his home it was a non-starter. In the end, they sacrificed the sitting room, which was large, had the advantage of being on the ground floor and had a separate shower and lavatory off it. It was the only room suitable for a bed-sitting room, which was – they innocently thought – what he would want. Francis made two trips to Surrey to help his father choose what furniture would suit, only to find when it came that Reggie had disregarded the list. An enormous sagging double bed arrived, with a bureau, six dining chairs, a sofa and two armchairs, three occasional tables, a sideboard, a glass-fronted bookcase, twelve photograph albums and a tea-chest packed with silver-plated cups and framed photographs of men, in military or sports uniform, usually with himself in the centre proudly holding a trophy. The removal men carted all this into the sitting room, drank their scalding tea and left.

'The place looks like an unsuccessful junk shop,' Francis had said. 'Well, he'll have to sort out what he wants most.'

'We can't just leave it like that,' she'd pointed out. 'We'll have to arrange it so he can sleep when he arrives.' They spent the day carting stuff to the outhouses and shifting the rest around.

'You wouldn't want a single book to furnish this room.' Francis sighed as they surveyed the result.

'And another thing,' he said, when they were back in the kitchen, 'His room leads directly into this one.'

'So?' Thomas was pouring drinks.

'So he can pop in here whenever he likes. There'll be no privacy.'

Mary could see he was getting distressed and guilty. 'Let's not worry too much.' She turned to Thomas. 'We agreed to try it, at least, didn't we?'

'We agreed. But I don't know about the trying part.'

'You mean he's burned his bridges? Well, he hasn't – quite. He hasn't had any offers for the house.'

This – mysteriously, she thought now – had seemed to cheer them all.

'Well,' Thomas said, 'perhaps he won't like it here. Quite sensible, really, not to burn his boats.'

Reggie had, in this short time, burned a good many other people's, she thought. The first evening he'd set out his stall. He didn't wanted to be any sort of bother, was perfectly prepared to muck in with everyone, only too anxious to help, just give him any little errand and if it was within his power he'd be only too glad. This was all fanciful hot air. He was obviously disappointed with his 'quarters', as he called them, and wondered aloud why they couldn't put some of his furniture into the sitting room.

'This *is* – was – the sitting room, Pa,' Francis said, as he heaved the huge leather suitcases on to the bed.

'Why are you putting them on the bed? What do you think that will do to the springs?'

'I thought it would be easier for you to unpack them.'

She'd followed them. A sort of back-up for Francis, she hoped. There was a brief silence while they watched him examining the room.

'I don't see any sign of my trouser press.'

'They didn't bring any trouser press.'

'It was certainly on the list. Did you check the list with the movers before they left?'

'We didn't have *your* list, Pa. We only had the one I made with you.'

'They must have gone off with it. You've put all my dining-room furniture into the dining room, I suppose?'

'We've had to store it, I'm afraid, Reggie. We eat in the kitchen.'

'The kitchen?' He was stunned, and Mary wondered if he might waver, a hope that died as she thought it. 'Sounds very jolly.'

He'd suggested, during supper, that perhaps there was a room he could use as his study, but Hatty pointed out the study was her father's. 'Nobody goes in it except him.' She spent a good deal of the meal observing her grandfather – a cool appraisal, of which he seemed quite unaware. He'd approached her with jocular patronage, and she'd been a child long enough not to respond to it.

'Doing well at school, are you?'

'I have no idea.'

He fell back on clichés grown-ups use with children.

Thomas had later suggested that he might do the household shopping and Mary gave him a list and directions for the butcher and the supermarket. He was gone for three hours and returned late for lunch and reproachful. He had obstinately chosen things he fancied and omitted the, notably, heavier items. 'Simply couldn't carry all of it – my back's dickey, you probably didn't know. I thought a spot of smoked salmon would come in handy. That? That's the best steak, they told me. Fillet. I bought the lot, because it's very good cold. They had bread at the supermarket so I didn't bother with the baker. What a marathon. Can't imagine why you need so much.'

It also prompted him to raise finances. 'Afraid I can't afford to foot the bill for everyone, Mary dear.'

'I think you'd better discuss that with Thomas.' Her voice trembled with rage, but he didn't notice.

He marched off to his room. 'Must take the weight off my feet – bit old for this sort of thing, you know.' The rebuke was evident.

'We can't afford smoked salmon and fillet steak.' She'd gone out to find Thomas on his tree plantation. 'He didn't take the slightest notice of the list. He uses a clean shirt every day, and expects me to bring him breakfast in his room.'

'Well, you offered him that.'

'I did, because it means at least one meal without him. He has a long rest after lunch, which means he's infuriatingly full of beans in the evening—'

Thomas started laughing. 'Oh, Mary, you really don't like him, do you?'

'I'm not alone, am I? Oh, yes, and when he said he couldn't afford the shopping for everyone, I said he'd better talk to you. About paying his whack, I mean.'

'Oh, Lord. I've no idea what would be fair – and he hasn't sold his house.'

'He says he's going to rent it, so he'll have that, apart from his pension and whatever else he's got.'

'I'm not much good at money. Ask Francis. Talk about it with him.'

But she knew Francis, already struggling with his feelings for his father, was blaming himself and feeling fantastically guilty for landing them with him. He wouldn't be able to handle this. And while it was she who managed their collective incomes, such as they were, she couldn't deal with it either.

Driving to Melton that afternoon, to complete the shopping, she decided that they would have to sort it out together some time when Major Reggie wasn't there.

His doctor had said he should take exercise, he'd told them earlier in the week at supper. Exercise was just the ticket when you were his age. If he didn't take exercise, his circulation would suffer, his muscles would seize up and in no time he'd be in a wheelchair, unable to be of any use to anybody. 'You have to look after yourself to prevent that sort of thing.' He'd looked round the table for agreement.

'Of course, you should be all right,' he said to Thomas, 'with all that manual work you do. No, I've decided to join the golf club – found out about it at the shop where I get my *Times*. Mary, my dear, I forgot to tell you that curry doesn't really agree with me . . .'

Well, he was golfing now, and the three of them could have a quiet lunch.

But when it came to it, they all found it difficult. Thomas, she suspected, was afraid of hurting Francis's feelings. Francis was nervous of starting a row. And she had come to fear her unequivocal dislike of the old brute.

Eventually Francis steeled his courage and said, 'Look. I know he's difficult. Well, hardly that, he's awful. He's had his own way all his life and bullied my mother, and he's not going to change. So I don't mind what you say about him. The question is, what are we going to do?'

'We're just discussing the rent. And I think Mary's the best person to decide. She's the housekeeper.'

She said, 'All right, but I agree with Francis that we need to talk the whole thing through. See if we have any other options. For instance, do you think he could go back to his own house if he had a lodger?'

'We should have thought of that before we moved him,' said Thomas.

'We didn't, but we have now.'

Francis sighed. 'Can you imagine a lodger who'd stand it for more than a week? Actually, he'd need more than one. He'd expect a cook, or cooking help of some kind. He told me he can't even boil an egg.'

Before she could stop herself, she exclaimed heatedly, 'He would say that. But if he was starving to death, he'd bloody well learn.'

Thomas was taken aback. 'I'd no idea you felt so strongly.'

'Well, she has him all day and he treats her like a servant. Exactly as he treated Mum. This house isn't big enough to have any kind of lodger, let alone him. He expects Mary to iron seven shirts a week for him.'

'Well, why did we agree to it in the first place?'

'I didn't,' she retorted. 'You both decided, then asked me to agree. It's not the same. We should've had a month's trial.'

'It's no good replying with what we should have done. It's what we do now we should decide.'

Then Francis said bitterly, 'When it comes down to it, we did this for Celia, really.'

There was a short, uncomfortable silence. Summoning all her courage, she said calmly, 'Celia's not here. And if she were, do you think – do you honestly think – that she would put up with him living here? Would she have expected us to have our lives completely changed?'

'No, she wouldn't,' Francis said. 'You're quite right.' He looked almost grateful.

'I don't see the need to bring Celia into it.'

'Thomas, I have to. That's why he's here.' She looked at Thomas's face, stony at the mention of his wife's name. 'Darling, what about Hatty? I know she's only had two days of him, but, apart from anything else, that's the room where she has her schoolfriends whenever they can't be outside. She's getting older. Her room's too small for them to be in.'

'We've made the most terrible mistake.' Francis was backing her up now, which made it easier for Thomas.

'Right. Options. He goes home and gets a lodger – or two. Or we find him somewhere nearby as a lodger. Or we get help. Mrs Peabody might do his laundry and he can pay for it.'

'I suppose we could, sort of, suggest the options to him. You know, put the ideas into his head.'

'Then he'll think we don't want him.'

'Well, we don't, do we?' Francis got up to put on the kettle. 'Maybe we should find him a wealthy widow – or any old widow. I never thought I'd long for a stepmother.'

Mary could sense slight desperation behind Francis's flippancy, but anything was better than agonized guilt. Thomas, too, had stopped worrying about eggshells.

But neither of them could handle the idea of negotiating with Reggie his share of the bills.

All afternoon she imagined his marble eyes bulging beneath his bushy oyster-shell eyebrows, his small tight mouth contracting under his ultra-military moustache. 'Good God, Mary, you must think I'm a millionaire.' If she asked for eighty pounds a month, all in – except for his whisky – she worked out that, with paying Mrs Peabody for his laundry, it would just about cover his food and a modest share of the household bills. They wouldn't make a penny out of his being there. She resolved to stand firm. Thomas thought it was too much and Francis nothing like enough. So, she thought crossly, she'd got it about right.

He behaved exactly as she'd expected. He even said he wasn't a millionaire. When she'd responded with some spirit that she never thought he was, and he couldn't stay anywhere for less, he capitulated. 'You've won!' he exclaimed. 'Beggars can't be choosers.'

THOMAS

It was too hot for this, thought Thomas, as he fumbled in his overall pocket where there might be some sort of rag to wipe the sweat streaming into his eyes. He had at last assembled the sacks of sand, compost, fine grit and concentrated manure, and the stacks of plastic pots were waiting to be filled. Business was quiet. Everybody had planted their hanging baskets and pots with bedding plants. The few that remained were on sale. When he'd potted up several hundred cuttings, he'd allow himself some less commercially viable experiments – perhaps taking cuttings from some slow-growing shrubs to see how that might work. This morning he was doing box in quantity, followed by a few camellias – magniflora and Cornish snow, an early white. His potting shed was too small, and he had to cart batches to the shaded polythene tent.

So, when he heard a car approaching, he was irritated at the interruption, covered the unpotted cuttings with a bit of damp sacking and went out to see who it was.

There was a white van from which emerged a small white-haired woman with a weatherbeaten face and a tall girl in a green dress, with bare legs and the sort of sandals Celia used to wear. He walked towards them.

'Mr Musgrove? My name's Plover. This is my niece, Persephone.'

She'd come to talk to him about his stock. She was reinstating a fairly large garden nearby, and would be requiring a good deal of hedging and edging, plus a fair number of trees. She wanted to know whether he grew his stock or bought it in. When he said that, with the exception of some bedding plants, he grew it, she was pleased. 'Good. I usually find that locally grown stock is more satisfactory.'

She asked to be taken round the nursery, and told her niece to get her notebook and come with them. They waited, and he watched the girl go back to the van. He noticed her long dark hair was tied back with a piece of green chiffon, the same colour as her dress.

Almost the same colour as her eyes, he thought, when – much later – they were all standing by the cash desk. He discovered, had half guessed, that the order was for Melton and it looked like being the largest ever to come his way. So her aunt was working for the rich shit who'd recently bought it.

'He's not going to turn the place into some sort of safari park, is he?'

'Nothing like that. He wants to restore the park and gardens to their former Victorian glory.'

Without thinking, he said, 'A lot of the garden was Edwardian, the rose garden and the largest glasshouse in the walled garden. All that was done just before the First World War.'

'Really? How interesting. I'm afraid the records relating to the grounds have disappeared.'

She – he couldn't remember her strange name – was looking bored, as though she wanted to go. 'As a matter of fact,' he said, 'the house used to belong to my family. I've got a few bits and pieces and old photographs. If you'd like to come into the house for a cup of tea, I could get them out for you.'

The offer was accepted, and they followed him along the cinder path that led them round the house to the kitchen door.

'It may be a bit of a mess,' he warned. He found himself minding about that, and a few other things that normally didn't matter. Would Mary be there to make the tea? She'd know if there were any biscuits or cake. Would the old boy be back from one of his trips to Melton? Was it one of Mrs Peabody's days? The door was open and he saw the polished flags at once, the scrubbed table, the absence of unwashed crocks, the neat bundles of herbs drying on hooks over the Rayburn, the white phlox and pale blue delphinium in the striped red and white jug he'd bought for Mary in their London days on the table. He saw it as though he'd never seen it before, with a kind of adventurous pleasure, and looked for an instant at the girl to see if she, too, saw it as he did.

'Hot raspberries,' she said, 'one of my favourite smells in the entire world.' She was standing beside the draining-board and a tray of cooling, uncapped jars.

'Mary's been making a lot of jam recently. Please, do sit down, and I'll see about the tea.' He was suddenly aware of his appearance, his sweaty shirt, his hands stained with compost, and the black crescents of his nails. How to get cleaned up and the whole business of getting the tea things on to the table? He looked wildly out of the windows, and there was Mary, thank God, coming out of one of the outhouses with a trug of tomatoes.

She saw him, and quickened her step.

'We've got guests – customers for trees. We all need some tea. This is Miss Plover and her niece.'

'It is very kind of you, Mrs Musgrove.'

Before Mary could reply, he said, 'Mary's my sister.' He paused and added, 'My wife's dead.' And then, aware of how bald it sounded, he added, 'So Mary looks after us, my daughter – and the family, generally. Miss Plover is dealing with the gardens at Melton, and wants to see what information we have about them.' And then he escaped and washed, scrubbed his hands and laved his face, then passed through to his study to collect the stuff about Melton.

When he returned, tea had been poured, a plate of shortbread was on the table, and Mary was saying, 'Part of the tree planting at the east side of the park recorded the battle formation of Nelson's fleet at the beginning of Trafalgar.'

The albums – there were two – did not yield much information. They consisted mainly of yellowing or sepia photographs of various people seated in basket chairs under the pergola, or standing stiffly on the front steps, or parties beside the tennis court, with the men in white flannels, the women in pale muslin frocks that showed their ankles and everyone sporting a racket. But one or two presented some vistas: of the fountain in the middle of the rose garden and one long view, through its open door, of the main glasshouse, showing an immense vine thick with clusters of grapes. There was also a rolled parchment with the design of a maze that was never planted in which Miss Plover was extremely interested. The girl was fascinated by the groups of people in the albums, some of which were cryptically captioned – 'Miss S. de W. Clementine. Fancy. Lord Heavyweather?'

Mary said, 'I think "Heavyweather" was my mother's name for a bore. Fancy was her spaniel. Don't know about the rest.'

Towards the end of this Francis appeared, and was greeted by the girl with obvious pleasure. 'I didn't know you lived here!' She said it as though he should have surely told her.

'Actually, I just biked up to Melton to see you because of the appointment with the Arts Council. I thought we should make some sort of plan before we go.'

'Yes, we should.'

She looked expectantly at him, and eventually, he said, 'Do you think, perhaps, that we should call another meeting before we go?'

'No. I think we should go – find out what they'll do for us, if anything, then tell the others at the next meeting.' When Francis seemed uncertain, she said, 'Could you come up to the house this evening after supper? Nothing much goes on after that.' And when he agreed, she looked at him and smiled, and

Thomas, merely the silent witness to this exchange, was none-theless struck by how the smile revealed her.

His attention was turned to Miss Plover, who wished to discuss some sort of timetable for delivery.

'We should be ready to do some of the planting by the middle of October. I should be back from London by then – and provided I can find the staff to do it. Do you, by any chance, have any people you can recommend?'

He said he would think about that. She said she would make a list of what would be initially required. Then there was a general move to leave. They were going.

'Any time after eight thirty,' the girl said to Francis, who accompanied them to the van. 'Jack is catching a morning flight to Málaga, so dinner will be early.'

When Thomas had finished his cuttings, and watered them, he walked back down the field, along the track that ran between the ranks of his young trees. The sun mellowed as it sank slowly behind the wood that bordered the west side of his plantation, leaving the golden sky around it streaked with rose-coloured wisps of cloud. The colony of rooks that roosted in the wood was travelling, black against the pale air, surging in uneven clusters, twenty, then two stragglers, then five, a pause, then a countless cloud, flying steady and purposeful towards their night. He stood and watched until they were gone. An evening routine he'd watched many times, but had never seen until now. The sight soothed his painful agitation and conflict.

'My wife's dead.' Saying it to total strangers – a matter of pure fact – had, without warning, changed everything. He saw now how grief, the endurance of it, had consumed him. Unbear-able, often resisted memories of Celia were entirely about his loss, rather than her. In six years he'd turned her into a painful, anonymous perfection who had suddenly betrayed him by dying. The drunken evenings with Francis, of which later he'd become so ashamed, had at least been honest mourning. They had shared anecdotes, little pieces of their memories of her. Once, late at night, his rage had overwhelmed him: 'Why, in God's name, did she drive – try to drive back so late? She could have stayed with you.'

Francis had looked at him for a while before he said, 'Because she wanted to be with you.'

Now, for the first time in years, he remembered his first sight of her, perched upon a bar stool in the foyer of a theatre, half listening to a man in a tartan shirt earnestly holding forth. Her eyes had wandered and rested on him. She'd gazed with a passive intensity, until she had said something to her partner, got off the stool and come up to him.

'How lovely see you. Again.' And she'd winked with a kind of gleeful conspiracy.

He'd played the game. By the time the interval was over, they'd agreed to meet after the play. Opposite each other, when they were seated, he asked whether she often picked up strange men in bars.

'Only when absolutely necessary.'

Later, he said, 'Was he an awful bore?'

'Yes, but it wasn't that.' They were the last people in the restaurant.

The weeks before they married slipped past like some miraculous dream where nothing was impossible, or even difficult, even the admittedly awkward introduction to her parents.

'I suppose you love me because I've got red hair and no prospects,' he'd said, as he drove them back to London in her car.

'Yes. I love you for everything about you.'

'She's very beautiful,' Mary had said, after they had met. She said it anxiously, as if Celia's beauty might be a trap.

'I know. But she knows how to be. She's not dazzled by it, and neither am I. For her it's just a bit of charming luck.'

And Francis. In a way, that had been the most uncertain

meeting. Francis was shy, and wary of him, and it was immediately clear he adored his sister. 'How long have you known her?'

And when he said about three weeks, Francis had muttered something about that not being very long, but then Celia had come back into the room and he said no more.

When they were alone, Celia had said, 'It's all right with Francis. He's just a bit protective.'

No, nothing then had seemed difficult. They lived in the sunlight of their mutual, increasing love, of a reciprocal passion that enchanted them both. If he *was* dazzled, it was by her generosity and directness.

'Do you think we'll always feel like this?' His question came back to him now, and he would never forget her answer.

'If we're grateful for it, why not?'

That was how it had been, and he'd buried it all when she died.

The rooks were long gone. A light breeze roused him as the sun went in, and as he walked back down the field to the house he realized the girl whose name he hadn't caught was the first person he'd actually seen – been really aware of – since Celia.

FRANCIS AND PERCY

'I don't think we did too badly. They didn't actually turn us down.'

'You were stunning. I don't think they were so keen on the art part of it.'

'Well, he said it wasn't his department. We have to see a Mr White for that.'

'He also said Mr White was on leave, so we couldn't have seen him anyway.'

'And then there's music and the theatre. I suppose Mr Black and Mr Blue are in charge of them. And if we'd asked to see them we'd have found out that one was on sick leave with glandular fever and the other on a cruise.'

Percy couldn't help laughing.

From the Arts Council headquarters in St James's Square, they had wandered aimlessly into Jermyn Street without speaking. Percy was thinking about sponsorship and how to get some, and Francis was overwhelmed with shyness. He'd had three bouts of it with the man who wasn't Mr White, and now, with that ordeal over, he was having one with Percy. The common cause of the festival had propelled him into an intimacy with her that survived only when they talked of it. It was she who broke the silence by suggesting that they had lunch. 'But where?'

'I do know a place off Shaftesbury Avenue that might be all right. It's quiet and not expensive and only about ten minutes' walk from here.'

Percy said, 'Fine. Let's go.'

So now they were seated opposite one another in an atmosphere of dusky plush, their faces illumined by the small table lamp between them. When Percy had started talking about the meeting, he'd relaxed once more, and when she laughed at his little joke, he felt more at ease and flushed a little with pleasure. They decided on the lunch menu and a carafe of house red. The restaurant was only half full, and the very old waiter who attended them made them feel that their choice was the best.

When they had begun their *pâté maison*, Percy said, 'The trouble is we don't know enough – music, for instance. I think I can manage the literary part of the festival, and you know about art and paintings, and I suppose the man with the girl's hair – Derek something – must know about theatre or he wouldn't be opening one, but we haven't got a music expert. I think your idea of portraits of various writers is brilliant.'

He blushed if she said anything encouraging to him, she noticed. Or perhaps it wasn't to do with her. Maybe he just wasn't used to being with people.

'It might be a good idea. Whether I'll be any good at finding the paintings is another matter.'

'Of course you will. I mean, obviously you'll get better at it as you go on. One thing leads to another with that sort of thing.'

How wonderfully confident and poised she was. She had every reason to be. She was one of the most attractive girls he'd met for a long time. Celia had sometimes worn small gold earrings, three little interlocked rings. Percy had silver dolphins, a bit larger, one in each ear. They set off her olive neck and dark hair, and undulated gently when she moved her head. On an impulse of pure admiration, he said, 'But you're so sure of yourself. I can't imagine anyone more likely to be unfazed—'

But here he broke off. Her face had changed, had paled and frozen. Her eyes had something near panic in them and he followed them to see a man with an open-necked floral shirt leading a tall blonde girl by the hand and saying, 'Very discreet.' The man saw Percy, blenched, recovered, then ignored her. They passed so close Francis could have touched them. He turned back to Percy.

'It's all right,' she said, with a small meaningless smile.

The old waiter had brought their casserole of veal, and returned now with a dish of vegetables. He refilled their glasses, glanced at Francis to confirm that all was well and padded away to the back of the restaurant.

'Have some wine.'

She picked up her glass and he saw that her hand was shaking.

'Do you want to leave? Shall I get the bill?'

'Of course not.' Then she added, 'But thanks for asking.' And then, seeing something of his helpless concern as he looked at her, she said, 'It was just someone I know – knew.'

Someone she loved, he thought. It must be. She doesn't want to talk about it. Got to get through this bit of time with her – help her not to cry. Distract her. Anything will do.

'Do you know anything about children's books?'

'Not much. The publisher I worked for did publish some, but I didn't have much to do with it.' She had started to eat her veal.

'Well, you might still be able to give me some advice. I've been telling Harriet, my niece, bedtime stories for a while now, and drawing pictures of the main character, and I suddenly thought perhaps it would make a book, that I could earn some money.'

She asked, as he'd meant her to, what the book was about, and he said a frog – a fairly magic frog. 'Has he got a name?'

'Greeny Hopper. Hatty thought of it.'

They got through the main course, of which she ate little. So when the waiter came to clear the plates he said, 'You wanted to go to your aunt's house to collect some clothes. Shall we just have some coffee and the bill?'

She assented gratefully to this, and shortly afterwards they were in the street, looking for a taxi.

Once she'd given the driver the address, he said, 'I used to live in Maida Vale with my sister. Before she was married.'

There was silence for a while, and then, more to keep the conversation alive than anything else, she said, 'Does she still live there?'

'No. She was Thomas's wife. She died – crashed her car driving back one night from London. The police said she probably went to sleep for a few seconds – a bend in the road and she just went straight ahead. Didn't hurt anyone else.' He stared blankly out of the window as he said it.

'Oh, Francis. How awful for all of you.'

He turned back to her and saw something of the same expression that had so struck him before – sweetness, whole-hearted concern.

'Shock,' she said, after a moment. 'The awful shock of it.'

'In the end, you sort of get used to it.' He wanted to stop talking, in case he discovered this wasn't true.

She seemed to sense no more was to be said, and by the time they arrived at Adelaide Villa they had slipped back to being new friends with a great deal of unknown ground between them.

Her aunt was out, so she made him some coffee and put him in the conservatory while she packed her clothes. A black cat came in, looked at him, sprang on to the table and inspected him further, its tail swaying gently as though impelled by a light breeze. He put out a hand to stroke it, but the cat evaded him and sat upright and severe at the far end of the table. His fur, with the sun on it, was the colour of Guinness. Francis got out his notebook and began to draw him.

When Percy joined him, he'd finished nearly four drawings. She thought the third was most like Marvell, as though he was an actual person. 'Floy would love it,' she said, so he tore it out of his notebook and left it on the hall table with Percy's note to her aunt.

'She's coming down to Melton next week. At least, I hope she is.'

In the train she told him her aunt had more or less brought her up, which led to a mutual enquiry about their parents. Each answered with such dismissive brevity that neither was much the wiser. He asked her what it was like living at Melton, and she said it was a bit like a nearly empty hotel. There were still workmen there, and she thought perhaps Jack, as she called him, was waiting until everything was finished before he invited friends to stay. 'Meanwhile it's just me and some of the time him, and Floy, of course, when she comes down and poor Mrs Fanshawe. And, of course, even poorer Hou-arn – as Mrs F calls him – who does nearly everything and is bossed about by the cook and Mrs Fanshawe. It's better for me now that I've got the festival to work at. Otherwise I would have gone weeks ago.'

'I suppose you would.' He smiled at her rather sadly – of course she would.

For the rest of the journey they talked about the festival. They agreed Francis would write a letter, to be enclosed with Percy's letters to publishers, outlining generally the proposed exhibition of portraits of writers, and asking for any information they might have, and that he should also write to Mr White for help and information.

'If you draft the letter, I'll type it up for you and run off copies as we need them.'

She dropped him off at Home Farm where Hatty was sitting on the gate.

'You didn't meet me at the station. And you're nearly late for supper,' she shouted, jumping off the gate and starting to open it.

'It's all right, we're not coming in.' He got out of the car. 'Thanks for the lift – and the day and everything.' He put his head through the open window. 'Or – would you like to come in for a drink?'

'She can't stay for supper, Francis, because Mary has made one fish for each person. I know Jesus could in olden times, but that was for thousands of people, and I don't suppose He would have thought it worth while for just one. But you could come on another evening, if you like.' Hatty had come round to the driver's window and was examining Percy with unblinking interest. She had the same high forehead as Francis, the same moth-like eyebrows above the same candid, strikingly penetrating eyes.

'Only we do have the drawback of Gramps. He's in for supper every night.'

'Thank you,' Percy said. 'I'd love to come some time, but I've got to go now.'

Francis watched her drive off, with Hatty tugging his arm.

'Francis, I've thought of a Gramps joke. Gramps and kidney pudding, minced Gramps pie, curried Gramps with rice—'

'Not a good joke.' He took her arm since she was giddy with laughing. 'It's not good to tell jokes that have to be behind the person's back. Tell me about your holiday.'

Which she then did at interminable length. It had clearly been a success. 'I got wounds on my knees from the rock pools. I had to use up twenty-three Band-aids. Meg's mother ran out twice. Twice, Francis. Are you listening? Because I want to ask you something quite difficult.'

'Of course I'm listening. There's no one else to listen to.'

'Well, the question is – does the sea join up everywhere?

'Not absolutely everywhere. Why?'

'Well, Meg and I each had our own special rock pool, and every day when the sea came in, it washed away the shrimps and crabs we were training to be pets, which was sad, but I sort of hoped that there might be a bit of different sea in them – like the Indian Ocean or the one where Robinson Crusoe had his island, only there's so much sea you can't tell if it's going anywhere. What do you think?'

He said it was an interesting thought, and he wasn't Jacques Cousteau, so he couldn't be sure.

'Well, ask Greeny, would you? He seems to know everything.'

'He thinks he knows everything.'

'That means he knows a lot more than the people who don't.'

They had stopped walking to the house during this exchange. 'I'll ask him,' he said, and set off again.

The tension at supper was worse than usual. Hatty, fresh from her holiday, wanted to tell everyone about it, which went down badly with Reggie, who'd had an altercation with the secretary of his golf club and, anyway, thought children shouldn't be much heard from. Thomas was strangely hostile – twice alluding to Francis gallivanting about London on a day he usually helped in the nursery. He speculated that, with this bloody festival, he'd have to expect more of this. Francis said it was a one-off occurrence. They'd got to the blackberry crumble and Hatty, having eaten hers very quickly, asked if she might get down as she wanted to ring her friend Meg. Mary said she could, but Thomas asked why she needed to ring someone with whom she'd just spent a fortnight. Her grandfather reflected loudly that in his day children weren't allowed to use the phone at all. Hatty said, 'It's not your day and Mary said I can, so sucks to you.' Mary made her apologize, which she did very fast with no punctuation at all so even that sounded rude.

He wanted, suddenly, to escape – to be sitting again on the train with Percy. Or, at least, to be alone so he could ponder the day he'd had, unlike so many other days. He wasn't the only one. Thomas muttered he had some paperwork to sort out and his father supposed he'd get out of everyone's way and make do with the wireless. So Francis stayed and helped Mary clear up.

'He says we're in a rut.'

'Who does?'

'Reggie.'

He looked at her face to see if this was a joke, but it wasn't.

'He asks why we don't entertain. We don't seem to have any friends. He wants to have regular bridge parties, but he can't have people to play bridge in his bedroom and fish doesn't agree with him at night, and why does a child of eight have to stay up for dinner?' She ran out of breath and scraped the fish bones into the compost bucket.

'And,' she said, rinsing the plate, 'we *are* in a rut. Nothing has happened since we had that talk. I did the money bit, but you haven't put the options to him about lodgers and everything. Have you?'

He hadn't. 'No. I will. I've been shirking it.' He stood by her and put a tray of water glasses on the draining-board, and as she pushed a strand of hair from her eyes, he saw how tired she was and realized how seldom he looked at her properly. 'I'll finish the clearing up,' he said. 'You make us some coffee.'

She said something about getting Hatty to bed, but he said he'd deal with her and they could have their coffee in Mary's bit of garden – a nice quiet time to themselves, which made her smile and everything felt lighter.

He dealt with Hatty easily, bathed and in bed in twenty minutes or Greeny wouldn't come near her. When he returned to the kitchen again, Thomas was there, wanting coffee made for him and complaining about Hatty having a bath exactly when he wanted one. 'She always used to have hers before supper,' he was saying. 'You'll have to speak to her about it, Mary.'

So they didn't go out to the garden, but sat at the kitchen table talking quietly in case it provoked an appearance by Reggie.

Harmony was restored, and though Francis reflected that no three people talk as any two might, it was still a comfortable end to the day. Thomas made up for his surliness at dinner by admitting he'd actually felt envious of Francis having a day off – meeting new people, going to a restaurant. Mary said if he felt like that, he should certainly go. 'You could take Hatty. She'd love it.'

Francis could see this wasn't what Thomas had had in mind, though he agreed he could, of course.

'What's her name, that girl you went with?'

'Percy. Her name's Persephone, but she's called Percy. Except her aunt calls her Zephie too.'

Mary said, 'I must say I liked the aunt. She looked so reliably sincere.'

'I thought she looked like a little indoor pirate.'

'It doesn't matter what you think, Francis. She's going to make our fortune. Does the girl, the niece, work with her?'

'No. She's between jobs. She works in publishing.'

'So she won't be staying here?'

'Off and on while the festival churns on.'

At the top of the stairs, he touched Mary's shoulder and, when she turned, kissed the side of her face, which seemed both to surprise and please her. 'Sorry about the rut.'

'Oh.' A small shrug. 'I'm sure we'll get out of it. You're such a tower of strength, Francis.'

This embarrassed him. 'I don't think so, but any other kind would be pretty alarming, wouldn't it?' And he escaped to his room.

Lying on his back in the dark, the easily suppressed and evaded anxieties came back to him. What on earth, precisely, was he going to say to his father? Tact wouldn't work. He was impervious. He'd either deliberately misunderstand or he'd— What would he do? Overwhelm him with his age, his poverty, his loss? Oh, God. Whatever happened there'd be a row and if he, Francis, didn't stand firm, the row wouldn't be the end of it. He realized then that never in his life had he stood up to his father properly. The scenes, and there had been so many over the years, usually ended with him walking out – nothing resolved – in a kind of surrender. He could deal with his father when Celia was there. She'd turned Pa from an object of fear and hatred to someone mildly absurd. Without her, he'd reverted.

It wasn't so much his father he hated, but the fear he engendered. It was this despicable, useless fear he really hated – it made him almost what his father thought him: cringing, passive, without the strength to stand up for himself, someone he most passionately didn't want to be. No, the rows had never resolved anything. He'd gone his own way, but he saw now that his idea of his father was forged from this fear, these commotions. He didn't really *know* him at all. Why did he behave like he did? He tried now to imagine a life, his father's, without affection – let alone love. It occurred to him that perhaps even his mother hadn't loved him, or maybe she'd tried and been repulsed. If you were unaware, ignorant of love, it would be as difficult to receive as to give. People married to be together, to have children, to be cared for and because they fell in love, and because it was expected of them.

But, then, even if one truly loved somebody, misfortune could intervene so easily and wreck it – wreck them all. As it had Celia. As it had Thomas, Hatty, himself – even Mary, who had sacrificed her own life to stop Thomas drinking himself to death and to mother Hatty. They were like survivors of a shipwreck, huddled on the same shore, salvaging what they could from the tragedy. Somehow they had made the shore into an island, not much inhabited by anyone but themselves.

JACK

'Melton.'

'Very good, Mr Curtis.'

Pressing a finger to close one side of his nose, he snorted cautiously and popped his left eardrum. He'd flown so much in the past week or so that his ears hadn't really recovered between flights.

Still, it had been a successful trip. The Toronto construction company in which he'd recently acquired a controlling interest now had a chief executive of whom he approved. The dead wood had been sacked and a leaner, more competitive company should emerge. He'd had a spot of trouble in Chicago, but a couple of hairy meetings seemed to have improved things. Now they just had to show they could do what they said they could. The Florida situation still had to be resolved. Late nights there and the faintly bizarre episode with a pneumatic blonde in a beach house had meant even less sleep. 'I think you're real cute,' she'd said, with a striking lack of conviction.

He yawned and looked at his watch. They were on the A4 and should be back in less than two hours. His dining room was finished at last, and he had invited Wystan and Amelia for the weekend. Miss Plover was due, and of course there was Percy. Their advent had really made him realize how sick he'd become of meals with Mrs Fanshawe. She was still useful – well, essential, really – as a secretary, she worked hard and reliably, but he wished now he'd employed her on a daily basis, rather than live-in. When he'd first come to Melton, still full of builders and decorators, he'd been glad of the company and someone who knew, as indeed she did, more about his business than anyone.

But since the Plovers' arrival, he'd increasingly wanted to be able to switch Mrs Fanshawe off – like a gas hob – and talk about trees and novels with the aunt and niece, as he sometimes called them. For nearly four months now he'd had the stimulus of their company, the aunt intermittently – she appeared every other week for a few days – but the niece, now that he'd made her the festival's director, a permanent guest. Percy had been the only person in sight able, or likely, to take on such a challenge. She had hinted that perhaps she'd look for a place in the village or even go back to London and visit every so often, like her aunt, but he didn't want her to leave. Why not? Partly it was nice to have someone to talk to in the evenings, and partly because the more the house became furnished and finished, the emptier it felt with just him and the staff in it. She wasn't his type – nothing like that.

He yawned again. God, he was tired. Still, it was only Wednesday, and he was looking forward to showing Wystan and Amelia the house, his estate, and – most importantly – his new friends, who in turn would see he had other friends. Yawning had popped his eardrums again: he was starting to feel human. As he dropped off, he visualized Mrs Fanshawe, who always happened to be in the hall whenever he got back. 'Welcome home, Mr Curtis.' She always managed to make the *o* in 'home' sound as though it was issuing from too small a hole in her face.

But it was Percy who met him, halfway up the stairs. 'You're just in time.'

'My plane was late. In time for what?'

'Dinner – well, supper, really. It was supposed to be grilled duck breasts but I put them on too early – my fault.'

'Why on earth are you cooking?'

'Miss Pomfret's left – the day after you went. Mrs Fanshawe's been trying to get a replacement. She did find somebody, but they only lasted two days. I was just going up to see if she knew your flight number so we could check whether you were actually getting back tonight or not.'

'Is your aunt here?'

'Oh, yes. She's been helping me in the kitchen, but she only got here this evening. Mrs Fanshawe's gone to bed with a migraine, and it's Juan's day off. We thought we might as well eat in the kitchen to save trouble.'

Rather dazed, he followed her through the baize door, down the flagstoned passage, through two more doors to the square room at the north end of the house that his architect had turned from a collection of storage rooms into a kitchen, equipped with every imaginable appliance and gadget. He'd only seen it once before when the architect had more or less forced him to inspect and admire it; then it had seemed satisfactorily like grand country-house kitchens in magazines with rows of handmade wooden cupboards, slate worktops, and a pair of porcelain double sinks flanked by hardwood draining-boards. Down the centre of the room the long pine table was laid at one end for supper.

'I'm resting your breasts under the turned-off grill,' Floy said, rather surprisingly, as she turned to greet him. She was wearing her roll-necked fisherman's jersey and corduroy trousers, tucked into her gum-boots, and was mashing potatoes.

'We've opened a bottle of wine,' Percy said. 'I hope that's all right. That's your chair.'

'Fine.' He sat down with relief and watched Percy light the candles, then turn down the ceiling lights. There was a bowl of various red berries on the table. It was all rather cosy and restful, he thought. What it would have been like to come back to a house with no food or staff, except Mrs Fanshawe in bed with a migraine, also crossed his mind.

'It's very good of you to do all this,' he said, as a plate of duck breast, mashed potato and buttered vegetables was put before him.

'You mean it's not our place, but it would be if we were anywhere else. Sorry about the duck. We had to have it because it was "on the menu", as Mrs F would say. She does the menus and we couldn't waste them. Actually, I think tough food can be quite interesting. I once went to a dinner party where the hostess had smashed everything up in a mouli – three courses – and it was like being a grown-up baby, all sloppy and dull. Floy taught me to cook,' she added, and he noticed that when she said this she glanced at her aunt with a fondness that changed her face entirely.

The duck was followed by an extremely good apple charlotte, then Percy cleared up while Floy gave him a report on progress outside. 'Trees are going in and a lot of the hedging. It's good, mild, damp planting weather. I've persuaded Thomas Musgrove to help me with the bigger trees. The bulldozers have finished with the kitchen garden, and work has begun on the big glasshouse. They can use the foundations, but the framework is nearly all rotted and it will be simpler to replace it all rather than attempt to patch. There's one very old vine, but I think we can save it. I've cut it back to the bone and we've covered it with sacking in the hope that it will survive until it gets its new roof.'

'Fine,' he said. 'You must take me on a tour tomorrow.' But his mind was on the coming weekend, and the worrying lack of staff. 'What are we going to do about the cook situation?'

'Oh, I'm sure one will turn up. Mrs Fanshawe has been on to several agencies, but the one she got came with very dicey references and there wasn't time to check them. So it might be a week or two.'

'Well, it can't be. I've got these friends coming for the weekend. That's in two days.'

There was a pause. Then Percy said diffidently, 'Well, I think

I could manage simple meals if we could get someone as well as Juan to help out.'

'But I've arranged a dinner party on Saturday night and you're meant to be at it. You have to be, because I've got someone who owns several pubs and might sponsor some of the festival. We have to find someone – a real chef – to do the job.' He realized he was sounding a touch hysterical and stopped.

Floy, who had been observing him calmly, suggested there was nothing they could do about it now. Better to have a good night's sleep and tackle the problem in the morning.

In bed, as he was on the point of sleep, he thought gratefully of how kind the two had been – like friends. Then the memory of Percy's face when she'd said her aunt had taught her to cook came back to him. Nobody had ever looked at him, and he'd never looked at anyone, like that.

MARY

On Thursday morning it was raining – had been raining most of the night and showed no signs of stopping.

'It's going to completely spoil my day,' Hatty had wailed. It was half-term and, of course, she was going to spend it with Meg.

'You can play Monopoly.'

'You can't play Monopoly on a bicycle. We were going to go to the forest to have a picnic.'

'I'll make you an indoor picnic. Anyway, it won't rain all day.'

'All right. But please don't put green stuff into the sandwiches.' She clomped off to phone her friend.

Mary sighed. At breakfast there had been a spat between Thomas and Francis. The latter had forgotten it was Thomas's day for tree-planting up at Melton and that he was supposed to field customers at the nursery.

'There won't be any in this weather,' he'd argued, and Thomas had snapped back that that wasn't the point: at this time of year people might easily buy plants for the weekend.

At that moment Reggie had emerged from his room. Something awful had happened to his top plate and he had to go to London at once to have it seen to. 'It's all right. I've rung my dentist and he's prepared to fit me in. Always helps the walking wounded, he said – jolly good chap.' With his teeth out, he looked rather like a tortoise. 'So all I need is a lift to the station,' he finished.

'I can't drive you, and Francis has to stay here. Take your own car and park it.'

'What about Mary?'

'What about her?'

'I'm not sure I feel up to driving.'

Mary was just about to give in, when Francis said, 'Oh, come on, Pa. You don't need your teeth for driving. If you really don't feel up to it, call a taxi.'

After grumbling that it was almost impossible to use the phone because the child was always on it, he decided to drive himself. An atmosphere of general ill-humour prevailed. It didn't improve when Francis said, 'I'll have to ring Percy. I arranged to go up to Melton. We've got a council meeting tonight and we need to prepare our progress report. I'll have to see if she'll come down here.'

This, Mary noticed, made Thomas crosser than ever. The thought had struck her several times lately that Thomas was very taken with Percy. He'd been quite keen on her coming to supper, which she'd done two or three times. He'd always washed and put on a clean shirt for these occasions. She'd observed that it irritated him when Percy and Francis talked about the festival, but he enjoyed asking about herself and her aunt, of whom he deeply approved. Once, when she and Mary were sharing their appreciation of Jane Austen, she had noticed that he was watching Percy intently. They were discussing the role Lady Russell played in dissuading Anne from an engagement to Captain Wentworth in *Persuasion*, which Mary deplored. Percy had pointed out, however, that her attitude was essential to the plot.

Just then Thomas had suddenly said, 'Would you marry somebody if your aunt deeply disapproved of them?'

And Percy, clearly caught off balance by the question, had turned to him in startled silence before she replied, 'I – well, I suppose I might. But Floy would never be like that. It just wouldn't happen.'

And Francis said, 'So nobody could write that novel about you.'

His voice had a kind of teasing solemnity and she responded in kind. 'Oh, no. I wouldn't do at all as an Anne.'

But Mary perceived the faintest colour rise in her face as she changed the subject and, also, that Thomas had noticed it too.

The trouble with these private intimations is that, unchecked by an audience, they race headlong to enormous conclusions. In no time she was imagining Thomas in love with Percy, engaged to her and married, and while part of her longed for him to be happy – to regain some of the energy and bliss Celia had inspired – another part was flooded with misgivings. Thomas had all the innocence of a full-blooded romantic and his experience of meeting Celia – love at first sight for both of them – compounded it. Percy might only want an affair with no commitment. And Hatty: no child took easily to a stepmother. It's a wearisome uphill task to overcome the hostility or indifference, and Percy might not be old enough to deal with it. I could help her there, she thought, and when things had settled down, naturally I'd go. Francis, too, would have to leave.

For a moment, a fantasy of Francis and her beginning an entirely new life together floated in her mind – and sank. She was bleakly aware of his loyalty and warmth, but he was seven years younger; she and he needed to make lives for themselves. Chance had thrown them together and chance would as easily part them. It was impossible, at this point, not to pair Francis with Percy, but what she'd seen of them together, and the way Francis spoke of her, seemed fraternal. No, it was Thomas she was worried about, had worried about as long as she could remember. The very familiarity of that was somehow soothing. She liked Percy. She liked the way her face was constantly lit up, her liveliness, the way she spoke about her aunt, her good manners to Reggie and, not least, her interestingly compassionate attitude towards Charlotte's marriage to Mr Collins in *Pride and Prejudice*. She had changed the linen on all four beds by now and struggled downstairs with an armful of sheets to find Francis and Percy coming through the yard door to the kitchen.

'It's all right. I've put a note on the shed telling people to knock on the front door here if they need help.'

'You know we hardly ever hear it. Hello, Percy. We ought to have the bell mended.'

'Do you want me to go and put "loudly" on the note?'

'Not much.' She dumped the linen in front of the washing-machine at the far end of the kitchen and noticed the first wash she'd put in wasn't washing. 'Oh, damn this thing. It's broken down again.'

'We need a new one.'

We need a new practically everything, she thought, as she fiddled with the knobs. Breakfast hadn't been cleared off the table, it wasn't Mrs Peabody's day, and she was irritated that Francis had brought Percy in to witness the mess.

Francis had begun to move the breakfast things and Percy was helping. 'We certainly need a new boiler,' he was saying. 'It was out again this morning. I'll go and ring the washing-machine man.

'Percy wants to ask you something.' And he went off to Thomas's study.

Percy was rinsing plates and mugs and putting them into the rack. She hadn't taken off her jacket and her hair, done up in a plaited ponytail, was glistening with rain.

Mary sighed. 'Sorry we're so untidy. I had to make Hatty a picnic before doing anything else. Would you like some coffee?'

'Only if you're having some.'

When she'd put on the kettle, she looked at Percy. 'What was it you wanted to ask me?' She spooned instant coffee into mugs. 'Please don't bother any more with the washing-up.'

'Well.' Percy moved from the sink to the table. She looked nervous. 'It was Francis's idea, actually. I mean I came to ask if any of you had any ideas and he said you.'

'Ideas about what?'

'He was out, of course, but I left a message with his wife. Have you asked her?' Francis came into the kitchen.

'No. I was just starting to explain.'

'It's quite simple. They're in a hole up at the house because the cook left suddenly and Jack Curtis has asked friends for the weekend and also invited people to dinner on Saturday night. They got another cook, but she only stayed a day, so Percy came to ask me if we knew anyone, and I said yes – you!'

'I can't cook properly, you see. I mean I can do a few simple things, but not a full-blown dinner. He wants it to be like that – you know, four courses and no holds barred.' Percy looked pleadingly at her as she said this. 'Francis says you're a professional, really, and you teach it. Jack said he'd pay anything. He just wants it to be wonderful for his friends – you can buy anything you want for it.'

The moment she agreed, a recollection came to her, hazy through time, of her childhood kitchen when her parents were alive. It was in the basement down dark stone stairs and along an ill-lit passage. The windows had heavy bars on them, adding to the dungeon-like effect. She remembered an enormous kitchen range, the tall hods of coke with which it was constantly fed and the curious zinc-lined box that contained the block of ice delivered by the fishmonger each week. The food never reached the dining room anything but fairly warm. She had braved the journey down there only if Thomas bribed her to extort a goody from the cook – gingerbread, fairy cakes, the odd leftover castle pudding – and then she'd get whiskery hugs from Mrs Allabone, whose apron strained over her vast bosom and who smelled of mushrooms and carbolic soap.

'Oh, that's wonderful. Jack will be so relieved.'

'I hope he'll be so relieved he'll pay Mary a terrific amount of money,' Francis said.

'I'll ring him now. How much do you want?'

She'd never done anything like this before and really didn't know. 'I'd want to do my own shopping for it, exclusive of the fee.'

'OK. Where's the phone?'

'One minute. Are they still using the old kitchen?'

'It's been turned into a wine cellar. The new one is on the ground floor and it's amazingly grand. Everything in it is new.'

'Ask him how many people the dinner is for,' she called, as Percy went.

'Mary, you're a sport. Sure we haven't bludgeoned you?'

'A bit late if you had. No, it'll be exciting to cook a serious meal for a change. I don't know what Thomas will think. He's still funny about the house – about not managing to buy it back.'

'Dear Mary, you can't live your life doing everything to suit Thomas.' He was ambling restlessly about the room and now reached the washing-machine. He gave it an aimless kick. It gave out a low moan and started its cycle. 'There you are, you see? Your very own live-in engineer. That's what's known as a kick-start.'

'What you should be giving Reggie.'

'Don't worry. I've started. I've put the idea of lodgers into his head – pointed out that with their rents he could easily afford a cook. I've even offered to help him rearrange the house so they have a sitting room to themselves and won't be in his hair—'

Percy broke in on this: 'He's awfully pleased, Mary. He's offered you fifty pounds for the dinner, but he wants you to help arrange the menus for the rest of the weekend – not cook it, just advise. Oh, and Francis, he's invited you to come to dinner too. He's postponed the festival meeting tonight until Monday. Mrs Fanshawe's telling everyone. So I could help you, Mary, with the shopping. If you like.'

What about Thomas? Mary thought anxiously. Aloud, she said, 'It would be. First thing tomorrow morning? And how many people? Did you ask him?'

'He said ten. And his friends arrive tomorrow, so it would be wonderful if you could think of something I can manage to do for supper – and the rest of the meals, whatever they are.'

Percy had the most beguiling smile when she wanted something, she thought, and wondered briefly if there was a plan she should cook all the meals. I won't do that, she thought. I'll help and advise, but I'm not leaving Thomas to cope on his own for the whole weekend – especially as they haven't asked him to dinner. But, then, Jack Curtis hadn't even met Thomas, whereas Francis was at Melton often because of the festival.

After Percy had left and Francis had gone back to the nursery, she stopped her chores and settled down to the enticing business of devising a meal that didn't, for once, depend in the least upon the cost of the materials, and the equally enjoyable thought that she could actually make fifty pounds from cooking it.

MRS FANSHAWE

Mrs Fanshawe had suffered what she called a really trying morning. Instead of a nice quiet time transposing Mr Curtis's notes from his American trip or, better still, taking dictation from him in person, she'd been told to ring all the council members to postpone this evening's meeting until the following Monday. It took longer than she would have thought possible, partly because so many of them hadn't left any phone numbers – which that Percy girl could have sorted out, but she'd gone off to Melton, shopping, without a word. Also, some of council members weren't at home, and when they were, they were variously aggrieved – very short notice, couldn't possibly manage the Monday, why was it being cancelled, anyway? It wasn't her fault. The only person who was nice to her was Admiral Connaught, a true gentleman. But Mr Curtis was cross about it. He said he'd asked her to invite the Admiral and his wife to the dinner on Saturday. Which he hadn't. That wouldn't have slipped her mind. So she had to ring him back. The Admiral was surprised, went to ask his wife, and came back to say they'd be delighted, and what time? And, of course, she hadn't asked, so she said a quarter to eight and hoped she was right. The rest of the morning she spent trying London agencies for a cook.

But what really upset her was that she was clearly not included in the dinner party and the chance to wear her new wine-coloured trouser suit with the black sequins was missed. It was the Plovers' arrival, she thought bitterly. Everything had changed when they came. Before, she'd dined with the boss often, but ever since she'd had that nasty cold and been indisposed, she'd been relegated to lunch. Of course, she knew evening tête-à-têtes with him couldn't be taken for granted, but she'd truly thought he actually wanted *her* company. Now she kept suspecting it could have been any old company.

That Percy girl was after him – very clever about it, gave no sign. Apparently came down to help her aunt, but now here she was, on her own, worming herself into a job, living in, making herself indispensable with her cooking and everything. And she was ordering everyone around about the guests who were coming and turning down *her* suggestions – like purchasing a nice bunch of carnations from the Melton flower shop to put in the guest bedroom.

These black thoughts were turning her into an insomniac. She'd lie in bed most nights now trying to recapture her earlier dreams of the future, but they would at once roll in, like a sea fog, obliterating everything. The romantic scenes she'd envisaged for herself and Jack – as she called him now – shrank before the reality of Percy with her glossy dark hair, her smooth olive skin that needed no makeup, her long slender legs – she didn't have to wear trouser suits to hide them – and eyes as green as a cat's. Percy was young, she concluded, with anguished envy. There was nothing she could do to counter that, except maybe take a little nip of the Johnnie Walker she'd been buying in half-bottles in Melton. She kept it in her underwear drawer. She'd also, since her cold, taken up smoking again. The smell of Miss Plover's little cigars had done it. She'd given up originally because the boss didn't smoke and she'd not wanted to upset him. But he seemed quite happy about the cigars, so she'd gone back to her Gold Flake.

So, after her lonely supper, brought to her by Hou-arn in the office, she decided she'd pop upstairs to her room, and after she'd taken off her makeup and creamed her face, she'd sit up in bed for a while with her drink and her fags and read her Catherine Cookson, until she thought she was dropping off. Of course, as soon as she turned out the lights she'd probably feel wide awake again, and go through the ritual all over again. Another little drinkie, cigarette and chapter. Sometimes she fell asleep with the light on and the book on the floor.

HUGO

'Well, thanks for telling me.' Hugo put the receiver back with relief. He hadn't intended going anyway. After a polite refusal from the only company who had seemed about to come up with some money for the festival, he'd given up trying. Instead he'd concentrated on his scheme to turn Easton into a luxury bed-and-breakfast establishment. He'd toured all ten of the spare bedrooms and the six large attics on the top floor. It was a bit dispiriting. He hadn't been over the house since he was a boy and he'd never seen some of the rooms. They had been shut up gradually over the years, and were in a state of depressing destitution.

The peeling wallpaper was punctuated by dark squares where pictures had hung before his mother had sold them off to pay bills. There was blistering paint on the doors and window-frames; the rugs and carpets had accommodated generations of moths; pillows and mattresses were devastated by mice; fireplaces were full of soot and dead birds. The bathrooms, ceilings stained with patches of what looked like maps of Oriental mountainous countries, had cracked tiles and viridian stains leaking from the taps. Wherever he walked, small clouds of dust rose courteously in front of him and subsided again in a kind of grimy salute. By the time he'd toured the attics – rat droppings everywhere like olive stones and one ceiling actually down – it was obvious money was required, and a good deal of it, if his scheme was to succeed. The only person with that kind of money was his brother.

He went back to his own room, kept warm by the extravagant use of a three-bar electric fire, put on his overcoat – he was perishing cold – and thought. Ashley was his only hope. But he'd pretty much resisted any previous pleas. He'd made an allowance to their mother that she scraped by on, and none to him. What if he asked – no, demanded money for house repairs? Surely he'd cough up. The roof, he thought. If the roof was actually in danger of falling in, he'd have to do something. Otherwise he'd have to buy another house for Mother to live in. He'd write . . . No, he'd compose a letter for Mother to sign. It should be both urgent and pathetic, and would contain two local builders' rough estimates. He'd better get on to it at once. On Lord Yoxford's behalf he should be able to persuade a builder to give him a rough written estimate. He could imply that without it they'd miss out on other lucrative work in the house.

That afternoon he set to work on the letter. It took him a long time. He had to abandon the idea of written estimates as no builder would give him one without a survey.

'But you must agree it's a pretty expensive business?'

'I should think that's likely with a big 'ouse like that.'

'Thousands?'

'Oh, yes, with scaffolding and all.'

'Ten thousand?'

'Likely. I couldn't—'

'Fifteen?' he said coaxingly, his hopes rising.

'Well, now, Mr Carson, wouldn't it be better if I popped over and had a look?'

'Oh, yes, of course you'll have to do that eventually. I just want to give Lord Yoxford a rough idea. I'll tell him it'll be in the neighbourhood of fifteen and then I'll be back to you.' He'd rung off. If Ashley insisted on a written survey, he'd have to make one. The thought of a spot of forgery, something he'd never tried before, was quite exciting. Come to that, he might as well do Mother's signature while he was at it. 'Your ever loving Mummy', she'd signed in her letters to him at school. Bet she did the same with Ashley. He'd taken over Ashley's old desk, and, rummaging through it, eventually found a letter from her to him, congratulating him on winning a prize at school. After a lot of practice he managed to produce a fair replica, only to remember she never used a typewriter. Either he'd have to forge the whole bloody letter or give a reasonable explanation for having someone else type it. He settled for the latter.

ADMIRAL CONNAUGHT

'Nonsense, my dear. It will do you good to go out.' He said it patiently – for the third time – while she raised the usual objections to anything unplanned happening that hadn't been discussed and worried over for days.

'I have nothing to wear.'

'Darling, that's nonsense. You've got that nice blue outfit you wore for the dinner—' He stopped there. It had been an evening to celebrate Christopher's passing-out at Sandhurst. Even mentioning his name upset her so usually he didn't. 'At Portsmouth – Captain Clegg's wedding,' he finished, hoping it was true.

They were in the kitchen and she was mashing potatoes while he collected things on a tray to lay lunch. He'd had an exhausting morning, taking Rosalie to the supermarket in Melton for the weekend shopping. Letty had given her a list, but she'd lost it. Lulu, who was teething, cried unless Rosalie carried her everywhere. So he'd bought things at random, hoping for the best, but he knew it wouldn't do. They were halfway home when Rosalie discovered the list in the baby's paraphernalia bag. They had to go all the way back for instant coffee, corn flakes, Fairy liquid and the rest. He suggested, this time, that his daughter and the baby stay in the car while he nipped in and got the necessary.

He'd thought, when Rosalie came to stay with the baby, that life at Pear Cottage would become easier, brighter, that Letty would enjoy having her grandchild about and that Rosalie would help her mother. In fact, Rosalie just drifted around doing almost nothing. She managed to feed and bath the baby, but she spent most of her time on her own appearance. It took her entire mornings to wash her long blonde hair and she spent hours on various Oriental exercises that seemed to exhaust what little energy she possessed. Beauty magazines were stacked high in the small bedroom she shared with her child, and piles of their clothes waiting to be washed or ironed. Although it was obvious she thought the meals her mother prepared were not digestible, she never offered to cook for them.

She'd never been very bright, he knew, but she had – all through her childhood – been extremely pretty and amenable. She had scraped through her O levels but even retaking her As had only managed one. The only thing she'd wanted was to go on the stage, an aspiration since she was six. Eventually they had agreed to let her go to a drama school. After several failed attempts she succeeded in getting into a rather obscure place in South London. Here she'd fallen in love with another student, got pregnant and married him, only telling her parents after both deeds were done. They had made the best of it. He had paid the deposit on a mortgage for a small flat and hoped for the best. But the husband, Irwin he was called – they only met him once – soon tired of the marriage, went off with someone else and stopped paying his share of the flat and the baby. The Admiral had paid for the divorce, and invited her home for a while to recover from the whole sorry affair. It was supposed to be a temporary arrangement, but during the summer he discovered Rosalie had sold the flat, was living with friends on the proceeds and had absolutely no idea what to do next. When asked, she just said she couldn't afford to rent anywhere, couldn't get a job when she had Lulu and her life was ruined. If Daddy thought she wanted to be cooped up in the country, unable to pursue her career, he must be out of his mind. So there it was. The cottage was already too small for the four of them. Lulu was now crawling – he'd constructed two gates at bottom and top of the steep staircase, which had to be undone every time they wanted to use the stairs. He'd also made a pen for her in the sitting room but she invariably wailed when put in it, and if she wasn't, she regularly wrecked the room by pulling books out of the book-shelves, knocking over Letty's pot plants and tearing up *The Times* so he couldn't do his crossword.

'You should make Rosalie pull her weight,' he said to Letty in bed at night. But Letty always had some evasive excuse. He concluded she was frightened of her daughter – had never, in fact, stood up to her selfishness and indolence. It had come to him, a few weeks ago, when he was in the garden shed making one of the gates, that perhaps Letty always gave in to Rosalie because she'd never really loved her; all her maternal feelings had been devoted to Christopher. So many people told them how astonishingly pretty Rosalie was, often in front of Letty, that she, whose appearance had depended largely on her youth, had become uncomfortable and eventually, he could now see, disaffected.

Their relationship hadn't really survived the teenage years – always more difficult with girls, he'd been told. He'd been away so much during that time he hadn't provided the rocky balance of power. And Letty wasn't well now. Her rheumatism was always there – on good days just tiring, on bad ones exhaustingly painful. He tried confronting Rosalie about not helping with the chores but, as usual, she just burst into tears, said she'd try to do better, and didn't he understand how difficult her life was? The sight of her streaming face, half shrouded by the long strands of golden hair, provoked his pity – a sensation he recognized as more familiar than love for her. The ensuing guilt made him silent. 'I'm sure you *will* do your best,' he'd said, without much hope of what that might be.

'It seems very odd to me that we should have been asked out of the blue like that. I suppose some other people can-celled.' Letty was draining the runner beans and asked him to get the mince out of the oven. Upstairs Lulu was crying, which meant that Rosalie was changing her nappy. He went to the bottom of the stairs, undid the gate and called that lunch was ready.

WYSTAN AND AMELIA

Wystan and Amelia Blunt had driven down from London, having deposited the twins with her parents in Barnes. They had not liked being left, and Amelia worried quietly about them through the Friday-evening traffic on the A4. Wystan said he was sure they'd settle, as though saying it *would* settle them, and no more to be said. She knew he was very tired, had already driven two hundred miles to and from the site, leaving the house at six this morning, nearly twelve hours ago. He'd recently had flu, and would far rather have collapsed at home for supper and an early bed. But he was really fond of Jack, and they both shared a feeling about him that verged on the parental. They wouldn't let him down. 'Besides, it'll be fun when we get there. I'm dying to see the house, now he's finished it.'

'It was an absolute wreck when I saw it. It couldn't have been restored on a shoestring.'

'But a million shoestrings have probably done the trick.'

'He got Mario degli Angeli to do it up, so be prepared.'

'For what?'

'Well, it'll be a bit over the top. You know how these guys love working for someone whose taste isn't much formed. They can do what they like.'

There was a pause while she unwrapped a bull's eye and passed it to him. Then she said, 'Oh dear. I should have offered to help him.'

'Darling, you couldn't have. Practically, you would've had to go and live there.'

Amelia, who was good at houses, sometimes did a little freelance work for Wystan's clients. Since the twins, there hadn't been time.

'Well, whatever it's like, we must admire it.'

They thoroughly fulfilled these good intentions from the moment they arrived – in the dark – through driving rain into the warm chandelier-lit hall, where Jack was waiting to greet them and conduct them himself to their room. 'I've put you in Ivy,' he'd said, unnecessarily, as he flung open the door. 'We're having drinks in the study – first right at the bottom of the stairs. Don't bother to change.'

When he'd gone, they looked round the room and Amelia giggled as she said, 'We'll both be Gothic ruins by tomorrow morning. All this ivy will come off the walls, up from the carpet, off the curtains and strangle us.'

'It is a beautiful room, though, you have to admit.'

'What would we have changed into if we'd changed?'

He put his arms round her small bony body to give her a hug. She had taken off her pea-jacket and under it wore black trousers and a black roll-neck jersey. 'You look like a little ski instructor,' he said fondly. He loved her and often told her so.

Downstairs in the library they were introduced to Floy and Percy and drank elaborate cocktails made by Jack, who seemed pleased and relieved they were all getting on so well with each other. Percy disappeared to do something about supper and Jack explained, with some embarrassment, that he was, temporarily, without a cook. 'Percy has come to the rescue,' he said, 'but I've got someone in to do the dinner party tomorrow. Tonight we're sort of roughing it in the kitchen.'

Amelia admired the amazing kitchen and they all settled down to Percy's fish pie. Looking at Jack's face during dinner, Amelia thought she'd never seen him look so alive with pleasure.

'Do you think he's in love with Percy?' she asked, when they were back in their room.

'I've no idea. I think he was just thrilled to have people in his house enjoying it all. He told me how glad he was to have us here. It was almost a sort of confession.'

'He told me, too. And that he couldn't wait to show us the rest – the gardens and everything.'

He'd got into bed and watched her wandering about the room. She was wearing her best white cotton nightdress and had let her hair down to brush it.

'Don't plait your hair, darling. You know I like it all over the place.'

'Like the first Mrs Rochester? I may be a bit drunk, but I'm certainly not mad.'

'I'm glad to hear it. We don't want the house burned down before he's shown it to us. Hurry up, darling – I've got my conjugal rights to think of.'

Later, as he leaned over her to turn off the light, she said, 'Well, she's certainly not in the least like Linda.'

'Who isn't?'

'Percy. He ought to get married and stop being so lonely.' He didn't answer. 'Anyway, it's so nice being married.' She thought he was asleep, but he wasn't.

'You really shouldn't generalize. It's nice being married to *me*.'

'Oh dear. There's no hope for him, then.'

'I'm closed,' he said, and seconds later, he was asleep,

JACK

Jack went to bed, but was unable to sleep. Usually, whatever business of the day or the week was on his mind, he could get into bed and switch off, sleep for seven hours and start the next day refreshed and in command. Tonight, however, was different.

Everything had gone beautifully; he'd been really delighted to see Wystan and Amelia again. He'd described them to the others as his oldest friends – which obviated the 'only'. Initially, he'd wanted them to come so he could show them his marvellous new house, his gardens, his park, everything he'd accumulated to illustrate his success. But his first sight of them in the hall, Wystan in his owl-like old-fashioned specs, his duffel coat, suede shoes and beads of rain in his ginger hair, Amelia in her fisherman's cap, trousers and bulky pea-jacket that hid how very small she was, instantly eroded his desire to show off to them. They both hugged him and as he awkwardly squeezed them back, he felt touched and embarrassed by their obvious warmth.

When he'd introduced them to Floy and Percy and saw they instantly got on, he was completely relieved. He'd made champagne cocktails to impress them, but there hadn't been any need. They didn't think less of him because they were eating in the kitchen – in fact, supper turned out to be rather cosy. He'd watched all of them with almost proprietary pleasure. Every now and then, he wasn't even a spectator: they drew him in and he became one of them.

The only thing he was anxious about now – probably

preventing his sleep – was the prospect of the dinner party. He'd asked Brian Hotchkiss and his wife – Amy, he thought she was called. He wanted Sir Brian to make a large contribution to the festival. Entertainment on any scale should always be connected to *some* business, he thought. He'd asked Richard Connaught and his wife, because he thought that the Admiral would lend tone to the occasion, impressing Wystan and Amelia and, more particularly, the Hotchkisses. But now he wondered if it was a mistake. Hotchkiss had made his money out of several free house pubs. His interests were alleged to be greyhound-racing and golf. He was also known to contribute to various local charities, but the festival couldn't really be described as a charity. Oh, well, it looked like being a good dinner. Percy had shown him the menu. She'd done a good job in securing a local cook who seemed to know what she was about. He'd got some good red wine and they'd have straight champagne to start with.

He remembered Amelia now, and how wonderful she'd been when he gave his first party – the one for his parents. It wasn't a great success, but that had been his parents' fault. They didn't like parties. Then he realized it was the last party he'd ever given. You couldn't count business dinners or breakfasts, or his *ad hoc* evenings with the Blunts – or, come to that, the parties Linda had given when he was married to her, full of people he didn't know and to whom he had nothing to say. He used to think they had made him feel inferior, but now he thought it was Linda who had – she'd probably complained about him to her friends. No, he hadn't had much practice at parties, but now he had this large house, and if tomorrow was a success, he thought he might go in for them a bit more.

MARY AND PERCY

On Saturday morning Mary fetched Percy to go shopping for the party.

'What are we getting?'

Mary handed her a notebook on one side of which was the menu, and on the other, the ingredients required.

'Salad,' she read, and then on the right-hand side, 'Prawn, avocado, cucumber and watercress. Halibut kebabs. Halibut, mushrooms and shallots. Roast partridge. Bread sauce, single cream for sauce, fried breadcrumbs. Brussels sprouts, potatoes lyonnaise. Chocolate profiteroles. Flour, butter, eggs, cream, bitter chocolate and one pint of double cream. Cheese – surely nobody will get to cheese?'

'Probably not, but we have to have them.'

'Not a dinner for Mr Woodhouse, then.'

'Let's hope he's not coming. If he does, I'll steam a very small piece of halibut for him.' They talked pleasurably for a while about Jane Austen and what a pity it was she'd written so little about food.

After a companionable silence, Percy said, 'I'm sorry your brother wasn't asked. By the time I mentioned it, Jack had asked ten people and didn't want any more.'

'Oh, well, I don't think he would have come. He's a bit odd about going to Melton.'

'Did he live there when he was married?'

'Oh, no. We only spent part of our early childhood there

before it was sold. But he's always dreamed of buying it back, when he'd made a lot of money and, of course, that was never likely to happen. He's always loved this bit of the country, so when they married, Celia bought a lease on Home Farm, and that was fine for him.'

'Does he mind helping Floy with the tree-planting?'

'I thought he might, but he seems to enjoy it. It gets him out, away from the nursery – and he loves your aunt.' There was a pause, and then she said, 'He likes seeing you, as well.' She glanced at Percy, but there was no reply.

On the way back, after they'd finished the shopping, Percy said unexpectedly, 'You know, I've never met anyone who loved somebody terribly and lost them. It must have happened a lot in the wars, but not much, these days.'

'Have you never been in love?'

'I thought I was but actually I just *wanted* to be – so much. Meeting someone like your brother makes me feel . . .' She hesitated, trying to find the right word. 'Well, a bit in awe.'

Mary felt obscurely irritated by this. 'You mean he's a type, rather than a person?'

'Maybe – though he's the only one I've ever met so he's a person to me.' Then, in a quite different tone that was barely audible, she said, 'I do feel so sorry for him.'

There was genuine sincerity in the way she spoke, which touched Mary. She took refuge – she thought afterwards – as we so often do, in breezy cliché. 'Oh, well. It's better to have loved and lost than never to have loved at all.'

Percy answered, in a small voice, 'I expect it is.'

*

'Take Rosalie with you, Richard. You know what I'm like when it's really bad.'

'Have you had your stuff?'

'Of course. But you know how it does me in for the day. If I just go to bed, I'll be all right tomorrow.'

'What about the child? Can you cope if she wakes up?'

'Yes, yes, of course I can. But once she's asleep she's no trouble, you know that. Just help me out of my jacket and blouse. I can manage the rest. You'd better tell Rosalie first – she'll want time to change.'

Rosalie was drying Lulu after her bath. 'I don't have time to wash my hair.' It hung in great golden swathes, obscuring her face and the baby's. 'Will that theatre man be there?'

'I don't know.'

'What's wrong with Mummy?

'Her rheumatism's playing up and she's had a migraine.'

'OK. I'll have to settle Lulu first.' She had laid the baby on her bed and fastened her nappy, was now thrusting her legs and arms into her sleeping suit. She looks like a little garage attendant, the Admiral thought, as Rosalie took the milk bottle out of its jug of steaming water, squirted a little on to the back of her hand and then, gathering her up, put the teat into the baby's mouth. Lulu sucked, her eyes peaceably on her mother's face. The room was so strewn with their discarded clothes that there was scarcely any space between the cot and the bed. 'Say goodnight to Grandad, then,' Rosalie said.

He bent awkwardly to kiss the baby's damp forehead.

'We need to leave at quarter to eight sharpish,' he said, as he left them.

FLOY

Floy had run herself a very hot bath in which she soaked until the water was disagreeably lukewarm. The day had been rewarding, but exceedingly tiring. 'Beginning to get past it,' she told herself. She'd spent the morning with Thomas, planting fruit trees. Of course, he had done the heavy digging, but she'd held each tree and its stake upright as he filled each hole and they'd both firmed in the roots with careful heavy treading. They'd planted three dozen – apples, pears, plums for the orchard, eighteen against the vegetable-garden walls, to be espaliered, and Morello cherries on the north wall, peach and nectarine on the south and west walls. And there was still room for more.

Jack had interrupted them, bringing his friends on a tour of the grounds, and it had fallen to her to introduce Thomas. Jack behaved as if he was a labourer and had been pretty graceless even when introduced. Thomas was just as bad, surly and awkward.

After they'd resumed their tour, he was quiet, worked doggedly on. In hope of lightening the atmosphere she'd said something about how good it was of his sister to help out at the party, but he burst out, 'Oh, the Musgroves are learning their place. No doubt about that.' His bitterness shocked her. Theirs had been such an agreeable collaboration. He had been eager to discuss and provide the stock and, on top of that, happy to help her with the heavy work. She'd assumed, incorrectly she now realized, his connection with Melton House was, by now, harmless family history. There were obviously layers of resentment and pride that she hadn't taken into account; his pride, she thought, that last refuge of most unhappy people, had been pricked.

Percy arrived with a Thermos and sandwiches for their habitual lunch, which they'd taken to eating in the new glasshouse. It was a more than usually welcome break. Floy sank gratefully on to her camp stool. Her back was aching and the prospect of the afternoon's work, reinstating the ancient vine that lay now in a tortured heap, seemed daunting. She lit her *café crème* and watched Thomas and Percy unpack the basket with wry amusement. They were aimlessly considerate to each other in a way that only happens with the mutually shy. Thomas was clearly smitten by Percy, and she – not usually shy now – was overwhelmed by what she'd told her aunt was the worst tragedy she'd ever encountered.

A memory of Othello's foreboding remark concerning Desdemona came to her as she watched them: 'She loved me for the dangers I had passed, and I loved her that she did pity them.' Yet somewhere in her was an urgent desire, almost a need, to see Percy established in an enduring relationship. Why? She was only twenty-four. She had plenty of time.

Percy asked what they were doing next. Thomas explained that the vine was to be severely pruned, then tied to the wires against the wall behind the glasshouse tables; the main problem would be teasing it back inside through the hole in the wall. He beckoned her to look.

Percy had been sitting on the table during lunch, but now got down and followed him outside. 'It's enormous,' Floy heard her say. 'It's like an awful pile-up on the M1.' She came back in and began packing up their lunch things. Her face was scarlet with an uncustomary blush that wouldn't go away.

Floy watched him studying her with a tender concern that transformed him into a charming, and much younger, man. He said, 'Oh, well. It's awfully old – I remember picking out the decent grapes for Mary when we were kids. I suppose I'm a bit sentimental about it. But if we prune it properly and set it up again . . .'

'And give it a pail of ox blood, if we can get it.'

He turned to her. 'Right, Floy. Then it might be grateful.'

'Ox blood and our sweat is what it wants. It can do without the tears – plants aren't sentimental.'

Percy's olive pallor had returned, but she still couldn't look at Thomas so hadn't seen his face.

Floy was out of the bath now, enveloped in a huge green towel bordered with unlikely clumps of holly berries. At least Percy had got over her love affair with that wretched man. Jack had been extraordinarily generous – the festival, providing somewhere for Percy to live and a decent salary – with no hint of the obviously inappropriate motive of seducing her. She probably wasn't ready for that, just now. His friends were reassuring too. She'd sensed, the previous evening, that they were affectionately determined to let him impress them and would do everything in their power to make the dinner party, which was so important to him, a success. But, Lord, she thought, she would give almost anything to curl up in bed with a supper tray and Mrs Gaskell's final novel. 'Anything but you,' she said aloud to Marvell, whose voluptuous occupation of her bed precluded anyone sharing it.

Marvell opened his eyes and slowly shut them. He was so inured to worship that he would only have noticed its absence.

SIR BRIAN AND LADY HOTCHKISS

Amy Hotchkiss took a long time dressing, partly because the dress she'd planned to wear turned out to have shrunk at the cleaners. 'Hold the top together before you zip,' she said. Her husband surveyed her fat back doubtfully and did as he was told, but the top of the dress wouldn't meet and when he wrenched, yet again, at the zip it broke.

'Damn thing's broken.'

'Oh, Brian.' Men were hopeless, they really were. She took a swig of her brandy and ginger ale, then pulled the dress off her shoulders. When she tried to step out of it, she nearly fell over.

'Whoops-a-daisy.'

He'd put out one of his huge paws to steady her, but she shook him off. 'Don't you use that tone with me.'

Wishing passionately that there was someone else here with whom he could use that tone, he backed off. She kicked aside the purple outfit and rummaged through the rack of dresses in her wardrobe. Most of them wouldn't fit her, he thought gloomily. She'd put on at least half a stone on the cruise and always wore her clothes on the tight side to show off her bust, which, in her day, had been pretty striking. Now it was kind of submerged by the rest of her.

'That kaftan you bought in Acapulco looked nice on you – very colourful,' he ventured.

'Brian, I can't wear a tropical kaftan in this weather. Sometimes I wonder if you're mad, I really do.'

'I'll leave you, then.' He made it sound like a concession, but her fleetingly fearful look touched him. 'Don't be too long. I'll be waiting for you in the lounge.'

He trudged down the stairs, stopping for a moment in front of the enormous gilt mirror in the hall to check that his tie was straight and to put his pocket comb through his ginger-grey hair. He looked finally into his eyes, watery, these days, but still quite shrewd, he prided himself – even if they were struggling somewhat to hold their own in the large florid folds of flesh that drooped down to the vast swag of his second chin. Dentures had reduced his lips to a thin placket, but his nose, always a bulbous feature, held sway, and his eyebrows, a pair of autumnal bramble hedges, still dominated the scene. He'd started in business as a publican in a free house, made enough money to buy it and others, had branched out into hotels and now owned various establishments, one in Melton where he'd elected to start his retirement. But apart from golf, which he played four afternoons a week, and the cruises he and Amy enjoyed two or three times a year, he wasn't sure how to fill his time so had postponed complete retirement. He still enjoyed making money. He was perfectly aware he'd been asked to dinner at Melton House because finance for some cause or other was required, but it didn't offend him: it confirmed him in his view of himself as a man of means, and therefore influence.

There was no denying that the cruises were the devil for putting on weight. His dinner jacket was straining over his shoulders and distinctly tight under the arms. He walked into the lounge, poured himself a stiff whisky from the cocktail cabinet and sank gratefully into his leather button-studded armchair. He'd give Amy another twenty minutes, then get her down here whatever she'd got on her back.

WYSTAN, PERCY, JACK AND AMELIA

'No, I can't really say that I cared for Acapulco. Not that much. Have you ever been there?'

Jack said, no, he hadn't.

'Brian didn't mind it as much as me, but in the end he had to admit he didn't think much of it either.' She popped a prawn into her mouth and called, more loudly but less distinctly, across the table, 'I was just telling Mr Curtis, Brian, that we thought Acapulco was definitely overrated.' And when her husband indicated his agreement, she finished, 'So you needn't bother with it, should it ever come up.' She was encased in a tight, red-beaded dress that had loose chiffon sleeves of the same colour. Her *décolleté* was such that the cleft between her breasts reminded Wystan, who sat opposite, of the Grand Canyon. She behaved as if the only person present was the one she was talking to. She turned now to the Admiral and gave him her opinion of the Caribbean, which was more favourable, although the islands were disappointing. 'Once you've seen one, you've seen them all.'

Wystan heard the Admiral reply courteously that he hadn't had much to do with the Caribbean. Since Jack had turned to the Admiral's striking daughter, who sat between them, he spun round to Percy, who sat on his left and had been working away at Hotchkiss about the festival: '. . . and I wondered which of the arts interests you most.'

Hotchkiss, munching his way steadily through the salad, stopped chomping to ponder this – to him – incomprehensible question before saying he quite liked opera, but since Amy couldn't stand 'people shrieking in foreign languages' he could only sometimes play it on his hi-fi system – he'd got the latest Danish speakers. They'd cost a packet, but on the whole he thought they were worth it.

Juan was taking the plates, stacking them precariously as he worked his way round the table. Amelia noticed this and, to help, quietly took Francis and Hotchkiss's plates and stacked them on her own. As he attempted to pick them up Juan dropped the ones he'd already collected. Francis leaped to his feet and Amelia, conscious of Jack's angry embarrassment, apologized fulsomely to Juan and took the blame on herself.

Floy – a real ally – declared what a delicious salad it was.

Rosalie revealed she'd been a waitress once and it was absolute hell. 'Never off your feet and I got so I simply couldn't face the food. I lived on KitKats and apples.'

Amy, turning back to Jack, said how difficult it was to find good servants these days. 'I sympathize. I really do.'

Percy slipped out of the room and ran to the kitchen, where she found Mary and Mrs Peabody dishing up the fish kebabs, to say she thought it might be a good thing if Mrs Peabody helped in the dining room.

After that things went more smoothly. Five bottles of Chablis were consumed with the fish, and conversation, though still sometimes strained, became more relaxed – dangerously so, in Amy's case, by the time they got to the partridges and the claret. Despite a ceaseless flow of talk her glass was always empty, and her bird was a wreck of bones before anyone else's. She was determined to wrest Jack from Rosalie, whom she eyed with quiet venom.

Rosalie seemed totally unaware of this. She gnawed her partridge bones with a delicate gusto while she told Jack how ill she had been when pregnant. 'People say you only feel sick for the first three months but I threw up throughout the whole nine. Your hair is supposed to get glossy and your complexion apparently blooms, but I was covered with spots and my teeth went completely to pieces. I was a wreck,' she finished, complacently pushing her blonde tresses over the bare shoulder nearest to Jack, where they lay in charming contrast to her waxen smooth flesh.

Any pause in this tide was seized on by Amy, who remarked how silly it was of young girls nowadays to starve themselves until they resembled darning needles. Jack really ought to try Cunard where the food and the service were the best you would find anywhere in the world. 'Such a choice. You only have to mention caviar or lobster, and it's there, whether it's on the menu or not.'

'But then, after hours and hours of ghastly labour – I just don't think any man can have the least idea what it's like – there was this amazing creature, damp and sticky with blood all over it. Can you imagine an enormous shrimp, but with hair, howling its head off? I felt a *real* sense of achievement.' She turned to gaze at him earnestly with her large, almost round blue eyes. Jack, who had stopped eating his partridge, poured her more wine before taking a large swig of his own.

Floy, who'd been listening to the Admiral's rueful description of his north-facing garden, saw how he struggled to maintain his composure while his daughter was holding forth – how, at one point, he had leaned forward as if to stop her, then thought better of it. To divert him, she asked if his wife liked gardening. But he said she had such severe rheumatism she was unable to be active in that way. Wystan, opposite, asked him now about his war, which enlivened him, and, when asked the same question by the Admiral, explained he'd just made it to sub-lieutenant three months before VJ Day. The Admiral smiled at him with positive approval.

Percy was still working away at Brian Hotchkiss. 'It looks as

JACK, FRANCIS, JUAN AND FLOY

Jack looked round the table with approval. His previous cook could never have produced such a meal. He'd observed Percy's foray with Hotchkiss and admired it – just the right touch, he thought, softening him up for the more direct approach he planned to make after dinner with brandy. Dinner parties were a bit of a strain, but definitely worth it. He looked down the table at Amelia, who smiled back as she said, 'What a wonderful dinner, Jack. You've done us proud.' They were his friends, she and Wystan, he thought, his real friends, and an unfamiliar catch in his heart made him silent, afraid it might reach his voice if he said anything. He nodded and raised his glass to her.

Mrs Peabody was asking him where he would like coffee served and he said in the drawing room. Wystan had called it that when they toured the house that morning.

Amelia accompanied Amy Hotchkiss to the loo, and Wystan did the same for her husband, while Percy and Francis almost collided in the passage to the kitchen where they found Mary and Mrs Peabody washing and stacking plates, while Juan arranged the coffee tray.

'It was marvellous,' Percy said, 'the best dinner I've ever had.'

And Francis gave her a hug and said, 'Well done, old thing. I just came out to say I'll drive Mrs Peabody home and come back for you, unless you'll be ready to come with us.'

'I don't think I will be – not for an hour, anyway. Oh, Lord, we forgot the cheese.' She'd tied her hair back, but strands had escaped and she kept pushing them off her face.

'Darling, we would have burst.'

Percy said, 'Thank you so much, Mrs Peabody, for helping in the dining room. Has Mrs Fanshawe been down for any supper?'

'Haven't seen her, I'm afraid.'

Percy reflected it must be difficult for her and felt vaguely uneasy.

'It's all right. I'll wait for you, Miss Mary – save Mr Francis the extra journey.

Francis said they'd better get back to the fray, so they did.

'You look very fetching in that dress,' he said to Percy, as they walked back to the drawing room. She was wearing a straight olive green velvet tunic that left her arms bare.

'It's my best thing. I bought it from Mary Quant in a sale.'

'It looks good on you.' It reminded him of Celia somehow, the kind of thing she would have chosen. He thought suddenly and anxiously of Thomas, his evening with Reggie and Hatty.

The drawing room was stately and white, with a lot of brand new gold leaf on the plasterwork. The walls were hung with large early-nineteenth-century mirrors and a pair of *faux* Canalettos – huge oils of Venice, the architecture looming over tiny clusters of people in cloaks and masks milling about. They must have taken a hell of a long time to paint, Francis thought.

The atmosphere was uneasy. People had been given their coffee and Amelia had brought Amy back from her excursion, makeup renewed, but rather unsteady on her feet. She was telling Wystan and the Admiral about the golf club where she often lunched with Brian after his round.

'There's a new member we've rather taken under our wing. A retired major – poor things, they don't get much of a pension, do they? He confided in me, as I find people often do, that he's reduced to living with his son-in-law, one room in a house that hasn't even got a lounge – not at all what he's used to. Before his wife passed away he had his own home and staff and everything. Brian says I'm soft-hearted, but when I hear him my heart bleeds – it really does. Of course, you wouldn't be in that position,' she continued to Richard Connaught, 'but we can't all be Admirals, can we? This poor man's got nothing. People are heartless, aren't they? I mean, really . . .' She stopped, because Francis had stalked across the room and now stood over her.

'You are talking about my father,' he said very quietly. Percy saw he'd gone white and his voice was trembling with anger. 'And if he has told you such things, let me tell you that they are quite, quite untrue. My brother-in-law and sister-in-law have given him the best room in the house and he has everything done for him that it is possible for us to do.'

There was a sudden, frightful silence. Then Amy, drawing herself up, said, 'You've no call to be so hoity-toity to me, young man. I am *not* accustomed to being spoken to in that manner. That's what he told me. Are you accusing me of lying?' She picked up her glass of brandy and drank it in a gulp.

'No,' he said wearily, 'I'm not accusing you of that.'

The Admiral said to his daughter that perhaps they should be getting back. Her baby might—

But Amy obviously regarded Francis's admission as some sort of triumph. 'I don't know what the world's coming to for a son to speak like that about his own father.' She turned to the Admiral, who had got to his feet. 'I'm sure you'd never have let a son of yours behave like that.'

'My son was killed in Cyprus,' he said, looking steadily down on her. 'Rosalie.'

Rosalie, who had been working her way quietly through a dish of Bendick's mints, got gracefully to her feet. 'You've got me, Daddy,' she said. 'And Lulu.'

Percy noticed Brian Hotchkiss and Jack now returned. They hadn't been in the room. Everyone, except Amy, got up to end the general discomfort.

The Admiral, having said goodnight to the general company, thanked Jack, who followed them out to the hall to help Rosalie into her coat. Brian, who perceived immediately that there had been trouble and his wife was the probable source, moved purposefully to the sofa where she sat and muttered something to her.

'I've been insulted, Brian, and of course you weren't there when you were needed.'

'Sorry about that, dear. Come on – time we got going.' He seized one of her arms and heaved her to her feet. 'Whoops-a-daisy. There we go.' She would have fallen if he hadn't retained a firm grip.

'Don't – use that – tone with *me*.' She tried to twitch away from him and fortunately failed. Everybody pretended not to notice, except Francis, who walked to the end of the room and stood looking out of the window. Somehow or other Brian contrived to walk her to the door where they met Jack.

'It's been a very pleasant evening,' he said to his host. 'Good night, all.' And to Percy, 'Pleased to meet you.'

And Jack, who now realized how drunk the wife was, followed them to help Brian get her into her mink jacket and see them down the steps outside the front door to their car.

While he was doing this, Francis joined the others. 'Sorry about that. I didn't intend a scene. Only I couldn't—' Words failed him, and Percy realized that he was, or perhaps had been, in tears.

Amelia said, 'It wasn't your fault.'

Wystan, hoping to lighten the situation, said, 'She managed to put both feet in it, didn't she? I mean with the poor old Admiral and his son.'

Floy, who had remained quiet until now, said, 'He told me

about that over dinner. He hadn't said goodbye to him properly after his last leave.'

But Percy burst in, 'I don't see how anyone can get over someone they loved being killed. Just because it happened to so many people in the last war doesn't make it better.'

Jack returned. 'Well, I think everyone's earned a nightcap. You all look as though you need one.'

But Floy thought she'd go to bed as she wanted to be up early and Francis supposed he'd see if Mary and Mrs Peabody were ready to go home. Percy said she'd go and say good night to Mary. As they left the room Francis apologized again – this time to Jack.

'What's he apologizing for?' Jack asked. 'What happened?'

His two friends exchanged a lightning glance. Wystan said, 'The wretched woman was drunk, Jack, and said rather a lot about someone she met at the golf club, who turned out to be Francis's father. It's all right, we knew she was drunk. The rest of the party went jolly well, didn't you think, Amelia?'

'Jolly well.'

He seemed relieved. 'Well, I wanted you to have a good evening. And it looks as though Brian Hotchkiss will cough up some money for the festival. Not that it was the point of the exercise,' he added hastily. 'The party was for you. To celebrate your first visit. Here's to many more.' And he finished his brandy.

Then they went to bed.

*

Juan was the last person up. After the two nice ladies had left, he collected cups and glasses from the drawing room, drew the fire curtains over the immense fireplace, where the logs still smouldered, turned out the lights and went back to the kitchen where everything was spotless. The Mary lady had been most nice to him all the evening – it had been a pleasure to work for her: she made no scene about the plates, and the Pea lady, who helped him, was also most nice. They had also made a good food for him before the party. He now poured the wines left in the glasses into a big glass and drank it, sitting with his bad feet up on the kitchen table.

Señora Fanshawe had been upstairs all the time. They had sent him to her room to tell her supper, but she said no – she no wants. Her, he did not like. Really, he hates. She say he lose his job if he not work more and this cannot happen as he have family to feed at home and must have money for it. She no lady at a single look. Anyone know that.

He finished the glass – he'd added the dregs of brandy to it so it tasted good strong for his bad feet. He washed up the things he'd brought on the tray and polished the glasses before putting them away in the pantry. He turned off the lights in the hall and crept up the stairs to the first landing, where it was dark, but he knew without eyes the baize door that led to the second staircase to top-floor landing – also dark. He passed Señora's room and saw light. She smoked so all the time that he could even smell it coming out from the crack and he could hear her radio – some big-band music. If he had a radio and played it at night she says he made her awake, but not enough money for radio. Bicycle he need – not two things.

He passed her room and went to the end of the passage where there was a small attic where he slept.

And so it wasn't until the early hours of the morning that Floy woke suddenly with the certainty that something was very wrong, and went out into the passage to find it full of smoke.

After

PERCY AND FRANCIS

'It's so complicated! I can't think why people find figures entrancing. They just make me cross.'

She was sitting opposite him at the enormous desk in what had become the festival office at Melton House. It was littered with piles of miscellaneous papers, bills and receipts, some imprisoned by vicious bulldog clips, some loose; the latter had an irritating habit of rising at the slightest breeze from the open sash window, hovering an instant, and scattering gracefully elsewhere. Sunlight, streaming into the room, made prisms of the dust they disturbed.

'Couldn't we just give them all to an accountant?'

'Oh, Francis. Yes, in the end, but we've got to make sense of them first and make sure they're all here, which is worse.'

'I don't think for a moment that, in my case, two heads are a blind bit better than one, but tell me your method, and perhaps I can help.'

'Come round here, and I'll show you.'

He got up and leaned over her, inhaling the lemony scent of her newly washed hair.

'This is the account book. One side says "Receipts", and the other "Expenses". I'm sub-heading it with each event. I've more or less done Angus Wilson because he was the easiest. We sold a hundred and fifty tickets – it was full, actually, so that came to seven hundred and fifty pounds. Then expenses. Fee fifty. Hire of church hall fifty. Posters and leaflets – well, there, you see?

The posters were for his event, but the leaflets were for other things too, so I don't know what to put. Anyway, that's the method. So could you do that for the exhibitions?'

'I'll have a go.'

They worked for a time in silence. It was a beautiful day. The view of the archway to the gardens was partially obscured by scaffolding. There were indistinct sounds from the men working on the roof, punctuated by small thuds as they chucked pieces of tile and masonry into the skip in the courtyard. For months a tarpaulin had covered the damaged area while Jack negotiated with the insurance company. The fire brigade had inevitably inflicted most of the damage. Both Jack and Wystan had tried to get up the stairs to the attic, but were overcome by smoke. It seemed an awfully long time before the firemen had arrived and then a further, increasingly agonizing wait while they erected their ladders, angled their searchlight and smashed two of the attic windows. They'd all watched, shivering outside, as one man stepped off the ladder and disappeared into the house, returning interminable minutes later with Mrs Fanshawe slung over his shoulder.

'Are you cold? Shall I shut the window?' She shook her head.

'How are you getting on?'

'I'm not, really. There are hardly any receipts at all here – oh, God, how boring. Do you think the whole thing was worth it?'

'Well, you sold a picture, Francis. And, anyway, it's the first time Melton has had anything like this. I bet if they keep it up, in a few years' time people will be saying, "We must go to the festival at Melton." Look at Edinburgh.'

'That doesn't actually justify it, Percy, dear.' He'd stopped work a while ago and was drawing her, elbows on her desk, hands in her hair. 'I mean, for a start there aren't really any venues for large audiences. What an awful word. *Venue*. Like *garment* and *tablet*. Isn't it nearly lunch time?'

'Am I asking you to lunch?'

'Are you?'

'Don't mind if you do.' When she smiled, her eyes became the shape and colour of horizontal diamonds – or rather like dirty emeralds.

Lunch was at one end of the enormous dining-room table: gazpacho and a fish salad laid out and waiting for them.

'Oh dear. I'm getting dangerously used to luxury,' Percy said. 'It'll be quite difficult, going back to London and awful office sandwiches.'

He looked up from his soup, startled. 'Are you planning to go back?'

'Well, I've virtually finished with the festival. Yes, I'll have to. I have to find *some* work. I can't really get any here.'

'Oh – couldn't you work for Jack?' She didn't answer, so he added recklessly, 'I rather thought you might marry him. That would solve the problem.' He noticed with dismay that she was blushing.

'As a matter of fact, he did ask me. Please don't tell anyone.'

'You mean till you've made up your mind?'

'I mean at all. I decided not to, you see.'

'It sounds as if it was rather a close thing.'

She hesitated. 'Well, not really. I mean, once I'd decided not to, it was obvious. But when he asked me there were one or two things . . .' She hesitated again but, after all, Francis in the last six months had become her close friend. 'Well, it may sound odd to you, but Jack . . . he's kind of vulnerable. I mean, in spite of being brilliant at making money, he's so lonely. The only friends he has are the Blunts. And Floy, she likes him. He's actually very kind. He was very generous about the festival.'

'But you can't marry someone because you're sorry for them and they're kind.'

She retorted, with slight irritation, 'I know – I know I can't. I've said I'm not going to. But when someone asks you to marry them and you don't want to, well, it's a sad thing.'

'Sad for them.'

'No, sad for both of you.'

'Oh, Percy, you've got a tender heart. He'll get over it. It would have been so much worse for him if you'd married him because you didn't want to hurt his feelings. And worse for you,' he added.

'Sometimes I wonder. I mean, there are so many of us and we live for such a short time, perhaps it doesn't matter what we do. We just think it matters.'

She got up from the table. 'I must get back to the sums. Jack returns from South Africa tomorrow, and Derek Mainwaring is coming to go over the theatre figures. And you said you had to help Thomas.'

He said he did and thanked her for lunch.

'Lucky you, being outdoors,' she called, as he got on to his bike.

He rode, very slowly, back to the farm, full of conflicting emotions. It was a terrific relief she wasn't going to marry Jack – and she'd been so adamant about it too. On the other hand it hadn't occurred to him she might leave so soon. The months they'd worked together on the festival had been increasingly enjoyable. They'd shared arduous and sometimes absurd situations, had laughed at the same things and had supported each other through various crises. Their relationship was comfortable and unthreatening. And she'd been the most welcome relief from the thunderous tensions at home.

He'd driven back on the night of Jack's dinner party, fuming at his father's treachery and unable to speak to Mary about it until they'd dropped Mrs Peabody off. When, finally, she was parking the car, he'd told her.

'The woman was drunk. She must have been,' she said.

'That's not the point, Mary. The point is that he goes around telling people we're awful to him.'

'Well, we probably *are*. We don't like him, *do* we? I had to stop Hatty singing, "Will you still need me, will you still feed me, when I'm sixty-four," the other day.'

'Mary, he's awful to *us*. We've tried – we've all tried. I know, I know, we agreed weeks ago he'd have to go. Well, after this, I'll have no problem telling him.'

'Yes, you will and, yes, he's a shit and he has to go. But we have to find an alternative for him. I'm too tired to talk about it tonight.'

She opened the car door and he saw in the light the violet circles under her eyes. 'Sweetie, I'm *so* sorry. Of course you're bushed. You did a marvellous job.' He gave her shoulder a squeeze, then stroked a strand of hair back from her face.

Only a kitchen light had been left on and they crept upstairs to bed.

FLOY

'It was very good of you to come, Mr Jenkins, and I'm most grateful for your advice.'

She saw her solicitor off and waited until he'd got into his car before shutting the front door and hobbling back into the conservatory. It was a very beautiful morning. Her garden was full of spring blossom and tender greens, and the wall of the conservatory that backed on to the house overflowed with jasmine, sky blue plumbago and a yellow tea rose. Marvell lay tastefully disposed in the sun on one of the large white squares of her marble floor. She remembered heaving the slabs – only twenty at a time – into her van and to the house. She couldn't do that sort of thing any more, she thought, as she lowered herself carefully – but not without pain – into the upright chair she'd dragged out of the sitting room. It was the only *comfortable* chair. She'd had back trouble before – an occupational hazard, she called it – but this was different. It wasn't a trapped nerve or a slipped disc, both of which she'd had before. Eventually, the pain would go away, as the crumbling vertebrae settled down, but there was no guarantee it wouldn't come back. She lit a cigar and stared at the papers on the table before her: the lease on her home, and a letter from the Eyre Estate confirming that, with only eight years to run, they weren't prepared to extend it. They also suggested obliquely that repairs to the property might have to be paid for at the end of it.

The house, when she'd originally found it, was heaven-sent:

the large back garden, the octagonal conservatory, decent rooms with lovely sash windows; everything about it had entranced her. It was enticingly cheap and pretty derelict too, which had only encouraged her. It was thirty-two years ago. At the time a forty-year lease seemed almost as good as a freehold, and she'd told herself if and when the time came, the Estate would surely renew. Now, it seemed, they wouldn't. Mr Jenkins had advised her to sell as soon as possible. There were people, he said, who wanted a short lease, provided it wasn't too expensive, people who'd rather live somewhere nicer for a short time than they could afford for a longer one. He advised her to get an agent to value it, then put it on the market. He was sure it would sell. He seemed to think, she reflected bitterly, that selling the house would end her troubles.

She surveyed her garden and the room in which she now sat as if they were already in the homesick mind's eye. I'm like a very old shrub, she ruminated. I shan't transplant easily.

And what about Percy? Maida Vale had been her home since she was twelve. She'd been raised here. She would be terribly upset – oh, she was just being sentimental. Percy would be twenty-five at the end of this month. It was time she left the nest. She'd even suggested, when Percy finally began to earn her own living, she might like her own place. Percy's response had been emphatic: 'I don't want to leave you *ever*. I honestly don't. Unless you want me to?' And, recognizing a flash of the appalling neediness that had so touched her when she'd fetched the angry, sulky child from the airport years ago, she'd reassured her: 'Of course this is your home for as long as you want.' She'd remarked then that they were like Stevie Smith and her Lion Aunt, and Percy had replied, 'Well, you're my Pirate Aunt. Anyway they were extremely happy together. I see nothing wrong with that.' No, nothing – except Stevie had had to cope with an extremity of loss when her aunt died. 'I shan't live for ever, darling,' she'd nearly retorted.

But she had no intention of dying in the immediate future and Percy was well on the way to being totally independent. The festival job at Melton had been a thoroughly good venture for her. She'd made friends with those nice Musgroves and Jack had treated her with impeccable generosity throughout. Her visits to Melton had confirmed that, while he clearly liked and respected Percy for the hard work, he had no – as she put it – designs on her.

But all this was coming to an end. She'd decided, the next time she went down, to impress on Jack that it was time to find and employ a full-time, experienced gardener to take on the estate. They'd finished the main planting in March – such a relief, because in her present state she'd be incapable of planting a dandelion and Thomas Musgrove had no more time from his nursery.

She'd been invited to stay during the festival, fortunately before her back had given way, and sat through a rather leaden production of *Hay Fever* with the Admiral's daughter playing the young girl in it. Rosalie Connaught had been striking to look at, but not to hear. She *had* enjoyed Nina Milkina's Mozart, Scarlatti and Chopin piano recital, and the two exhibitions organized by Francis Brock, but not the afternoon of opera excerpts. She'd bought one of Francis's paintings. The flower show in the town hall was a revelation, with remarkable house plants, ferns, bulbs, cacti, various flowering shrubs and a quantity of hideously ingenious flower arrangements. She'd seen that the festival had been a success for Percy, even though it had suffered from lack of audiences. 'Not bad for a first-year effort,' Jack had said. 'It just needed a bit more publicity than we could afford.'

She was due to go to Melton this weekend, but given the state of her back, she doubted it. She couldn't drive and the thought of the train – with Marvell protesting in a basket too heavy for her to carry – filled her with dread. He'd sprung on to the table and was making it clear he expected his lunch. I suppose this house is too large for me anyway, she thought, as she struggled to her feet and began the slow, agonizing descent of the basement stairs.

MARY

She'd got Francis to drop Hatty off at school and Reggie had gone, as he more and more frequently did, to his 'club', as he called the place where he played golf. It was a great relief he'd found somewhere else he wanted to be. After the dinner party Francis had held firm and confronted his father, though, at the last moment, he'd begged her to be there, which she'd thought a mistake. It made him lose face.

'It's obvious you aren't happy here—' Francis had begun.

'Who says?' he'd interrupted. 'Who says I'm not happy here?' His eyes had bulged at the suggestion and shifted uneasily round the room.

'You aren't.'

There was a silence, which, it seemed, might never be broken.

Eventually, Mary said, more gently than Francis, 'I think you know it's true.'

'I don't complain.'

But Francis was relentless. 'Yes, you do. You've been telling people at your golf club—'

He blustered, denied everything and accused Francis of heartlessness, of scheming to get rid of him; none of them realized what it was like to lose a wife and home; he was getting old; they all wanted to put him in some home where they could forget about him; he'd read about that sort of thing in the papers; never, not for one moment, not in his wildest dreams, had he imagined it could happen to him. Francis stormed out of the room shouting – as people often do when they've lost their temper – that his father had to get out before he did. Reggie had slumped into a kitchen chair, combing through his yellow-grey hair with his knobbly fingers and stared at the table. He'd looked up at her. 'To think that my own son . . .'

Despite the cliché, she could see he was badly shaken. 'I think you'd rather be back in your own home. If you'd let me, perhaps we could go through your finances and see whether we can do that.' She added, 'I know how difficult it is to work that sort of thing out, but I've had to do it quite a lot and, if you'd help me, we could at least see what might be done. Shall we have some coffee? I'll make it and perhaps you could get your papers.' It was a mark of how shaken he was that he went off to his room quite meekly to fetch them.

He'd returned, just as she'd started to think he wouldn't, with a battered briefcase that he emptied, with some difficulty, on to the kitchen table. Papers literally sprang from it as he released the catch. 'I keep everything in one place,' he said, as bank statements, unpaid bills, letters, a copy of Anne's will and much else, not immediately identifiable, were revealed. It took the rest of the morning to sort them into relevant piles and the results were disquieting. In spite of two pensions, the rent from the house and income from a few shares, there was hardly anything in the bank. It was the bills that appalled her, the red notices and various threats. There were bills from his tailor, his wine merchant, his shirt-maker, plus old phone bills, bills from his Surrey garage, his insurance company and his lawyer. He hadn't paid his road tax. 'Anne used to see to that sort of thing,' he kept repeating pathetically. She must, Mary thought, have paid most of them from her own income. The case contained a quantity of cheque stubs, but he'd almost never filled in the counterfoils, so it was difficult to know what he'd paid. Two things became clear to her during that arduous and frequently irritating morning: it would take months to pay his debts, and – far more alarming – once he'd done so, he wouldn't have enough income to live separately and pay a housekeeper.

She'd sent him off with a sheaf of bills to pay, but he was soon back: there were only two cheques in his chequebook and he'd forgotten to fill in the form to get a new one. He had to go now anyway for an appointment at the club. 'Well, fill it in and be sure to post it on your way.' He came back with the envelope. He was out of stamps. She found him one in Thomas's study. 'Better buy yourself a book. You're going to need them.'

'It's no good losing my temper with him,' she said to Thomas, over their soup and cheese.

'I don't know. Might do him good.

'Why did Francis storm off and leave you to deal with it?' he asked after a while.

'Reggie's his father. It's all too difficult for him.'

'I suppose,' he said, over coffee, 'we've been lucky not to have parents. I mean, of course we had them, but they weren't around. We just had each other.' He leaned across the table and took her hand. 'I don't know what I'd have done without you,' he said. 'Your hands are like sandpaper. You ought to put some stuff on them. All that money you spent on the fridge and the washing-machine and none of it on you.'

'Hatty's cross I didn't get a television. She says all her friends have one. I think perhaps we should.'

'She's never here, these days.'

'Exactly. Life hasn't been much fun for her since Reggie came. She doesn't like bringing friends home in case he's here and I can't stop her going to them – it's the holidays, after all.'

'I'll think about it.'

And do nothing, she thought, after he'd gone back to the nursery.

JACK

'What you should do, darling, is marry and have a family.'

Like most well-meaning advice this presented him with what seemed insurmountable problems. He'd had business in London and, on impulse, had dropped in on the Blunts before driving home. Wystan was out and Amelia was giving the twins their supper. She'd taken him upstairs to the bathroom – 'I can't leave them.'

The children sat at each end of the bath eating drumsticks from the plate placed between them. 'Much easier to clean them up after they've finished, but I'll get Marika to finish them off. This is your Uncle Jack.' They gave him one piercing but noncommittal look and returned to their chicken. The au pair was called and they went down to the sitting room where she poured them glasses of white wine. 'So, how are things?' she'd said, in the tone of one who sensed they weren't very good.

He'd told her about Floy wanting him to get a gardener, which meant she wouldn't be going to Melton much any more. About Mrs Fanshawe, still in a nursing-home where her burns, her alcoholism and accompanying nervous breakdown were still being treated. Then, more reluctantly, about Percy having to get back to London to find a job now the festival was finally wound up. But the immediate problem, he'd said quickly, was Mrs Fanshawe. He certainly didn't want her back, but she was unlikely to be able to get a job with anyone in the foreseeable future.

'I think it's very good of you to feel so responsible for her,' Amelia had said.

Oh, well, she'd been a good secretary in her way. He'd no idea she'd a crush on him. 'She thought *I* rescued her – did you know?' The hideous night flashed through his mind: helping the fireman carry her moaning on to the drive; her hair and nightdress burned off; her screams as they tried to cover her; the ambulance and her looking up at him and whispering, 'My hero. Always knew – you cared – deep down.'

'None of it was your fault, Jack.' But she could see that, in some baffling way, he felt it was.

'Percy said . . .' he began hesitantly '. . . I hadn't treated her as a person. And that if I had done, I'd have known.'

'What?'

'Oh, I don't know. How miserable, how desperate she was. She thinks that.'

There was a silence. Then, looking away, he said, 'Everybody seems to be leaving. I'll have to get somebody else, I suppose.'

It was then she'd made the remark about his marrying and the two embarrassing scenes with Percy came back to him. Oh, well, the humiliation had to be lived through yet again. 'If you're thinking of Percy, it's no-go. I asked her and she turned me down.'

She said she was sorry, but somehow her sympathy and care grated. She made it sound as if it was just a small, temporary setback. What could Amelia know, he thought, as he began the long drive back to Melton, from such a settled, successfully cosy spot? How could she know what it felt like to sense the need of something without knowing precisely what it was? A companion of some sort, he'd presumed, someone who would ease his growing sense of isolation. And he'd thought Percy would fill that gap.

The idea had dawned on him slowly; he was hardly aware

when it began. He'd liked her at first out of respect and fondness for her aunt. He was impressed by her hard work on the festival, and even more so on the night of the fire. She'd tried to penetrate the upper staircase after calling the fire brigade. She'd called the ambulance, too, and, with Floy, had looked after the wretched Juan, holding the oxygen mask over his face, crooning to him in what turned out to be Greek. 'I knew English wouldn't be any good. He just associates it with being told what to do,' she said afterwards. Once out of hospital, Juan had returned with a devotion to Percy that was apparent to everybody – if she left, he realized, Juan might go too. But ever since then he'd felt differently towards her. She wasn't really his type: he'd usually liked blondes with more of a figure. This, and that she was Floy's niece had stopped him making a pass. But she fitted in so well with the whole place, knew where everything was, and had helped him find a couple to cook, a local part-time secretary, and through her friend, Mary Musgrove, somebody to come in and do the housework. When she occasionally went off to spend a weekend with Floy in London, the house seemed extraordinarily empty. It rapidly became obvious that he should ensure she stayed in it. This decision, once taken, had magnified her charms. It also had about it the kind of excitement – where risk was involved – he often felt before a big business deal. He decided to set the scene, and do the thing in style. He went to Asprey's and bought a rather large cabochon emerald ring surrounded by diamonds. He booked a table at the only reasonably good restaurant nearby and announced he was taking her out to dinner 'for a change'.

She was in her office, writing never-ending thank-you letters to those who had participated in the festival.

'One second. Are there two *c*s in Puccini?'

He hadn't the slightest idea and shrugged kindly.

'Oh, well, it'll be in the programme.' She was wearing a loose knitted sweater over her jeans, a kind of mossy green, and her silver dolphin earrings. He was right about the emerald, he thought. He'd get her more proper jewellery.

But when she finally realized he was inviting her out, she said, 'Oh, good. When?'

'This evening.'

'Oh, sorry, I can't. Thomas Musgrove is taking me to the cinema.'

'Couldn't you change it?'

'He asked me last week.'

'Well – tomorrow, then.'

She'd agreed. The wait had made him quite nervous.

Later that day she'd asked him if he thought the letter of thanks to Sir Brian Hotchkiss should, in fact, come from him. 'He did underwrite the opera event and, though quite a lot of people went, it still lost money. So I have to send him a bill as well as thanks.'

'You write it and I'll sign it.'

'And there's another bill for Mrs Fanshawe's nursing-home.'

He told her to write the cheque and he'd sign it. He rang the restaurant to change the date and order their dinner. Caviar, lobster and raspberries seemed appropriate to him. He made it clear he wanted a good, secluded table, and their best champagne, preferably Krug but Dom Pérignon would do.

Then he immersed himself in a succession of calls to South Africa and, later in the day, Florida. Throughout, he felt mounting exhilaration. He dined alone, almost enjoying his last dinner as a single man, and spent the rest of the evening struggling with *Mansfield Park* because she'd been rereading it and had told him so enthusiastically to try it. Apart from Mrs Norris, whom he rather enjoyed despising, he found it heavy going. A snobby lot, the family, but he took pleasure in comparing the two houses, the one in the book and his own.

Melton now had glasshouses and a large formal kitchen

garden, and there was no mention of these in the book. And while the Bertrams seemed always to have lived at Mansfield Park, had probably inherited it, he'd worked bloody hard to get Melton. He'd had it done up inside by professionals, had had the grounds freshly laid out and planted. He had all this to give her. It only remained for him to ask her.

This he did the following evening in suitably romantic circumstances: candlelight, gardenias floating in a bowl on the table and champagne glasses. He put the open box with the ring on the table. The emerald and diamonds glinted as he stretched out his hand to hers while he told her she could have anything she wanted, would never have to do dull office jobs again, that he was sure, fairly sure, Floy would approve and that he would look after both of them for ever.

But he never reached her hand. She withdrew it and, as she looked down, her loose dark hair fell over her face so that for a moment he couldn't see it. When she looked at him once more, he saw that her eyes were full of tears.

'Don't cry. Don't – darling.' The word so surprised him. He'd never used it before in his life.

'I'm sorry. It's tremendously kind of you, but I can't. I'm so, *so* sorry,' she repeated. She was looking anxiously at him now. She brushed away the tears and tried to smile.

For a moment he was stupefied, shocked by this completely unexpected response. He couldn't think, or feel, or comprehend, or accept anything. Then he remembered he'd had to fight for everything he'd achieved with patience, toughness and never taking no for any answer.

'I've been too abrupt. I've upset you. You probably don't believe me – you need time.' And when she shook her head, he continued, 'Tell you what, we won't talk about it any more now.' He refilled their glasses. 'This was meant to be a treat to thank you for all your hard work for the festival.' The small lie deceived neither of them but afforded a precarious route back from the abyss. She fell in with it gratefully and they picked at their lobster, but it all seemed unreal to him. It wasn't really happening – and it certainly wouldn't stay this way. He'd steer her towards him somehow.

Towards the end of the meal, as the ring still lay on the table, he picked it up and, with deliberate lightness, said, 'At least let me try this on your finger. Just to see if I got the right size.'

She let him. It was far too big and slipped round so the emerald faced her palm. With a small shrug, she gave it back to him. 'It's a very beautiful ring.' She said it politely but he noticed her colour rose.

'Well,' he said, as he put it back in the box and into his pocket. 'I've got one small request to make.'

'What's that?'

'Would you just consider for a bit before you finally make up your mind? Just give it a short time?'

'All right. But I don't think—'

'No. Just say you will.'

'All right.'

But the next day she came to him and said she'd thought about it, as he'd asked, and it was still no. She asked if he'd rather she left Melton. She could finish the accounts and all that in London, but he'd said, no, no, finish them. Anyway, Floy had rung to say she was bringing down a possible gardener to be interviewed the following week.

'Why don't you ask your friends the Musgroves for dinner?' He didn't want her to think he was angry and he thought he might as well get to know them.

'I'll ask them, but it might be difficult for them. Or, at least, all of them.' She explained that Harriet, the child, had to be babysat and they were having trouble with Francis's father, who lived with them. 'They don't seem to go out at all,' she finished.

'But I thought you said Thomas took you to the cinema.'

'He did, but Mary held the fort. I'll see if she can come. I must go, Jack. Mrs Quantock is due with her accounts for the flower festival, and I've got to work out the expenses before she arrives.'

She'd behaved, he thought now, as if nothing had happened between them. As he parked the car near the house, empty this evening as she was having supper with the Connaughts, he reflected drearily that she seemed to have made all sorts of friends of whom he knew practically nothing.

After his solitary supper, served in the library, he looked at his half-read copy of *Mansfield Park*, and put it back on the shelf. Not much point in going on with that.

Instead he went steadily through *Autocar* magazine and decided to buy himself a new car.

MRS QUANTOCK

'I'm going out now, dear. I'll be back in time to give you your tea,' she yelled. Mother had the telly on so loud she hardly heard anything else – or pretended not to. She was still perfectly able to accuse her daughter-in-law of abandoning her without a word, though. So she tried again.

'No need to yell like that. You're interrupting me – you go out all the time with your silly excuses.' She hunched herself more firmly in her chair. 'I'd be better off with Beryl,' she shouted, as a parting shot.

Oh, no, you wouldn't, Elsie thought, as she got into her little car to see Miss Plover. Beryl doesn't have a television. Since it had all gone colour, Fred had bought one and his mother was, as he put it, a different woman. She watched from lunchtime until nearly midnight. She probably watched the test card until children's telly at five. She watched everything: news, pop shows, highbrow programmes about books, people being interviewed and comedy. It stopped her complaining all the time, but Elsie could hardly hear herself think with the constant noise, and if she wanted to read she had to resort to the bedroom. It was a relief to get out, and she was looking forward to her afternoon with Miss Plover, whom she'd come to like more and more during the festival. The festival. If you'd told her six months ago she'd actually be sorry it was over, she wouldn't have believed you. But it was the truth.

Because Miss Plover had been ever so nice about the flower

part of it, really helpful, she'd decided she'd go to the other events in solidarity. That had been a revelation. The theatre enthralled her, not so much the play, which was about a lot of people she didn't really know, but being there when the actors were acting, seeing them at it, being part of an audience laughing and listening. You could've heard a pin drop when they weren't talking. It had excited her in a completely different way from seeing a film. And then she'd forced herself to go to the lecture on Dickens. Again, although some of what the nice man – Mr Wilson, he was called – talked about was a bit of a mystery, he read some passages from novels and she became hooked, had got *Great Expectations* out of the library and read it right through and had started on *A Tale of Two Cities* the next day.

But perhaps the most marvellous revelation had been the music. It was all of a kind that she'd never heard in her life. The pianist, a very small woman in a long black dress, had sat down before a huge great black piano, laid her hands on the keyboard and started playing with magical brilliance. The Scarlatti stuff left her a bit breathless, but the woman had played some bits twice and that helped. The best of all was the Chopin – dreamy and romantic: it had made her remember her youth and feel glad and sad at the same time. And then there was the opera evening, the lady and gentleman, sometimes singing separately, sometimes together. She couldn't understand the words, but it was all about love, no doubt about it, and a lot of it was tragic, according to the programme. Sometimes they were joyfully united, sometimes they were dying because of it, and this had reduced her to tears, while at the same time she felt this was life as it ought to be and wasn't. Not in her experience, anyway . . .

She remembered a time when she was thirteen, just before the war, and she and Violet had stayed out late. They'd each saved a bob to go and see Fred Astaire and Ginger Rogers in *Carefree*, and when she'd got back there was her father, in his shirtsleeves and braces, puffed up with anger. 'Where have you been?' he began, and when she started crying and told him, he screamed, 'I'll give you something to cry for,' and slapped her so hard on the side of her face she nearly fell over. And he'd gone on and on at her until she'd run out of the kitchen up the stairs to find Mum, but she was in bed with the light out. All she said was, 'Go to bed, Elsie – quick. Go to bed.' She'd known then Mum was afraid too, wouldn't protect her. Hours, it seemed, lying in the dark, afraid he'd come, but eventually she heard him stumbling up the stairs and he didn't – went off to their bedroom and everything was quiet. Ever since then, she'd thought crying was what you did when something was awful or sad. She hadn't known you could cry for other things. It had taken those opera songs for her to find that out.

She'd cried from all sorts of things in her life – when Violet's dad was killed in the Somme and her brother a few weeks later in the same battle. She'd been lucky, really, Fred having something wrong with his feet. It had meant they didn't call him up and he'd just gone on working for the railways, although they did let him join the Home Guard, which gave him a lift.

Well, she'd done her bit for the festival. The flower show had been quite an achievement – best one ever. The arrangements were spectacular – you wouldn't believe what people could use for them: the first prize went to a desert oasis, with cactus, sand, a bit of mirror glass, two camels and tiny palms the lady had grown from date stones, a real work of art.

The only bit she hadn't really cared for were the art exhibitions. The portraits had been of people she'd never heard of and not like anyone she'd ever seen. They didn't seem anything like as good as photographs. She couldn't see the point of them. Painting was obviously very difficult, and judging by the few pictures she'd seen at school – she remembered one of Jesus called *The Light of the World* and another of a lady drowning in full evening dress – people had got worse at it.

They still had scaffolding on the house. People said it was

lucky it hadn't burned down. It was the secretary smoking in bed – fond of her drink too: Violet said her cousin Joan, who cleaned three mornings a week, said the room had bottles in it, empty and full, so it was pretty clear what had happened. Anyway, no lives lost, that was the main thing.

She parked her car at the back as she'd been told and walked round to the front with her carrier-bag full of the flower-festival accounts.

THOMAS AND MARY

'I thought I might take Percy to the cinema.'

He'd said this casually to Mary, almost as if he was trying the idea out to see if it sounded as daring and unlikely as it felt.

'Good idea. Have you asked her?'

'Not exactly. But I've found out they're running a season of Ealing comedies and I asked her if she liked them and she does.'

'Well, fine.' She returned to the papers on the table. They needed to be sorted for the tax accountant.

'How are we doing?'

'Much better than last year, but that's because of all the stuff we sold to Melton. And it won't go on. Stop walking about and sit down. I want to talk to you.'

He sat. He knew what she was going to say. He was trying to do too much without enough help; the business was too big for one man.

'We're only just keeping our heads above water and you can't work any harder.'

'Well, what, then? What can I do?'

He thought she wasn't going to answer and, with a kind of irascible triumph, repeated it. What was the point of saying we were in a mess if she couldn't see a way out of it?

She looked at him, at his lined and sunburned face, the once auburn hair now fading to a dull greyish-brown, at his anxious angry eyes. Unspeakable affection filled her. She said, 'I've thought about it. You need a partner, somebody who would put some money or time into the nursery.'

It was so unlikely but it was a straw to be clutched at. 'It's an idea,' he said. 'Can't think how I'd find one . . .' There was a pause. 'I did ask Floy if she thought I had the makings of a garden designer. After all, she seems all right. I'd have to go to London and take a course, though, which costs, and the nursery would go to pot.'

Another silence. Then, careful of her words, she said, 'Floy told me they're looking for a head gardener at Melton.'

'She told me too – asked if I knew anyone, which of course I don't.'

He got up and was doing what he'd come into the house to do: filling his Thermos flask with water from the fridge. In a minute he'd top it up with a trickle of lemon barley water from the bottle and be gone.

'I wondered if it might be just the thing for you.'

He turned to face her. 'What on earth made you think that?'

She told him. It was a good, steady, interesting job. He'd be working on land he knew and loved. It would be well paid and he'd enjoyed working with Floy, who would find people to work under him.

'You must be mad. Do you seriously think I've sunk so low as to be a paid employee on an estate that ought to be mine? Have you forgotten everything? I may have made a mess of things, but I still have some pride. Have you any idea how humiliated I'd feel working for that man – some rich shit who could sack me on a whim?'

She had expected he would argue, but this torrent of pent-up rage was too much. Trying to keep her voice steady, she said, 'I don't think he is a shit. He doesn't treat people as you say. I'm sorry you feel that way. It was just an idea. I thought it might stop us having to worry about money all the time.' She put her hands over her face and pressed her cheekbones hard – she really didn't want to cry.

He came over to her, pulled up a chair and sat beside her. 'We don't do so badly. You said this year was much better. You worry too much, old thing. It's Reggie who's got you down. I know you've had an awful time with the old bugger.' He brushed her hair aside and gave her a quick kiss. 'Sorry I flew off the handle.'

A bell rang in the kitchen; a customer had arrived at the nursery. 'Got to go.'

As he reached the door, he said, 'You'll think it extravagant but I'd like to take Percy out to dinner after the movie – somewhere really nice. Where should we go?'

She said that the Black Swan at Eyesham was supposed to be good.

'Right. I'll give them a ring. When I've asked her.'

After he'd gone she allowed herself a small weep. She *did* worry about money. She *had* to. Her small teaching salary just about paid for Hatty, her clothes, her extras at school, her pocket money, and the dentist – all those things. Francis paid his whack as a lodger and did some part-time work for the nursery, but they were in debt at the bank when Thomas had bought the extra stock for the Melton job, and by the time they'd paid the interest on it, the profit had been modest to say the least. There was never any money to spare, to replace things, for maintenance of the house. She looked at the new washing-machine they would never have had if she hadn't cooked that dinner party. Neither she nor Thomas had taken a holiday for years and, until the festival, neither had even gone out for the evening. She'd seen to it that Hatty went to everything; she and Thomas had taken it in turns and she'd lashed out on tickets for Hatty's friend, Meg, to pay back some of Meg's mother's hospitality.

Although nothing had been said, she was perfectly aware

Thomas was smitten by Percy. Supposing he married her? She herself would have to go, would feel free – Oh, there was Hatty, of course. She'd have to go slowly, give Percy and Hatty time to settle down with each other. Then what?

HUGO

Hugo's plans to get his brother to cough up some dough to spend on Easton Park hadn't been entirely unsuccessful. He'd failed to convince Ashley the house needed a new roof, largely because he'd failed to get any builder to provide an estimate for this without a survey of the job.

But when Ashley had finally agreed to a survey, dry rot had been discovered. News of this was sent to Hong Kong and Ashley had released the sum of five thousand pounds, irritatingly to Lady Yoxford's bank. However, Hugo knew how to deal with that. He explained to his mother that Ashley was all for them making rooms available to festival tourists, which he'd said would generate a good income. The fire at Melton had exasperated him. Why on earth hadn't he thought of that? It would have produced far more money, and a spot of arson would have been exciting.

Too late. He'd got in decorators and had already set about modernizing one ancient bathroom and installing a second. This, plus the renovation of two bedrooms and a dressing room on the first floor at the opposite end of the house to where he, his mother and Betsy slept, would provide room for three lots of visitors at twenty pounds per head per night, which would provide an income for yours truly, he hoped for long after the festival was over. He'd enjoyed overseeing the job, arranging the better pieces of furniture, hanging the walls with murky portraits of what were doubtfully family ancestors. Faded elegance was what he'd been after, to which end he'd taken some of the taffeta and velvet curtains from reception rooms that were not – and had not been for years – in use. He filled bookcases with rows of leatherbound volumes of Walter Scott and eighteenth-century sermons Betsy said nobody would want to read. 'It doesn't matter. It's the look of the thing,' he'd responded, to this and any other objection she made. Most of the rugs had been attacked by moths, but he arranged them cleverly so chairs and tables covered the worst bits. The builders hung three enormous foxed mirrors he'd discovered stacked on the attic floor.

Betsy toiled faithfully after him. She'd been much encouraged by the prospect of the splendid breakfasts to be offered to guests, which, naturally, the family would also enjoy. 'Eggs scrambled, fried or boiled, bacon, sausages, mushrooms, porridge if desired, orange juice, toast, homemade marmalade and the rest of it,' he'd told the cook. It was going to make a lovely change from corn flakes and instant coffee. The outlook even animated Lady Yoxford, who offered to arrange flowers when the time came.

What neither Hugo nor anyone else had realized, until a couple of weeks before the festival was due to start, was that they hadn't arranged any publicity to inform tourists of the event. In spite of a leaflet hastily printed and sent by Percy to all the main travel agencies and some hotels in London, tourist bookings were minimal. In the end all he got was a middle-aged American couple and their daughter, who stayed the whole week, were voracious sightseers and called him 'Your Lordship', which he very much enjoyed – he primed Betsy not to disabuse them since it gave them almost as much pleasure as it gave him. They wanted their English breakfast at seven thirty, which was a great strain on the household, as the cook, who only came in by the day, wasn't prepared to turn up so early, and Manningtree, butler since his father's day, was only really up to making tea and putting out the corn flakes and, in any case, was usually hung-over in the mornings. However, he gave everyone a pep-talk: it was only for a week. He didn't let on about his longer-term plans. It was for the honour of the house, he told his mother, and when that didn't galvanize her enough to forgo her usual breakfast in bed, he bribed her with a box of Bendick's peppermint creams to invite the Americans to take tea with her one afternoon.

The guests used up all the hot water, but went off for the day and covered an amazing amount of cultural ground, apart from going to every festival event. They were in awe of their surroundings, he thought happily. He was unaware that they were in awe of the splendid discomfort: the tepid bathwater; the absence of showers; the beds like padded toast-racks; the drapes so rotting that they could hardly use them – and, above all, the extreme cold. Even on fine sunny days the house, when they returned to it from one of their excursions to Stonehenge, or Wardour Castle, or Wilton House was – as their daughter Kimberly was heard to remark by Betsy – like 'coming back to an ice-box'. They clung to the discomforts as being 'genuine', and 'genuine' was what they'd come so far and paid so much to experience.

He hadn't got much else out of the festival, unless you counted Rosalie. He'd gone to the first night of *Hay Fever*, in which she played the young girl. With her glossy blonde hair and long legs – perfectly set off by a scarlet mini-skirt – she was just his type, on top of which, he discovered early on, she was Admiral Connaught's daughter. He thought he might be on to a good thing. He went to the play again – committee members got free seats – sent her some flowers and a note suggesting he take her out for a drink after the show. This was a success. They went to the Crown, sat in a dark corner of the saloon bar and he listened while she told him what hell rehearsals had been and how her part didn't give her the chance to show her range.

'If only I could have been Judith,' she said, 'but Derek said I was far too young.' She'd gazed at him with her mournful blue eyes. 'The trouble with the theatre is that they do so much type-casting.'

This first date was so fraught with misinformation about themselves that it only increased their interest. She was staying with her parents as her mother wasn't well and Daddy needed help, so she'd put her career on hold and when Derek, from the theatre, realized she was there, she hadn't been able to resist accepting the part. He early established that he lived in Easton Park where his family had lived forever 'and you can imagine what it's like trying to keep up a house like that, these days – impossible to get staff and my mother, Lady Yoxford, is getting rather past dealing with all that. So it falls on me.'

'Is it a very large house, then?'

'Quite large.'

'How many bedrooms?'

He laughed disarmingly, 'Do you know, I've never counted. A couple of dozen, I guess.'

She still gazed at him, but slightly less mournfully. 'Cor.' She picked a piece of cucumber out of her Pimm's and chewed it thoughtfully.

Shortly after, he offered to drive her home. 'But, actually,' he said in the car, 'I thought I'd drive to somewhere quiet for a bit first.'

'OK.'

He drove to a cart track off a little-used lane, backed into it and turned off the engine.

After a strenuous pause, she asked, 'Are you in love with me?'

'I'm mad about you. How about the back seat?'

'OK.'

When they were installed, she said, 'I think it's terribly important not to repress one's feelings, don't you?'

'Terribly.'

'Like our parents – they must have missed so much.' He

agreed. 'Even if they fell in love, they'd have been too repressed to express it.'

He agreed again, hoping to stall these ruminations.

'I mean, I can't imagine them—'

'Don't try,' he interrupted. 'Imagine me.' He'd undone her blouse by now and his own trousers, and found the zip of her skirt.

'Are we going to . . . ?'

'Absolutely.'

That was the beginning, and after the festival, they met two or three times a week. She was keen to see the house, and eventually he took her there – late enough for his mother and Betsy to be safely in bed. Gradually, he learned she'd been married, now divorced, and had a baby. One visit – to pick her up from the cottage – revealed her father couldn't be well off. But neither of these things made too much difference. It meant, of course, marriage was out of the question but, so far, the subject hadn't come up. Fortunately, there was still quite a bit of money left from the five grand, so he took her out to dinner every now and then. He'd given up the idea of spending any of it on the dry rot – the builders said it was no good doing part of it: it was all or nothing. Meanwhile for once in his life he had some cash to spend as he pleased.

Betsy kicked up about the money, saying she ought to have a share as she'd worked just as hard as he to get the tourists' rooms ready, so he gave her twenty quid to keep her on his side and she was both surprised and content.

She'd spent it immediately on buying another pony, which she described as an investment. 'I can take four people on rides, so that's an extra fifteen shillings an hour. Anyway, Bumble's getting so old I can't use her for much. But if you get more guests, I think I ought to have more,' she added, 'because Mummy says I need new clothes – not that I care much about them, as you know.'

As he certainly knew, he thought. She lived in jodhpurs or jeans, faded Aertex shirts or heavy oiled-wool sweaters depending on the season, her seldom-washed hair in a single plait, her shiny freckled face scrubbed with soap and water, her hands cracked and sometimes raw with chilblains in winter – she refused to ride in gloves as 'you can't feel a horse's mouth if you wear them'. For a moment he actually had a pang of conscience about her. She asked for so little and put up with so much. Ashley should provide her with some sort of allowance, he thought. Her riding school just about paid for itself with nothing to spare. Then he reflected he couldn't possibly write to Ashley about it since it was safer not to communicate with him just now or the dry rot would rear its head. On impulse, he gave her another twenty-five pounds.

'Oh, thanks. I can get a new pair of boots at least. Mine are done in.'

'I can't guarantee there'll be any more.'

'I'm sure we'll get more people to stay. They gave Manningtree a huge tip, so he's quite keen. I think you ought to give Cook something, though. She didn't like having to come so early to do the breakfasts and we'd be done for if she left.'

'Good idea.'

Good irritating idea, he thought. It was extraordinary how, the moment one had any cash, everybody seemed to want to lift it. Well, if it hadn't been for the festival, he wouldn't have had a bean of it.

PERCY

'Oh, it's so lovely to be home.'

She lay in the basket chair in the conservatory, and Floy sat upright in the new chair she'd dragged there for the purpose. She'd come up for the day to go shopping and also to drive Floy down to Melton as two gardeners were expected for interview. They were having what Floy described as a picnic lunch of sandwiches, grapes and iced coffee. They hadn't been alone like this for some time, and both were still selecting which bits of news to tell the other. Percy had been shocked by her aunt's appearance. She seemed washed out and weary, and was clearly in more pain than she admitted. 'Oh, it comes and goes,' she said. 'I had to go to Clifton Nurseries yesterday and stand about with a client who couldn't make up her mind what climbers she wanted. The doctor says it will settle down – just a bit of rest. He's given me three lots of pills. I'll be quite all right. I want to hear about you, darling. Did the festival come out all right financially?'

'Well, we didn't make any money, so the sponsors just about evened things out, but everyone agreed, if they continue next year, it should do much better. Still, I learned a lot. And Jack gave me a decent salary – if he hadn't, there wouldn't have been enough to pay me.'

There was a pause during which Floy lit one of her little cigars. 'So there's nothing more to keep you there?'

'No.' She presented Marvell with a scrap of ham, which he examined very carefully before discarding it.

'As a matter of fact Jack offered me Mrs Fanshawe's job.'

'No-go?'

'No-go – like he asked you to be his head gardener. I think he's just lonely and dreads us leaving. He even asked me to marry him. Took me out to dinner and tried to give me an enormous hideous ring.'

'And that was no-go?'

'Yes. I mean, no, it wasn't. He asked me to think about it, and I said I would, but I didn't need to. I do feel sorry for him, though.'

'That's not a good reason to marry someone.'

'I know. But apart from that, would you have thought it a good thing?'

'There isn't any apart about it.'

'But you do like him?'

'Yes. And I agree with you he's lonely. But that's something he'll have to sort out, don't you think?' She winced as Marvell jumped heavily on to her lap.

'I did have a good idea for him . . .' Percy stopped for a moment, and Floy wondered if she was more entangled than she realized. 'I thought . . .' Percy began slowly ' . . . it would be a marvellous idea if he married Mary.'

'Thomas's sister?'

'She'd run the house perfectly and she's very fond of children and he said he wanted a family. It used to be her home so it would be lovely if she could go back to it. She wouldn't have to work so hard and worry about money all the time, and do her boring job teaching girls to cook.'

'Do they know each other?'

'No, but I thought I could easily arrange that. And I could get her to take a bit of trouble with her appearance – she's really rather beautiful in a Burne-Jones-ish way. Floy, don't laugh, I'm serious.'

'You sound like Emma Woodhouse to me. Knowing what's best for other people is a dangerous game.'

'But I love Mary. Why are you so against the idea?'

'I'm not against anything. But I wonder if you've thought about her brother and the child, what would become of them. And don't tell me love will find a way, because love is often exceedingly bad at that.'

'All right, I won't tell you anything. It's just sometimes I feel so sorry for her.'

'Percy darling, you're always feeling sorry for people because you wouldn't like to be them. They may feel quite differently.'

'That's a cop-out.' She was feeling sulky and cross and got up to clear the lunch things. 'What time do you want to leave?'

'As soon as we can, don't you think? I've put all Marvell's things in the small shopping-bag.' She started to haul herself to her feet and instantly Percy was beside her, collecting the stick that had fallen to the floor, holding her other arm. 'Oh, Floy. I'm so sorry. I'll do the kitchen. Why don't you just sit while I shut up the house, or would you rather not go?'

'I'd rather go. It's quite all right. It's good for me to walk a bit. I've got to go upstairs, anyway, to finish packing my case.'

'Well, I'll bring it down for you. Just shout for me.'

In the van, with Percy driving and Marvell in the back in his basket, they listened, by mutual consent, to Glenn Gould playing preludes and fugues. Floy ruminated on the fact that she hadn't told Percy about the house. She'd have to tell her but not yet, she told herself – not until Percy had finished with Melton and found some work. The whole dreary business loomed in her mind: selling, finding somewhere to live, probably without Percy, and doing everything in her power to stay independent. Ageing, she concluded ruefully, was an arduous business, requiring increasing effort, with less and less to show for it.

Percy, ostensibly intent upon driving and listening to the music, was anxiously considering her aunt. She was getting worryingly frail, but also, for the first time in years, Percy had withheld a piece of news that now felt more important for withholding: she hadn't said a word about her evening with Thomas and the confusion it had caused her. She ran the evening over and over in her mind, like a clip from a film, until she thought she knew every word, every gesture by heart. He'd picked her up, smartly dressed in a dark suit, deep blue shirt, darker blue silk tie and highly polished shoes. The film had been *Kind Hearts and Coronets*. Her favourite, she'd said, and he'd agreed. 'I haven't seen it for years,' he said. 'It'll be like the first time again.' He seemed both festive and shy, and she felt awkward. Every now and again, he laughed out loud, and she was suddenly aware that she'd never heard him laugh before. Often, when she turned to him, she found him watching her, as though he was anxious she should enjoy it.

Afterwards they drove to dinner and he told her how nice it was to be out of the house. 'I expect Mary's told you about Reggie.'

'Yes. Actually, I had rather a wild idea about that.'

They'd arrived at the restaurant and he'd cut the engine.

'You know Jack had that secretary, the one who started the fire? Well, she's recovering, sort of, and is apparently well enough to leave the nursing-home, but not to take up her old job. I wondered if she couldn't be a sort of housekeeper for him in return for her keep. If the house is big enough he could take in a lodger as well. She'd be terrific at paying the bills and looking after all that sort of thing. And she plays bridge.'

As she thought of it now, all the things Mrs Fanshawe couldn't do came to mind. But the poor woman had nowhere else to go. It was, at least, worth a try.

'What an amazingly kind person you are,' he'd responded, after a pause, and she had felt vaguely uncomfortable.

'Shall I speak to Mary about it?'

'And Francis,' he said indulgently. 'You could talk to both of them.' In the restaurant – ironically the same place she'd been to with Jack – he'd talked about his favourite bits of the film. 'I particularly like Guinness as the clergyman, and that bit when he sinks, saluting, under the waves, his wonderful unwavering face.'

When she declared it was really as good as *The Importance of Being Earnest*, he agreed. 'I saw that with Celia before we married, before we came down here. She loved the theatre – took me to lots of plays.' Then the waiter came for their order and they hadn't chosen. 'You must have whatever you most like,' he said.

This time she saw from the menu it was an expensive place. She knew money was tight in the Musgrove household, so she chose soup and chicken breasts because they were the cheapest and he said jolly good choice, he'd have the same. They decided on red wine and the waiter left. They were on their own again.

'This is fun,' he'd said. 'I haven't done anything like this, well, since Celia died.'

She was unsure if he wanted to talk more about Celia or if he had mentioned her to ward off questions. She'd been crumbling a roll in her fingers, and when she looked across the table at him she saw he was smiling. 'It's all right,' he said. 'I don't mind talking about her with you.'

'When did she die?'

'Six years ago. It was the shock, really, that was so difficult. I mean, if she'd been ill, or something, at least I'd have known what we were in for. But out of the blue like that, without any warning, it seemed my whole life had been swept away. The funny thing is I couldn't believe it. Of course I *knew* it had happened, but at the same time I couldn't take it in – didn't even have a chance to say goodbye. She could have stayed the night in London with Francis, but she wanted to get home to me. That's what happened.'

Tears were hot in her eyes and she could say nothing.

At this point, the waiter brought their soup.

'I didn't mean to upset you.' He'd said it very gently, with real contrition. 'It – well, it just seemed important to tell you what it was and to tell you also that it isn't like that any more.'

She'd managed to say she was glad he'd told her.

During their chicken he asked her about herself. 'Have you liked living in the country all these months? You're really a London girl, aren't you?'

She told him about her childhood in Greece and then about being brought up by Floy.

'What about your parents?'

She told him about them, adding the latest news that her father had finally divorced her mother, who was living in Brazil. 'But they've never seemed much like parents, so I don't really care what they do.'

'Mary and I had parents like that. They left us quite early on and we were farmed out. But I always had Mary – and you always had Floy. She must have made up for your parents.'

'She did everything. I love her more than anyone in the world. I can't imagine what I'd have done without her.'

'Francis said you'd be going back to London soon.'

She explained she had to get work.

'But you might come back and run another festival?'

'I don't know. I don't know if there'll be another, and even if there is, I'll probably be working and couldn't get the time off.'

'I suppose you wouldn't.'

He sounded so disconsolate that she said, 'I'm sure we'll be back from time to time. Floy won't be able to resist coming to look at the garden. It's the biggest commission she's ever had and she'll want to check whoever takes over is sticking to her plans. She told me she hoped it was going to be you.'

'Did she? Well, it won't be. I don't fancy working for somebody else – apart from anything.'

The waiter came with their pears in red wine, so she missed the chance of asking him what the anything might be.

He had asked if she'd like some coffee and a liqueur – and here her memory failed her. She did recall a growing awkwardness between them, that whenever she glanced at him he instantly averted his gaze, and as it dawned on her that he was going to tell her he'd fallen for her, he swallowed half of his brandy and began, 'You know I was telling you about Celia and how it had been and that it wasn't like that any more?' And before she could make some small gesture of assent, he went on, 'Well, it changed because of you – that first afternoon when you came with Floy. I fell in love with you at once. I didn't even know it at the time, but I do now. No, don't say anything for a moment. I didn't mean to bombard you on our first evening like this, but now you're going away and suddenly there seems to be no time so I *have* to tell you – that I love you, want to marry you, to have your children, to live with you for the rest of our lives.'

At that moment time stopped for her. It was as if they were frozen, without speech or movement, as she was immersed in a flood of confusion, of conflicting emotions. It was as if somebody had placed a great weight on one side of some scales and the other had shot into the air. His certainty, his sincerity were beyond doubt, as was the startling fact that she was deeply touched by both. Nobody had ever spoken to her in such a way – without the blandishments of praise or endearments, without the false humility: just a plain statement that was undeniably of love. Eventually she heard herself saying his name.

'This is where nice girls blush and say, "Mr Musgrove, this is so sudden,"' he smiled, and she felt a rush of gratitude and warmth.

'Blushes don't show much on my olive skin,' she said. 'And those nice girls also say, "I'm deeply sensible of the honour you have done me." But, dear Thomas, it *is* sudden and I can't – I don't know what to say except that I don't love you enough to say yes.'

'You don't dislike me?

'No.'

Perhaps you'll think about it. Please, take all the time you want.'

'It's not that I'm in love with anybody else.'

'I knew that,' he responded, 'or I wouldn't have asked you.'

That was it. On the way back to Melton, he talked of ordinary everyday things, about how he was thinking of asking Floy's advice on garden design, and about Hatty, who was mad about riding and spent all her spare time with Betsy Carson up at Easton Park. 'She just adores grooming and feeding ponies and is pestering me to get her one.'

'And will you?'

'I'll see what Mary thinks, but not until we've got Reggie sorted out. I know Mary's told you about him.' He said it absently. They'd arrived at Melton and there was a short silence, during which the earlier part of the evening became uneasily, overwhelmingly present and she was aware only of needing to go, to escape and be alone. She began to thank him for the evening, but he put a hand on her arm and turned her towards him.

'Persephone, Percy, Zephie – I like the name your aunt calls you best. It's what I call you to myself. Listen, before you go, would you – may I? I have no idea, you see – but I long to have, at least, kissed you once.'

How could she refuse? He took her head in his hands and looked intently at her whole face before kissing her, a long kiss that was as intense as it was tender. 'Thank you. Now you must go.'

He took her up the steps to the door. 'Darling, beautiful Zephie,' he'd said, before she left him to go into the house.

In the hall she waited until she heard him drive away before she ran up the stairs to her room and lay on her bed in the dark.

Before Denis she'd been used to men, people she worked with or casually encountered at parties, flirting, making passes, making it obvious they wanted a quick lay. They'd tell her how beautiful she was, hint at their sexual prowess or even sometimes openly boast about it. And it was easy for her to brush them off. But she so wanted to be loved, and she was easy prey for anyone experienced in seduction – hence Denis. She'd been attracted to him and he'd been happy to amuse himself with a romance, if that was what she wanted. He'd told her how much he loved her and how, if he wasn't already a husband and a father, she'd have been the love of his life. He knew, in fact, how to seduce and keep a mistress, and for months she had resigned herself to it. When Jack had proposed to her she'd realized Denis no longer meant anything to her at all, had just been an awful, humiliating mistake. Jack had touched her, not because of everything he offered but for what he hadn't perceived to be missing. She thought then of the airy plan she'd concocted for Mary to marry him, the practical advantages she'd put to Floy, as if that was all that was needed. Why should Mary be content with them, if she wasn't?

Thomas was different. He loved her. All her life she'd longed to be truly loved and here it was. He was someone who really understood love – he'd cherished Celia and, according to Mary, was nearly wrecked by her loss. 'Take all the time you want,' he'd said, but she couldn't do that. She couldn't string him along, raise his hopes, while she tried to discover if love could grow out of friendship, of approval, of pity and respect rather than it be the bolt of lightning she'd always dreamed of. Surely I should know, she thought. She was beginning to feel both irritable and sorry for herself.

As she drifted into sleep, she indulged in a sweet and easy dream of Mary happily married to Jack, and she to Thomas, each having discovered what they really wanted, living nearby so their friendship could remain and increase for the rest of their lives. Her last thought, before oblivion, had been of Francis. What would happen to him?

He'd always be there – always.

REGGIE

Reggie sat in his car in the dark, stupefied. He couldn't believe his luck. If anyone had told him that morning – just another day of golf, a sandwich at the bar, find someone for a round in the afternoon before nipping back to the farm and sprucing up for dinner and bridge with the Hotchkisses – if anyone had even suggested things would turn out as they had, he'd have told them they were mad. Even now he found it difficult to take in. It had begun that morning. As he was having a quick pee before lunch, the chap next to him suddenly remarked, 'Pity about old Brian. We've probably seen the last of him.'

'Brian?'

'Oh. Haven't you heard? He's been caught out having a bit on the side in London. Poor old Amy's in no end of a state.'

When he'd asked how on earth he – Travers, he thought his name was – knew that, the man just put a purple finger to his nose and winked. 'Mum's the word,' he said, long after it clearly hadn't been.

At first he'd just thought bang went his evening. All the same, he decided after his sandwich and pint that perhaps he'd better ring up and see how the land lay. After all, Amy had been most sympathetic when he'd told her his troubles.

'I've told you I don't want to speak to you, Brian, and I mean it.'

'It's Reggie. I was just ringing to check what time this evening.'

'Oh – Reggie. Oh – seven thirty as usual.' He'd detected a slight hesitation but, as she said nothing else, he decided he'd better go, pretend to know nothing and wait to be told.

He didn't have long to wait. She was in the room with all the leather sofas, lying on one in a long black dress with a deep V-neck, sporting a brassière that enhanced her striking cleavage. Her hair and face were immaculate, and crimson toenails peeped from her high-heeled golden sandals. A tray loaded with drinks was on a low table well within her reach.

'Help yourself,' she said, 'and top me up, there's a dear. Just brandy, I don't want any more ginger ale.'

He did as he was told and she said, 'Cheers,' with a kind of portentous cheerlessness.

'You seem a bit upset,' he began.

'You're right I'm upset.'

'Where's Brian?'

'He's gone, never to darken these doors again, if I've anything to do with it.'

And then the whole story came out. He'd been cheating on her. She'd heard him on the phone, chatting up someone called Lois, and she'd gone through his suits and found a letter from the bitch with a phone number. So when he was away 'on business in London, the bastard', she rang the number, pretended to be his office, anxious to get hold of him, and the bitch said he wasn't there but was expected soon. She'd confronted him two days later, when he came home from his bloody business. 'I had no idea your business was called Lois,' she'd begun. It turned out he'd been cheating on her for years. For years they'd been laughing about her behind her back. Well, *she* was going to give him something to laugh at: she wouldn't just be divorcing him, she'd be taking him to the cleaners. 'If he dares to come crawling back to me I won't have him,' she finished, at the end of her first, but no means last, outburst.

They had a few more drinks while he told her he couldn't

understand how any man could treat *her* in such a way. He'd perceived dimly that her rage was shot through with anxiety.

'I mean, to look at me, Reggie, would you say I was the kind of woman who deserved to be treated like that? Would you?'

No, he wouldn't. He wouldn't say she was that kind of woman, and he certainly wouldn't dream of treating her as anything but a lady. The mollifying helped her anxiety, but fuelled her rage. She went over it again and again. He was getting rather hungry and had by now surreptitiously eaten a whole bowl of Twiglets.

'It's not the money,' she said, more than once. 'I'm not short of a bob or two. It's the humiliation.' He'd taken particular note of that and fulsomely agreed that money wasn't the point at all. By the time they were on their fourth drink, she'd become a bit tearful – what a good friend he was. Brian had left her in this back-of-beyond and she'd lost touch with all her chums. He, Reggie, was a true godsend, he really was.

Still starving, he had a brainwave. 'You need to get some food inside you,' he said. 'I bet you've been too upset to eat all day.' She could say that again, she hadn't fancied a thing. Trust him, it was just what she needed. Should he . . . ? No, just ring the bell. Maurice would bring a tray the cook had left.

The tray held two bowls of jellied consommé, a pile of smoked-salmon sandwiches and a bunch of grapes. 'I thought a light snack would be best in the circumstances,' she said, meaning her own.

He thought she should sit up for her soup, and as she did so, one of her breasts made a wild bid for freedom. She crammed it back with a petulant gesture.

Though she didn't stop talking, she matched him sandwich for sandwich and the meal was consumed in no time. Between fulminating about Brian and various possibilities for revenge, there were more encouraging remarks. It was *wonderful* to have someone who really understood her. She'd always thought there was more to him than met the eye, she really had. Brian had never been what she'd call a sensitive man, but if you were married, you had to put up with the rough as well as the smooth – though there'd been precious little of the latter. She thought she'd like just one more drink now and there was a box of choccies on the shelf by the cocktail cabinet, if he'd be a dear and fetch it.

So they had another drink and ate a whole box of Black Magic, while she told him that if it hadn't been for her Brian would never have had all the money he had now. They'd started by running a pub together, and everything had gone from there. And she'd had to hand it to him, Brian knew how to make money. But what was money for, she'd told him over and over again, if it wasn't to enjoy yourself?

Full of brandy and chocolate, and with all the effort of commiserating and agreeing, he was exhausted – longing for Bedfordshire, in fact – when she suddenly said, 'That reminds me. We were due to go on the *Sea Queen* for a Far Eastern cruise next month, a suite on a deck – lovely ship. Six weeks.'

'I suppose you won't want—'

'Oh, yes, I will! I've got the tickets and, what's more, I've got his passport and I'll see to it he won't find it. *He* won't be able to go – or take his floozy with him.'

And then, without warning, she burst into tears, strident, racking sobs. He got to his feet, rather unsteadily, and put an arm round her shoulder, which felt like upholstery, patting it and telling her, rather hopelessly, she mustn't cry while searching in his breast pocket for the foulard handkerchief he wore on evenings out. She groped for it and mopped up. Her tears – like a jungle shower – had stopped as suddenly as they'd begun, making her look rather sweet, a bit like a clown. 'That's better,' he said. 'You'll feel better after that.'

And that's when it happened – the chance of a lifetime. Just after she said, 'I must look a sight.'

'Of course you don't.'

'Do you know what I'd like?'

Of course he didn't.

'I'd like you to come with me on the cruise. Not to share the suite – nothing naughty or I won't get my settlement – in a separate cabin.'

Demurely he said, 'My dear, I'd love to, but I really couldn't afford it.' He already knew he wouldn't have to.

'Oh, I'll pay. You can be my walker. I just can't face going alone.'

He protested, mildly. He knew it wouldn't put her off and it didn't.

Now he was in the car, trying to take it in. It was as if Father Christmas – or some such personage – had waved a wand and, hey presto, he was on the threshold of a new and glamorous life. He luxuriously pondered the previous dreary alternative: being manoeuvred by the family into going back to his house in Surrey with some wretched lodger in return for domestic service; being treated like a schoolboy with inadequate pocket money for months until his bloody bills were paid. Not on your nelly. And all because Anne – wretched woman – had had the cheek to leave her money to that irritating little Harriet. Not for the first time he wondered if she'd done it to spite him. Then he thought, of course not, she wasn't a bad sort, though maybe he didn't really know what sort of stick she'd been at all. Well, he didn't need to worry about any of that any more, because everything had changed.

He started the engine and wove slowly down the Hotchkisses' drive, but he forgot his lights and was well into a rhododendron bush before he remembered them. By the time he got back to Home Farm, he had a thundering headache.

Luckily, they'd all gone to bed. When he reached his and lay down, disjointed visions of life on a cruise came to him and the whole room seemed to be moving about, much as if he was already at sea.

FLOY

One of the disadvantages of age, she reflected, was that people never stopped asking advice. Not in order to take it, of course, just to thrash out their own indecision until they discovered whatever it was they wanted to do. It was attention they needed, to be listened to, to be taken seriously, and it was difficult to do that without the energy of affection.

It was early evening; she and Percy had only been at Melton for a night and a day, but almost from the moment they'd arrived, her opinion had been sought, chiefly by Jack, which was reasonable up to a point as she'd come to help him interview the two gardeners earlier this morning. But there had also been the discussion at dinner the night before about Mrs Fanshawe's future when he'd asked earnestly what she thought – and Percy had intervened. In fact, she half suspected the earnestness had been partly for Percy's sake, for her approval. Percy, she thought fondly, had always been so deeply moved by other people's misfortunes, often beyond what was called for. She wept not so much about them as for them, but the saving grace was the practical trouble she was prepared to take on their behalf. Mrs Fanshawe's terrible accident had appalled Percy. She'd visited her in hospital and helped Jack arrange for the subsequent nursing-home. Now she had this strange idea that the Musgroves' father-in-law could provide her with a home and a job.

'If they didn't get on, he could just kick her out and then what? Though Mary says the only *real* problem is there would be no money to pay Mrs F any sort of salary, unless Reggie took in lodgers. And I'm not sure either of them could handle that.'

And Jack, who had listened carefully to everything Percy said, had turned to her, Floy, and asked, 'What do you think I should do?'

She'd said perhaps Mrs Fanshawe needed a small part-time job that could provide her with at least some income and independence, but before he could reply to this, Percy burst in: 'The very best thing would be if she had some income she didn't have to earn, wouldn't it? An allowance, maybe?'

Floy thought this was outrageous of Percy, in the circumstances, a kind of teasing moral blackmail, a positively Emma-like interference with other people's lives. She looked at Jack, whose expression was unfathomable, and said there wasn't much point planning Mrs Fanshawe's future until she herself had been consulted. The subject had been dropped.

'Why were you cross with me at dinner?' Percy had asked. She'd come into Floy's bedroom as she was getting into bed.

'Because I thought you were putting Jack in an impossible position. He's already done far more for that poor woman than he need have. More importantly, you were using the fact that he wants to marry you. He deserves a little more consideration from you, don't you think?'

'I *am* being considerate.' Amusingly, Percy was twisting her hair round her finger, something she always did when being ticked off. 'He doesn't *really* love me, so I can't have been using him. I was just a suitable candidate.' She said this with a hint of scorn.

'That makes me feel truly sorry for him.'

'I can't marry someone just because I ought to feel sorrier for him than I do.'

'Zephie – of course not.'

'And he's got so much money, giving Mrs F some wouldn't make any difference to him.'

There was a silence. Like most people, Floy thought, Percy didn't like being in the wrong. She began to say she was tired and wanted to turn in and Percy, who had been wandering round the room, suddenly came and sat on the bed.

'I'm sorry. It's much . . . easier to consider some people than others. Sometimes, I think . . .' Her voice died away, but she still looked distracted. 'There's something else I haven't told you and I don't know what to do about it. You might know.' And then she told her about Thomas. 'I know he's serious – he really means it. I don't know what it will do to him. I just couldn't bear to make him unhappy. He was so— Oh, I can't tell you what it was like, except that it wasn't at all like Jack. I just don't know what to do.'

'Do you love him?'

'No. I mean, I do like him, very much, but not enough to agree, you know, to marriage and all that.'

'You told him so?'

'Oh, yes. I told him exactly that. And he said I could have all the time in the world to think about it.'

'Well, then . . .'

'But I can't keep him waiting and hoping if, in the end, all I can say is no. The longer I do that, the worse it will be for him. This isn't at all like Denis either,' she added.

A great many thoughts slipped through Floy's mind. Thomas Musgrove was a nice, honourable man. Zephie, perhaps, wasn't really mature enough to settle down with anyone. And their home, what about their home? As usual, Zephie was taking far too much responsibility for herself and Thomas, and she hadn't even said if she found him attractive.

'What shall I do? What *should* I do?'

'Darling Zephie, if he said take your time that's his responsibility, not yours, or certainly not entirely yours. You don't know each other very well, do you?'

'We don't. But I do know he loves me.'

'That can be a powerful trap.'

'You don't believe me. He does.'

'Darling, I do believe you. I meant being loved so much by someone can be confusing – a kind of intoxication – where you're so aware of his feelings you lose sight of your own. You need to sort out *your* feelings.'

There was a silence, and then, just as she was about to suggest bed for both of them, Percy said, 'I've been wondering, lately, if it matters what we do. I mean, if decisions we make are actually important. They sort of veer between being awfully serious and rather pointless – in the end. I'm not sure . . . I mean, I'm just one out of millions of people. Nothing I do will make much difference. I can't stop bombs or war or people starving to death, so why make a big deal about who I spend my life with? It won't change anything, really, will it?'

Floy didn't immediately respond and when she did, it was with a studied mildness. 'Well, darling, decisions have consequences that have to be lived with. And, of course, the choices we have come in different proportions. We may not individually be of much significance, but we still have to do the best we can. It's the only contribution we can make – small, perhaps, but not to be despised.' She reached for her niece's hand, and gave it a little shake. 'To be too grandiose or unduly humble is merely paralysing. So don't you go persuading yourself into spending your life with someone just because they want you to. Now, kiss me and go to bed. I've got a heavy day tomorrow.'

But when Percy had gone, sleep did not come easily. It was impossible, when alone, not to worry about Maida Vale. She'd done nothing since the meeting with her lawyer. The first obvious step was to find out from an estate agent what the property was worth, but she hadn't taken it. She'd told herself she wouldn't do this until she'd spoken to Zephie, until they were both back in London. But in two days they would be and she'd have to face it. And Zephie needed to find a job that wasn't just marking time, something that interested her as the festival had done. A little distance from Thomas wouldn't be a bad thing; it would stop her agonizing about his feelings. She was determined to remain strictly neutral about the outcome of that. He was a good man, but that was hardly enough. A part of her longed for Zephie to break free and lead her own life. If that meant relinquishing her to someone else, well, it was right it should be so.

None the less, living without her – alone – would be a challenge she couldn't help dreading. She'd done it before, so long ago that she'd buried the fear and grief, but here in the dark, in the summer night's silence it came back to her. In the summer of 1916, when she was seventeen, she and Antony had met at a dance, halfway through his leave from France. They'd hardly time to speak or touch one another before the magic certainty that each was the one for the other had struck. After the dance they'd walked slowly through the empty streets to the house where she was staying and stood mute before it, unable to part, until he said, 'Tomorrow. How early may I fetch you?' and she said as soon as her shift at the hospital was finished, six the following evening. It was then he'd kissed her – an unimagined rapture.

He'd had ten days left of his leave, and after their second evening, she took the time off from the hospital and spent all of it with him until they parted each night. They went for long walks in the London parks, sat on benches, went to *thés dansants*, danced later in the evening at nightclubs – dancing meant they could touch in public. And they talked and talked, about their families – his widowed mother in Sussex and two sisters, one still at school – about everything except the war, about which he was resolutely silent. She stopped asking questions, after one or two attempts: he wore a Military Cross. The only time it came up he said how ridiculous it was he didn't have the time to marry her. 'My next leave, though,' he said. The day before his leave was up they spent the night together in a small anonymous hotel, whose name she couldn't now remember, and the next morning she went with him to Victoria to see him off – a long train packed with men. She'd stood before the open carriage window, her hand stretched up to hold his, he'd bent to kiss it, until the train started to move. As the train gathered speed he was obscured by the men leaning out from other windows, waving, waving, then gone. The platform, so crowded before, so full of bustle, of jollity and shouted messages, of snatches of song from a distant band, now fell silent, and those who were left – women, some with children and a few old men – turned, a sad, reluctant tide, and drifted towards the barrier.

The war was two years old by then, and she'd realized, with a shock, that these departures were so frequent that the faces she now saw – so touched by resignation, grief, endurance or despair – must have been dreadfully commonplace. But then she was full of blessed hope, with a faith that Antony would survive. She wrote to him, got one letter back, and then . . . silence. After weeks of suspense that slowly evolved from increasing fear to terrible dread, she could bear it no longer, tracked down his mother's address and wrote to her. After some delay she had a response. Antony had been killed on the second day of the still raging battle of the Somme. He'd been seen to go down under heavy fire but, sadly, there was no body due to the heavy shelling. She was sorry to send such tragic news and was having a tablet put up in her local church in lieu of a grave. He was her only son. She was hers, sincerely, Grace Downing.

She clung to her work like a rock in a sea of anguish. And then sickness overcame her. She couldn't go out in the morning without throwing up. The smell of food in the canteen nauseated her. Once she fainted, while standing in the queue to collect her food. 'You are pregnant, my dear,' the old doctor to whom she was sent announced. 'Your husband?' She'd shaken her head mutely and he took it to mean she was widowed and said kindly, 'Well, now you have something to live for.'

Yes, she'd thought bitterly, as the difficulties of bringing up a child on her own assailed her. The only person she could have told was her brother and he was in France. Her parents would have insisted upon adoption. No, somehow she'd have to manage on her own. The child was all she had left of Antony. She remembered now how she'd made herself eat, rest when she wasn't working, and save every penny possible. She bought herself a wedding ring to wear when she had to visit the doctor, and gradually the sickness went away and she began to sleep heavily at night. Someone to live for, she'd told herself, touching her belly, *something* left remarkable beneath the visiting moon.

She miscarried at three months, and that was the end of it all, of the child's life and, she felt, her own. The future lay before her: a desert, uncharted, endless and bleak.

She'd made something of it. Her intense desire for independence prevailed. With so few able men by the end of the war, she easily obtained a job at Kew where she learned her trade. Gardening, growing trees and plants, was a solace. And then, when she was in her mid-fifties, twelve-year-old Percy had come into her life and imperceptibly her affection, her love became engaged to a degree she would earlier have thought impossible. And they'd lived together and she'd been rewarded by having a second person in her life whom she loved unconditionally. The next step is for Percy to discover that I'm not indispensable, she thought – if I can show her that – but then she pondered that one couldn't teach people anything that really mattered.

Marvell landed with a heavy, relaxed thud on the bed, settled and resettled himself between her neck and left shoulder, his purr thunderous in her ear, interrupted by sudden vigorous grooming. She was smiling as she fell asleep.

FRANCIS AND MARY

Francis was painting Mary sitting at the kitchen table shelling peas. He'd been working on the picture for what seemed to him like weeks, but was in fact only about six sittings, during which she'd variously hulled strawberries, podded broad beans and let down the hems on several of Hatty's summer dresses. He could only do it, he'd explained, when the early-evening light reached a certain point and the sun made a chequered pattern on the kitchen flags in exactly the same place. She was wearing a faded pink shirt of his because, he said, he liked the colour. He had rolled up the sleeves for her himself, since she never got them just right. He had also made her take her hair down and it kept getting in her eyes as she bent over the peas. She complained, but not much, for really she loved these times, his attention, his company and the desultory, easy talk between them. They were disagreeing about Reggie. They'd been stunned by his news about the cruise. He and Thomas had been jubilant – he'd be off their hands at last – but she was wary.

'It could easily be a temporary thing. She'll get tired of him and he'll be back with his tail between his legs.'

'Not if he can help it. Anyway, he's not coming back, tail or no tail. That simply won't happen.'

'Percy has some idea of Mrs Fanshawe going to be his housekeeper.'

'Mrs Fanshawe? Oh, yes. How do you know?'

'She told Thomas about it. The night they went out.' There was a silence while he rubbed a bit of canvas with a rag.

'Don't fiddle with your hair, it's just how I want it.' Moments later, he said, 'Funny, his taking her out like that. He hardly knows her.'

'It's not funny at all. He's in love with her.'

'Ha. That makes two.'

She made a clumsy movement and the pods in her lap fell to the floor. Stooping for them, her face hidden, she said, 'What do you mean?'

'I probably shouldn't be telling you but I am anyway. She told me Jack had proposed to her.'

'Oh.' She shovelled the pods on to the table.

'Do you want a rest? You look all white and tired.'

'I'm fine, but poor Thomas.'

'She turned Jack down.'

'Oh, well, perhaps Thomas has a chance, after all.'

'I doubt it. I can't see her marrying him and he wouldn't settle for less, would he? He's an all-or-nothing man, as we both know. It would be too much for her.'

'Why do you say that? I love Percy. I think she's rather marvellous.'

'She's not going to throw everything up and settle down in the country with someone like Thomas. Think of all she'd have to take on, all the things you do to keep everything going – Hatty, the housework, the cooking and ironing and laundry, stretching the money, doing a part-time job you don't particularly want to. *You* are a treasure, Mary, dear, and he's so used to you he doesn't notice.'

She felt herself blushing and rubbed her face briskly to hide the cause.

'Celia did it, settled down in the country.'

'That was different. That was love at first sight.'

After a moment, she said, 'Do you think that's the best kind?'

'I've no idea. I think it's probably more unusual, but certainly not much fun unless it's mutual. Don't look at me, Mary, look at the peas.'

A few silent minutes later there were sounds of people in the courtyard.

'It's Betsy bringing Hatty back from her ride.' She could see the two ponies. Hatty dismounted and gave her reins to Betsy, planted a kiss on her pony's nose, then watched them turn and ride away.

'I rode Betsy's new pony,' she announced. 'He's rather frisky, so I rode him with a pelham. It's different from a snaffle. We did bending and Betsy says I might ride him in the gymkhana in August if I practise enough. Can I have some lemon barley and a flapjack?' She pulled off her black velvet hat and put it on the kitchen table. Her face was shiny with sweat.

'Not there,' Francis said. 'I don't want it in the picture.'

Mary told her the lemon was in the fridge and the flapjacks in a tin on the dresser. When she'd helped herself, she leaned heavily over the back of Francis's chair to look at the picture. 'It's quite good, isn't it? The shirt is awfully good and the peas. Of course I know it's Mary. Other people won't, but it doesn't matter.'

'Thank you for your unstinting praise.'

'You look very hot, darling. Why don't you go and have a bath and change into something cooler?'

'I can get cool without changing.'

'All the same, I'd like you to – before supper, anyway.' Hatty, without moving, crammed the last piece of flapjack into her mouth and muttered something.

'I can't hear you with your mouth full.'

'I said wouldn't it be a good idea if you painted a picture of me on Brandy?'

'I'll think about it. Move – you're getting in my way.'

After a moment, when she didn't, Mary said, 'Harriet, did you hear me?'

'I didn't, actually, because I was pretending you were talking in a foreign language. I do it at school when the teacher's boring. It makes English sound quite exciting and difficult, but it means you don't understand anything, of course.'

'Well, understand me now. Upstairs, bath, and change.'

Halfway up the stairs, Hatty called back, 'There's a terrifically smart car in the lane. It's coming in.'

They both turned. It was Jack Curtis. He'd got out of the car, and walked slowly towards the kitchen door looking up at the house. Mary wondered why he'd come, and Francis thought perhaps he'd lost another cook, but neither said anything.

'May I come in?'

Francis put down his brush, Mary her pea-pods and Hatty plonked herself on the stairs to watch.

'I'm afraid I'm interrupting you . . .'

This, though clearly true, was denied. 'We've done enough anyway,' Francis said, and Mary, getting to her feet, offered him tea. When he hesitated, Francis said, 'Or a glass of wine? Fine. I'll get it, Mary. My sister-in-law – I don't think you've actually met. Mary, this is Jack Curtis.'

'You haven't met me either,' said Hatty, from the stairs. 'But it's jolly good you've come because I wanted to ask you something.'

'Harriet, come downstairs and say how do you do properly.' While Mary twisted her hair into some sort of bunch at the back of her head and Hatty came downstairs to do as she was told, Francis, rummaging in the fridge, said, 'Are we out of drink?'

'Oh. Yes, I'm afraid we are.' As we usually are at the end of the month, she didn't add. She'd pulled out a chair. 'Do have a seat, Mr Curtis.'

'Jack,' he said. He spoke tentatively, as if it would be kind of her. 'There might be some cider,' she said to Francis.

'I should have lemon barley, if I were you. I know that's there because I've just had it. What I wanted to ask you is could

Betsy and I ride in your park? She said we couldn't without asking you and she keeps not doing it.' She was sitting on a corner of the table now, kicking one leg of it with her boot. 'It would only be two ponies, so I don't see how you could possibly mind.' Her smile was the more engaging because of a gap in her front teeth.

'I couldn't possibly mind.'

'Thanks awfully.' She jumped off the table. 'Mary, can I go to Dad's study to ring up Betsy and tell her?'

'When you've had your bath. No, I mean it, darling, off you go.' And she did.

With her absence, the awkwardness returned. Francis produced the remains of a bottle of cider. Then Jack said, 'I've never thanked you properly for that wonderful dinner you cooked before the festival.'

'Oh, well, you sort of did. I was very well recompensed.' They were both, she realized, smiling with a mutual shyness. It's a slightly odd situation, she thought and just as she was wondering what, in fact, he'd come for, he said, 'As a matter of fact I've come because Percy and her aunt are leaving on Monday for good and I want to give a farewell party for them. I want it to be a surprise, so it seemed better to come, or risk her hearing me on the phone. I hope all of you can be there – I mean Francis and you and your brother.' It was almost as if he was pleading – he wasn't at all as she'd imagined him.

'What a good idea.' Francis, who had poured the cider, now took a swig. 'Oh, God, I'm afraid it's flat. We're not much cop as hosts, are we? On the other hand, we're pretty keen guests. Thank you, I'd love to come.' He looked at Mary, who said, yes, she would too. She wasn't sure about Thomas, whether he—

At this moment Thomas appeared, hot, dishevelled and clearly not in a very good mood. 'The bloody connection on the hose has gone again. Just snapped off this time. I'll have to get a new one. I've tried taping it, but no luck.' Then Mary saw him take in the scene: Jack, cool in his spotless white shirt and dark cotton trousers, and he in his old check shirt, the sleeves cut off, dark patches of sweat, khaki shorts, his freckled arms dotted with insect bites – everything bit poor Thomas – and his threadbare desert boots with their muddy laces. It was bad luck, she thought, that he should meet this particular man at such a disadvantage.

'Thomas, this is Jack – Jack Curtis.'

'I know. Good evening to you.'

Before she could say anything, Francis took charge. 'Jack is giving a surprise party for Percy and her aunt and he's invited us to go.'

'It's a farewell party, actually. Floy wants to leave on Monday, or Tuesday at the latest, so I thought tomorrow evening. They'd both want you all to be there.'

So he does know Thomas might be difficult, Mary thought, and her opinion of him grew. She noticed also that Thomas's expression softened at the mention of Percy's name.

'A surprise party – um. I didn't realize they were leaving so soon.'

'I'm afraid so. Floy only came down to interview gardeners for me, but she has commitments in London, and Percy wants to get on and find a new job. So, there it is.' He got up from the table. 'I thought about seven thirty, if that's all right?'

'We'll look forward to it,' Mary said, and Francis went out with him to the car.

There was a brief silence while Thomas went to the sink, ran the cold tap and washed his face in the running water. Then he said, 'I'd no idea they were leaving so soon. As a matter of fact, I wanted to ask Floy about garden design.'

'You can ask her tomorrow.'

'Yes. Yes, I can. What were you all drinking?'

'The rest of the cider, but I'm afraid it's gone flat.' He took a glass from the rack and filled it. 'Poor man's drink,' he said, and downed it.

Neither of them mentioned Percy. I suppose he thinks I don't know, she thought, as she cleared the table for supper. Well, until he tells me, I don't.

He went upstairs for a bath and Francis, returned from seeing Jack off, began scraping his palette. 'He's a funny chap, isn't he?'

'How do you mean?'

'Well, of course, you don't know him at all. But running the festival meetings or talking to some long-distance tycoon, he's smooth and assured, completely in command, and then, just now, he was almost – you know – shy of us.'

'Perhaps he's not very used to people, non-business people, I mean. After all, he hasn't met Thomas or me before.'

'Thomas is coming, then?'

'He didn't say he wasn't. He's upset about them leaving so soon.'

Francis, who was now swirling his brushes in a murky jam jar half full of white spirit, said, 'Has it struck you that if Thomas did make it with Percy, our lives would have to change?'

She was kneeling by the fridge, pulling peppers and an aubergine out of the bottom drawer, and didn't respond immediately.

On her feet again, she said, 'Yes, it has struck me.'

'I suppose I'd go back to London and design rich old women's flats and you – I know – could go and be Reggie's housekeeper. It's a joke, darling. Don't look like that. Perhaps I could do rich old men's houses and find you someone nice to marry. Meanwhile, we could share a grotty little flat.' He picked the picture off the easel and placed it carefully, face towards the wall. 'Well, it's not going to happen, anyway,' he said finally.

THOMAS

It was extraordinary, he thought, how little he actually remembered of the house. The outside, of course, the chequered marble floor in the entrance hall, the curving staircase with its ironwork balustrade and dark wooden rail down which he used to slide, but when they'd arrived and were ushered into a room called the library, he didn't recognize it at all. Of course, the whole thing was so done up like a stage set it wouldn't have been familiar, but he was quite unable, now, to remember how it had actually been. But, then, neither he nor Mary had had much to do with what they called their parents' quarters. He had consciously to search for the sentimental nostalgia he'd been expecting, dreading, rather than be overwhelmed by it. Bit of a relief, really – perhaps he'd been making too much of it.

The other odd thing was that revisited childhood homes are supposed to feel smaller. Here, he felt the opposite. The ceilings, with their elaborate plasterwork, seemed dauntingly high and the white marble chimney was wide enough for an enormous, elaborate carving of two facing chariots drawn by a pair of horses. But perhaps Curtis had put that in – there was nothing he couldn't afford, it seemed. The curtains alone— but then Zephie came in. He didn't see her at first, just sensed her presence. She was wearing a dress of pale green silky stuff, a pleated mini-skirt that flared a little as she moved, and her dark hair streamed down her bare back. He noticed everyone fell silent for a moment as she came in. She was sorry to be late, hadn't known about the party, had

had to wash her hair. He gazed at her as she kissed Mary. 'Hello, Francis. Thank you, Jack,' as he handed her a glass. 'What a lovely surprise. I bet you knew, didn't you, Floy?'

Then, 'Thomas,' a pause – anxious and tender, he thought – and she said, 'I'm so glad you've come.'

She knows I'm the one who loves her. Everyone loves her, of course, he thought, but not as I love her. She doesn't know that yet. Time . . . he thought, but she's going away. All evening, he tried not to stare at her, but all evening he saw nothing but her. There was a peculiar joy in watching her with other people present. At dinner he was placed between her and Francis and listened leniently as they teased each other, inventing the most boring subject people could be an expert in, a game that recurred spasmodically throughout the meal. Benevolence streamed from him. He responded to Mary's earlier anxious look with a grin. He told Jack how delighted Hatty was to be able to ride in the park and how good it was of him to agree. He discussed the best methods of protecting young trees from squirrels and rabbits with Floy, and let slip, casually, that he'd be grateful for her advice about something but wouldn't bother her with it now. All the while he was conscious of her beside him: the small wafts of her scent as she turned her head; her slender, polished shoulders accentuated by the narrow green ribbon straps; her husky voice erupting with a throaty giggle as she or Francis scored a point in their game. 'Early kirby-grips – beat that.' They were like children, he thought, siblings, and they could be for ever, as far as I'm concerned.

When, at the end of dinner, Jack proposed a toast to Floy and to her 'and may they often return', he drank to it with genial enthusiasm. Their departure was insignificant; it was unreal and couldn't dim the radiance that now protected him.

Earlier, when the others were talking among themselves and she was silent beside him, he sensed she felt awkward, shy, with him, guessed she was deeply conscious of what had passed between them, uncertain how to treat him now. 'You know,' he began, 'when you made that kind suggestion about Mrs Fanshawe and my father-in-law?'

'Yes. But Mary told me you'd sorted it out.'

'*We* didn't sort it out. Reggie did. He located a rich lady at his golf club whose husband ran off with someone. In no time they were on a cruise together. He's left us cock-a-hoop, full of cunning plans for the future, and we're off the hook. Maybe it sounds hard-hearted but, honestly, Reggie is someone who is as awful when things are going his way as when they aren't. We've cleared out his stuff and got our sitting room back. It's changed everything.'

Safe ground. She tried to defend Reggie: surely he must have some good in him; there must be some in everyone. Maybe he was badly treated as a child. Events, he responded, shaped people only as much as they allowed themselves to be shaped. People had to rediscover the goodness for themselves, if they had it. 'But I suppose,' he added, 'this doesn't help your Mrs Fanshawe's future.'

'Well, it doesn't. We're still trying to sort it out.'

Then Francis had leaned forward and said, 'I've thought of the most boring subject to be an expert in. Me.'

And she laughed and said, 'Oh, Francis, you're not as boring as that.'

It wasn't until they were gathered in the hall ready to leave, and she had kissed Mary and hugged Francis, that she turned to him, uncertain of the right gesture. He took both her hands, raised them to his lips, and whispered, 'Nothing's changed. You know that, Zephie.'

It never occurred to him that he hardly knew her, that he'd only ever spent an evening and a few fleeting moments alone with her. What had happened with Celia, what they'd had together, assured him that love – real, serious love – happened at first sight.

JACK

The three of them watched the car round the bend in the drive until it was out of sight. Then he said – quickly, before they could escape, 'Let's have a nightcap.' He wanted to discuss the party, to be reassured they'd really enjoyed it, but above all, he didn't want it to end.

They followed him back into the library. Floy surprised him by asking for whisky; Percy stuck to wine.

'It was a lovely dinner, Jack,' Floy said, as he bent to light her small cigar.

Percy laughed. 'And isn't it lovely to know it won't end in a fire?'

'Don't be too sure. I expect Marvell will take up smoking any minute, and if he does, he'll undoubtedly smoke in bed.' Floy grinned at Percy, and said to Jack, 'How did you get on with Mary?'

'I liked her, very much. She wasn't at all what I was expecting.'

'Which was?'

He turned to Percy. 'I don't know – something of an old maid, I suppose. All I knew was that she was a very good cook. I'd somehow thought she'd be difficult to talk to, a bit dull. She's not at all like her brother, is she? Is it her daughter who wants to ride in the park?'

'No. She's Thomas's child. His wife died in a car accident.'

'But it was a long time ago and he's getting over it,' said

Percy, and he noticed she glanced eagerly, anxiously, at Floy. Then she turned back to him and said, 'She looked very pretty, don't you think?'

He hadn't thought about it, so he agreed and went on, 'She told me the house used to belong to her parents, but they left it when she was very young. It must have been strange for her, coming here after all these years. I must seem something of an interloper.'

'Oh, well, I suppose you've interloped in a way, but you aren't a stranger any more. And now, my dear Jack, I think I must retire.' Floy gathered up the long skirt of her kaftan. 'Thank you for giving us such a nice farewell party.'

When she'd gone Percy, who had also risen, put her glass on a table and said, 'She's gone to bed with George.'

'George?'

'Eliot. She's reading *Middlemarch* for the millionth time. She always calls her favourite novelists by their Christian names – though, of course, it wasn't her actual name. She was called Marian, poor thing.'

There was a pause, and he knew she was poised to leave as well. 'Don't go. There's something I want to ask you.'

'Oh, Jack. I've told you, it wouldn't be any use.' He was standing close to her and she looked steadily at him for a moment before she said, 'I won't change my mind about marrying you. I *do* like you – you're a very kind and good person – but I don't love you.' And then she said gently, 'And you don't love me. I know you think you do, but it's the idea of it you want – not me.' There was a short silence during which he felt impelled, but was unable, to protest. She then said, 'I've had a wonderful, wonderful time here, with the festival and living in your amazing house, and I do thank you for that.' She put her arms round him and kissed his cheek.

'How can you be so sure? How do you know?'

'I've been there myself, Jack. It's a bit like a false pinnacle on a mountain. You think you've got to the top and then you see the real one a long way ahead. Good night.' She slipped away from him and out of the room.

For a while he stood where she'd left him, trying to marshal his thoughts. To be told he wasn't loved was one thing, but to be told he didn't love was quite another. How could she know what he felt? She had no idea. But the resentment dissolved and he was overwhelmed by the hopeless realization that, in truth, he knew nothing about what people called love. He knew now he'd never loved Linda. He'd wanted her and thought she was suitable, but he could see now how inadequate that was. He thought of Wystan and Amelia. Undoubtedly they loved one another and they were fond of him, as he was of them, but affection wasn't going to fill this vast, empty place and it was becoming rapidly clear that he didn't know how to live alone in it.

He turned off the lights and went slowly up the stairs. The house was entirely silent. The long passage was lit by regular pairs of sconces that dimly illuminated the set of sporting prints the interior decorator had acquired on his behalf – beleaguered stags, fleeing foxes, gasping salmon, Labradors with dead birds in their mouths. Mario had assured him they were appropriate country pursuits, suitable as what he'd called passage pictures. Percy would never have chosen those, he thought bleakly, noticing them properly for perhaps the first time. Until now they'd just been a bit boring, but in fact they were pretty revolting.

He'd reached his bedroom or, rather, suite – it had a separate dressing room and a bathroom. The latter was all mahogany and gold fittings, black and white tiling, a thick white carpet and a Victorian shaving mirror that extended out from the wall, but was too low for him, so he had to stoop to shave.

He had chosen the house for its size, the number of rooms, the grandeur of a park – even its decay had pleased him: he'd be responsible for restoring its former glory with his well-honed skills with builders. With the furnishings, he knew that he knew nothing; hence the famously fashionable Mario degli Angeli.

His bathroom led into the dressing room, walls covered with tobacco-coloured hessian and carpeted in lemon yellow with curtains to match. There were huge cupboards and drawers and hanging space for far more clothes than he had. In front of the window was a desk with a phone where he sometimes worked very late or early as business hours around the world dictated. His vast bedroom had a double aspect as it was at a corner of the house. The walls here were sea-green silk with striped curtains, a darker green and cream, and the carpet a pale turquoise. The furniture was pale satinwood and boxwood, Mario had explained, and the enormous French bed was carved from pearwood. These walls were decorated with Chinese prints, of flowers, birds and occasional richly robed individuals. How amazed and thrilled he'd been when first he saw the finished effect of these rooms. They were the culmination of his effort and work, the reward for years of determination to succeed, to transcend his shabby, tedious background – a stage set suitable for the brilliant life he was due to live.

And he'd cherished showing the results to Wystan and Amelia, revealing it all to them, enjoying their astonishment. But now, after more than a year in the house, the novelty had worn away. The triumph he'd felt during his first weeks, and the pleasure of showing it off to Floy and Percy, then the Blunts, had come and gone. Yes, the gardens and the festival had kept him occupied and excited. But now even they were completed, almost fulfilled. And as a result the Plovers were leaving. He had become deeply attached to both of them. Marrying Percy had been an ideal solution to a problem. It hadn't occurred to him she would turn him down; he couldn't believe a penniless girl would refuse a life of such splendour and ease.

'And you don't love me. I know you think you do, but it's the idea of it you want – not me.' Then that sisterly kiss.

Life for him had been a succession of hurdles to be overcome; clear, tangible bars to success. Marriage, as far as he'd been concerned, was another of those hurdles and then, after one or two false starts, he'd come upon attractive, appropriate, suitable Linda and their marriage had withered as they ceased to be status symbols for each other.

His first ever sight of Percy hadn't been encouraging: a pale, thin girl with dark circles under her eyes, quite shy, he reflected. He'd never even really ached to go to bed with her but, after Linda, he'd thought that was probably no bad thing. He had definitely, during those months of the festival, grown to like her hugely, to respect her and have genuine fondness for her – surely that was love.

Clearly not, he thought bitterly, if she's right. She obviously feels the same way about me, but doesn't call it love. So whatever it was, this lacking thing, this component outside his experience, presented him with a challenge and he was much used to them. But, for once in his life, he had absolutely no idea how to meet it.

FRANCIS

He took a long, last look at them, Floy, Jack and Percy standing on the steps of the house and waving, three figures almost, but not quite, silhouetted against the amber light that streamed uncertainly from the hall behind them. 'Goodbye,' he called and Mary, beside him, repeated it. Thomas, in the back, was silent. It was a warm still night and the headlights lit the trees, arching the avenue down the drive, creating the romantic effect of a set for *Les Sylphides*, he thought.

'It was a good evening, wasn't it?' he said, glancing at Mary. He had earlier helped her put her hair in a French plait, pinned up, which showed off her slender white neck. She wore the old navy blue dress she'd had ever since he could remember. He'd made her shorten it to make it more fashionable.

'I can't wear a mini-skirt, Francis. I haven't got the knees for it.'

'Nor have most people, sweetie. The girl in the Co-op has one so short a giraffe could see her crotch. I'll get it just right.' He'd knelt on the floor with a ruler, pinning it for her to hem. He'd helped her, and she'd helped Thomas, washing and ironing his best blue shirt, insisting he wear the darker blue silk tie she'd given him for Christmas. He never worried about his clothes: a clean white shirt and his old moleskin trousers did him perfectly well. Hatty had inspected all three of them rather sulkily. 'I suppose you realize I'm the only person in this house who hasn't been asked.'

And when Mary had consoled her with the prospect of having Meg for supper and the night – fish cakes and strawberries and cream with Mrs Peabody – she'd insisted on putting on her party frock 'and your court shoes, Mary. They fit perfectly if I stuff the toes with paper. Then it will really feel like a party.'

So, one way and another, there had been unusual excitement in the house, and now it was over.

'It *was* lovely,' Mary said. 'I thought Floy looked a bit tired, though.'

'She'd spent the morning tramping round the place with the second candidate for the gardening job,' Thomas said. 'And the day before dealing with the first one. Quite exhausting in this heat.'

'Have they chosen one?'

'Well, she didn't think either was perfect, but she's plumped for the younger. She said the older one clearly knew more, but she thought he wouldn't be much good with people under him.' He relapsed into silence, and nobody said anything until they got back to Home Farm, where they found the girls and Mrs Peabody playing a rather lackadaisical game of Old Maid.

He offered to drive Mrs Peabody home, but she said thank you, Mr Francis, she had her bicycle and it was downhill all the way.

'Bed, you two. I'll be up in five minutes to tuck you up.' Meg, who had never been known to utter a word in front of any of them, scuttled up the stairs, but Hatty lingered.

'Did you have a good time? What did you have for dinner?'

'Dragon's tail soup and roast python. We'll tell you about it tomorrow.'

'You know, Francis, you don't stick to the truth much. The older I get, the less I believe you. It's funny, isn't it?' she went on, as Mary was shepherding her on to the staircase. 'You wouldn't think you could be as old as Mrs Peabody and only know one card game. Good night, Dad. You can see I'm not allowed to say good night to you properly, so I just have to shout it.

'I didn't wear your shoes for long,' she continued, as Mary got her to the top of the stairs, 'because I'm afraid a heel came off, but it was all right because in the end Meg decided we'd just wear bare feet.'

PERCY

She'd thought she was being discreet, but before they reached the lodge gate at the end of the drive Floy said, 'There's some Kleenex in the glove compartment . . .'

'The one that doesn't open?'

'It does now. I put a screw where the handle was.'

When she'd mopped herself up, she said, 'It's not that I'm especially sad. It's just endings, departures, seem to me – particularly gloomy. Oh, Juan and the mixed carnations – that was pretty weepy. He must have gone especially to Melton to get them.'

'Yes. That was touching.'

'And poor Jack. What do you think he's going to do for the rest of the day?'

'What he usually does, I imagine. A great deal of telephoning, and he's seeing the builders about getting the lodge ready for the gardener. I think he'll survive.'

'Of course he will. But just surviving isn't much fun, is it?'

'Better than not.'

'Aren't you a bit sad all your work there is finished?'

'I'm deeply relieved. I've been neglecting everybody else because of it. I'm getting a bit old to run a one-man band.'

Silence. Then Percy said, 'I've been thinking. Would it be a good idea if I became your partner, sort of? You could teach me what to do and I could do the hard stuff. I've got to do something, after all.'

'No, darling, I don't. Gardens don't really interest you and I think you'd quickly get bored with all the things you'd have to learn about a subject you haven't chosen. It wouldn't work. Besides, I don't want to expand the business, I want to start retiring from it.' There was a pause and then she said, 'Your father's written to say he's getting married again. He's in Rome. He mentioned you might like to meet his new wife.'

'I wouldn't. I don't regard him as a parent at all. Thomas's parents were hopeless in just the same way. He said they had an awful time being abandoned. I felt so sorry for him.'

'Well, he had Mary.'

'And I have you. You're my family; you always have been. I can't imagine what would have happened to me without you.'

'Yes. Well, you did have me and you're grown-up now. I wonder if you might have reached a stage where you can forgive him.'

'You think I ought to?'

'No, Zephie. It's entirely up to you.'

'I don't like things being entirely up to me.' As she said this, she could hear how childish it sounded. 'I can't say I forgive him if I don't, can I?'

And Floy just said, 'No.'

A bit later, she offered to drive and, to her surprise, Floy accepted.

'Is your back worse?'

'No, but it will be if I don't give it a bit of a rest. Don't drive too fast, will you? You know Marvell doesn't like it.'

It's not Marvell, it's you, she thought, as she started to drive. Anyway, the old van didn't care to do much over fifty, as she pointed out.

'Just the right speed.' Floy settled herself with her back cushion and went to sleep.

When we get home, I'll find some lunch and make her have a rest after it, she thought, glancing anxiously at the beloved aunt whose red woolly hat was slightly askew. Not her Lion Aunt – hardly her Pirate Aunt – but someone older, more vulnerable, her skin streamed with minute lines, like a map of well-watered country; only the small beak of her nose, stretched over the sharp bone, was bare of them, and her resolute mouth, softened and slightly open in sleep. It was the hat that made her look piratical.

The rest of the drive home she made resolutions: to do the cooking, the shopping, to take Floy away for a holiday. She'd saved money during her stay at Melton, but she really needed to find work as soon as possible and that would take time. Meanwhile, it was enough to be coming home to familiar life with Marvell and Floy, and until she got a job she'd take over all the domestic chores to give Floy a rest.

★

But two weeks later, in spite of innumerable letters to publishers, then magazines and newspapers, she still had no work.

The Arts Council, by whom she'd been interviewed, had said they would bear her in mind. One publishing house had offered her proofreading, on trial for a month, and several others had taken her particulars and said they'd let her know if anything turned up. She was soon on edge about the post and dashed to collect it each morning as it thudded on to the mat. And so, one morning, when Floy was at the far end of the garden taking lavender cuttings, she ripped open one of the several typewritten letters addressed to Miss Plover and read the following:

Dear Miss Plover,

Further to your instructions, we have now viewed your property, and can inform you that in our opinion the remaining lease could go on the market for the asking price of £15,000.

We agree with you that the house has certain amenities, such as the conservatory and a large garden, but we have to point out that the lease having only eight years to run with no guarantee from the Estate of renewal, plus the fact that its fabric, let alone its decorative condition, leaves much to be desired, it is by no means certain that the asking price will be achieved.

However, if you wish us to put the property on the market at the price we have estimated, we shall be happy to act for you.

Yours sincerely,

Cyril Catchpole

She read it twice. What on earth was Floy doing? And why hadn't she told her? Tears of rage stung her eyes. She'd opened the letter because it was addressed to Miss Plover and Floy didn't get many letters. What if she hadn't opened it? Presumably the next thing would've been crowds of strangers 'viewing' the house, arranged for when she was out? And what was to become of them when the house – her home – was sold? Was that why Floy wanted her to visit her father? To get rid of her? Floy, of all people. These and a flood of the same kind of unbearable questions possessed her until she reached a high tide of panic.

She walked slowly through the hall and sitting room to the open door of the conservatory from which she could now see Floy slowly returning with a barrowload of lavender.

'Help me up the steps with this, would you, darling?'

'No. I want to talk to you – now.'

Floy looked up at her, standing at the top of the steps with a letter in her hand. 'What's the matter?' She picked up an armful of lavender and began slowly to climb the steps. 'What's wrong, Zephie? You look awful. What on earth has happened?'

'What's happened is that I opened a letter addressed to you by mistake.' She held it out. Floy dumped the lavender on one of the peat trays and took it.

'How could you make all these plans behind my back, not telling me?'

Floy looked at her with concern and said, 'I think we'd better both sit down, I because I'm tired and you because I've got a lot of explaining to do and you won't hear me properly if you're shaking like that.' She felt in her jacket pocket for her little tin of cigars, chose one and lit it. 'I'm sorry I didn't tell you before—'

'Before what?'

'Zephie, don't interrupt – it won't help. I haven't known so long. About a month ago, as I was sorting things out with my solicitor, he drew my attention to the fact the lease I'd bought on this house had only eight more years to run. I said I wanted to renew and he wrote to the Eyre Estate, but they replied they weren't prepared to issue a further lease until this one expired and couldn't guarantee they'd do so even then. Mr Jenkins then said I should therefore sell the remainder of the lease as soon as possible. I have some savings, but not enough to buy anywhere else without the extra capital selling here would bring. So there's no choice. I knew it would be a blow to you, but I couldn't face telling you during that last weekend at Melton. I'm sorry you found out as you did. It comes of us both being called Plover, but,' she attempted a smile here, 'there have been some advantages to that in the past, don't you think?'

It was the attempted smile that did it – collapsed her fiery rage to ashes round her heart. 'Poor Floy. Obviously you don't want to leave either.'

'I want to leave as little as you do. Or Marvell, come to that.'

'You don't think it's worth having another go at the Estate?'

'I don't. Try, if you like. Anyway, darling, even if they do agree, they're almost certain to want too much for it. No. We're going to have to draw in our horns and find somewhere smaller and more modest.'

Floy looked round the conservatory with its jasmine and plumbago, its pots of cymbidium and cyclamen waiting to flower, to the garden, with its small alley of topiary yew lollipops that ran up its centre to the ash, and the yew arch beyond, and the beautiful Davidia she'd planted thirty years ago, which now produced its cream, sweet-scented handkerchiefs and nutmeg-shaped fruits every year. The garden was full of treasures too mature to be transplanted, all to be left to unknown and possibly indifferent owners. She was momentarily overcome by the weariness of grief.

Percy was asking how they should set about finding somewhere. 'We'll start with a good map,' she said, 'and then we'll make a list of our requirements.'

'A proper garden for you.'

'And a whole floor for you, Zephie. I want you to have more room to yourself, so you can have your friends without me in your hair.'

'I want you in my hair.'

'Well, I don't want to be in it, darling. And we must find somewhere not too far out, so you don't spend half your life travelling to work.'

For the rest of that day they tried to concentrate on the practical aspects of what lay before them. Floy got out maps, rang the agents and Mr Jenkins and told them to go ahead. Percy made lists. Occasionally, the cracks showed. When Percy speculated, 'It would be lovely if we could find another conservatory like this one,' Floy said, yes, it would. She didn't add that, in all her experience of London houses and gardens, she'd never seen such a thing, but Percy noted her tone was as mechanical as it was hopeless.

In bed that night she tried to think of ways in which they might hang on to the house. She could go and see the Estate managers – plead with them to extend the lease. Her father might loan her money if she guaranteed to pay it back from whatever salary came her way. She'd never thought seriously about money until now. All her childhood and schooldays her father had paid not only the school fees but also some money to

Floy for keeping her. Out of this Floy had given her pocket money and, when she was old enough, a dress allowance. She hadn't wanted to go to university, though Floy had suggested, and encouraged her to consider it. When she was twenty-one, all finance from her father came to an end.

At one point, just as she was drifting off, she wondered if she should ask Jack for the money, but she knew at once she couldn't possibly bear to and Floy would intensely disapprove. And as sleep finally overwhelmed her she was trying, but not very hard, to imagine a new home for them that would become as loved as this one.

MARY

She woke late and the house was full of sunlight and silence. She'd slept, without waking, for nearly seven hours, with hardly a dream or at least none she could remember, merely gentle, familiar fragments that had skittered across the surface of her memory to sink back into her past. Such refreshment was rare for her – perhaps, she thought, for everyone. She felt a kind of ageless well-being, an uncharted hope – not any particular expectation, just a feeling that whatever might happen was going to be good.

And perhaps the best thing was that she could just lie here, watching the tiny atoms of dust seemingly agitated by the bar of sunlight streaming through her open window; she could lie here as long as she liked. For the first time she was alone in the house. Hatty had been taken by her friend's mother for a pony-trekking holiday on Dartmoor. Thomas was in London on a garden-design course and Francis was on a well-paid commission in the South of France. The nursery garden was closed, and except for regular watering, she had no responsibility for it. She could actually do as she liked.

It had all come about by degrees – by a series of chances. Hatty's holiday had been long planned. Hatty had infected her new friend Agnes with the pony bug. She was an only child and her mother was anxious to arrange holidays that involved her best friend and something interesting to do. She was well-off and generous, and insisted on giving Hatty the holiday; this year it was ponies, an offer that couldn't be refused. Mary tried to pay for Hatty, but Mrs Bowman was both adamant and tactful. 'You'd be doing me such a favour and look what you did for Agnes when she had that accident in the park.' In the end, Mary had gratefully agreed.

Thomas, increasingly restless after Percy and Floy left, had spent a couple of nights in London consulting Floy about garden design and had promptly joined a three-month course. He'd closed the nursery for a month, but what was supposed to happen after that wasn't clear. He assumed Francis could hold the fort. Relations between her and Thomas were strained; he was spending what profit they'd made from Melton on the course in London. He'd never been realistic about money and over the years had relied on her, then Celia, then her again. She suspected he really wanted to be in London to see and be near Percy, but since he'd confided nothing, she didn't dare say so. In short, to avoid a total breakdown of relations between them, she'd had to mind her own business, without being entirely sure what was happening. So, she'd seen him off at the station in his new clothes: 'Please give my love to Floy – and Percy.' He'd smiled then, the first time for weeks, hugged her and said he would.

She had looked forward to a lovely quiet time with Francis and Hatty, but an offer then came for Francis to go to Paris for a week, guiding a group of students round the museums. So he was off, too, for the first week of Hatty's holiday. That week alone had been taken up with pleasurable duties. It was a good chance to clean the entire house, to make raspberry jam and crab-apple jelly, to mend the linen and sort out Hatty's chaotic room. Two days before Francis was due to return, he rang from Paris to say he'd been offered the opportunity to paint portraits of an American family in their house in the South of France, an extremely lucrative commission he couldn't turn down. He'd let her know, once he'd settled in at the château, how long he thought it would take. She had realized then how much she'd been looking forward to his return, had put down the receiver, eyes stinging with tears, berated herself for being a fool to be so disappointed and indulged in a good cry 'to get it out of her system' and pull herself together. She stopped crying, but there was nothing much else in her system, nothing much left for her to pull together. An immense languor ensued; she had no desire or energy to do anything at all. That evening, she drank the whole bottle of wine she'd saved for Francis's return. She remembered nearly falling on the stairs, then nothing. She woke the next morning, with a pounding head, fully clothed on Francis's bed. A shock – and one she determined to ignore.

She had spent the next few days and evenings sleeping. Fatigue rolled over her like a sea mist, blotting out the ordinary routine of the day – mealtimes, baths, clothes; any small effort produced fresh torpor. One morning, she woke to find Mrs Peabody by her bed with a tray. 'I've done you an egg, Miss, dear. It's plain you haven't been eating much.'

Kindness was too rich. She tried to thank her and Mrs Peabody was both bracing and comforting. 'All this living for others, it takes it out of you. But what can you expect with men?' She bustled about the room, arranging the tray on a chair by her bed.

That had been a turning point. After a bath and with her hair washed, she had sat in the sun combing it dry when Mrs Peabody came out to tell her Mr Curtis was on the phone. He needed someone to help with the laundry, did she know of anyone, and then, after a pause, he'd asked her to dinner – well, that evening, in fact, as he had to go to Zürich the next day for a couple of days. She said yes, not so much because she particularly wanted to go, but because she sensed he very much did.

The prospect of a night out, of almost any kind, was pleasant, but daunting. She had come to like Jack since the Plovers had left – especially since the accident in the park a week or so before. Since then he'd rung her once or twice for advice on various domestic matters. Was there anyone local who could be a part-time secretary? He didn't seem able to keep one. Did she know someone who could fix a Hoover? And to ask after Hatty's friend who had fallen jumping her pony in his park. That had been the first time he'd rung. Hatty had come up to Melton House for help, Agnes was lying on the ground and wouldn't get up because it hurt too much, and Jack was unsure whether to move her or not. He'd met her at the entrance to the drive, 'Harriet's gone back to be with her. It's only about a hundred yards from here,' and as they ran through the long grass she remembered thanking God it wasn't Hatty, then immediately thinking perhaps it was worse – she felt so obliged to Agnes's mother.

They found Agnes lying awkwardly on her side, Hatty squatting anxiously beside her and the two ponies tethered to a nearby tree, unconcernedly chomping grass.

'I keep telling her Betsy says the best thing to do when you fall off is to get on again at once, but she won't.'

'I can't. I keep telling you I can't.' Her face was streaked with dirty tears and she was shivering.

As she knelt down to examine her, memories of a first-aid course from years ago came to her rescue. 'It's all right, Agnes, I don't think your arm's broken.' She was loosening the belt on her jeans as she spoke. 'I'm going to strap your elbow hard against your side and you'll see it will be much easier to get up.'

This was done, but Agnes still resisted moving. In the end, Jack bent down, put his arms round her waist and lifted her to her feet.

'I don't want to ride. You can't make me.'

'I'm not going to make you do anything. I'm going to take you home. Hatty, take the ponies back to Betsy's and I'll come and collect you later.'

'I didn't make her jump. I only betted her.'

'Yes, well, we'll talk about that later.' A little guilt wouldn't come amiss, she thought, anxiety assuaged by relief and anger. It could have been so much worse.

Jack offered to fetch Hatty. Agnes's mother behaved very well and Mary left them as they set off for the doctor.

When Jack returned with Hatty, he'd brought a bottle of wine with him and, in the end, she'd asked him to stay to supper.

That first evening was so dominated by Hatty they'd scarcely talked to each other at all. She'd run into the house before him and burst into tears. She was so sorry – she hadn't meant anything bad to happen. Was Agnes's mother very angry? Would it mean they wouldn't go on holiday? Oh, Mary, don't let her not go. Could she ring Agnes to say sorry?

The idea of the holiday being cancelled hadn't occurred to Mary, who also acknowledged now how very much Hatty had been counting on it, and how helpless she was either to make it happen or provide an entrancing alternative if it didn't. She took refuge in being calming and soothing. She could ring Agnes, but they needed time to get back from the doctor. Meanwhile she'd better have her bath. Jack, in the interim, had put the bottle of wine on the kitchen table and retreated to the sitting room.

'Things better?'

'I think so.' She was too tired to explain about the riding holiday being in jeopardy.

'You look as if you could do with a drink. Would you like me to open the wine? No, you stay there. Just tell me where the corkscrew and glasses are.'

She had sunk gratefully into the battered old sofa whose springs had gone. The room faced west, and was suffused with soft golden light that dealt kindly with the worn carpet and yellowing paint of the bookshelves, carefully refilled with the paperbacks that had been stored in boxes during Reggie's sojourn. Above one, Francis had hung his unframed portrait of her shelling peas in his pink shirt, with several large water-colours, framed and glazed so their subjects, with the sun on the glass, couldn't be seen. The large window at the far end of the room was filled with fields and sky, intermittently darkened by the hazy patterns of returning rooks.

'Harriet told me Thomas is away and Francis is off to Paris next week.'

'Yes.'

'So if she goes on this holiday, you'll be on your own.'

'Yes. Only for a week.'

He had opened the wine and handed her a glass. 'Tell me. What do you do when you're on your own?'

She looked at him, startled, but he seemed serious. 'Well, I hardly ever am. I imagine it will give me the chance to catch up – you know – household chores, that sort of thing.'

'But if you didn't have them, what *would* you do?'

'Goodness.' The idea was a strange one. 'I'd like more time for reading. And I really like gardening.' She came to a stop there. It was something she hadn't considered for such a long time that her more colourful pleasures had receded into fantasy. 'I used to go to the opera quite a bit, and to the Proms, and the theatre. But that was when I lived in London. I enjoyed the festival here very much.'

'But what do you ordinarily do in the country?'

She looked up then, and saw he was regarding her intently. He wasn't just enquiring after her, she realized, he was seeking information. She thought of the large house, scarcely recognizable now as the faded and comfortable cavern of her childhood, now furnished and decorated until every room gleamed – everything new and nothing used. And then she thought of being alone in it.

'I just wondered,' he said.

Hatty burst into the room. 'It's OK, Mary. I rang Agnes and her shoulder is perfectly OK and her mother said that we *are* going on the holiday and I apologized so everything's fine. What's for supper?'

She said it was macaroni cheese and Hatty could lay the table. As Jack got to his feet, she asked him if he'd like to stay. After all, she'd thought, Francis was in London for the evening and he seemed to need company.

He accepted and they withdrew to the kitchen. She'd made a salad, and Hatty went out to the garden in the courtyard and picked some roses for the table and got a thorn in her finger that had to be squeezed out and plastered. 'One of the things about me,' she'd said, 'is that I'm slightly braver than Agnes.' Later, Hatty said she had a favour to ask, looking firmly at Jack, who immediately asked what it was.

'It wouldn't be any trouble for you. In fact you'd hardly notice because you mostly stay indoors, don't you? The favour is, in a week I'm going away for three whole weeks, and it's very boring for my goldfish in his tank by himself, so I wondered if you'd mind if I brought him to your house to go in the pond you've got. It would be a nice change for him to have more water to swim in and you don't absolutely have to feed him much – just a few ants' eggs about every two days. And the eggs wouldn't cost you anything, because I've got them. It's only one fish,' she finished, with another of her winning smiles.

Jack had said he couldn't see a problem and Hatty replied it would show he was kind to animals, which was a good thing. She hadn't, of course, wanted to go to bed, but by the time Mary put her foot down it was dark and Jack had to get back for some calls from America and she remembered now that as she finished clearing up she was so tired she was grateful he hadn't stayed.

It had been an effort to get ready for the dinner at Melton with Jack, and while she was deciding which of her shirts looked least worn, she'd realized she hadn't gone out to dinner *à deux* since her London days when she would spend ages choosing what to wear and how to do her hair. And makeup: in those days she had used eye-shadow and mascara and a pale, discreet lipstick. Now the shadows were natural – but *under* her eyes – and her hair, long so she could avoid the hairdresser, had a few, discernible white streaks, which was a bit much when you were only thirty-five. She wondered then whether Francis thought of her as middle-aged. He was nearly seven years younger, so he probably did.

Celia had kept her makeup in an old biscuit tin with a picture of men galloping to their death in some Victorian battle on its lid. She'd come across it clearing out Celia's clothes, which she'd done when Thomas was out, with his tacit, silent agreement. She had kept the tin, partly because she planned to give it to Hatty when she was older and also because she was naturally frugal. It seemed such a waste to throw the little pots and sticks and brushes away. She rummaged in it now in an effort to find something to reduce the violet shadows and something to put on her lips, but the lipsticks were dry, and the foundation creams had congealed. She'd have to make do with her own face powder. The tin gave off a faint theatrical odour of sugary chalk and something indefinable. Just as she closed the lid, she saw a tiny phial of scent, half used. She opened it and the faded, sweet aroma intensified, and she realized it had been leaking very slowly. It was years since she'd possessed any scent.

The evening had been pleasant, though by the time dinner – three courses and coffee – had been consumed, she was so full of food and drink she longed for bed. Conversation had revolved around the festival and friends. She learned his parents lived in Bexhill-on-Sea, where his father had elected to retire, and she gathered Jack had bought them a bungalow, but he hardly, if ever, saw them. They hadn't really hit it off, he said. But then, when he asked about her family, she couldn't come up with much more – Thomas and Hatty, of course, but no known cousins, and her parents so distant she could hardly remember them.

'But, then, you have friends, apart from a family life. I expect you have a good many having lived here so long.'

'Not very many.' Almost none, she thought, with a small shock – something she hadn't really considered. 'Of course I know people I work with, Mrs Peabody and people at Hatty's school . . .' She faltered then as the discovery completed itself: in fact there were no friends, no friends at all. 'It's time, you see,' she said. 'I really don't have much time for things outside the family. My brother has become rather reclusive since his wife died. Well, I suppose he was before, really. He was totally wrapped up in his marriage, and when Celia died, he was – he was devastated. It shattered him.'

'Is that when you came to live here?'

'Yes. He couldn't cope with Hatty. She was only three and he couldn't manage. Well, of course he was working very hard, trying to make a go of farming, and farming anything single-handedly is pretty difficult.' She didn't add that, at the time, Thomas did practically nothing but drink and rage with grief. There was a silence and she felt he understood she'd left things unsaid.

'This is supposed to be good with puddings,' he said, pouring her a glass of Beaumes de Venise. The pudding was a kind of mousse in a small white pot.

'I haven't drunk this for ages. It's lovely.'

'I always thought living in the country would mean more friends, you know, with no distractions like theatres and cinemas and so on, but it doesn't seem to be like that.'

'People come and stay with you, don't they?'

'A few. Of course, when Percy and Floy were here it didn't really matter. And then with the festival, I suppose I thought, with all those meetings, I'd get to know people. But I didn't take to any of them, really, except your Francis and the Admiral – strange, considering I know nothing about painting or the navy – so here I am.'

'You don't have to be,' she said, before she could stop herself. She really didn't feel up to advising him on how to make friends, but luckily he hadn't noticed.

He carried on: 'Making friends and influencing people. I can do the latter. That's what business is about – making money. I know how to do that.'

She nodded. She was overcome with fatigue and had no reply.

Coffee had arrived and he began to talk then about refurbishing the lodge for the new gardener and his wife. It had needed much more doing to it than he'd thought. He'd put in a damp course, rewired it, replaced several windows whose frames had rotted, and painted the interior. He'd like to show it to her some time. In fact, the builders had more or less finished, but there wasn't a stick of furniture. Would she help him, when he was back, to make a list of what was needed, or even help him shop for it? She would? Well, they'd make a day of it and he'd take her to lunch.

With the coffee drunk, she said it was a lovely dinner and she should be going, and fell asleep in the car as he drove her home.

She'd had these two dinners with Jack because to refuse them would have seemed – almost – unkind. He was clearly so short of company. And she certainly had nothing better to do. Yesterday morning, she remembered, as she languished in bed, she had found she was actually looking forward to what Mrs Peabody called a day out – something Mrs Peabody occasionally did with the Women's Institute. It was a hot, golden day, but after thunder and rain in the night, everything was refreshed. When she opened the kitchen door, the enormous cobweb on the climbing rose trembled with glittering drops, and she could smell the peppery, familiar scent of her white phloxes from the central bed of the yard; except for the soft, insistent, incessant courting of a pair of ring doves, the air was full of a contented silence. All this, and the absence of chores, of routine, the absence of any need to consider other people's happiness gave her the unusual opportunity to consider her own, to look forward to the day with light-hearted anticipation.

She had dressed in jeans and a T-shirt, very old but of a faded coral colour she'd never been able to replace and, on impulse, hadn't put up her hair, just tied it back with a silk ribbon from a Christmas present Francis had given her years ago. Then, remembering what the day's mission was about, she put a note-book and a tape measure in her bag.

He was waiting for her outside the lodge, apparently designed, like so many of its kind, for small people, its darkness enhanced by a high, sprawling hedge, its diamond-paned windows the merest concession to light, and its nail-studded door reminiscent of some minute Gothic prison.

'Bit dark, isn't it?' he said, as they went in.

'Trimming the hedge down will help a lot.'

The door opened straight into the sitting room with windows at the front and back – the back overlooking a small, overgrown garden. There was a fireplace, a flagged floor and a second door that led to the kitchen, which had nothing but a large shallow stone sink set between a pair of stainless-steel draining-boards.

'Perhaps we should start making our list here.' She got out her notebook and tape. 'It looks as if they've wired it so the cooker will have to go in this corner. And the fridge, I suppose, over there.'

'The door through there leads to a sort of cupboard room. I wanted them to put a lavatory there, but it's against the rules.'

Mary opened the door. It had clearly been a larder, since it contained a tiny window and a stone slab. 'We'd better measure the rest of the kitchen to see what size table would fit – with four chairs, I should think. Everything else comes in standard sizes.'

'How practical you are,' he said, as he took one end of the tape.

'It's what you asked me for,' she answered. She felt slightly defensive.

'And the company as well,' he said. 'Apart from being terrible with this sort of thing, I find it much more fun doing it with someone.'

There were two bedrooms up the steep, narrow staircase, one very small, and a third, also small, that had been turned into a bathroom. The whole place had been painted white and the floors were boarded.

'Pretty cramped, isn't it?' Jack said as, having measured the dimensions of the two bedrooms, they tramped down the stairs.

'The worst thing will be getting a double bed up the stairs because they're so narrow. And the windows are too small to do it that way. We'll have to get one that comes in pieces.'

His car was parked a few yards up the drive in the shade, a dark grey, with black leather seats and a beautiful walnut dashboard.

'Is this a new car?'

'New for me. I got it a few weeks ago. I've always wanted an old Bristol, from their glory days, so it took me a while to find one in really good condition. Are you interested in cars?'

'I don't know anything about them. It seems very comfortable,' she added, realizing ignorance sounded like lack of interest. 'Are we just getting the bare essentials? Appliances and beds and tables and chairs? Or is it to be fully furnished?'

'What do you think? I told Moult, the new gardener, it would be furnished. So I suppose that means pots and pans and blankets and things like that. Can't we get everything at the same place?'

'Somewhere like Peter Jones, you mean?'

'Good idea. London, then.'

She got out her notebook. 'I'd better start making a proper list.'

And so, while he drove, with a speed and concentration that clearly denoted enjoyment, she struggled with a list that grew all the way to London until it became a truly daunting prospect. Neither Thomas nor Francis would stand for shopping on this scale, she knew, and men were notoriously impatient when faced with even half an hour buying things. She began to feel unfairly responsible, to dread Jack's likely resentment.

But it turned out to be surprisingly easy. He was in his element: he enjoyed choosing and buying, made decisions quickly, deferred to her when it came to linen and the kitchen equipment, was generous when she suggested that a couple of electric fires and a standard lamp for the sitting room might be a good idea, and added an unflagging energy to the day that, in the end, she couldn't match. By the time he'd paid and organized the delivery of everything she was exhausted and stumbled on the escalator. He caught her arm.

'Sorry.'

'You must be tired. You need some lunch.' It was nearly three o'clock.

'It *is* a bit late, isn't it?' She was clutching the rail as they sped down. 'I'm sorry, Jack, but could you keep hold of me? I'm feeling a bit odd. I'm not sure I'll get off this thing.'

He moved to the step below her. 'It's all right. I'll get you off. Just hang on to me and take a step when I tell you.'

When they got down, there was nowhere to sit.

'Can you make it to the car?'

She nodded. He took her arm and they walked slowly and in silence out on to the hot street into the petrol fumes and dust. She felt him darting looks of concern.

'I'm so sorry I put you through such a marathon,' he said, when she was in the car. 'Now – lunch.'

But lunch proved far from easy to find, and after trying a number of places that were either closed or no longer serving in varying tones of apology and triumph, they settled for a small Indian restaurant in Chiswick, a dark, narrow room crammed with small tables, each with a vase of plastic carnations, and not a single customer. The waiter, deliriously happy to see them, invited them to choose a table and returned with two greasy tomes from which they might select their food. She said she'd like some water and it was brought at once, the waiter placing the glass tenderly before her as if she and it were precious beyond belief.

'Would you like some lager?'

That, too, was brought at once, with a plate of poppadoms and a dish of various chutneys. In spite of the elaborately dark red flock wallpaper and the distant, almost subliminal, meandering wail of a girl enduring some sort of romantic dream, the place seemed restful, pleasantly quiet.

Drinking the water, she soon began to feel better. 'I'm so sorry—'

'No, it's me. I should apologize for dragging you around for so long. And I meant to give you a really proper lunch somewhere posh—'

Both stopped.

'I'm enormously grateful to you for coming with me and being so practical and helpful.'

'I enjoyed it,' she said, not quite sure how true that was. 'The last time I did this, furnished a place from scratch, it was the first flat I had with Thomas and then it was all just make do or do without.'

'But your parents sold Melton, didn't they? I would have thought—'

Here, the waiter came back for their order and with her assent he ordered one chicken and one lamb curry and some rice.

'No, we didn't have much money. We left Melton when I was six. Our parents went abroad and we lived with an aunt in what used to be the dower house of the estate – the nursing-home to the east of the park now, which, I suppose, it more or less was before. Aunt Gertrude was a professional invalid – but she did leave us a little bit of money.'

'Did anyone live in the lodge then? It was in an awful state.'

'Two old gardeners when we were children, and they stayed on with the new owner. They didn't do much and loathed each other. I should think it was in pretty bad nick when they were there.'

'So you didn't have much of a family life when you were a child.'

'I had Thomas. When we were with Aunt Gertrude, he used to tell me he'd make a fortune and we'd go back to the house.' There was a pause. 'All nonsense, of course,' she finished, as their food arrived.

For a while they ate in companionable silence. 'So, this flat you had together,' he said. 'How long did that go on for?'

'From when he was at university until he married. About five years, I suppose. They lived in Celia's flat until she got pregnant. Then they moved to Home Farm.'

'And you went with them?'

'Oh, no. I stayed on in London.'

Without warning, she was back in that time: Celia's amazing beauty at the wedding, Thomas glowing with joy, and their mutual happiness, like sunlight irradiating everyone in their orbit. She had watched them leave for their secret honeymoon destination, though Thomas had told her it was Venice. Refusing the offer of dinner with Celia's parents, she had caught a bus back to the flat she would henceforth inhabit alone. She remembered trudging up the stone staircase, opening the door and standing for what seemed ages in the silence. The flat was full of him, full of his absence. The battered but beautiful kilim and the enormous gilded mirror that had caused their first real argument, the rocking-chair he'd bought her for a birthday present, 'so you can rock and read', his unfinished breakfast still on the table – a half-drunk pot of coffee and an unopened boiled egg. His bedroom was full of discarded clothes, the Quimper bowl, full to its dusty brim with his copper change, a rack crammed with shoes he hardly wore, the unsteady pile of paperbacks on the floor by the bed, the large, yellowing photograph of Melton, taken before he was born, and the scent of his Floris aftershave clinging to the air.

She remembered looking down at the rather unsuccessful dark blue silk dress she would never wear again and telling herself aloud she must get out of these clothes and start clearing up—

'He wants to know if you'd like another lager.'

'Oh. No, thank you.'

'It wasn't a bad lunch, was it?'

She said it was delicious, but there had been so much of it she couldn't eat any more.

Washing her hands in the ladies', she examined her face in the small, cracked mirror and wondered if she wasn't too old now to wear her hair down. When she'd asked him Francis had said no, it might be for some people, but not for her. 'You look good both ways,' he'd said, possibly just to please her, but it had anyway. While she undid the ribbon to recomb her hair she reflected how little these skirmishes of curiosity actually revealed. She had stayed on in London, as she'd told Jack, but that had said nothing of her desolation, her loss, the slow, painful acknowledgement that, until he married, Thomas had been her life, the one person she'd loved and cared for – had lived for, really. Of course she'd been glad for him, and sincerely so. She liked Celia, saw she was as much in love with Thomas as he was with her, and had no doubts about them living happily ever after.

But afterwards she had had to contrive a life without her brother. After a series of jobs, she landed a post at Claridge's. It was interesting, demanding and enjoyable, and she became very good at it. She was reliable, tactful and discreet, and the manager rewarded her by raising her salary. She learned to drive and bought a Mini. Friends were more difficult. The people she knew outside work were all Thomas's friends. She'd been happy to cook supper for them, but she was shy, she was Thomas's sister – and, anyway, they came and went as often as Thomas ricocheted from one enterprise to another.

Adrian Greenway was her first serious date. They had met at a Prom, stood next to one another during Verdi's *Requiem* at the Albert Hall. He was a tall, sallow man with spectacles, a good ten years older than her, with a voice so quiet she could hardly hear him. 'I was asking you if you'd like to have something to eat with me,' he'd repeated patiently, looking as if he very much doubted she would. This made her accept. Over dinner she discovered he'd studied to be a violinist, had been called up and sent to Burma where he'd been captured by the Japanese and spent four years in a prison camp. When she asked if he was playing now, he put his hitherto unremarkable hands on the table. One index finger was missing, and the others, on both hands, were a misshapen, trembling bunch. 'So now it's a case of those who can't do, teach,' he'd said, with a small, ironic smile that pre-empted any response. Compassion, and his rejection of it, made him a hero to her and fabricated a strange kind of love between them. For months she put up with his moods, his pessimism and his neurotic lethargy. He hated his job, his barren little flat. Nothing she could do would calm him, but he sulked if she was inattentive. He would tell her she'd changed his life, he couldn't imagine it without her, how her love kept him sane.

Then Celia died. Leaving Adrian hadn't been so hard – awkward, yes, difficult, but ultimately unpainful. She'd got by for too long on crumbs and from a poor man's table to boot. He went through the motions, offering his lifelong devotion, but it was merely a gesture to convention – a moral prop to support his pride.

She finished with her hair in the mirror and almost bumped into Jack when she came out of the ladies'. He was on the phone at the bar. After listening for a bit he hung up and joined her. 'I was ringing Amelia and Wystan – thought we might call in on them on our way home, but there's no reply. I wanted them to meet you. You cooked that splendid dinner when they came to stay.'

'Oh, yes. Percy said how nice they were.'

'Well, they'll be down some time.' But he seemed deflated.

They walked out of the cosy gloom of the restaurant into the hot haze of the street, littered with plane leaves, sweet wrappings and, every now and then, abandoned office furniture, bikes or wilting vegetables from grocery displays.

She fell asleep in the car, only waking when he stopped for petrol.

'Don't apologize. I'm afraid I wore you out. You sleep as much as you want.'

He was really very nice and kind, she thought, as she dropped off again.

And so, when he'd asked her, she agreed to have dinner with him that evening in his house. He'd fetch her, he said, so she wouldn't have to drive.

THOMAS

After two weeks in London, he was in despair. The course wasn't at all what he'd imagined, nothing serious, like the RHS or the Chelsea Physic Garden or Kew, simply a pair of cocky young men – photographers – who'd devised the thing purely to occupy bored wealthy housewives and make some money. They held it in their studio in Fulham, showing endless pictures they'd taken of famous gardens and dropping loads of snobbish innuendo about the owners. For the rest, they took it in turns to give talks on things like planting, the arrangement of colour, structure, suitable shrubs. Either he felt he knew it all, or it wasn't worth knowing. He'd paid for the course, which made him hang on longer than he should have. He hated being in London, in August of all months. It was full of traffic and noise, and he hated the grotty little hotel in Pimlico that smelled of stew and cabbage.

But Percy was in London and, as the futility of the course became clear to him, he realized he'd only done it to be near her – more than that, to see her, to be in her orbit.

He'd refrained from ringing her for those two weeks and then he had to try several times before anyone answered, and it was Floy. Percy was out – no, she hadn't got a job yet, and how was he getting on? He didn't tell her. Then she asked if he'd like to come to supper and he said he would. Come at seven, she said, and told him exactly where they were. 'Take a bus up the Edgware Road to Carlton Vale. We're the other side of the road.'

It was a small semi-detached brick house with a slate roof set back from the road, with Floy's old van parked in what had been a small front garden, and a flight of steps leading up to the stained-glass front door. It was where Percy lived.

The door opened – and there was Floy. His anticipation that it would be Percy spilled over and he bent to kiss her. She looked faintly surprised. 'Very nice, Thomas. Percy is doing things in the kitchen. Come and see my conservatory.'

He followed her through the sitting room, which had honeysuckle-patterned wallpaper that he remembered from his childhood day nursery at Melton, into a surprising and beautiful place at the back of the house, filled with the chlorophyllic scent of freshly watered plants and the perfume of jasmine. There were four basket chairs and a table littered with papers, a mug full of variously coloured crayons, glasses and bottles.

'Get us both a drink,' she said. 'Whisky for me.'

'This place is perfect for you. I'd no idea that London houses have such conservatories.'

'They very seldom do – at least with small houses like this one.' She'd sunk into her chair and was clearing the papers. 'Tell me about the course. I gather it isn't quite what you expected.'

'Who told you that?'

'You did – by not telling me when I asked you.' So he told her then how disappointing it was. 'And you're staying with friends?'

He told her about the hotel. 'I lost touch with everyone I used to know when we moved to the country.'

There was a short silence while she lit one of her small cigars, and he wondered why Percy hadn't joined them, if she dreaded seeing him. She was saying something about having had doubts about the course he'd found, and it being a question of going the whole hog to get formal qualifications ' . . . or muddling into it, as I did,' she finished. 'But I expect things are different now. There wasn't the competition when I started.'

Then Percy arrived. She wore white trousers and a pale grey shirt, and she was carrying a bottle of wine. His heart lurched and he couldn't look at her while it rearranged itself and greetings were exchanged.

She settled at the table, poured herself some wine and asked how he was getting on, and when he said not very well so far, she asked after Mary. 'She's all alone, isn't she? Francis is painting portraits in France.'

This was news to him. 'How do you know?'

'He wrote me a lovely letter – very funny. He says the family he's painting are all exactly alike, like a set of little spanners, he said, just different sizes. He writes very good letters. I've tried to ring Mary once or twice, but she seems to be out.'

There was a pause and he noticed she was looking at her aunt with some concern. 'I thought we'd have supper in here – it's much cooler and, anyway, it will save you the stairs. Oh. I'd better nip out and do some watering.'

'I've done it.'

'Oh, Floy. I said I would.' She turned to Thomas. 'She's supposed to be taking things easy.'

'I am.'

'You're not. She's just agreed to do a whole garden in Hampstead from scratch. It's too much, with everything else going on.'

Floy said, 'He doesn't know about the everything else, Zephie. What about dinner? I'm sure Thomas will help you with the trays.'

Of course he would. He followed her into the hall and down a flight of stairs to the kitchen, where they found a cat sitting morosely on the kitchen table with a saucer of untouched fish before him.

'Marvell thinks our fish is probably nicer than his, so he's holding out for some. I forgot to make the salad. Have a seat, I won't be long.'

He watched her whiz about, tearing lettuce leaves into a bowl, fetching sliced tomatoes from the draining-board, sprinkling them with fresh basil from a pot on the window-sill and shaking the dressing vigorously in a small jar until, conscious of the silence, she saw how intently he was watching and said quickly, 'The everything else is bad news, I'm afraid.'

Then she told him about selling the house and how she'd tramped all over London looking for somewhere else. 'I only take Floy to one or two possible places, but she hasn't liked them. Meanwhile people come traipsing all over this house pondering and eventually deciding they don't want it. And now she's taken on this huge new commission—' She stopped. He sensed sudden confusion in her, a consciousness, perhaps, that she was treating him intimately, heartlessly, like an old friend. And he knew she was remembering what he'd said to her on the drive back to Melton and the kiss that had been asked for and given.

'Sorry. I didn't mean to go on like that. It's just that I worry about her.' She was putting knives and forks and plates on a tray and didn't look at him.

'Of course. Let me do that.'

She'd opened the oven door and handed him the oven glove.

'They were supposed to be fish cakes, but they fell to pieces when I tried to fry them, so now I'm afraid it's just a kind of fish splodge. I'm not a marvellous cook like Mary.'

As he carried the tray upstairs, he had a pang of guilt about his sister. He'd only rung her twice – once to say he'd found somewhere to live, and once to say he was getting on with the course. He hadn't told her what was actually happening. He didn't want to admit to failure. But not knowing about Francis being away had shaken him. He knew Hatty was on holiday for three weeks, so Mary was alone. He recognized, with a further pang, that he'd have stayed in London anyway – because of Percy. He decided it was Francis's fault for changing his plans.

In spite of their troubles, both Percy and Floy were very good company. Percy told stories about the awful houses she'd seen and the one or two nice ones that were too expensive. 'There was one in Camden Town, very noisy, but only on two floors with a huge balcony looking on to a really decent-sized garden. But the moment we made an offer, the owner raised the price. She did it twice and the agent said she was gauging what her house was worth. It would have suited us, wouldn't it, Floy?'

'It was on the small side, but otherwise, yes. I'm afraid property brings out the worst in people. I think we shall have to go further afield than we first thought. In any case, we really must sell the lease on this first.'

Percy asked him about his course and he described the two photographers who ran it. 'One of them never stops saying "stunning" and the other one "wizard". They're called Lionel and Raymond and they keep telling us how good each other's "pics" are. The rest of the students are rather bored women who spend their lives taking courses – in fact, one told me she did just that.'

'How depressing. I'm never going to be one of them.'

Floy said, 'Why is it such a bad thing? Apart from there being a number of reasons why people seek distraction through learning something, a world full of professionals and experts would be rather smugly dull, don't you think?'

'But Thomas says it's such a rotten course.'

'That's another matter entirely. That's bad luck.'

Then, he didn't know quite how it happened, Percy was dispatched to make coffee – no, she didn't want help with the trays – and he was to be shown the garden by Floy.

She went ahead of him down the small iron spiral staircase on to the gently winding path of beautifully trimmed topiary yews and past pillars of clematis, blue and purple, still flowering, and banked on either side by white tobacco. Further on there was the Davidia she'd planted thirty years ago. Two-thirds of the way up the garden, under an enormous ash tree, the path ended with an arch made of yew flanked on either side by two stone lions. Beyond it were beds of old-fashioned roses, still announcing their identity with some flowers. 'Bit late for them, but so wonderful in their month.'

Further on, at the end, were two large herbaceous borders broken by a small rectangular pond at the back of which was an old wrought-iron bench. The borders were crowded with day lilies, phlox, cosmos, delphiniums, white and blue agapanthus and Michaelmas daisies, not yet in flower; and the whole was edged with lavender and backed by two or three old fruit trees. 'I shall have to sit here for a bit if you don't mind.'

Marvell had mysteriously joined them and when they sat, he plonked himself on a small round plot of nepeta, rolling from side to side in it, his mouth slightly ajar, the better to inhale the marvellous smell. 'That's his own bed,' she said fondly.

The garden took his breath away with its charming blend of order and carelessness. 'Do you do all this yourself?'

'Yes. It isn't so labour-intensive as I like to think it looks. Cunning, you know, and things well established. Plants are far less trouble if you put them in the right place, and *that* one learns from trial and error. But it's a gardener's garden. I wouldn't design it for a client unless they were keen to work in it themselves and you don't get many of them.'

He said, 'I don't know how you can bear to leave it,' and as she answered steadily, 'I shall have to bear it,' he thought, How stupid, how crass of me. There was a pause while he watched her gazing at her cat.

'I—' He felt suddenly humbled by her, uncertain how to proceed. 'Would you mind if I asked you for some advice? Oh dear – how can you answer that?'

She turned to him then and smiled. 'I expect I shall find a way. I suspect you want to ask me if you should abandon your course.'

'Yes. That's one thing.'

She was silent, but he sensed she was seriously considering . . . something. At length she said, 'It's generally unwise to change horses without fresh ones to hand, as it were.' Another silence. The ball was back in his court.

'Well – I was wondering – Percy said you've just taken on a new job that would involve lots of heavy work she doesn't think you should do. It occurred to me, perhaps, you could take me on to do the heavy stuff and at the same time I'd learn what it's like to do a garden from scratch. I don't expect to be paid anything, just learn from you for a month or two.'

'What about your nursery?'

'Francis and Mary can hold the fort for now. We earned a good bit from the stuff we sold you for Melton. We can coast on that.'

She'd been looking at him intently. Now she said, 'I think it's a deal. We could perhaps be of some use to one another. I warn you, it will be very hard work.'

'I'm not afraid of that.'

She agreed that he wasn't. Then she said, 'And the other thing?'

Until this moment, he'd believed he was longing to talk about his love, to confess it, to ask for reassurance. Now, suddenly, he was afraid of what she might say – his poverty, the fact that he was, what? twelve, thirteen years older than Percy flooded his mind and he sat miserably clasping and unclasping his hands, unable to look at her, unable to speak. He heard her start to say, 'You don't have to—'

'I do. I love her. I asked her to marry me, but she said no, said she didn't love me enough. Then, when you both left Melton, I thought if I could see her, she might get to know me better, might love me more. I suppose that's really why I came – but I also thought I should make a better fist of earning my living. Seeing her tonight was like . . . well, like being in the sunlight – you know? Just seeing her . . .' After a pause he said, 'I wanted to tell you, to ask you, to see if you thought, well, I couldn't come and work for you without— False pretences, wouldn't it be? But perhaps you knew already, perhaps she told you.'

'She did tell me.'

'And do you think she might – might change, get to love me?' He could feel himself becoming craven, but couldn't stop it. 'If you thought I could make her happy—'

'My dear Thomas, I'd be in favour of anybody I thought could do that. But it's not my business. It's entirely between the two of you.'

Then they heard Percy call that their coffee was getting cold and started to walk back; she took his arm. The yellow lights from the house sharpened the dusk to near darkness and the white flowers of the tobacco became stars, and within a few steps he would see her again.

HUGO

'Luncheon is served, Mr Hugo.' He said this every day at precisely the same time – two minutes to one – in a funereal tone, as if, Hugo sometimes thought, he might well be saying, 'I'm afraid her ladyship has recently shot herself in her boudoir,' or 'A tiger has inadvertently entered the hall and is in the process of consuming your sister.' He enjoyed such mental play, but this morning he was too bored and dispirited to try. Since the bed-and-breakfast venture, he'd spent hours making it look profitable. There *had* been a trickle of guests throughout the summer of various nationalities – some earnest Belgians who wanted twice as much breakfast as provided, a crowd of French, only one of whom spoke English but all of whom expected a tour of the house and took pictures of each other in every room, and more Americans, including a brash young woman who claimed she was writing a book about English decadence and cross-examined him about British royalty. One and all, he was glad to see the last of them. In desperation, he'd invented a haunted bedroom, another where Princess Margaret had stayed, and fearsome death duties involving recent relatives who'd died untimely deaths, which accounted for the more serious decline of the house. The scheme *had* made some money, but nowhere near enough to reach the five-thousand mark that would put him in the clear about the dry rot.

As he got to his feet for lunch – sure to be better than usual as he'd run over a pheasant in the drive – it suddenly occurred to him. Despite his usual lugubrious tone, Coleridge had been grinning. This, he knew from bitter experience, did not bode well.

*

'I can't see why you're so upset.'

They had graduated from the back of his car to a rug on the floor of a dilapidated summerhouse in what had once been the walled garden at Easton. She lay on her side, head propped in one hand, the other absently curling a strand of her long silky hair.

'I mean I should think you'd be pleased.' She closed her eyes for a moment and said dreamily, "Peer Marries Hong Kong Heiress". I expect it'll be in the papers, won't it? Why be upset?'

'Well, apart from anything else, he says he's bringing her back to see the ancestral home – to find out if she wants to live here.'

'He told you?'

'No. He wrote to my mother.'

'I bet she's pleased.'

'You bet right.'

'Well, then, why are you so upset?'

'Rosalie, if you ask me once more I may seriously consider strangling you.'

'Oh, all right, darling.' There was a pause and she said, 'It's only that I wanted to know.' Her large, extremely blue eyes were fixed on him. She had one of those faces that were prettier the closer you got to it. Now she said, 'So when are they coming?'

'I don't know. Soon, she said. He wrote to my mother, not me.'

'Well, she is his mother.'

'It must have slipped my mind.' But sarcasm was lost on her.

She ran her raspberry-coloured tongue over her moist upper lip. 'Shall we have some more sex? Would that cheer you up?'

It was like being offered the last sandwich on the plate, he thought morosely. 'No, thanks. I must get you home. I've got a lot to do.'

'OK.' She sat up and buttoned her shirt.

As she got out of his car, outside the cottage, she bent down to look at him through the open window. 'It's only because I care. Men find it so difficult to express their feelings. I *do* know.'

In the second she hesitated after this, he knew she expected him to lean forward and kiss her. Instead, he stretched out his hand and patted her cheek. 'Be seeing you.'

Being understood was the last thing he wanted. It usually led to some kind of humiliating exposure, and to be understood by someone clearly not all that bright was worse. He decided he couldn't face going home to the feeble and pointlessly festive ruminations of his mother and Betsy. The obvious alternative was the nearest pub.

There, after a couple of double Scotches, he tried again to think of one, or several reasons why Ashley's money hadn't been spent as he'd ordered. He could produce the bed-and-breakfast scheme as evidence, but he knew Ashley, who'd always regarded him with profound distrust – dating back to when he'd smashed his older brother's china pig to get at his pocket and Christmas-present money – would go into every detail. Nothing had been done about the dry rot and he'd gone through . . . well, about three thousand, not counting the meagre profits from the bed-and-breakfast project. For once in his life he'd had a few months when he could take Rosalie out, buy himself some decent clothes, get some drink into the house and generally comport himself as he felt was his due. His mother's allowance to him only ever covered one of these things, or less of more of them.

Meanwhile, there was Ashley, no doubt already as rich as

Croesus, getting hitched to an heiress he really didn't need. It just wasn't fair. Stuck as he was in Melton, how could he find an heiress? The memory of that humiliating drive to Paddington with what's-her-name came back to him now. Swamped by injustice, he ordered a third Scotch.

FRANCIS

He'd never been much of a one for making decisions, preferring them, as he'd once told Percy, to arrive ready-made, like pork pies or teabags. But these last few weeks in France had made a mysterious difference. The time had come for him to acknowledge that, unless he did something, he would spend the rest of his life painting when he had time, hoping people would chance along and buy the results, doing his share of the chores at Home Farm and wondering from time to time if anything significant would ever happen. He assumed this faintly uneasy feeling had started with the festival and working with Percy – he'd enjoyed it all: collecting the works for the exhibitions and generally helping her. But then, when it finished, she had gone back to London to get some other work and seemed so enviably in charge of her life.

Then he'd had the offer of the Paris trip, a last-minute thing: Gerry, whom he'd known at art school, had rung up out of the blue, his summer travel-guiding job was going to fall through unless he could find a partner – the original bloke had got shingles. 'They won't allow me to do it all on my tod, there has to be two of us.' He'd told Mary it was well paid, which it wasn't, and felt a bit guilty about leaving her, with Thomas away. But the money wasn't the point: to be paid at all just to look at paintings, many of which he'd only seen in reproduction, was a captivating prospect, and to go to Paris, where he'd been only once before, when his mother had taken him and Celia for a week, was irresistible.

Paris had been a revelation. He couldn't imagine why he hadn't spent more of his life there. 'God, I wish we could stay longer,' he'd said to Gerry, on the third evening. They'd found a café to frequent after the students were fed and watered and had taken to sitting for hours over Ricard, and coffee in little thick white china cups. He'd been drawing a nearby couple immersed in courtship.

'Well, why don't you?'

'We can't, can we? We have to take them back.'

'Only as far as Victoria – I'm nipping straight back on the next boat train.' He stubbed out his Gitane. 'I have an assignation not to be missed. You could have one or two yourself, you know.' He signalled to the waiter. 'Same again? Don't mind if you do.'

In the course of three evenings, Francis had heard a good deal about Gerry's love life, which seemed as incessant as it was varied.

'Gerry, I couldn't afford it. I don't have a private income like you.' He looked up from his drawing to see his friend's brandy brown eyes, amused, appraising.

'My dear, my income is so private even I have no idea what it is. Things happen. If I don't enjoy them, I go on to the next. One of the good things about this job is that you meet people. And the second good thing is that you're on the move.' He picked up the little water flagon and topped up the new drinks the waiter had brought. All his movements had a kind of powerful grace. He was always at ease, fully aware he could charm people of either sex, but with genuine kindness, and it made Francis, at least, simply like him more. They talked a bit that evening, inconclusively, about what he might do if he stayed in France, and when they parted in the corridor of the small hotel, Gerry put a hand on his shoulder and said, 'Leave it to me. I might come up with something.'

And, amazingly, he had.

So here he was in an enormous rented villa on Cap Ferrat, painting portraits of a family of American children, whose tiny bird-like mother was infatuated with Gerry. Her husband was away making even more money somewhere else, and Gerry was employed to teach the children French, which he did rather carelessly at meals. The rest of the time he spent with their hostess. Sandra Gatkin was an heiress in her own right, had married young, some kind of tycoon – Francis never discovered what he actually did – and produced five children, including a pair of twins until, like Mrs Carmichael in MacNeice's poem, she was through with overproduction, and had turned her colossal energy to preserving her youth and having a good time. Gerry was currently the good time. They spent hours at the swimming-pool, hours on excursions to Cannes, Nice and Saint-Tropez, and would return with intensive shopping booty – yet more clothes for her and extravagant presents for the children. From time to time Francis was given things, shirts, shorts, an amusing hat, dark glasses. It was clear Gerry was also much favoured. Afternoons were spent having – in Gerry and Sandra's case – lengthy siestas. The children, after a morning's rioting in the pool and an enormous lunch, were usually herded to their rooms by an au pair and were dormant until early evening, when one would be summoned to sit for him.

He spent siesta times lying in the shade on a terrace overlooking the dazzling, well-behaved sea. The luxury, the indolence of this interlude – he called it that to defend himself against its unreality – was something he'd never experienced before. 'Scott Fitzgerald stuff,' he'd called it, inwardly. He kept meaning to write to Mary, to explain why he was here, to say when he'd return, but the days passed and sloth prevailed. He didn't write to her.

But as the days passed, strikingly similar, he began to feel uneasy, isolated, to want someone there who might feel as he did – Percy. If she were here it would be quite different. They would be enjoying it as onlookers, laughing at the way Sandra had to organize everything for her pleasure; the smallest deviation from her intricate house rules provoked her. It would be fun, sometimes, not to do exactly as she wanted, and he knew with Percy it would have been a kind of game they could both play.

He was having trouble with his commission. 'No, I don't think so. I don't think that's an accurate picture of Harvey. I know him better than you do. He's a very sensitive child. No. You'd better try again.' An 'accurate' picture of eight-year-old Harvey would turn him into a chocolate-box fop, he'd thought crossly. But he'd done as she wished and hated himself for doing it. He wrote to Percy, to entertain her, describing his employer – he put it like that – as a blonde toothpick and the children so much alike, quiet as mice at meals, while his friend Gerry made them speak only in French. He told her of the affair that seethed with the barest pretence it didn't exist. One of the older children had said, 'Mom likes to have people in bed with her, but I have a bear for that.' When he tried to describe the place, he got lost in postcard clichés – umbrella pines against the sunset, the cloudless morning skies in the pine-scented villa garden, the coarse green freshly watered lawns, the house dripping with purple and cream bougainvillaea, the lunches on the terrace overlooking the sea with amazingly arranged platters of hors d'oeuvres: the black and green olives, the piles of rosy prawns and terrines ready sliced in their square dishes, anchovies, cold dressed yellow and red peppers, cornichons and thick yellow mayonnaise. 'You can see, I could have just sent you a set of postcards that would show you better.' He ended, as such letters so often do, with queries about her, had she got a job? Had she heard from Thomas? Give his love to Floy. 'This writing paper was in my room – just like an hotel. Now I shall have to summon up all my energy to find a stamp and somewhere to post it.' He added, suddenly finding that this was truer than it sounded, 'I miss you, Percy. So love, etc.'

It wasn't until several weeks later, when he'd completed four of the five portraits to Sandra's satisfaction, that he realized this interlude was coming to an end and he'd have to make decisions, or at least one decision, about what to do next. Back to Home Farm was the obvious choice, but he felt vaguely uncertain, uneasy. Perhaps he should go back and then work out what to do. It might take some time. Meanwhile he could continue at Home Farm, helping Thomas with the nursery, teaching Hatty to draw, lending Mary a hand with the odd maintenance job and perhaps getting her advice—

He must, must write to her. Except for one postcard, he'd been really terrible about keeping in touch; she might think he didn't care about her, which wasn't so. She had filled the gap Celia had left, had encouraged him to paint. She'd be the first person to help and advise how best to go about doing it more seriously. She was so practical – would see the difficulties of professional portrait-painting stuck in Melton. Just the idea of writing to her about it fired him up, clarified what he wanted and gave him the courage to take the plunge.

He wrote that night and felt much the better for it.

MARY

Two weeks into the autumn term, and she was still on her own, except for Hatty. The routine was established. Hatty cycled to school and back, at least until the end of double-summer time, when it would be the car run once more, twice a day. On Tuesdays and Thursdays she taught at Abbey Court, a new school year with another set of Charlottes and Carolines and Emmas: how to make soups, pastry, basic sauces, and the principle of making a stew, dividing the classes into three groups and rotating them each week so that everyone had a crack at everything. Two mornings were enough. Every evening there was a battle with Hatty to do her homework before she went riding. 'Agnes always does hers after, so why can't I? And Agnes's mother will bring me home so you won't have to do it, Mary darling. Wouldn't that be nicer?' In the end she gave in over this, largely because she didn't want Hatty riding alone.

All these weeks, and still neither Thomas nor Francis had come home. She'd had one postcard from Francis, a highly coloured photograph of a huge plate of hors d'oeuvres, prawns, mussels and the like. 'You can see I'm not starving here. Marvellous weather. Am working on five portraits. Lots of money. Love Francis.' At least he wrote, she thought, and it sounded as if he was enjoying himself.

Thomas had rung to say he was coming down for a night to collect more clothes. He said he'd given up the course, but was working with Floy and staying with them at Maida Vale. He'd tell her all about it when he saw her. Could she collect him off the six o'clock train?

He strode along the platform towards her and even from that distance she saw the transformation. He was charged with a kind of energy and excitement she hadn't seen in him for years.

He hugged her with enthusiasm. 'You look well,' he said, as if he hadn't expected it. 'All golden from the sun.'

In the car he told her about the new garden Floy was designing and how her arthritis made it hard for her, and that Percy had agreed help was needed and wanted him to be Floy's aide. 'She loves Floy so much,' he said. 'She worries dreadfully about her health. She's almost given up trying to find a job because of looking after Floy and the house thing— Oh, you don't know about that . . .' and he told her. 'She says it's breaking Floy's heart to leave the house— The most wonderful garden. Floy has genius and, by God, I'm learning a lot from her. But I think I'm being some use to them, earning my keep as it were. And Percy spends days tramping all over London trying to find something with a decent garden they can afford, as well as showing people their house all the time, which isn't much fun, but she's awfully good about it.' He was running out of breath. 'So, everything all right at home?'

She told him the nursery was ticking over. She was keeping it open at weekends only, and Mrs Peabody had kindly agreed to do Sunday afternoons on the till, and she was doing one day a week for Jack Curtis. For some reason, she didn't feel like telling him about their trip to London or the evenings they'd spent together.

'Not cooking again for him, are you?'

'No. He has a perfectly good cook. Too good, really – the man hasn't enough to do. No, just secretarial stuff, getting his papers sorted for his accountant and finishing the lodge for the new gardener to move in.'

'I hope he's paying you.'

'Of course. He's very easy – generous – about that sort of thing. I'm saving up to buy Hatty a pony.'

'Oh, Mary, she'll never look after it. It'll be one more chore for you. And they cost money to keep – food, vets and tack.'

'It won't be a problem. I've made an arrangement with Betsy Carson, the Easton Park girl, her riding teacher, that the pony can stable with her on the understanding she can use it for pupils and Hatty has first call on it. But it's a secret, Thomas. I want it to be her surprise Christmas present.'

'Right. I won't say a word.'

It was a windless evening with a light mist rising from the meadows on either side of the lane, the hedges – already decorated with wild rose hips, hawthorn and black bryony berries – an intricate background for the pale green seed heads of cow parsley waiting to ripen. When they got out of the car he stood for a moment. 'Oh, gosh, the sweet air – and the rooks.' They were flying in their rambling patterns, silhouetted alternately against a sky whose pale blue, molten with the setting sun, was streaked with aquamarine and drifts of peach-coloured cloud, a combination, she remembered Francis once saying, that could only be brought off by the celestial.

'Oh, it's so good to be home.' He took her arm. 'Dearest Mary – and how is Hatty?'

'She seems fine. She's moved up a form, but with her mates. She doesn't like being Hatty, by the way.' She started to laugh. 'As a matter of fact, she wants us to call her Tracy.'

'Good Lord. No, I can't do that.' They were walking towards the kitchen door. He said, 'Celia started calling her Hatty – thought it sounded less severe than Harriet.' She'd never heard him speak in such a matter-of-fact way about Celia.

The moment they got into the kitchen, he saw the tank of tropical fish. 'Where on earth did they come from?'

'They're Hatty's. I'll let her tell you about them herself. She'll be back any minute.'

She was already back, came thundering down the stairs. 'Hi, Dad.' She gave him a perfunctory hug. 'Come and look at my fish. A man called Jack gave them to me. He's very kind about fish because he let me put my poor old one in his pond when I went away because I thought he'd like it but he didn't and he died, which was awfully sad but he had a proper funeral under the cherry tree out there and he said he'd get me another one but what he actually got was this whole tank with these amazing fish in it – they're tropical and they have to have sea water and not much food but he gave me a book about them so I can tell you what they are if you like.' She stopped for breath.

'Tell me.'

'Those beautiful stripy ones are angel fish and those three small ones are guppies, that lovely black one is a black molly and I'm the only person at school who actually owns tropical fish but Agnes is quite kind about it because her mother gave her a cat. Those bubbles are oxygen. They don't look as if they breathe but they do it from the sides of them – gills.'

There was a short silence while they admired them together and she could see Hatty was pleased, and during supper – chicken pie and blackberry crumble – she deluged him with more about her life until, eventually, Mary made her go upstairs for her bath and bed. When she came down from tucking Hatty in, she found Thomas had cleared the table and was washing the dishes. 'Percy has house-trained me,' he said, with a sheepish smile. 'It's not too bad when you get used to it, is it?'

'Not too bad. Let's have coffee in the sitting room. I want you to see it – I've cleaned it up.'

'Goodness, the egocentricity of the young. You'd think theirs was the only life in the world.'

'Well, in a way, it *is*, for them. It shows she's happy – far, far better than being withdrawn and sulky, not wanting to tell us anything.'

'Of course it is.' He moved to her, the teacloth flung over

one shoulder, and turned her round to face him. 'You have been the most wonderful mother to her, Mary darling. I can never thank you enough.'

There was something valedictory – more threatening because he seemed unconscious of it – in his manner that made it difficult for her to say anything. She gave a little shrug and thought she smiled.

If Percy is to become her new mother, what will become of me?

A thought, unsaid.

'Here. Let me take the tray,' he said.

'You've painted it all,' he exclaimed, when she'd lit the two lamps in the sitting room. He admired the pale aquamarine of the walls, and noticed the white-painted bookshelves with the newly arranged books. 'And not a sign of Reggie,' he added, which lightened the air. 'I really think that's one of Francis's best pictures,' he added, 'and it looks just right there. Gosh, you've done a lot. Have you heard from him? Percy got a long, funny letter. He seems to be enjoying himself.'

'I had a postcard. He said he was earning a lot of money, which is good.'

'Don't let's talk about money tonight. It only makes us both cross. I know things are going to turn out all right in the end.'

The warmth that had invaded her when he'd mentioned Francis's name evaporated as quickly as it had come. 'A long, funny letter'; 'a postcard'. They were sitting at each end of the sofa and he'd taken out a small cigar and matches. 'Floy put me on to these,' he said. 'Much better for you than cigarettes . . . Mustn't stay up too late,' he said, once his cigar was lit. 'I've got to catch the early train in the morning, so I suppose I'd better pack my clothes tonight.'

It was obviously up to her. 'Please tell me,' she said, 'about Percy. Please.'

'I'm in love with her. I've meant to tell you—'

'I've known for ages—'

' – but I haven't been sure enough, you see, not about my love for her but about how she feels. I did ask her to marry me, but she said she didn't love me enough, and then I thought if I could be with her more she'd get to know me. And I think that's happening.' He was silent for a moment, and she watched him clasping and unclasping his hands, a familiar gesture when he was moved.

'She's begun to confide in me, a little. Told me she didn't think she'd ever been in love, or thought so once and came a cropper. She says she's over it, but she's very young, and I think it's left its mark.'

'What does Floy think?'

'Well, she says, quite rightly, that it's up to us, Percy and me – not in the least her business. But if she was against it, she'd have said something discouraging. I think she's on my side, actually.' He fell silent again. Then, in a voice she could barely hear, he said, 'I never thought anything like this could happen to me again. She is so – lovely, so completely the person I want to spend my life with. It seems such a chance, a miracle to have met her.' He was looking at her now, his eyes so full of apprehension and joy she could hardly bear it.

PERCY

She'd stopped writing letters or scanning advertisements for jobs. There just wasn't time to follow them up. Since Thomas had come to stay with them, going off to work every day with Floy, it was left to her to hunt for somewhere else and be at home when people wanted to – as the agents put it – view the house. Floy was keen they should find somewhere to buy, but it was increasingly clear they couldn't afford a place with a good garden unless it was further out. A lease, provided it wasn't too long, would be cheaper; she was advised something between thirty and forty years. At least this produced a new batch of properties to see, and she spent at least three days a week searching. If she found somewhere she thought at all possible, she took Floy – and sometimes Thomas – to see it during the weekend. As a result they lost the one she'd thought most desirable: a ground-floor sprawling studio flat with a large unkempt garden facing west – just what Floy would have wanted. She had been promised first refusal, but the agents reneged as another buyer came along prepared to pay over the asking price.

This had upset Floy deeply. 'We should have nothing more to do with that agency,' she said, but Percy asserted they couldn't do that, they specialized in an area they liked, and, anyway, they were probably all the same. They had had a bit of a row, while Thomas had his bath and she and Floy were getting supper.

'One has to make a stand.'

'It won't make the slightest difference.'

'It does to me.'

'Are you saying that if someone offered more than we're asking here and someone else had already offered the asking price, you wouldn't take the higher one?'

'Certainly not. Dishonest.' She lifted a saucepan full of mashed potato out of the sink but dropped it suddenly. 'Oh, damn.'

When Percy got to her, she was massaging her right hand. 'It's my hands, Zephie. Sometimes they just won't work. I'll clear it up in a minute.'

'I'll do it. You've done quite enough for the day, too much, I expect. Darling, go and have a peaceful drink. Go on, I'll be back up in a minute.' Alone, she stood for a moment. Floy's sudden tears of pain had shocked her.

Supper was muted. Thomas had been carting new topsoil into the Hampstead garden all day and there had been trouble with the owners because he could only get from road to garden through the house; Floy had gone to deal with an old client whose roses had arrived unexpectedly and was determined they should be planted at once. The lost garden flat weighed upon Percy's mind. Lost, it now seemed twice as desirable. It might be weeks before anything as good turned up. Meanwhile, there was the uncertainty about their sale. Nothing was resolved, despite weeks of effort and the suspension, she felt, of ordinary life. And then there was Thomas.

She'd come to realize that without him Floy could not have taken on the new project. Floy really shouldn't be working, but Thomas had been a godsend. His approach with her was exactly right and she obviously trusted him, had even become very fond of him. She'd turned over to him all her looseleaf books of designs and plantings, with explanations of why she'd done such and such, and follow-up notes showing both the successes and the mistakes. She taught him, he protected her; it seemed an ideal partnership.

As soon as supper was over, Floy said she was for an early

night and left them. Percy had been peeling a pear and was about to offer him a piece, but the utter silence made her glance up to find him observing her steadily with such a blaze of love, of adoration, even, that she was speechless.

He'd come back from Melton that morning and she took refuge in it, asking about Mary and Hatty. He answered her naturally, but then another silence fell.

She told him about Floy dropping the saucepan in the sink. 'She always says the arthritis is only in her hands or her back but, really, it's everywhere. She ought to have a complete rest, to stop working. Don't you think?'

'She told me she has no plans to retire. She's determined not to stop. And she's mourning the loss of this garden. She needs another to take its place.'

'But you know what that means. It's too much for her.'

'Yes. But I'm here, Percy. I can stop her doing too much by doing it myself.'

'Yes, but for how long?' she cried, before she could stop herself.

'That depends on you.'

She felt trapped, angry. 'That's blackmail, isn't it?' She felt as furious with herself as with him. 'It's not on.'

'No, it isn't. I – I'm sorry.' He looked suddenly defeated. 'I didn't mean to make you angry.'

'What did you mean?'

'I meant that . . .' He thought for a moment, then began again. 'When I asked you to marry me you said you didn't love me enough. Of course I understand that. But I knew there was no chance of it happening unless we saw more of each other. So I came to London. And then, it seems to me, things fell out my way, if you like. Floy's taking me on, living here and seeing you every day might mean you'd get to trust me . . . like – even love me more. No, don't say anything, darling. Let me just say it all now. I've come to believe it's not possible for someone to feel as I do about you for nothing. That you can't in the end— Oh, I don't know.' Here he attempted a smile. 'Look, I only propose marriage every two or three months or so. You have as long a reprieve as you like now,' he ended.

At that moment, she really felt she loved him. Impulsively, she held out her hands and he kissed them.

'You're tired out,' he said. 'I know, because Mary gets little violet smudges under her eyes when she's done in. Go to bed. I'll clear up.'

Long after she heard him climb the stairs to the attic bedroom where he slept, she lay awake. All these weeks she'd been trying to keep a kind of balance between friendly familiarity and the fear that she was giving him false hope. In one sense, his outburst had cleared the air, but in another not at all. She didn't feel like she had the first time he'd proposed. She felt not only more tender of his feelings but also more uncertain of her own. She *did* like him and, in any other circumstance, she would have admitted she loved him, but her love was so poor a thing compared with his. It was as if he'd laid a great golden mantle upon her that weighed so heavily she felt very small. She felt unworthy, not up to it. She couldn't fault him: he was tender and honest. His sensitivity belied his rather worn, outdoor façade. She had noticed his protective kindness towards Floy and been moved by it many times. And she knew he wouldn't attempt to separate her from Floy. She imagined the three of them together and, of course, Hatty too – but it faded; she couldn't think where this would happen. In London? At Home Farm? Or somewhere else?

It occurred to her to wonder why was she thinking about it at all, and then she found she was too tired to think about anything.

JACK

Once he'd come to the decision, it seemed extraordinary he hadn't come to it before. But then, he thought, taking time over it showed it was serious. It had grown naturally out of a situation he'd found increasingly agreeable – and right. This time he surely wouldn't fail. His decision was well considered, the odds far more on his side. He could offer everything with the certainty that, if it was accepted, it would be with both gratitude and integrity. The more he thought about it, the less he could imagine it wouldn't happen. He did think of asking Amelia, to test the idea out on her, not just what she thought of *her* but perhaps for advice on the best way of going about it. But he decided against this, wanted to do it his way and on his own. He wouldn't say things he didn't mean, wouldn't exaggerate or pretend what he did not feel. He would put it plainly, be honest at all costs, but he'd list the – he felt formidable – collection of positives. And he did feel *real* affection . . . and respect, and a kind of comfortable ease that was entirely new to him. No more blondes with breasts. He'd been green then. He knew now that money, though useful and he wouldn't be without it, was by no means the answer to a good life.

There were certain rituals he couldn't dismiss. He went to London, walked slowly down Bond Street looking in windows at the trays of rings on display. Before, he had thought a large ruby or emerald set in diamonds was the thing – it had been Linda's choice. Now that didn't seem right. He wanted something less obvious but didn't know what.

Inside the shop they had many more rings of every description, but another customer was having a necklace shortened, sitting in a chair, holding a mirror while an assistant adjusted it round her neck. It was made of large, multi-coloured stones that looked like glass to him. She saw him looking, and said, 'They're glass – foiled glass. There was a lot of it in the eighteenth century.' On impulse he told her he was looking for a ring, but had no idea how to go about it and she offered to help. He left the shop with a little box containing an antique ring, a cinnamon diamond set in a rectangle of small plain diamonds, *circa* 1740, they said, and the necklace lady said it was what she would have chosen. He drove home assured that he'd made a successful and discriminating choice.

When he was nearing home, he decided he didn't want to get there just yet so he drove into town to buy some flowers. There could never be too many – something else to buy and use up some of the hours until the evening he had planned.

But on the hill, about half a mile outside Melton, he came upon – nearly ran into – a battered car that had clearly broken down in the middle of the road. A small child strapped in a pushchair on the verge was smearing its face with a chocolate bar, and an older man seemed to be attempting to push the car backwards into the side of the road. The man looked up when Jack got out of his car, and he recognized Richard Connaught.

'Oh – Curtis. Just let me get the handbrake.' He stuck his head into the car and heaved. 'Not that it seems prepared to move an inch. I wonder if you could help me push it somehow into the side of the road – dangerous where it is. Have to move it backwards because at least it's downhill.'

'If you release the handbrake and cope with the steering, I'll push from the back.'

Their combined efforts produced the necessary result and the car settled rather drunkenly half in a ditch. The Admiral took a large grey handkerchief out of his tweed pocket and wiped his face. 'Mission accomplished. I couldn't have done that without your help.'

'Can I give you a lift?'

'It would certainly be most kind. The thing is, you see, I was in a bit of a quandary – got my granddaughter with me and I can't abandon her to get help. Anyway, I'm afraid it's a garage job.'

'Shall I take you both home and then you can ring your garage?'

He seemed doubtful. 'The thing is I was on my way to the Yoxfords' place to pick up my daughter, who seems to have got stranded there. Then Letty wanted me to do some shopping, so now I'm late.'

'Don't worry, I'll take you to pick her up and then home.'

'That's really decent of you. I can't tell you how grateful I am. I've had trouble with this hill before, but this is a new car, well, not new, exactly, but new old, if you see what I mean. The garage swore it was a real bargain.'

Only the old boy would have believed that, Jack thought, as he moved the shopping bags into his boot while the Admiral went to retrieve the child, who was now chewing the Mars bar wrapper.

'If you don't mind, it's probably best to put the baby straight into the back and the chair in the boot, if it'll go.' He'd attempted, with the grey handkerchief, to clean up some of the chocolate, but his efforts just dispersed it further and were strongly objected to. 'She'll pipe down when we get moving.'

This turned out to be true. The drive to Easton Park wasn't a long one, but by the end of it Jack found himself wondering what on earth it must be like to be Richard Connaught, something he'd never considered about anyone he'd ever met before. His questions became quite reckless in an effort to find some lightness, some interest indulged, and some pleasure in the old man's life. He knew his wife was an invalid already. He liked golf, but the club subscription ruled it out. He used to love sailing, but that was a no-go area. He spoke of expenses in a way that sounded as though he never stopped paying them. Rosalie, his daughter – whom he'd brought to dinner with Jack, did he remember? – had been through a difficult divorce. Yes, she was their only child; his son had been killed in Cyprus. There was a lingering silence after this. The Admiral said he'd been thinking of motoring down to the coast somewhere for a week. His wife seemed to benefit from a spot of sea air, but he really wondered if the car was up to it. Before Jack could reply, they'd reached the entrance to the drive of Easton Park, and there was the girl, sitting on the ground hugging her knees, her face concealed by long strands of golden hair.

She looked up when the car stopped. 'I thought you'd never come.'

Her father told her about the breakdown and said how kind it was of Jack to rescue them, and mentioned the dinner they'd been to.

'Oh, yes. I remember you,' she said, as though this was something of a feat.

She climbed into the back of the car with the child. 'Lulu,' she cried, as if she'd just discovered something. Jack turned the car, saying, as they set off, that he would need directions to get them to their home.

Not much was said on the journey. The Admiral asked him if he knew much about lawnmowers; the one he'd picked up in a sale was astonishingly difficult to start, and he didn't know anything about them. The girl was silent, but once, when he looked in his mirror, he saw tears falling down her face, and when she met his eye, she put a finger to her lips for him to stay quiet and he did.

The cottage squatted behind a high yew hedge, in the middle of which was a rickety gate. When he helped her with the pushchair, she'd stopped crying. 'Thanks for the lift,' she said, kicked the gate open and disappeared up the path. She was wearing very faded, very tight jeans, he noticed.

He helped with the shopping, but the Admiral insisted on carrying it all himself. Having loaded himself up, he put it all down again while he thanked Jack once more for his decency. 'I'd like to ask you in,' he said untruthfully, 'but perhaps another day.'

'Phew.' This unexpected encounter had shaken him up rather – he didn't know what to make of it, but he felt uncomfortable in some indefinable way. It wasn't as if the old boy had been whingeing – he had said everything apologetically, almost as if it was all his own fault. He obviously couldn't afford a decent car or lawnmower and that was a dank little place he now lived in – an invalid wife and the daughter, Rosalie . . . Why was she crying and why didn't she want her father to know?

He'd learned to weed out the con-men from the straight ones in business because getting that sort of thing wrong could be expensive, but he'd never applied this acumen outside work. There hadn't been much point, but now, as he was embarking on an entirely new life, he could see it might constantly be needed. Marriage would mean children, a family and friends, a full house, like a good hand in poker. The excitement, and also the faint, but surely very faint, element of risk had made him unexpectedly aware of other people – a sensation he was enjoying. He would soon become like Amelia and Wystan. He'd be joining the club.

MARY

Ever since Thomas's visit she'd been trying to think calmly of the implications, and though she told herself again and again it was by no means certain, she always concluded that Percy and Thomas would marry, and if – when – it happened, she would have to leave the farm and start a new life. And Francis would also leave and the grotty little flat he'd dreamed up would become a reality. She would linger at this point – the flat wouldn't really be grotty. She'd go back to work and he'd have a studio in which to paint. They'd be free to explore the delights of London, go to concerts, plays, films and, of course, exhibitions. She'd be earning a proper salary again and he would get commissions, have a show and come altogether into his own as a painter, with her support and encouragement. They'd have friends, holidays together – she hadn't been abroad for more years than she could remember. At the centre of it all they would have each other, and then at last Francis would, Francis might understand – everything.

But none of this, she knew, was certain, until Thomas's situation was resolved.

She thought a good deal about Hatty, also, and how she could be eased very gently into this change. She felt she could trust Percy here, and Hatty could come and stay with her and Francis in London and they would return regularly for weekends. For the rest, she had her best friend and, hopefully, her own pony, and there would presumably be siblings and a father who was demonstrably happy. Her going, she thought, might actually be easier for Hatty than it would be for her.

Whenever she was alone, she thought these things through, but with teaching, her work for Jack, now two mornings a week, the nursery and Hatty's crowded schedule of school, her riding, ferrying her to and from Agnes's house, there never seemed enough time to resolve them.

She'd seen Hatty off to school and was making beefburgers for her and Agnes when the post arrived: one letter she could see at once was from Francis – a real letter, not a postcard. 'Francis.' She heard herself say his name aloud. She slit open the envelope, spread out the sheets of pale blue paper on the kitchen table and sat down to read.

She read it all very fast and then a second time, more slowly. The first page was about his life there, descriptions of the place and the people and an account of his routine, all light amusing stuff. She turned the paper over:

– I realize it's been good to get right away for a bit. It's made me think, for the first time in years, what on earth have I been doing with my life? The answer I came up with, bugger-all. Drifting, just doing what came to hand without any plan, is how it now seems to me. I've not worked seriously at anything, notably painting, but if I'm to call myself a painter that is what I should at least try to do.

So I've decided, Mary dear, that it's time I leave Home Farm, which, thanks to you, has been such a secure refuge, and strike out on my own. I've just enough money left from the sale of Celia's flat for rent and the rest. I don't expect to earn my living from painting for some time, at least, but will take odd jobs to tide me over. If, at the end of five years, I still can't make out as an artist, then I'll just have to think of something else, but at least I'll know I've tried. I do hope you understand all this. I've always been rotten at decisions and this is perhaps the most serious attempt at one I've ever made in my life. I wanted to tell you first and hope you'll be able to explain it to Thomas. Of course I will always come back and see you all. You have been such a marvellous support to all of us – a mother to Hatty, an incomparable sister to Thomas, and to me a sister as well as a friend. Away from you now, I can see all this so clearly, how you picked up the wreckage left by Celia's death and made all well. Apart from anything else, I wanted to tell you that.

I expect to be back at the end of this month and shall spend a couple of days in London. My friend Gerry says I can kip in his flat. He'll be away. Then I'll come down to collect my stuff.

All love,
Francis

Paralysed, unable to think, she picked up the envelope to return the letter to it and a small piece of thyme fell out, the leaves dry, falling off the stalk. She picked it up and held it to her face. It smelled more strongly of thyme than any she grew.

He was going. What she had most dreaded was happening. And throughout it he'd said 'I'. She wasn't part of his plan.

Then it hit her. Of course he knew nothing about Thomas and Percy. Of course he'd assume she had to stay. Naturally he'd assume that. She pulled the letter out again and read the second page a third time. There was something of a farewell about it, a signing-off, that perturbed her, as if she'd been given a reference for a new job: 'an incomparable sister . . . and a friend'. Somehow, the gratitude tainted the obvious affection: there was something threadbare about it that frightened her. She was so used to suppressing her most private feelings, had always been afraid, unable to give words to them; they had lain, lay now, like a foreign language or a code imprisoned in her heart that escaped only in shameful tears or hesitant gestures. She'd got drunk and found herself in his bed. She'd cared so much when he'd suggested she go to be Reggie's housekeeper. The closest she'd ever got to any of it was clichés: 'You're seven years older, not much of a catch, are you?' But he was definitely coming back –

to get his things. When he knew about Thomas, he'd know she couldn't remain, know she couldn't stay on after they'd married.

She was refolding the letter when the phone rang. It was Jack, asking her to supper. She hesitated and he said he'd got oysters, please come. A distraction she accepted.

★

Some hours later she stood at the kitchen door, watching Jack turn his large car in the yard, momentarily dazzled in the headlights, guessing he was waving and waving back, and followed the red tail lights as they receded to the bend in the lane and were no longer to be seen.

The kitchen was tidy, the house quiet. Mrs Peabody had said goodnight and gone home. The girls hadn't only cleared up, they'd gone to bed – or, at least, they weren't about. That was a relief, but still she didn't feel absolutely safe until she reached her bedroom and had shut the door.

There had been champagne and oysters, and the table was decorated with an enormous elaborate arrangement of flowers and silver candelabra. The room was dusky beyond their light except for the rosy glow from the fireplace. It must be a special occasion, she'd thought, and asked if it was his birthday. He'd laughed – a nervous sound – and said, no, it wasn't.

It wasn't until Juan had brought in the main course – roast quail with all the trimmings – and had poured their first glass of red wine that they were alone. He said he had something he particularly wanted to ask and should he do it now or wait until they'd finished dinner? And she'd said, why not now? She'd looked up from dissecting her bird as she said this, without the slightest curiosity, but when she found him staring at her with extreme and, for him, remarkable anxiety, she did feel that something unexpected was going to happen – but not, most certainly *not*, that he was going to propose marriage. Nobody had ever asked her to marry them before and she sat stunned while he presented his reasons. 'Please,' he'd said, 'let me explain what I feel before you say anything.'

He'd begun by saying how the more time he'd spent with her the more he'd wanted to spend. He'd come, in these last weeks, to admire her more and more. He'd never met anyone with whom he'd felt more at ease, and for whom at the same time he felt so much affection and respect. He didn't, he added – and this was when she felt the most fondness for him – know much about love, but he thought it probably grew out of the feelings he knew he had for her. He wanted to look after her, to give her the life he felt she deserved. He'd worked extremely hard to get where he now was, but he'd come to see it was pointless without a partner, a wife, a family. He looked forward to bringing up children whose childhood would be so much happier than his own had been. He'd seen her with Harriet, so he knew how good she'd be at that. And if she wanted Harriet to live with them he'd be happy – in fact, he honestly wanted her to have everything. 'This house was your home once,' he ended. 'It seems so right you should return to it as its mistress.'

There was a moment's silence. 'And now you're going to tell me you don't love me enough,' he said, before she could.

'Oh, Jack. Yes, I was going to say that.'

'If you like me enough I think we could find a way – both of us. I've surprised you.'

'Yes – yes, you have.'

'What I ask of you, *all* I ask of you, is that you'll think about this, you won't simply dismiss it. Please, please, don't do that. You can have all the time you need to decide – only don't decide now.'

She said she'd think about it. To refuse seemed both unkind and belittling.

A silence followed, during which they both attacked the, by now, distinctly cool little birds and she sensed that he, like she, was desperately casting around for something neutral they could talk about. She drank some wine to embolden her, but before she could ask how things were going at the lodge, he said, 'I'm so sorry. I should have waited, and now I've spoiled your dinner.'

'It has become a rather different sort of dinner.'

'Shall we do what we usually do?'

'Usually do?'

'I usually ask your advice about things and you usually produce all the right answers.'

'Do I?'

'Of course you do. I keep a notebook which has an "Ask Mary" page. It's never empty.'

She looked to see if he was laughing at her, but he wasn't. He was simply trying to make things easy between them and she felt a rush of gratitude towards him for that. 'So? What's on the list tonight?'

'Well. I've been thinking this establishment needs a dog – perhaps several. Only what kind? I don't know the first thing about them, only that I don't like the small yappy types.'

'I don't know a lot about dogs either. My father had Labradors here because they were useful for shooting. They were very good-tempered, but awfully greedy – would eat anything, except birds. They were trained to bring them back after they'd been shot.'

'Did you like them?'

'I didn't get to know them much. They had kennels in the stables. They weren't house dogs – they could be, of course.'

She picked up a quail leg to eat with her fingers, and after a moment he copied her. 'I'm so glad you did that,' he said. 'I wasn't sure if it was the done thing.'

'It depends, really,' she said, clinging to the subject, 'what you want a dog for. Dogs can be very good faithful companions.'

'I think I might want one of those.'

And so the evening limped on. Soon after they'd finished dinner, she said she'd like to go home, had to be up early in the morning to get Hatty and her friend off to school, and he said, of course, he'd take her back at once. When they reached the farm, he turned to her and said, 'I did get a small present for you, but I don't suppose you'll accept it,' and took a box out of his pocket, snapped it open to reveal a glittering ring, 'but I do wish you would. It needn't mean anything specific, only that I'd like you to have it.'

She looked from the ring to his urgent, persuasive face and was torn between not giving him false hope and not hurting his feelings. 'I think you should keep it for now,' she said, as gently as she could manage. 'But thank you.'

He put it away with such direct resignation, that she was touched, again, to warmth for him.

'You will think, won't you?'

'Yes. I promise I will.'

And then she'd escaped.

But now, lying in her bed in the dark, confusion overwhelmed her. Marriage meant commitment, something she recognized her nature craved, life with one person, her own children, babies. A memory came to her of visiting Celia in hospital with the day-old Hatty in her arms, of Celia's face as she gazed at her baby, and a wave of absolute longing to be like her, to bear a child that was hers had overcome her and congealed to quickly suppressed envy. That feeling still recurred in dreams, never quite the same, never resolved, occasionally with an exquisite sense of fulfilment, more often with the sharp desolation of loss. She loved Celia's daughter and had come to feel she was indeed her mother, but now she knew that the craving for her own children had never been vanquished. She was thirty-five – her years for babies were running out.

And she'd been touched by Jack, by the absence of either arrogance or pretence on his part that made everything he said more credible. He hadn't tried to touch her, and he hadn't used the word 'love'. He had certainly provoked her affection. It crossed her mind how extraordinary it would be to have some freedom in her life after all these years tied down with money worries. Marriage to Jack wouldn't only bring children of her own, but the ease, the intense comfort of knowing she came first in another person's life – an idea so seductive it was intoxicating.

If Thomas married Percy, she would naturally, properly, be usurped. And as for love— But she did love. For years she'd concealed this admission with harmless names or phrases: fondness, companionship, a member of the family, almost another brother. It had seemed to her that as long as she kept it secret, not only from the others but most of all from herself, there was a hope, the faintest hope, it would become reality. It was as if she'd been moving through an endless desert with a distant oasis she'd insisted was a mirage. Admitting now that she loved Francis was a shock, but of course it wasn't really. She had loved him for years. Fear of rejection and a kind of shabby pride had induced her to bury it so deep that it was now a revelation.

She knew now she loved him totally unconditionally. She didn't have to think about or weigh up the advantages of being with him. The 'grotty little flat' would do perfectly for her. If they were together, she would always have the chance he might come to love her, a possibility that made her feel faint.

Just before she slept, she realized that if she had just told Jack she loved someone else, everything would have been far simpler. She wouldn't now be lying in the dark beset by the confusion poor Charlotte Lucas must have had: her own establishment with a dull and foolish man or the doom of spinsterhood and poverty.

PERCY

The day had begun with the promise of an Indian summer – heavy dew, a cloudless sky and pale yellow sunlight that lit up but barely warmed the still air. Floy said they must make the most of it. The shrubs and climbers ordered were due to be delivered in Hampstead, so she and Thomas left the house before eight. They had trouble starting the van, and then with Marvell, who wanted to go too, but Percy scooped him up and held him safely while they puttered away. He leaped from her arms and made for the breakfast table where he found some toast in the rack, which it was just worth his while to knock over. When she came back with a tray, he'd found the milk jug and had thrust his paw into it, but the milk had been warm with a skin on it that was now cluttering his face in what he clearly felt was a most distasteful manner. She put some milk into a saucer for him, but it was ignored. Her next job was to get the house into the state of unnatural tidiness urged upon her by the estate agents.

She planned to ring them to find out if anyone was coming to see the house today, before trekking up to Dartmouth Park Hill to see a garden flat. But, promptly at nine, they rang her. The Andersons had made an offer, five hundred pounds below the asking price, but they had the cash – there was no chain – and she was strongly advised to accept. 'Only one stipulation, Miss Plover.' Mr Catchpole's voice implied he hardly thought it was one. 'They would like to complete as soon as possible, and as we have the searches, I told them it should be possible in six weeks. In view of the fact this is the only offer we've had, after a number of viewings, I really feel we should accept and go ahead. A bird in the hand, you know.' She said she'd have to consult her aunt, who was out for the day. Mr Catchpole said he'd call again that evening. 'Must strike while the iron's hot. If I called about seven, would that suit?'

She said it would. Well, it was what they'd wanted, what they'd been after for weeks now, but she felt neither exhilaration nor relief. She thought of those six weeks and panicked. How on earth were they going to find somewhere to move into in six weeks? Even if the one she was to see that morning was suitable, buying the lease was bound to take longer. Everything in the house would have to be packed and stored. And they were bound to be moving somewhere smaller, so a great deal had to go. She'd taken the breakfast tray down to the kitchen and now poured the dregs of the coffee into her cup. She hadn't really thought what clearing up the house would entail, but looking round this one room she began to realize at least some of what lay ahead. One long wall was lined with a large dresser that had drawers and deep cupboards. Apart from the Rayburn and the large porcelain sink below the one barred window, every scrap of wall space was filled with shelves and hooks and a large, shallow, glass-fronted cupboard designed for glasses. She'd done some tidying for viewers, just bundling stuff into the already pretty full drawers and cupboards.

Floy – and it didn't apply only to the kitchen – found it wasteful to throw things away as they might easily be needed again. There were collections of small corroded screws wrapped in weak, ancient newspaper, cracked salad servers, huge saucepan lids, whose pans had long since gone, sieves whose wire had collapsed, and a shoebox containing some parts of an old-fashioned mincer. One cupboard, when she opened it, simply spewed out a collection of empty washed jam jars, minus their lids.

She spent the morning sorting the useless stuff, cramming it into old shopping bags and making a pile of things she thought should go, but Floy might want to keep, on the kitchen table. Then she realized she'd be late for her appointment at Dartmouth Park Hill unless she took a cab.

It was a garden maisonette with five rooms, a forty-year lease just over their price. The garden, though it faced west, was full of the lime and sycamore trees she knew Floy abominated, but otherwise it fulfilled their list of necessities. It was possible, but in no way thrilling. Nothing will be after this, she thought, as she trudged back to Maida Vale with the shopping for dinner.

By the time she'd tidied the kitchen enough to cook in it and given Marvell his supper, she felt a little weak and faint and realized she hadn't eaten since breakfast. She'd just made a cup of instant coffee and got a Ryvita with a rather weary piece of Camembert when the phone rang. It was Thomas.

'Is Floy there by any chance? No, I didn't suppose she would be. I can't get hold of her at Hampstead. The van's broken down. I mean seriously – it's kaput. It happened in the middle of nowhere, so it's taken ages to get a garage to tow it in.'

She asked if he was coming back by train and he said, no, he couldn't because of the plants. 'The garage thinks they can get me a van to hire some time tomorrow. I did tell Floy not to wait for me in Hampstead after six in case I got held up. Tell her I'm sorry about the van. The man here says he's amazed it's lasted as long as it has. How are you, Percy, are you all right?'

She was fine, she said. Somehow she didn't want to tell him about the house. She felt obscurely irritated with him, which was unfair: the breakdown was clearly not his fault. After she'd rung off, she realized she hadn't said a word about how boring and disagreeable a time he must be having.

Mr Catchpole rang on the dot of seven and Floy still wasn't home. She suggested he ring again in half an hour. By now, her coffee was lukewarm and Marvell had got hold of the

Camembert, which he had successfully separated from the Ryvita and was eating with the professional speed of an experienced thief. He was addicted to smelly cheeses although they didn't agree with him. She tried to catch him before he threw up in the house, but she failed and he was copiously sick on the stairs. By the time she'd dumped him outside on the conservatory steps and cleaned up the mess, the phone rang again, and she took it in the hall just as she could see Floy's silhouette through the stained glass of the front door.

'Hold on, Mr Strapp, my aunt has just arrived. Let me just explain to her . . .' She turned to Floy.

'We've had an offer – five hundred pounds below what we're asking, but we have to agree to it now or let it go.'

Floy shifted her heavy canvas bag from her shoulder and dumped it on the ground. 'What – now? This minute?'

'I'm afraid so. I thought you'd be back much earlier and the deadline was seven.'

'How extraordinary. Do you think we should accept?'

'I think we should. I'm sorry. I thought there'd be more time to talk about it.'

'Thomas didn't turn up. I had to come back on three buses.'

'The van broke down. I'll tell you in a minute. We have to clinch with Mr Catchpole first.'

'Why haven't you done it, then?'

'I thought I should ask you.'

'You're not asking me anything. You're telling me.'

'I'm not. I'm asking you.'

'Oh, just tell him yes, then.' It was a retort, rather than capitulation. Trying to make it my fault, Percy thought, but didn't say so, as she dealt with Mr Catchpole.

Floy, who had divested herself of her much-worn windcheater, had wandered off to the conservatory and now returned with Marvell in her arms. 'His cat-flap was jammed.'

'I know. I locked him out. He was sick on the stairs.'

'That's not like him.'

'It's exactly like him when he gets hold of cheese.'

'Well, you know not to leave it around.'

'I didn't. I was going to eat it when Thomas rang. I'd better get on with supper or we'll never have any. Marvell's had his, by the way.'

But Floy followed her downstairs to the kitchen, saying if he'd been sick, he'd want more supper, and then she tumbled over the bulging bags of rubbish. 'Good Lord, what on earth have you been doing?'

'Clearing out things we don't want to take with us. The stuff on the table is for you to sort out.'

'Oh, Percy. I really don't feel up to doing that now.'

Then she explained that the condition of sale was they had to be out of the house in six weeks, adding that she'd seen a place she thought might do. She got the particulars out of her bag and put them on the table. Floy had been hunting for Marvell's food in the fridge and had put a haunch of rabbit into a saucepan with some water. 'Poor treasure – it should have been cooked for you this morning.'

'There was some cooked and he's eaten it, presumably thrown it up with the cheese. He could have a tin.'

'Not after he's been sick. It won't agree with him. Six weeks. We really should have found somewhere before we agreed to leave here.'

'I've found two places, but we don't have to settle for either of them. We could rent somewhere and go on looking.'

'Then we'd have all the bother and expense of storing our stuff.' And she added, 'A rented garden isn't the slightest use to me.'

Percy didn't say she'd not thought of them renting anywhere with a garden.

'And, anyway, renting is simply money down the drain.'

Percy was chopping onions, which helped diffuse the

sickeningly sweet smell of the cooking rabbit. 'Please look at the stuff about the maisonette.'

Floy got her spectacles out of the case slung round her neck and sat down. There was a silence while Percy put some oil in a pan to heat for the onions.

'And what's all this about the van?'

'Thomas said it was wrecked, finished, kaput, he said.'

'What? Did he have an accident?'

'No. It just broke down. And the garage said it can't be repaired.'

'I've had it for nearly ten years and it's been perfectly all right.'

'Exactly. It's just too old. It was bound to happen eventually.'

Floy said, 'Everything is bound to happen eventually.' She pushed aside the papers and added, 'We really should have settled on somewhere before we agreed to sell this.'

Here we go again, she thought. It had been a long day and she was tired of the whole house thing, of looking at places, of placating people, of trying to get Floy to make up her mind, of the horribly unusual atmosphere of recrimination. She had been quite looking forward to losing her temper, to feeling less responsible for everything, but she thought she'd have one more go. 'We have found two possible places. I just need you to say which you like.'

'Darling, please stop talking to me as if I'm wonderful considering I've got no arms or legs.'

'OK. You're not wonderful. I've spent weeks and weeks trying to please you, to find somewhere you'd like, and all you do is dither and criticize. On top of that I've also been on the receiving end of all the awful people who come here making inane remarks about only one bathroom or the garden being labour-intensive or the wallpaper being old-fashioned or the house being on a main road. I can't get the people who are buying it to agree to take possession any later. Mr Catchpole said we should be glad they want it, because it's such a short lease. I'm sick of being blamed for everything.' By now she'd run out of breath and temper, but the air wasn't cleared and the atmosphere remained. 'Why on earth don't we just stay here?'

She watched Floy extract the last of her small cigars from its box and light it. Her hands were shaking. They looked at each other directly for the first time and, catching sight of her aunt's distress, her anger dissolved. 'I just don't know what you want,' she said, with some gentleness, because it was true.

'We can't stay here, darling. That's the one thing I do know. But I really had no idea how difficult it would be to find somewhere even remotely similar to this garden and house. I suppose most people who haven't much money find that and then adjust to it. And I've put it all on you, which I can see is hardly fair. You know we talked about a place with a decent garden, enough room for you to have some privacy, a life of your own, and not so far out that you'd have to travel miles every day for whatever job you find – all that? Well, then I thought perhaps a lot of that may not matter any more. I thought perhaps you and Thomas—'

'No,' she said. 'No. I'm just glad he's helping you.'

After a short silence Floy said, 'If you're sure of that, perhaps you should tell him.'

'I should. I will. But at least now you can make a decision. I don't want a flat of my own. I want to go on living with you.'

This caused a fleeting smile that came and went so fast it just highlighted the anxiety and distress, which, Percy realized now, during the last weeks she'd written off as mere – or pure – fatigue.

When Floy put out her cigar she said, 'I think another reason, possibly the only real reason, I've been so unhelpful is that the whole thing seems utterly unreal to me. I've always felt I owned this house outright and, above all, the piece of earth that goes with it. I can't even imagine myself living anywhere else. When

I came in tonight and you told me it's actually sold and we have to leave so soon, well, reality struck. Always frightening if one's been avoiding it, as I'm afraid I've done. I'm so sorry, Zephie.'

The air was clear. 'I was crosser than you.'

'Let's not have a competition. Give me the rabbit, darling, and I'll bone it. Where's he gone, by the way? It's not like him to leave when there's rabbit about.'

'If you undid the cat-flap, I expect he's in the garden, chasing moths.'

'I was only cross about the flap because of that horrible marmalade tom that terrorizes him. The flap is his means of escape.'

She put the mashed potato, onions and corned beef together, and Floy dealt with the rabbit, using a knife and fork because it was so hot, and they talked about Thomas hiring a van for the plants and Floy going to see the garden maisonette and the sycamore trees and the idiocy of tree-preservation orders that took no account of the size of garden or the kind of tree or, indeed, the kind of owner. She suggested a glass of wine and supper upstairs, but Floy wanted to go for her evening prowl in the garden first before it got too dark. 'I shan't be long.'

'It's very nearly dark now.' She really didn't want her aunt to leave: she wanted her to stay in the kitchen so they could go on with their desultory conversation. Because of Thomas, she realized then, they'd had very little time on their own recently; tensions had built up. She wanted to make the most of it now, but it seemed too absurd to say so. Floy always went into her garden when she came in from work, and the rapidly fading light meant she wouldn't be long. 'Put your jacket on,' she called, but Floy was already clomping down the conservatory stairs and probably didn't hear her.

The phone rang twice as she carried the supper trays from the kitchen to the conservatory, but she was halfway up the stairs each time, and when she'd dumped the tray and got to the phone, whoever it was had rung off. Wrong number, she thought, or maybe Thomas ringing from a callbox.

So Floy had thought she might go off with him. How strange. When she'd said that, Percy's own uncertainty had suddenly vanished. He wanted marriage, total commitment, and she'd learned in these weeks not to doubt the strength and sincerity of his love – but she couldn't return it. She had become increasingly fond of him, and was grateful for the way he'd worked with and looked after Floy – had even almost loved him for that – but her 'almost love' was as nothing to the depth and weight of his feelings. If I married him, I could never keep it up, she thought. I'd end up lying and resent having to, and however much I pretended, he would know. And if he became wretched, as a result, I'd despise him; if he became angry and indifferent I'd hate him. Perhaps I'm just no good at loving people – at serious, deep love. But then she thought of Floy – her darling Pirate Aunt – pottering about on the piece of earth she loved and she knew, with a blessed, grateful certainty, this wasn't true at all.

It was no longer dusk outside. When she lit a lamp in the conservatory, the sky had turned from grey to charcoal. She opened the door to the garden and called that supper was ready. She heard no answer and took the torch that always lay on the sill beside the door and went down the iron stairs, calling again. The torch needed a new battery and emitted a weak, buttery circle of light that did no more than highlight the gathering dark. By the time she reached the yew arch and the lions, she'd stopped calling. Something had happened: Floy must have fallen, hit her head, was unconscious somewhere, unable to answer. She started to run past the roses and reached the stone coping round the pond. There, beyond the strip of black water, was the bench and her aunt in front of it.

Floy was on her knees, her left hand hooked round the armrest of the bench, her head caught between the angle of the armrest and its back and her face hidden, until Percy lifted and turned it. Her eyes were open. She looked surprised. She was dead.

Percy saw this and would not believe it – felt fruitlessly for a pulse in her wrist, in her heart, cradled her, beseeching her to come back, to wake up, showering her with a torrent of endearments and tears until eventually her incredulity froze and she was left with no choice. Shock made her passive. She did not know how long she sat there with her aunt in her arms. She remembered closing Floy's eyes and wiping the small rusty stain of blood from the side of her head where she must have hit it on the iron of the bench. But gradually she became aware that she was shivering with cold and she had to move, and move Floy if possible. She got stiffly to her feet and tried to lift her aunt, to carry her, but though Floy was small, her inert body was oddly heavy. She tried to lay her comfortably and went back to the house. The torch had finally given up and she stumbled up the staircase to the conservatory, to its mellow light and the cosy supper laid on the table. The sight of it stunned her afresh and she went into the sitting room. There were so many things she should do – she should call doctors or ambulances, but they would just cart Floy away. The only thing she knew for certain was that she wanted her aunt in the house, but she needed someone to carry her. Without Thomas she could think of no one and even if she managed to drag her up the garden, there was the staircase. There was no way she could manage that. I can't leave her cold and alone in the dark. I can't—

She realized she was trembling all over, felt so shaky she could hardly stand. She went into the hall to the cupboard of boots, jackets and Floy's gardening clothes, found her fisherman's jersey and, rolled up in one corner, Thomas's sleeping-bag. She took them to the conservatory and put the jersey on. Then, seeing the open bottle of wine, she slopped some into a glass and drank it. The torch lay on the table, and she had to go back to the tool drawer in the hall in search of new batteries. The wine steadied her, made it easier to quell the tears intermittently scorching her eyes and blurring everything. She was determined to do what next had to be done. Armed with the sleeping-bag, a seat cushion and the torch, she went back into the garden.

At the bench, she shone the torch on her aunt's pale, composed face and felt, at first, that she hadn't the heart to disturb her. She knelt beside her: one or two leaves from the fruit trees had dropped on to her hair and she seemed mysteriously younger, more vulnerable. To move her, to shift her at all, seemed a gross invasion. But it had to be done. She stroked the cold face – damp now from the dew – plucked the leaves from her hair and kissed her, but it was like embracing stone. Absence was all there was, an ache that howled and burned in her heart.

She began on her task trying to be gentle, to be delicate, but it was no good: she had to push, heave and shove with what became an agonized impatience – she wanted nothing more than to get it over, and eventually it was. Floy lay safely encased up to her neck, with the small pillow under her head. Then, pulling from the head end, torch in one hand, she managed to heave her off the bench and drag her in the sleeping-bag, backwards to the house, stopping every few yards. Her mind was besieged by a crowd of painful questions: how did she die? Was it a heart-attack? Could she have saved her if she'd found her sooner? Had she been secretly ill and said nothing? How could she have been so irritable, so horrible to her when she came in? Maybe the strain of that killed her.

Eventually, she reached the foot of the iron stairs, the light from indoors streaming into the night, but at least she could see them. In the garden, she'd thought this last part would be impossible, but somehow she must do it. She had to stiffen her resolve, tell herself not to feel, empty her mind and concentrate on bringing her aunt up each step.

She wanted to lay her on the sofa in the sitting room, but when she finally reached the conservatory her strength gave out.

She resettled the cushion under her aunt's head, picked some pieces of jasmine that climbed the wall outside the conservatory, undid the sleeping-bag and put them gently in Floy's stiffening fingers. 'That's all I can do,' she said aloud, to no one. She was shaking, parched; she drank water from the jug on the supper tray and wandered back to the sitting room, with a vague idea that she might perhaps manage to get Floy on to the sofa after all, but the sight of it reduced her to tears once more and, too exhausted to face the enormity of what had happened, she threw herself on to it and sank into oblivion.

*

She woke because a bell was ringing insistently and someone was knocking on the front door. Thomas, she thought, as she got up to answer it. She shrank from facing him, telling him. But it was daylight and everything had to be faced.

It wasn't Thomas. It was Francis.

'I tried to ring you several times last night, but either you were engaged or you didn't answer – Percy, what's wrong?'

'Oh, Francis – Francis.' She started to try to tell him, to tell him calmly, but could not get beyond the one awful fact before weeping overcame her. He said nothing, but she felt his arms round her and relief that he was there. They stayed like that until she was able to tell him more, though not very coherently.

'Shall I go and carry her in for you?'

'She's in – in the conservatory. I couldn't leave her out there in the dark all night. I knew I couldn't do that.'

She took him to Floy. 'I tried not to hurt her dragging her in. I tried to make her cosy.'

'Dearest Percy, you couldn't have done more.'

'But what shall I do now? I don't know what I'm supposed to do.'

'I'll help you. First thing, when did you last eat anything?'

She tried to think and realized it was breakfast yesterday, but she wasn't hungry.

He said he'd make some coffee, if she could show him where the kitchen was, but first they needed the phone number of Floy's doctor.

She followed him downstairs to the kitchen. He was so steady and clear about everything – the only person, she thought, whom she could bear to be with, to rely upon and to trust. Partly, she realized, this was because she knew that, when Celia died, he'd lost the person he loved most in the world too.

MARY

'Mary? It's Thomas.'

He was ringing from a callbox. He sounded very odd.

'I haven't got much change on me so I'll have to be quick.'

'What's happened?'

'Something awful. It's Floy. She—' They were cut off.

She put the receiver back and waited. He rang again.

'She died last night – very suddenly.'

'Oh, Thomas. Poor, poor Percy. Where are you?'

He said he was in a pub somewhere near Northampton. The van had broken down when he was collecting plants. He'd had to hire another for the plants and now he was taking it back to the garage so he could catch a train back to London.

'Is Percy all by herself? I should—'

'No need. I'm going back there as fast as I can.' There was a pause, and then he added, 'Francis is with her.'

'Francis?'

'Apparently he'd been ringing them – they were engaged for ages, and then there was no reply – so the next morning he went to the house. She couldn't ring me, you see, she didn't know where I was. We'll get cut off in a minute, I've no more change. Anyway, Francis will hold the fort until I get back.' There was a pause and then he added, 'At least I know what it feels like.' And they were cut off.

To hear someone you know has died suddenly is always to some degree a shock. Though she hadn't known her well, she had liked and admired Percy's aunt and could hardly imagine what poor Percy must be going through. If she was dealing with it all on her own, she would have called her to see if she wanted her to come to London, but she had Thomas – and, it seemed, Francis.

Francis was back – but he *had* said he was going to spend a few days in London before coming down. It was natural he should get in touch with the Plovers – natural and very fortunate for Percy, given Thomas wasn't there. How did Floy die? It felt almost vulgar to want to know, but it was the question that sprang irresistibly to mind. She wasn't very old, though she had that ageless appearance some older people have, as if she'd always been in her fifties, so it was possible she was much older. It hardly mattered. Now, she thought, Thomas will get his heart's desire. The symmetry of what they'd each lived through, each losing the person nearest to them, would surely bring them together. The thought of Thomas happy again, transformed once more by requited love, brought tears to her eyes. All her life she had wanted him to have what he most desired, long, even, before she knew at all what that might be.

She thought of Francis. Perhaps it was a good thing he was with Percy and Thomas. It would become clear to him and then surely he'd realize their marriage would free her – free them both to start a new life . . .

It was one of her days at home and she'd spent it top-coating the woodwork in Thomas's bedroom. Helping Jack get the lodge in order had made her see how shabby the farm had become. Nothing had been done to it decoratively since Celia's day, and she'd used these weeks when the house was comparatively empty to do as much of it as she could. She had started with the sitting room, partly to banish the memory of Reggie's stay, and then, cheered by Thomas's appreciation, she'd gone on to do Hatty's room with much clearing-out and acrimony; when she'd pointed out that surely thirty-two bears, monkeys and frogs were more soft toys than any one person could need, Hatty had replied coldly, 'They need me.' Now she was finishing the big room in which Thomas had continued to sleep after Celia died. It had been painted a pink that had discoloured to a faded peach. Once she wouldn't have dared to change it without consulting him, but now she felt free to do so. The room faced south, so she painted it the palest green with white windows and doors. All the bedrooms had coconut matting on the floors and there was no money to change that, but she planned to replace the faded cretonne curtains.

She'd just finished the windows, and was taking the brushes down to the kitchen to clean them, when the phone rang again. Francis, she thought, as she dumped the jam jar on the table and rushed to answer it.

'Is that Mary Musgrove? This is Richard Connaught. We met during the festival. The thing is, I, or rather my wife and I, are having a little sherry party this evening – got everything ready for it – but we've just discovered that, through some oversight, no one has been invited. It must sound idiotic, but I thought Letty was doing the inviting and she thought I was. So it's very short notice, I'm afraid, but I – we – should be so very pleased if you could come. I'm afraid it will be rather a small party due to the oversight, but Letty has taken so much trouble over the canapés I fear she'll be very disappointed if nobody comes to eat them.'

So she said of course she'd be delighted to come. 'All three of you, I hope. I don't know your brother, but Francis and I were on the festival committee together, so I thought—'

She explained that both of them were away.

'But you will come? Six o'clock. Our cottage is about a mile and a quarter outside Melton on the Wickstead road, at the bottom of the hill – so good of you to come at such short notice.'

Life goes on, she thought, sudden death and sherry parties.

She didn't in the least want to go, but she'd heard the desperation in Admiral Connaught's voice. It would have been heartless to refuse.

There was another phone call half an hour later that wasn't Francis either. It was Jack.

'That nice old boy Admiral Connaught has just rung to ask me to have sherry this evening. He seemed so desperate for me to come I said I would. I guess he's asked you, so I wondered if you'd like me to fetch you?'

She said yes, that would be fine. He was at such pains to make her feel at ease with him that she was anxious to seem so. Also, she had to admit, she felt warmed by his continued attention.

'There's some very bad news, I'm afraid,' and she told him about Floy.

'How awful. What on earth happened?'

She said she didn't know, only that it was very sudden and she was expecting to hear from Thomas when he got back to London.

'Will you let me know? I don't feel I can ring Percy somehow. It must have been the most terrible shock for her.'

She said of course she would and she'd felt the same about ringing.

'Let me know if there's anything I can do. She was the most remarkable person I've ever met, I think. Can't imagine her not being there. Here, I suppose I mean.'

The afternoon dragged by. She ate a tomato sandwich, made a stew – supper for her and Hatty – and bottled some of the plentiful Victoria plums. Still nothing from Francis. She reread his letter. She so wanted to speak to him, but felt she couldn't call Percy's number just now and she had no idea where he was staying. Surely by now Thomas must have got back. Maybe she was being too ridiculously melodramatic. Would Percy really throw herself, sobbing, into Thomas's arms for Francis to witness? She'd be in shock, after all. It occurred to her briefly then that, while she knew what Thomas felt for Percy, she had no idea how Percy felt. But no one, she thought, could be indifferent to Thomas. Francis had once told her, 'I'm one of life's onlookers.' Well, by now he must have seen quite a lot in London and he was, she knew, extremely sensitive to people's feelings. He may not have noticed hers, but that was because she *had* taken great trouble to hide them.

She decided she had to write a note to Percy. Francis had once told her that Floy had become her entire family – her parents were much like her and Thomas's – and the realization of what she must be feeling at such a loss, with no brother to share it, drove her to it. A letter might not comfort, but it could do no harm; at the very least it was an acknowledgement of her bereavement.

'Sorry I'm late. Why are you crying?'

'I'm not really crying, just a bit sad,' and she told Hatty about Floy.

Hatty came over to her at once and gave her hug. 'Poor her. And poor Percy. I'm not surprised you're crying a bit. You know that girl I told you about called Anna who had a garter snake? Well, it died in the holidays and the whole form decided to write her a condolence card. You get them at paper shops. I nearly cried writing my name and saying I was sorry, and I absolutely loathed that snake, so I quite understand. Floy was nice, wasn't she? She told me to call her Floy and that shows you. Could I have some tea before supper? I'll get it. Would you like a cup of tea? It's supposed to be good for sad people.' She was blundering about getting milk out of the fridge, putting the kettle on the stove and selecting mugs from the dresser. She'd grown a good deal in the last few months and wasn't at all used to her body.

'She wasn't Percy's mother, was she?'

'No, she was her aunt. But she was Percy's only real family.'

'Like you? With me, I mean.'

She nodded. She found herself unable to speak.

'But you're far, far younger than Floy. She was pretty old.' There was a pause, and then in a studiedly casual voice, she said, 'I would really hate it if you died.'

She said, as briskly as she could manage, 'Well, I've no intention of dying. I'm going to a drinks party instead, but I'll be back in plenty of time for supper and if you've finished your homework and Mrs Peabody says you've been good, we'll have a game of bezique.'

'Oh, good.'

When she got upstairs to change out of her painting overalls, Hatty followed her, and a few minutes later appeared in her room. 'Is the drinks party at Jack's?'

'No, it's with some people called Connaught.'

'Is Jack going with you?'

'Yes. He's coming to collect me.'

'Dad's in London with Percy, isn't he?'

'Yes, he's been helping Floy with a garden.' Hatty had brought her trousers and a jersey in with her and was now divesting herself of her school uniform, which she dropped about the room.

'You look very nice when you do your hair like that.' There was a pause while she came and leaned on the dressing-table chair so both their faces were reflected in the mirror. 'I've been thinking,' she said. 'It might be a good thing if you married Jack. He seems very fond of you and he's got such a huge house there would be plenty of room for me. And then I thought Dad could marry Percy and now she hasn't got her poor aunt it would be a good thing for her. And Francis could take turns to stay with us all. Don't you think that's a very good idea? It would be all right for Francis, because I don't think he's the marrying type. And I could be a bridesmaid twice, which would beat everyone else in my form because they're always boasting about being bridesmaids and I never am. What do you think?'

Their eyes met in the reflection. Hatty watched her carefully and – taken aback by Hatty's simplicity and shrewdness – she couldn't at first think of a diplomatic response. She applied her party lipstick rather slowly, then said, 'Well, that all sounds very neat and tidy, but we can't arrange other people's lives. You have to leave it to them, really.' Mercifully then they heard Jack's car.

*

'Well, it was a good thing we went,' she said, some two hours later when they were safely in the car again. The party, through feverish appreciation from the guests, hadn't been a failure, but it couldn't be described as much of a success either. Great efforts had been made in the small sitting room. A gate-legged table had been pushed to one end and was laden with assorted glasses and plates of water biscuits upon each of which was perched a slice of hard-boiled egg and an anchovy fillet. There were bottles of sherry and a half-bottle of gin, another of vodka, larger bottles of tonic water and a bowl containing ice-cubes that had stuck together in the crisis of meltdown. Rosalie, in a most becoming black dress that invited appreciation of her charming and rather large breasts, produced bridge rolls thickly smeared with sardines.

Mrs Connaught, dressed in foulard whose pattern in no way resembled a zebra, though that animal had clearly been the designer's inspiration, stood near the door being introduced by her husband to each new arrival to whom she painstakingly explained that Richard had forgotten to invite them until the last moment. At its height, the gathering consisted of a dozen people, mostly retired couples whom she didn't know.

Everybody, she noticed, did their best, ate as much and drank as little as they could – the gin and vodka soon ran out and the sherry was designed as a drink to toy with – and ran through their array of small-talk with well-worn ease. They knew enough of one another not to want to know any more, but all were true to the idea of a social event and were also, she noticed, genuinely fond of their host. So it seemed mandatory to stay at least an hour and a half. By then, the room was hot and smoky, the ashtrays were overflowing with olive stones, sausage sticks and cigarette ends. The Admiral had more or less stopped topping up people's glasses, Rosalie had ceased bringing yet more food round, and had knocked back two large sherries, which she'd asked Jack to pour for her, and Mrs Connaught had subsided into the only armchair where she sat smiling weakly at nobody in particular. People began to thank their hosts and go. Jack caught her eye and they followed suit.

'Yes. Poor old boy. She was taking it out on him, wasn't she? Telling everyone he'd forgotten to invite people. I think their daughter has rather a thin time of it.' And he told her of the lift he'd given and her crying in the back of the car. 'Boyfriend trouble, I suppose – or does she still have a husband?'

'I think they're divorced.'

There was a companionable silence, and then he said, '*Not* speaking of divorce, I wondered if you've thought any more about – about us?'

'Of course. I've thought about it a great deal.' She had a sudden urge to tell him about Thomas and Percy, but resisted. He'd only think there was even less reason for her to refuse him, and she couldn't possibly tell him about Francis when she knew so little how he'd feel. 'It's just I'm not sure of anything at the moment, with Thomas and Francis away. I'm sorry, Jack, to seem so feeble.' She felt overwhelmed by fatigue and worried that any more words she uttered might be the wrong ones.

'At least, you haven't said no. Would you like some dinner?'

'I can't. I promised Hatty I'd play bezique with her after supper tonight.' She didn't ask him to join them. The mere thought of a threesome after Hatty's earlier remarks was too tricky for her to endure. When they were back in the yard, she reached to touch his hand on the steering-wheel. 'Don't bother to get out, and thank you for taking me.' She wanted to thank him for more, but words seemed either to have a double edge or to be meaningless. 'I'll be in touch,' she said, as she took away her hand and got out.

Hatty had laid the table for dinner. Her hair was washed and it lay in glistening strands over her shoulders, soaking her shirt.

'Francis called. He didn't talk long. He said Percy's house was sold and there was an awful lot to do and Dad is finishing off the job he was doing for Floy. He said he's coming down the day after tomorrow because he needs some clothes.'

'Thomas is coming?'

'No, Francis.'

'Did he leave a number?'

'No. He said he'd catch the nine o'clock train. He said you'd know what time to meet him. He doesn't want to leave Percy too long. Was the party nice?'

'Yes. It went very well, I think. Is he staying with Percy, then? I thought once your father was back . . .'

Hatty was getting the stew out of the oven. It was dark brown, and drips from her hair sizzled on the top. 'He didn't say. I don't think I much care for social life,' she said. 'Standing up and talking to people is so boring. I like one person at a time, and sitting down or in a tree. Then you can talk properly. Can we start? I'm really nearly starving.'

'I meant to cook some spinach.'

'No need. I know it's good for our complexions, but I only seem to like food that brings me out in spots. And you're so lucky, you don't get them.'

'You'll grow out of it. And you'll grow into eating more vegetables and then you won't have *any*.'

'Oh, thanks very much.'

They finished their meal with baked apples stuffed with sultanas; then Mary cleared up while Hatty laid out the bezique.

'Three games only,' Mary said, 'and that's assuming you've done your homework.'

They played, and Hatty won, which was satisfactory for both of them, and eventually she was tucked up, smelling sweetly of toothpaste. 'I love our evenings,' she said. 'Especially when I win.'

Alone, what she called her Charlotte Lucas thoughts plagued her. She couldn't think or feel clearly about anything. She so longed for Francis to come, to speak to him, to find out more of his plans, to discover if, now he'd seen Percy and Thomas, he included her in them. If he didn't, what would she do? Start all over again or marry Jack, who was offering her everything that a part of her, she knew, craved – a household of her own, freedom from financial anxiety, a companion and, above all, children? To these, she felt, purely selfish desires, she could add Hatty and Thomas near and happy. She could also see that she had something to give that Jack so clearly needed.

FRANCIS

I don't know what made me go to the house that morning. I'd got back in the early evening the day before. Gerry had given me a key to his place, a basement flat in Pimlico, the entrance down the area steps in the front. I'd been looking forward to getting back – breaking away from Sandra was more difficult than I'd anticipated, but I did manage to leave before Gerry, so I missed the abandoned-waif routine. I had produced the requisite number of portraits of her children – only one of which had any merit; the rest were unspeakably sentimental, but they seemed to give her satisfaction and I came back with a really indecent sum of money.

But the flat was enough to dampen anyone's spirits. It had one room, a kitchenette and a shower and was pitch dark, unless you turned on all the lights, and when you did it was ugly and unkempt, the carpet covered with coffee and wine stains, an unmade divan with slate-grey linen under its orange sateen eiderdown and an armchair with broken springs and a small table that rocked. I took a quick look at the facilities, as they're called, and found what I expected: dirt, grease and absence of anything to clean it with. The contents of the fridge, when I opened it, looked like they might well make a lunge for freedom, they'd been there so long. There was nothing for it but to eat out and spend the night in my clothes. It was depressing, an anticlimax after the heat and luxury I'd left in France. I turned on the two-bar electric fire, and when I saw the phone, I thought I'd ring

Percy. I'd brought back some scent for her and thought they might just ask me round. But the phone was dead – cut off, I imagined. Gerry isn't a great bill-payer. So I went out to a callbox. The line was engaged and I waited outside the box and tried again. Still engaged. So I waited a bit more and then it just rang and rang and nobody answered. They must've gone out to dinner, I thought. Just my luck. I went and ate pizza in a dreary alpine joint nearby. I tried again and it still rang with no answer.

I was dead tired by then, and decided to sleep on top of the eiderdown in my clothes. I *had* planned to spend a few days in the flat while I looked for somewhere to rent, but clearly I was going to have to waste at least a morning cleaning.

I dozed off at once, but woke a couple of hours later, some time after twelve. For some reason I started wondering about why the Plovers hadn't answered the phone. Of course, there might be all kinds of reasons, but it nagged away at me. I wouldn't have worried if they hadn't been engaged the first two times. Burglary and robbery with violence is increasingly common and Floy and Percy aren't, or weren't, exactly robust, either of them. I did kind of know these were just late-night incoherent insomniac thoughts, but I couldn't calm down or think of anything else. They just wouldn't go away. Anyway, through those late and subsequently early hours I went from simply wanting to see them to feeling it was imperative I go to their house and check they were all right.

It was even colder outside the flat and I went back to get a jersey. It was so early I decided to walk – along the edge of Hyde Park up Park Lane to Marble Arch and on up the Edgware Road, which I knew turned into Maida Vale and those Edwardian semi-detached villas where the upper classes apparently used to keep their mistresses. Percy told me about that. It's not far from where Celia had her flat, so I know the area well. By now I was convinced my night-time fantasies were just that, so walking meant I wouldn't arrive too early to be welcome.

Before I reached the front door, I could see all the lights on the ground floor were on. I rang the bell, and when there was no answer I was suddenly perturbed. I rang again, longer this time, and eventually pounded on the knocker and kept my finger on the bell until, eventually, I saw through the stained glass someone was coming.

Almost before she'd opened the door I began to explain myself but the sight of her stopped me. I started to ask what was wrong and she managed to say that Floy was dead, before she was racked by a fit of sobbing so violent, so heartrending there were no words to comfort her. I could only put my arms round her and hold her through it.

Eventually she began to tell me about finding Floy in the garden, and when I offered to carry her in she said she'd done it, and took me to the conservatory, where her aunt lay in a sleeping-bag with jasmine in her hands. Looking at the steps down to the garden I just couldn't imagine how she'd done it. There were two trays on the table with a meal clearly untouched upon them. Percy was kneeling by her aunt. 'I wanted to put her on the sofa next door, but I couldn't do it.' She didn't know what to do, and I realized exhaustion was overwhelming even her misery. It turned out she hadn't eaten for about twenty-four hours, so that, and then calling the doctor, seemed the place to start.

She stumbled on the stairs to the kitchen and I took her arm.

'Oh, Francis,' she said, 'I'm glad it's you.'

Their cat was in the kitchen eating rabbit out of a saucepan. 'It's all right,' she said. 'Floy boned it for him. It was the last thing she did.' Her eyes filled with tears again and slipped down her face, but silently now.

I made her sit at the table and tell me where everything was and I made coffee, some toast and scrambled eggs, told her we were both going to eat. She asked about the doctor and I said if she gave me the number, I'd ring him, but only after she'd eaten something.

'But he can't do any good, can he?'

Later, she said, 'If I'd rung him last night, when I found her, would he have been able to do something?'

I said no, though of course I didn't know. I could see she was starting to blame herself and there was no point in that. A self-inflicted wound was the last thing she needed.

'You must eat. Drink some coffee. You can eat your eggs with a spoon, if you like. I'm watching. I want you to eat.'

'You know what it's like, don't you? Celia. Mary told me you loved her more than anyone else.'

At once feelings – which I'd thought long distant now – of grief, of utter and final loss reverberated with power so raw and immediate I couldn't answer. Then, looking at her poor ravaged face, swollen and red-eyed, and seeing her obediently picking at the food on her plate, with no choice but to embark upon the bleak wasteland that lay before her, I was possessed by a protective tenderness for her and I knew then I had to see her through at least the worst of it.

'When you've finished your coffee, you're going up to bed to sleep. That's the next thing to do.'

She hardly protested. I went upstairs with her. 'I don't think I can sleep,' was all she said, and I told her not to think, just to trust me. She told me where the address book was and I rang the doctor, who said he'd come as soon as he'd finished his surgery.

I went to look at her ten minutes later and she was out for the count.

Just then Thomas rang – I hadn't realized he'd been working with Floy and living with them. I told him what had happened and he said he'd get back as soon as possible. 'Poor Percy. How is she?' Then he asked lots of questions I couldn't answer about

Floy, and why I was there and I told him. He wanted to speak to Percy, but I told him she was asleep. He was clearly very shocked, but for some reason his questions irritated me. 'I'll get back as soon as I can,' he said. 'Sorry, my money's running out. Give her my love and say I'll get back as soon as I can.' And that was that.

Then, the doctor came, a middle-aged man with thinning white hair and tired eyes. I gave him a brief account and took him to the conservatory. 'And her niece is . . .'

'She's asleep. It was horrible for her and she had all the struggle of getting her aunt in from the garden. Hence the sleeping-bag.'

'And you are?'

'Just a friend. I came round because nobody answered the phone.'

There was a silence while he knelt by Floy's small, rigid body. Her face looked as if it was carved from some soft pale stone; only the nose was sharp.

'There wasn't anything that could have been done, was there?' I asked, because I knew Percy would ask me, but I was praying he'd say no.

'I doubt it. Her heart's been a problem for some time now.'

'I don't think her niece knew that.'

'Very likely not. It wasn't easy getting her to acknowledge it. The last time I saw her I told her she needed a really good rest, but she said it wasn't convenient. Advice seldom is. A lot of my job consists of giving inconvenient advice.' He'd got to his feet. 'And now, I need to ring the police.'

'The police?'

'Yes, Mr . . .'

'Brock.'

'Brock. That's the procedure when someone dies suddenly without having seen a doctor for two weeks. There has to be a post-mortem and that involves the police.' I took him to the phone and waited while he made the call. Then he said, 'I'm afraid you'll have to wake Miss Plover. They'll want to question her.'

I could see there was no point in arguing, so I did as he said.

She was deeply asleep. I sat on the bed, stroked her shoulder and repeated her name gently. When she opened her eyes I couldn't help seeing that fleeting moment of innocence before she remembered what she was waking up to.

I did my best to be both matter-of-fact and gentle, and she responded with mechanical docility. Yes, of course, she'd wash her face, get dressed and come down at once.

She was like that throughout the whole, awful ensuing business, as we sat at the table in the conservatory. There were two policemen, one who asked the questions and the other who stood by looking respectful and bored. Eventually, the questioner closed his notebook, made some sign to his partner, who left the room to return moments later with two more men and a stretcher. Percy said, 'What's happening?'

'We have to remove your aunt now for the post-mortem. Perhaps you'd rather not be here while we do that.'

'No – I want to be there.'

I held her hand while we watched them ease Floy's body out of the sleeping-bag on to the stretcher and cover her with a sheet. As they lifted it, she stopped them and they waited while she lifted the sheet and kissed Floy's forehead.

We – she and I – followed the men, watched while they loaded the stretcher into the Black Maria. The police went after them, and I saw the inspector caught her extreme anguish as the doors of the van were closed.

'I should think you could do with a nice cup of tea,' he said gently.

She watched until the black van was out of sight, and when I closed the front door we stood exactly as we had so many hours ago. The sense of *déjà vu* was heightened by the fact she was wearing the same jeans and fisherman's sweater and her hair was scraped back and fastened with a clip – only now she wasn't crying or anywhere near it.

She turned away from me and wandered hesitantly back to the conservatory where the discarded sleeping-bag lay scattered with pieces of dying jasmine.

'Got to put it all away,' she said. She picked up each dead flower and laid them on the table. I helped her roll up the bag. Best to keep doing things, I thought, so I asked if she knew the name of Floy's lawyer, and she said Mr Jenkins and his number was in the address book. 'I suppose he should be told,' she said, and I said, yes, Floy might have left some instructions about her funeral in her will. I asked if she wanted me to ring him for her, but she said, no, she'd do it and she did, at once. 'He was out to lunch, but I left a message.

'I was trying to sort out the kitchen,' she said. 'I suppose I'd better get on with it.'

The kitchen was full of everything but food, but I found a tin of consommé and there was enough bread left for two slices. She was still so stunned that if I told her to do things she just did them, so when I said, 'Consommé break,' she sat down at the clear end of the table. I told her Thomas had rung and I'd told him about Floy and he was on his way back, and she said, 'Oh – Thomas. I'd forgotten about him.'

'There's not enough food for three people. Do you think we should go shopping?'

'I don't know. Could you go, Francis? There's so much to do here. The whole house to clear up and I've only got six weeks . . .' She saw my incomprehension. 'We sold it yesterday. Floy agreed the price, but we have to get out in six weeks or the people won't buy.'

Everything she said was more painful, more difficult.

'I was going to take her to see a flat today. We had an appointment at eleven. I should think someone else has taken it by now. It doesn't matter. I don't particularly want to live there.' There was a pause. 'It had a garden, you see. That's why I wanted her to see it. She was so upset about leaving this one.'

The phone rang. It was Mr Jenkins and I handed him over to Percy.

'He's coming tomorrow morning,' she said, after a brief conversation.

I decided to leave the shopping until Thomas was back. It wasn't a good idea for Percy to be alone. She started feverishly emptying drawers and cupboards and putting loads of ancient cooking implements into boxes that I carted upstairs and down the front steps to the space where the Black Maria had been.

And so the first bleak and dangerous hours of her grief passed. I remember after Celia died I took to walking for hours, all over London. I walked all day, north to Highgate and Hampstead Heath, east to the City and the marshes, west as far as Richmond, and south to Camberwell and Blackheath. I'd get back to the flat we'd shared before her marriage, quite late at night sometimes but safely exhausted, just about able to shed my shoes and jacket before falling into bed for some mercifully unconscious hours, if I was lucky. Other nights I'd lie there with hopeless, useless thoughts of what might have been. Sometimes these notions concluded in fits of weeping, of rage as well as grief. 'Rachel weeping for her children, and would not be comforted . . .' That's from the Bible, I think, a remnant from school, meaningless at the time. But I understand it now.

We'd just about finished the worst of the clearing-up, when the front door banged and she said, 'That'll be Thomas.'

I went up to the hall where he was getting out of his windcheater.

'How is she?'

'Just about managing. We've started clearing things up. She's got to be out of the house in six weeks – they sold it yesterday.' By now I was following him down the stairs.

She was standing at the sink washing her hands. I watched him go straight up to her and put his arms round her as he said, 'Zephie. My poor darling.'

'Please don't call me that.' She'd turned towards him, her face smudged with grime from pushing strands of her hair back. 'I can't talk about it now. Francis will tell you. I think I'll have a bath.' She slipped from his arms with a fleeting expression that might have been an apology and left us.

There was a silence until we could no long hear her. Then he said, 'God. I can hardly believe it. Was it a heart-attack? Was Percy with her? What happened exactly?'

So I went through it, and he said, 'If only I'd been here. She must have had the most awful night on her own. When did you turn up?'

I told him.

'If only there was something I could do. I was very fond of Floy. She was a really remarkable person.' His eyes were full of tears. He repeated, 'If only there was something I could do.'

'Well, there are one or two things. There's no food in the house and we need to get some.'

He said he would do that, only he was clean out of money. I had a couple of five-pound notes and some loose change so I gave him the notes.

When he'd gone I went upstairs to see how Percy was getting on. She came out of the bathroom just as I got to the top of the stairs. She was wrapped in a large bath towel and her hair was pinned on top of her head with a toothbrush.

'Is Thomas . . . ?'

'He's gone to buy us something for supper.'

'Oh.' She sounded relieved. 'Francis, there are so many things – so many things I wanted to ask you.'

'Yes?'

'Can you stay for a bit? Not leave me? Just till things get sorted?' She was both insistent and uncertain.

'Of course I'll stay.'

She put out her hand to touch mine. She said nothing, but her look of instant relief was enough. I said, 'I'll stay as long as you want. You get dressed and then we'll have a drink.'

Thomas came back with lamb chops, vegetables and a bunch of grapes, and somehow we got through that first uneasy evening. It wouldn't have been easy anyway, but Thomas made it more difficult: though his intentions were clearly good he persistently struck the wrong note. He treated Percy like an invalid who couldn't know what was best. It started when he announced he'd bought a bottle of whisky and poured her a stiff one.

'I'm sorry, Thomas, but I don't like whisky.'

But he put the glass into her hand and said, 'Of course I know that. Treat it as medicine. You need it.' And he stood over her with an overbearing tenderness till she had obediently gulped half of it.

His voice, when he spoke to her, was mournful, church-like, hushed. He wouldn't let her help make dinner, so she sat, idle, unhappy and alone, in the conservatory while he – who'd never cooked anything in his life – tried to help me. At one point, our plates of food in front of us, he suddenly declared, 'Francis told me how you got Floy out of the garden into the house. How amazing. I can't tell you how much I admire you for that.'

'I wanted to.'

'I only wish I'd been here to help you.' Another little cul-de-sac.

To ease the tension I asked him how much more there was to do to the Hampstead garden and he said he thought one full day would get the final planting done. We were on the bottle of wine that hadn't been drunk the previous evening when he asked me where I had to get back to.

Percy said at once, 'He's staying. I asked him to.'

'I'll have to go back some time, just to fetch my stuff.'

I could see he was taken aback and I realized immediately why Percy wanted me to stay.

'Oh, well,' he said, 'I really ought to deliver and put all the shrubs in tomorrow.'

'Tomorrow we'll find some movers and get tea-chests or boxes to pack the books and things in, after Mr Jenkins.'

'Mr Jenkins. Is he about the – the funeral?' He looked anxiously at Percy.

Percy said, 'No. He's Floy's lawyer. He's coming about the will. And I expect he'll help with the other things. She may have said what she wanted.'

'Of course. Well, it's good you're going to be here, Francis. For tomorrow, anyway.'

Nobody said anything for a bit, then Percy said she thought she'd go to bed. 'Oh. Francis, there's a room on the top floor, but the bed won't be made up.'

'Don't worry about that. I know where the sheets are, and I'll give them to him.'

I'd started to clear up supper, but he said, 'Don't bother with that. I'll do it before I go off in the morning. The sooner I go the sooner I can get back. Don't leave her alone, will you? She adored Floy, adored her. It's obviously the most horrible, horrible shock.'

As we reached the foot of the stairs together, he said, 'You might as well know. I'm in love with her. I never thought I could love anyone after Celia, but I do. So when we've got through this awful time, she'll be all right in the end because I'll look after her.' I couldn't tell him it was obvious.

'Well, we've got to get through all this first,' I said. Fatigue had hit me. I was incapable of emotional response.

'I just wanted you to know,' he said.

We tramped up the stairs, he gave me the sheets and told me the room on the left at the top would be mine. He was going to have a bath, he said. I'd noticed there was no light coming from Percy's room and guessed he wouldn't disturb her.

The rest of the week was a nightmare. Mr Jenkins came as arranged and read the will. Floy had left everything to Percy, but it was all frozen until after probate had been established, which made Percy feel duty-bound to find the cost of the funeral. Mr Jenkins suggested that perhaps Percy's father, Floy's brother, could help with expenses and could be reimbursed when probate was granted. How awful and strange that death could produce such administrative complications. I could see Percy was reluctant to get in touch with her father, but when Mr Jenkins pointed out that he had to be told in any case as next of kin, she agreed to telephone him. Mr Jenkins, who seemed to have grasped – or perhaps already knew – how it was between Percy and her father, suggested it would be a good thing if she rang while he was present. Percy seized on this. 'Would you tell him? And tell him about the money and everything, and then if he wants to speak to me I'll do it?'

It's difficult to refuse Percy sometimes and he agreed.

We found the number in Floy's address book and the call went through surprisingly easily. Mr Jenkins did his stuff, then handed the receiver to Percy. He indicated we should leave her to speak to her father in private and we went to the conservatory.

'Had the elder Miss Plover entered into any arrangements about new accommodation?'

I said she'd been going to see a flat with Percy the morning after she'd died. I added that Percy didn't want to live in it on her own.

'And arrangements for the funeral? As you heard, Miss Plover expressed a wish to be cremated. Perhaps her niece should put a notice in the newspaper announcing her death and stating any particulars about the funeral. If she'd like, I could arrange that for her.'

'I think she'd be most grateful. It's all been such a shock to her.'

He stood by the conservatory door. 'It's a lovely garden,' he said sadly. 'I once told Miss Plover I was having trouble with slugs eating my delphiniums and she advised me to put coarse grit a foot round each of them and the slugs never went near them after that.'

Percy joined us. 'He's sending me three thousand pounds. He said we should put a notice in *The Times* and the *Telegraph* saying when and where it was to be.' She stopped there, and Mr Jenkins offered to compose the notice and read it to her over the phone before he sent it off.

'And if there's anything else I can do to assist you, Miss Plover, you have only to call. In the mean time, I'll do my best to facilitate probate.'

When I'd seen him off I came back to find her standing by the conservatory door, staring out at the garden. I started to say something about how helpful Mr Jenkins had been. She turned to me, and I think she was trying to smile, but she was overcome by another fit of racking sobs and, again, there was nothing I could do but hold her.

'Sorry,' she said eventually. 'A lot of the time it just seems unreal, and then it suddenly doesn't.'

'It's good about your father.'

'He asked me to go and stay with him in Jordan.'

'That might be something to do.'

She shrugged. 'I don't think so. Actually, I don't want to do anything.'

I told her I had to get my stuff from Gerry's flat and she could come with me, unless she'd rather stay put.

'I'd rather go with you.'

So we did that. Took two buses to Victoria, had some lunch in a small, noisy Italian restaurant, picked up my luggage from the grubby flat. 'The sheets are like dirty washing-up water. Poor Francis, what a horrible night,' she said. We went back to Maida Vale in a taxi. The for-sale notice outside the house now had a sticker saying, 'sold' on it, and the cat was sitting reproachfully on the front-door step. 'How awful. He's had no breakfast. We'll have to get him some proper food. He really hates tins.' So we set out to do another local shop.

When we got back, there was a message from the undertakers, wanting instructions about the funeral. When that was settled – Golders Green in a few days' time – she rang Mr Jenkins to tell him, and he read out the notice for the newspaper to Percy. 'It seemed all right,' she said. 'I told him I wanted the funeral to be private, but he seems to think there are people who'll want to come to it, so I agreed. I do know lots of her clients were very fond of her. I've got to choose some music so we could sort through her records. They said three pieces.' So we spent the rest of the day listening to bits of Bach and a Scarlatti sonata she said Floy particularly loved, and packing books from the sitting room until we ran out of boxes. When we got to the formidable row of Dickens volumes on the shelf, she said, 'Floy used to read *A Tale of Two Cities* aloud to me. I'll never forget poor Dr Manette saying, "A hundred and five North Tower," when they asked him his name. She did his trembling old voice so well – she was a very good reader-aloud.' In spite of her saying she didn't want to do anything, activity seemed the best thing for her. There was a long shelf of gardening books, which we didn't pack. 'I think I'll give them to Thomas,' she said. 'They'll be useful to him. Floy became very fond of him, you know.' She gave me a quick look as she said this and I realized then that she knew Thomas was in love with her, but then I thought, of course she knows: how could you not know if someone loved you? But it was to do with the future – all too confusing, too much for her now.

Well, we made a chicken casserole for dinner that night. Thomas came back, saying he'd finished the job, and almost immediately she went off to have a bath.

'You've tired her out,' he said, as he set about watering the conservatory.

'It seemed the best thing to do,' I said. It's funny: I've known him so long, through so much, and it seemed odd that things were so uneasy between us. He asked me when I was going home and I told him I'd decided to start up on my own and would be looking for a flat in London. He seemed to think that was a good idea. 'One of us ought to go home,' he said. 'The bulb order will have arrived and Mary's held the fort long enough. But I don't want to leave Zephie now, not with the funeral pending and getting out of here. I can't leave her.'

Two days later I went down to Melton.

JACK

'. . . so I know it's very cheeky of me, but you have lots of them, so I wondered if you could possibly lend Daddy one, just while his is being mended and Mummy's in hospital?'

There was a pause, and then she said, 'I'm asking because I know Daddy never would – in fact, he'd be furious with me if he found out I'd asked you. The thing is he has to keep taking cabs to visit her and he can't afford them.'

For a moment he looked at her, confounded. The pram stood in the drive. She'd walked – something like four miles – to come and ask him, whom she scarcely knew, to lend her father a car. Her long golden hair was streaked darker with sweat. She wore a corduroy skirt and a T-shirt with a psychedelic image on it that undulated across her breasts. 'A mother to see you, sir,' Juan had said, and he'd come out to find her – Rosalie. It was quite a cheek, but the simplicity of it intrigued him, and now her large dark blue eyes, trustful and direct, were fixed on him.

'You'd better come in and have some tea.'

'I'll have to bring Lulu.'

'Juan will bring the pram. Juan.'

Juan turned out to love babies. He provided tea in a flash and practically begged to have the baby. 'I know them. My sister have them all the time. I look after her.'

Tea was in the study.

'I'm sorry your mother's ill.'

'She's not ill, exactly, but she hasn't been very well for ages really. They've taken her to hospital for tests. Golly, what a lot of books you have. Have you read them all?'

'Very few. I'm working my way through them.'

'They look nice and, I suppose, that's the main thing.'

'You must be tired after that walk.'

'A bit. Babies mean you're usually tired anyway, but since the car broke down I've been walking into Melton practically every day for the shopping.'

As he poured her more tea, she said, 'Sorry. That sounds like I want the car for myself, but it honestly isn't that. I can't drive.'

'Well,' he said, 'I'd be happy to lend your father a car. And if the one he's got is no good, perhaps I could help him find another more reliable one.'

'Oh. That would be great. That would be—' But her eyes suddenly filled with tears, which streamed down her face, and she became incoherent with apologies.

He produced a large white handkerchief as he remembered her crying in the back of the car, and waited, uncertain what on earth he could say to her. Some love affair gone wrong, he thought: the man who ran the theatre or perhaps that young ne'er-do-well Hugo Carson. He remembered how boring she'd been about her pregnancy when she came to dinner and how attractively the strands of golden hair had lain on her smooth white shoulders – and that was all he knew about her.

She was getting over it, snuffling in a childish way into the handkerchief for which she'd thanked him. The last thing he wanted was a blow-by-blow account of her unhappy love life.

'Look. I'm going to drive you home and I'll have a car sent over for your father first thing in the morning.' He rang the bell for Juan.

In the car, she said, 'Thank you for not asking me – about crying and that. I used to think you should say everything you felt, but actually it only makes things worse. And especially thank you about the car. Can I tell Daddy you thought of it? Then he won't be cross with me.'

'Of course you can.' Generosity, even of the smallest kind, was beginning to feel like some kind of refuge.

The faint but perceptible sense of oppression, familiar to him now, on his return to his large well-ordered house arose as he turned into the drive whose trees, already copper-coloured, were beginning to drop their leaves. There were lights on in the gardener's lodge and he caught a whiff of the radio as he went by. This oppression irritated him. He should have got used to being alone and, in any case, it was only for one more evening. Amelia and Wystan and their children were all arriving the next day for the weekend, and Mary was coming to dinner that night to meet them. He had great hopes that, in some way, this would precipitate her into agreeing to marry him. He wasn't sure why he should think that, but he was sure they would all like one another and mutual approval must, he thought, reflect well upon him.

But when he got back it was to a phone call from Mary saying she was terribly sorry but she couldn't come. 'Francis is down – just for one night,' she said.

'Bring him.'

'Jack, it's terribly kind of you, but I can't. There are things he wants to talk to me about and he can't stay long because he's looking after poor Percy. He has to get back.'

'I see.' He didn't, of course, but the mention of Percy silenced him.

'Well, the Blunts are here till Sunday evening – how about Saturday?'

'On Saturday evening there's a concert at Hatty's school. Sunday would be better. Could I perhaps come to lunch and bring her?'

'Whichever you like.'

But not what I like, he thought, after the call. He'd ordered a really festive dinner for Friday, and while it could have been postponed until Saturday, it was definitely unsuitable for a lunch with children. It would be nice, he thought, if I was the most important person, if somebody couldn't do other things because of me.

The next morning he decided to ask Richard Connaught and his daughter to dinner.

FRANCIS

He went to sleep, woke with a crick in his neck and a fleeting uncertainty of where he was, but the familiar landscape and the deceleration of the train made it clear he was about to arrive at Melton where Mary would be waiting for him. He felt vaguely grumpy at having spent the journey asleep. He'd been looking forward to being on his own and making some practical plans for the future, like where he should live, picking up his car, and how to set himself up as a working painter – thoughts he hadn't been able to contemplate since arriving in Maida Vale.

The last few days had taught him something obvious, but it had struck him with a fresh and awful clarity: that however hard you tried, it was impossible to know what it was like to be somebody else. Of course he had tried, had seen at once that, in losing Floy, Percy had lost her whole family, her background, the framework of her life, and there had been no warning, no chance to prepare for it. He'd done everything he could to sustain her, but had been forced to stand by helplessly, watching as, again and again, she retreated into some private hell where she could be neither reached nor comforted. Often, on these occasions, she'd shut herself into Floy's room, sorting her belongings, her clothes and the contents of her desk – all part of the grim business of clearing out the house. She would emerge dazed and silent, unnaturally quiescent to any suggestion he made. So they spent several evenings going to the cinema, to films Thomas carefully vetted, and afterwards eating out at a small Greek restaurant where they got lots of attention because of her fluent Greek. The funeral loomed – now only three days away – and he thought maybe once it was over she might start to consider her future.

There was Mary, shading her eyes and watching for him.

'How brown you are.'

'That's the South of France for you.' He gave her a hug. 'Thanks for meeting me.'

In the car they exchanged news. Hatty was well, 'But she's spending the night with her friend.'

'Shan't I see her, then?'

'You will for tea. But I thought it would be nice for us to have an evening on our own. How is Percy?'

'She's still pretty shocked. She asked me to thank you for your letter.' And he filled her in with what had been going on at Maida Vale. 'It's one reason why I can't stay. I really don't like to leave her at the moment.'

'Thomas is there, isn't he?'

'Yes. He's been marvellous at arranging for people to come and store everything, working like mad, coping with the undertakers and dealing with the lawyer. I never knew he was so practical.'

'Well, he's in love with her, isn't he? So of course he would – do anything.'

Some asperity in her voice made him turn to her.

'He's got to come back soon. I really can't cope with the nursery on my own. I've had to pay Mrs Peabody's son to man the till. We can't afford to be closed so much at this time of year. And my term has started and, though it bores me, we can't afford for me to give it up.'

There was a short silence, but just before he'd thought of something to say, she said, 'Sorry, Francis. I do understand about you wanting to get your life going. It's just that all our lives seem to be in a state of flux, including mine. Don't let's talk about it now, particularly not in front of Hatty. We've got the evening for that.'

So the day passed. They had lunch and Mary said she had to go and sort bulbs for the nursery. He spent the afternoon packing up his car, clearing his room of his clothes and his painting gear. It was quite surprising, he thought, that his effects, after all these years, would fit into something so small. But as he carted things from his room to the car he was weighed down by a feeling of unease, that he was abandoning the set-up at Home Farm, leaving Mary to cope. Should he feel guilty? Surely not. He'd come originally to support Thomas, to help Mary with Celia's child and because Mary herself needed help with both of them. And it had worked. He'd done what he could, but the need for it was gone now and he had to think of his own life and career. Surely nothing wrong in that. I've always been something of a spectator, he thought, which is one way of not facing up to my own life. I've never taken the risk of living for myself. Rather disgustingly I rationalized that what I was doing was more important. And perhaps it was, but it's over now. As soon as I've got Percy on her feet I'll start sorting out my career as a painter. And if I'm no good, I'll just have to find something else to do. He was sure Mary would understand, but all afternoon the faint dread he felt about doing so persisted.

Hatty came back from school and was clearly pleased to see him. She gave him a tumultuous hug and launched at once into news of her life. The death of the goldfish and the arrival of the tropicals, the pony she rode, her friend Agnes, how much everyone in her form loathed Miss Williams, the new English mistress, who made them learn masses of soppy poetry by heart . . .

'Not all poetry is soppy,' Mary said.

'It prob'ly isn't. But she's soppy. She reads it in a hushed, churchy voice that stops it being about anything. I prefer prose.'

They were having tea and he was amused to see how she

could talk so much and eat at the same time. She elicited a promise from him to take her in his car to the riding stables after tea to see her jump, then on to Agnes's.

'Guess what.'

'What?'

'Betsy's older brother is a lord and he's come back from Hong Kong with a slightly Chinese wife and Betsy says they're going to spend thousands on the house because she wants to live there only not with any of them. So Betsy's mother and Betsy are going to live in the coach house, which is jolly small and only has an outdoor lav, but Betsy says they'll put in an indoor one, and Hugo's being sent to Hong Kong to a job in a bank there.'

'Poor Lady Yoxford.'

'Oh, no, Mary. She's going to be much richer, Betsy says, because she won't have to keep paying Hugo money. And they're going to repair the stables and let Betsy have more horses – not just ponies. I shall be a great help to her.'

'Well, be a great help to me and clear up tea before you go off. And make sure you pack your school clothes for tomorrow. I must go and see that Jimmy has shut up the greenhouses.'

He said he'd go with her.

'Don't worry, Francis. Agnes's mother is fetching them, so you needn't stay longer than to watch a few jumps. And then we can talk.'

'How's the nursery going?'

'Well, it's ticking over – just. Thomas placed a huge order for bulbs, which I've had to pay for, and we had a sale of herbaceous stuff that went quite well. But I can't be there all the time and Jimmy Peabody is still learning the names of everything. Do tell Thomas he must come back after the funeral. But we'll talk later.'

Each time she said this, he felt some kind of dread without quite knowing why. Perhaps she had news that was going to ensnare them again – Reggie, perhaps? But nothing had been heard from him since he'd gone off on the cruise. Well, he wasn't prepared to do anything about him and he wouldn't allow Mary to either.

For the following two hours Hatty occupied his attention. She had grown since he'd been away. The bones in her face were more defined. She was becoming more like Celia had been at her age, the same high oval forehead, the same marvellous eyes. Then he realized she was inspecting him.

'We neither of us have any eyebrows to speak of, do we? Just little moth-like streaks. Of course, when I'm older, I expect I'll pull them out and paint proper ones, but you can't do that. Can I come and stay with you in London? By myself?'

He said she could, but he had to find somewhere to live first.

'And you'll come back here, won't you?'

'I'm sure I shall.'

So he watched her pony ambling over little jumps constructed near the stables, and when he said he had to go, she bent down from her pony, put an arm round his neck and kissed him. 'I do *actually* love you, Francis.'

'*Actually*, I feel the same.'

'I thought you did. But people like people to say it, don't they? Then they can be sure.'

'That's it.'

When he got back, he noticed Mary had changed into a blue dress, and done her hair in a French plait. There was a bottle of vodka on the kitchen table, which was laid for dinner, with a bowl of white chrysanthemums and two red candles each side of it.

'It all looks very nice,' he said. 'Festive – that reminds me.'

He rummaged in the rucksack he'd brought with him and produced the present he'd brought back from France for her.

'Oh, Francis. I haven't had any scent for years. L'Air du Temps.'

'I hope you like it. They sprayed things on my arm and this smelt the nicest.'

'I'm sure I will.' She undid the stopper and sniffed.

'There's a spray attachment. Put some on.'

'Yes. I will.' She was smiling with pleasure and a simple excitement that touched him. She wasn't behaving like someone who got many presents. 'You do it for me.'

He walked round the table and took the scent spray from her. She kept still while he sprayed her behind each ear and then her throat, but as she tilted her head, she looked up at him and suddenly flung her arms round his neck, drawing his head down until their faces were almost touching; her eyes, so close to his, shone, and through her arms he felt her trembling. For one mad moment he thought she was going to kiss him – on the mouth, something they'd never done. He did kiss her – on her cheek – because he had to do something, and then he straightened up, and felt her arms immediately release him. 'It's a lovely present,' she said, in a small voice. 'The nicest I've had for years. Now I think it's time for an enormous drink.'

Over dinner she asked about Percy and he explained about the house and Percy having nowhere to live.

'I suppose Thomas might bring her down here.'

'I don't know. I think if she did she'd feel committed to him, and I'm not sure she's ready for that. I think he has to be very patient, and wait.'

'So we'll all have to wait, then. Well, you don't, because you've made up your mind, but I shall have to.'

'How do you mean?'

'Well, obviously, if Thomas does marry her, I'll have go – get out. It wouldn't be fair on her if I stayed. And I wouldn't want to anyway.'

'What *do* you want to do?'

'Well, I'd have to find some way to earn my living and London's the obvious place for that.' There was a pause, and then she said, 'Do you remember you once said we might end up in a grotty little flat in London?'

'Did I?'

'I always remember it because you said "grotty".' There was a pause, and then she said, 'Because afterwards I always imagined myself making it *un*grotty. I'd have a job as well, of course. I wouldn't be in your hair all day.' She offered him the vodka bottle, but they'd already had two strong drinks and he shook his head.

'I mustn't drink any more or I'll be too drunk to drive.'

'You're not going back tonight, are you?'

'I promised Percy.'

'She's not alone. She's got Thomas.'

He nearly told her Percy wanted him more than she wanted Thomas, but thought better of it.

'I do think,' she said, after a moment, 'she'll marry Thomas in the end. He has so completely set his heart on it. I couldn't bear it not to work out right for him. What do you think?'

'It's their business, so it doesn't matter much what I think.' Then, feeling he'd been unduly severe, he said, more gently, 'You worry too much about Thomas, Mary dear. You always have done. It's time you thought about yourself for a change.'

'Is it?' They were eating an excellent fish salad and she pushed the dish towards him; to please her, he took some more. 'And how do you think I should do that?'

'Thanks. It's delicious as always. Well, think what you want for a change. Go on. What *do* you want?'

She picked up her glass of wine and drained it. 'Well, to start with, I'd like you to stay one more night here. Go back as early as you like, but stay now. We've hardly ever had an evening on our own, have we, in all these years? A chance to talk properly, that's one thing I'd like.'

'Mary, darling, I can't. I promised Percy, and in her present state I can't let her down. But I don't have to go just yet.'

'Are you in love with her?'

The abruptness of this question startled him.

'In love with her? Good Lord, no. I'm not in love with anyone. I just happened to turn up at the most awful moment of her life and she asked me to see her through it. Like you, I seem destined to look after people. I probably learned it from you because you've always been so good at it. No – I meant what do you *seriously* want?'

She regarded him steadily, with no expression he could decipher. She shrugged and said, 'It doesn't really matter. Do you want some coffee before you go?'

'That would be good.'

She got up from the table and put on the kettle. While she was making the coffee, and with her back to him, she said, 'Jack has asked me to marry him.'

'Jack – Jack Curtis?'

'We don't know any other Jacks, do we?'

'Sorry – it's just such a bombshell. Why didn't you tell me before? Are you going to?'

'I think I might. What do you think?'

'If you love each other, I can't think of anything better.'

As she came back to the table with the coffee, she said, 'No, there couldn't be anything better than that, could there?'

While they drank the coffee she told him how Jack was happy to include Hatty if she wished to live with them and he interrupted her: 'I suppose you haven't accepted him because you're worried about Thomas. Well, don't be. Do what *you* want for a change. Oh, Mary, I'd be so happy to think of you being cared for and loved and, I'm sure, if you love him, he must be exceptionally nice.'

It seemed a good moment to make his departure. He finished his coffee, collected his rucksack and together they walked to his laden car, where he put his arms round her and gave her his usual hug. 'I wish you'd told me earlier,' he said, when he'd got into the car. 'We could have celebrated more.'

'Please don't tell Thomas.'

'OK. Of course you should be the person to do that.'

'You promise? As seriously as you promised Percy?' He crossed his heart and hoped to die.

She was illuminated in his headlights for a moment before he turned the car, and he blew her a kiss, but the lights must have blinded her, as she didn't return it.

PERCY

It was over. She'd walked to the front row of the ugly little chapel, past about twenty people she didn't recognize, and sat staring at the coffin on which lay a wreath she'd made of autumn flowers from the garden while the recorded music – Gérard Souzay singing 'Ich habe genug', which Floy had always loved – soared above the mournful grandeur. Then the vicar arrived and everyone stood. She'd been asked whether she'd wanted anyone to speak about Floy, but she only wanted the words of the funeral service. They knelt for the Lord's Prayer and then it began, and she heard her aunt's full name for the first time – Florence Hortensia Plover. Eventually the vicar blessed the coffin, pressed a hidden button and it slid slowly through opening curtains and out of sight. Francis gripped her hand when the coffin began to move. That was the worst moment – she stared at its inexorable disappearance with an anguish beyond tears. Eventually the curtains closed again, and it was done.

Outside, it was raining, a fine spiteful rain, and people were waiting for the next service, huddled beneath umbrellas. Thomas took her arm. 'We have to go and look at the flowers,' he said, and she allowed him to lead her to various displays of wreaths and bunches with cards attached to them. Jack had sent an enormous wreath of white freesias and roses, and Mr Jenkins, hovering in the background, another of red and yellow carnations, but the others were all from people unknown to her, one or two of whom approached her to say a few words of condolence. She was touched and found herself smiling and thanking people for coming, while icy breezes rustled the dead leaves in the garden on to the terrace and round their feet. It was another milestone in an endless journey.

Then she was in Francis's car with Thomas and they drove in silence back to the house with its tea-chests and boxes packed, its premature air of desertion. They had soup and cheese in the kitchen, and Francis said he was going to look for somewhere to live and did she want to go with him? 'We might find somewhere for you,' he said, and Thomas said she ought to get away somewhere first. She said she was tired and just wanted to sleep. She'd hardly slept at all the night before, dreading the funeral, but now she wanted more than anything to be alone. Thomas said he'd do a bit of gardening.

When she heard Francis leave and could see Thomas in the garden from her bedroom window, she went into Floy's room where Marvell lay on the bed. Ever since she'd begun clearing up Floy's clothes and papers, he'd followed her there. The packing made him profoundly uneasy. He'd prowled around the boxes in a fidgety, querulous manner, jumping into some and scratching at the newspapers. But he always ended up on Floy's bed and she had taken to leaving the door ajar for him. During the last few days she'd cleared out Floy's modest wardrobe. It and the chest of drawers were now empty and she'd almost finished with the desk where Floy had kept her papers, gardening diaries, letters from clients and sketchbooks. Percy kept all of this, putting it into a suitcase, except for the contents of a hidden drawer she'd found. It contained a single large yellowing envelope – unsealed – in which were two letters, each within its own envelope, addressed to Floy. The first had a pressed poppy pinned to one corner. The pin had rusted and the poppy had faded to the indistinct papery brown of dried blood. The paper had clearly been torn from a looseleaf book and the letter was written in pencil.

My darling, my dearest love,

This will only be a note, a very poor expression of how much I love and care for you, how much those ten days with you meant to me, how you are always with me and, perhaps particularly, how much I treasure our night together. To know that you love me and trusted me enough for that has given me more joy than you can imagine.

I don't think many people have the amazing luck we've had in finding each other and both knowing so immediately we are meant to spend our lives together, at least I haven't come across them. I think more than anything I love your beautiful generous heart, your warmth and directness.

Oh, darling! You are always yourself with me and what more could anyone want? You give me the strength to face all that goes on here and everything to live for. I can't write more now. I send you a poppy as they are everywhere here and I know you love flowers.

All love,
Antony

PS A letter from you! I will answer it properly as soon as I can, but of course we shall have children – I suggest four as a good number, only I'll have to finish my training to afford them. But yes, meanwhile, we can make do with a cat, if you love them so much.

The second letter, in a blue envelope, contained a letter on paper to match.

Dear Miss Plover,

Thank you for your letter enquiring about Antony. I am indeed sorry to have to tell you that he was killed on the second day of the Battle of the Somme – was seen to go down under heavy fire – but unfortunately his body was never recovered due to the heavy shelling.

I am so sorry to have to tell you this.

I am having a tablet put up in our church in his memory in lieu of a grave. He was my only son.
Yours sincerely,
Grace Downing

She'd wept when she first read the letters and had been haunted, ever since, by the revelation that Floy, her Pirate Aunt, had had a lover who was killed, a distant tragedy of which she'd known nothing. Floy was always self-contained, independent, someone for whom marriage was almost unthinkable. But now it seemed she had loved someone passionately, and had had the assurance it was returned just as passionately – then silence. She thought now of Floy waiting for the second letter that never came, and the bleak heartbroken note from the mother confirming what must have been the increasingly terrible fear that all was lost, at an end.

She'd taken the letters out of the desk to read again. It was another way of mourning her beloved aunt – four children and a cat, if she wanted one. There had been, she knew, four cats in Floy's life, Herbert, Wyatt, Marlowe and finally Marvell, who now lay on Floy's bed beside her. And as for children, she, Percy, had been the only child.

Marvell got to his feet and shook his head. He appreciated the warmth of her body, but not the tears that fell on his face and into one of his ears, so he resettled himself further down against her knees. He was her cat now, and whatever she did with her life, he must be in it. The thought was curiously comforting. It implied some sort of future – survival. Floy had survived and so must she.

But I don't love Thomas, she thought, carefully folding the brittle paper of the letter with the poppy. She had none of the passionate certainty, the unconditional love contained in that letter – and she might never have it, but at least she knew now it was possible.

MARY

She watched and then listened as his car disappeared, until there was silence. That was that. He'd gone and she would never see him again with any vestige of the secret hope she had contained for so long. He felt nothing for her but a kind of brotherly love and nothing she felt for him could change that. She turned back to the house, but her tears so blinded her that the yellow light streaming from the open kitchen door was a blur as she stumbled on the path towards it. He hadn't even remembered the grotty little flat, and when she wanted him to stay one more night he'd refused because of Percy. At least he wasn't in love with her – he wasn't a threat to Thomas.

She sat at the table, in his place, put her hand round his coffee cup, still warm with the dregs, and groped for his scarlet checked napkin to mop her face. She had imagined it all. There was not, had never been, any proof either that he felt as she did or knew she loved him. Telling him about Jack had been a kind of last throw. If he loved her he would have protested, but he didn't. He'd be so happy to think of her being cared for and loved – by anyone except himself. At least she'd got him to promise not to tell Thomas. She hadn't burned her boats there.

But now he was gone, after all these years. Thomas, she was sure, would succeed with Percy. It was only, as both he and Francis said, a matter of time and she would then have to leave what had been her home for nearly seven years and make some sort of new life. The choice before her wasn't simple. Finding somewhere to live, some work to earn a living – starting again – alone. Or Jack.

She extinguished the candles and cleared the table, drank the last of the wine and finally went to bed.

On Sunday evening, after a convivial lunch party with his nice friends and their children, whom Hatty took over as their nanny, as the Blunts packed themselves into their car to go back to London and she was alone with Jack for a moment, she told him she would marry him.

THOMAS

All she needed was time. After all, if after Celia died someone had turned up desperately in love with him, he wouldn't have been able to deal with it. And her love for Floy, though it was different, must mean it was just as much of a shock. He'd lived with both of them long enough to know that. And she was losing her home. It was no wonder she had no time, no room in her heart, for anything but grief. And it was no good telling anyone they'd get over it – if anyone had said that to him about Celia he would have ignored them completely. No, time was what was needed. He mustn't mind that he couldn't comfort her, that all he could do were the mundane and practical things. He'd done all he could in that way: the movers, the packing, the solicitor. He'd also taken on some of Floy's clients, initially out of fondness for Floy but also because it earned him some money and enabled him to pay his way. More importantly, perhaps, it gave him a reason to stay on, to continue to be with her. He knew he ought to go back to Home Farm, that it was hard for Mary to deal with it alone, but now she'd got Jimmy Peabody in to help it should be all right for a bit longer, until after the funeral and the closure of Maida Vale, although what would happen then was obscure.

The night when Francis went back to Home Farm he'd had his first night alone with Percy; he'd taken her out to a film and dinner at the Greek restaurant she liked. He'd hoped the restraint between them would dissolve when Francis wasn't there. He wasn't jealous of Francis exactly, but he envied the easy way he had with Percy, the way he trod with matter-of-fact assurance through the minefield of her grief – he could even make her laugh sometimes. And he always seemed to know when to leave her alone and when to deflect her away from the curious fidgety stupor of her pain.

They'd gone to a French film with Alain Delon, which, in spite of his rusty French, he'd enjoyed, and so, he observed with some pleasure, had she.

'We did this the first time we went out together,' he said, when they'd ordered their food in the restaurant.

'What?'

'Went to a film and then had dinner.'

'Oh, yes.'

She was wearing a black sweater and her silver dolphin earrings; her hair, scraped back from her forehead, accentuated how thin her face had become. He watched her pick an olive from the small saucer between them. It was the same colour as her eyes. He'd ordered retsina because he knew she liked it and, in time, he thought he'd get to like it too.

'Some people have parties after funerals, don't they? I can't think how they can bear to.'

'I don't know. I think they feel some sort of celebration of the person's life is necessary. I wouldn't want one.' There was a pause, and then he said, 'It will be better when the funeral's over. It's another stage.'

'I know.'

'It's impossible to contemplate the future until it's done.'

'No.'

The waiter brought their lamb cutlets and salad. When he'd gone, he said, 'Have you thought at all about what you'll do?'

'I – I don't know. You just said it's impossible.'

'I didn't mean the future. I just mean what you want to do next.'

She looked trapped, cornered. 'I don't want to do anything.'

'I know, darling Zephie.'

'Please don't call me that. That was only Floy's name for me.'

He saw she was on the brink of tears. God, I'm no good at this, he thought. 'I'm sorry. I promise not to again.' A ghost of a conciliatory smile. 'You could come back to Home Farm. Mary would love to have you.'

But she shook her head. 'I'd just be putting things off.' She drank some wine. 'My father has written inviting me to stay. He's in Amman – for another two years, he said.'

'You wouldn't want to go for two years, would you?'

'More like two weeks, I should think.'

'Oh, well,' he said, relieved, 'I should think that might be a good thing to do.'

'I don't know. He's only asking because he thinks he ought to.'

He remembered how bitterly stubborn he'd felt about his parents and was silent. 'Perhaps it's a kind of olive branch.'

'Even if it is, I don't know whether I could face it. He can't even get away for the funeral – his own sister. Not that I specially wanted him to come.'

She was intent on not having it both ways.

'Well,' he said at last, 'it might be a good way to pass the time. You could always come home if you didn't like it.'

'Home?'

The way she said that, the satirical bleakness, was almost too much for him. 'You could come back to me. I long to give you a home, to look after you, to stop you feeling so desolate and abandoned.'

She looked at him, for the first time that evening, and he saw she was moved. Then, with an attempt at lightness, she said, 'You make me sound like a Battersea dog.'

'Well, some come to a good end, you know. You might be one of them.' I'm for it now, he thought, I must go for it. 'I know this is an awful time for you but it will get better. I'll wait for as long as it takes and when it does – I don't think you know how much I love you, my darling, and that gives me the faith to believe—'

'What?'

'Oh. That you'll want to be with me in the end. Something like that,' he finished, rather lamely. 'But there's absolutely no need for you to worry about it now.' He was suddenly afraid of an outright rejection, not that he would have accepted it as final but because it might make it harder for her to change her mind.

She didn't want any more to eat and the old waiter who served them removed her plate, still laden with meat and salad, with a glance of mournful indulgence. He loved her because she spoke Greek with him and he brought them two coffees without being asked. '*Metrio*, *kyria* Persephone.' And she thanked him. Thomas loved to hear her speaking Greek – there was a husky, liquid tone in her voice, reserved for that language.

'I expect Francis will be back,' she said, as they left the restaurant. 'He promised he would be.'

'You rely on him a lot.'

'He's like a brother,' she said.

'Francis is everyone's brother,' he replied. It felt a magnanimous thing to say – and safe.

In the cab going back, she said, 'I thought you might like Floy's gardening books and her notebooks. She was very fond of you. I'm sure she would have liked you to have them.'

'I'd love to have them. I got to love her too, you know.'

For the first time in the evening she turned to him impulsively and pressed his hand. 'I love other people to miss her.'

He longed then to take her in his arms, but didn't dare.

Later, lying in bed, he relived that moment, her eyes shining with spontaneous warmth, her hand on his, and he felt all was not lost. It *was* just a question of time.

FRANCIS

After three weeks of intensive searching, he found a large, dilapidated maisonette on Muswell Hill, whose owner, an Italian engineer, was frantic to sell quickly as he was about to go abroad. After two more visits, one with Percy, he knew he wanted the place. It was in an Edwardian family house and had six large rooms and french windows on the ground floor that looked on to a long, narrow garden; one of the upper rooms faced north and would make a decent studio. He didn't mention to the owner that in ten days' time he would be homeless – would either have to rent somewhere or, if it was free, return to the seedy little flat in Pimlico. Percy would also be homeless. She still hadn't made up her mind about Jordan, had asked him once if he would go with her, but he felt it was a bad idea and nothing more had been said about it.

On their third meeting Signor Pasquini had come up with what seemed to him initially a mad scheme. If he would sign legal paper to say he would buy flat and pay a deposit, he could move in and pay rent until the deal was closed. How about that? 'Then you move today – or now if you like. This would suit all.'

He thought long and hard for about two minutes before he agreed to it. It was the first place he'd seen that was just within the price he had got for his old flat when he'd sold up to move to Home Farm, and the money from France would go some way towards decorating and repairs. Of course there was a risk but, like everything else he had in mind, it seemed worth taking.

He got back to Maida Vale, excited to tell Percy all this. Thomas had, that morning, finally left for Melton and his nursery, and he found her in the conservatory alone with Marvell on her lap.

'I can't possibly go to Jordan,' she said. 'I can't leave him.'

'Well, you'd both better move in with me. Just as a temporary measure. If you like.'

'I suppose I could help you get things straight. And we could take some things from here, like chairs and beds.' It sounded grudging, but he saw the relief that flitted, for a moment, over her face. 'And we could fit a temporary cat door for Marvell.'

'It'll be the first thing we do.'

At supper that night, she said, 'One thing is worrying me rather – Thomas.'

'His being in love with you?'

'He's so – intense about it. He wants to marry me and all that.'

'Well, at the moment, I don't suppose you want to marry anyone.'

'No. But he seems to think, in the end, I will. He said something like that just before he left.' She waited a moment but he said nothing. 'I asked him if he'd told Floy and he said yes, and I asked him what her reaction was. She apparently said it wasn't her business, it was mine. But he thinks she was in favour of it, really.'

'Well, she was right, wasn't she? It only matters how *you* feel.'

'Yes . . . but I've come to feel I just don't know much about being in love. And Thomas seems so *sure*. He says he feels just as he did about Celia. I'm so relieved he's not here. Not being able to talk to Floy about it makes it so much worse.'

'It doesn't really,' he said gently. 'I mean, you know what Floy thought. It's your business.'

★

The last evening before they had to leave the house, she asked Francis to go round the garden with her. It was a fine bright evening; the air was sharp with a suggestion of frost. They walked slowly and in silence up the winding path past the tobacco and clematis, still sparsely flowering, through the yew arch and past the stone lions, the roses now brilliant with hips and the white, pink and purple borders of Michaelmas daisies to the small pond and the bench where Floy had died. She stood for a moment, then indicated they should sit. She broke the silence by saying, 'I haven't been out here since she died. And the new people will sit here and they won't know, will they? To them it will just be a nice garden seat with a view.'

'Gardens and houses must be full of that kind of thing: histories unknown to their owners.' After a pause he said, 'Adelaide Villa – I expect someone called Adelaide died here and whoever built the house for her sold it to people who knew nothing about her.'

'People don't really live on after they die, do they? Unless they leave something behind. Floy always said gardens don't last unless people preserve them, and that doesn't happen often. I suppose people who have children leave them behind, but Floy only had gardens to leave . . .' She paused. 'And me.'

He took her hand and held it. 'Yes, you. You *are* a part of her legacy.'

'It's awful how you can love someone so much and think you know them so well, and be wrong – be unaware of the most important things about them. There was someone she loved, who really loved her, and he was killed in the First World War. I found the letters in her desk. She never told me. And I never realized how tired she was – if I'd known I could have stopped her working. I didn't know.'

He put an arm round her. 'Loving someone doesn't mean you can organize their life for them. You loved her and she knew it.' He wiped the tears from her face with his fingers. 'You aren't responsible for her death. If you start thinking that, you're just making less of her, and perhaps too much of yourself. You can love other people, but you can't *be* them.'

On the way back to the house she stopped by the stone lions, stooped and stroked them.

'Do you want us to take them?'

'No. They were here when the new people saw the garden. She wouldn't approve of our moving them now.'

Marvell met them at the top of the steps, wondering urgently if they realized nothing had passed his lips since lunch time.

'You'll have to make do with a tin,' she said, as he wove through their legs.

'He won't be alone. We're down to baked beans and the remains of the bacon.'

Later, as they finished their frugal supper, he said, 'If you've decided not to go to Jordan, don't you think you should tell your father?'

'Yes, I should. I'll write to him. I'll tell him I can't go away now, but would like to stay with him later. I don't want to hurt his feelings.'

He had emptied the drinks cupboard, the dregs of several bottles – Tia Maria, Campari, cooking brandy and a sickly sweet sherry that had, she said, always been there in case it came in handy for something.

'What'll you have?'

'Campari? Oh, there's no soda water. I don't know.'

'I'll make a cocktail. There's still some ice left.'

He got a jug and poured various drinks into it with all the ice that was left and several slices of lemon.

'It ought to have a grisly little umbrella sticking out of it,' he said, as he poked a finger into the mixture to taste it. 'Mm. Unusual. Not bad, actually. I drew the line at the sherry. Think of it as a superior cough mixture,' he added, after a cautious swig.

'I haven't got a cough.'

'No, but you might feel one coming on if you don't drink up. You'll soon get used to it.'

They both had a go.

'I think it could grow on me.'

'Awfully slowly. Oh, Francis, it's so good being with you. I don't know how I could have got through all this without you.'

'Well, you didn't have to. Don't start being grateful, it'll only make you cry. It's been fine for me. I love being needed.' He smiled at her, and after a moment, she smiled back.

They had two drinks each, then gave up, and he poured the rest down the sink.

'We should have an early night. Tomorrow is going to be a very busy day. The movers come at nine. I must say, I'm glad you're coming too, Percy. It would be rather dreary moving into that huge flat on my own.'

He could see this pleased her.

'Yes, but I promise I won't just become a fixture. I'll only stay until I've got a job and then I'll find somewhere.'

'Or you decide to marry Thomas?'

They had reached the first floor, and were standing outside Floy's room, and she turned to face him, suddenly, unexpectedly, angry. 'I don't want to talk about that. I don't even want to think about it.'

'All right. It's not my business, I know.'

'No, it isn't.'

'I'm sorry, Percy – sorry I brought it up.'

'OK.' She softened. 'I'm accepting your apology.' She leaned towards him and kissed his cheek. 'Good night.' And that, for then, anyway, was that.

JACK

She had looked so tired and strained when she joined them for lunch that he was almost cross with her: he so much wanted to show her off to the Blunts, and she wasn't looking her best at all. Her face was puffy, with mauve smudges under her eyes, and instead of the rather charming plait at the back of her head, she'd scraped her hair into a loose bun from which tendrils kept escaping. She wore an old corduroy skirt and a faded washed-out darker blue shirt with palpably frayed cuffs. He was afraid she'd look dowdy and dull to his friends as at first she made little effort to please or attract attention from any of them. But as lunch progressed, he could see that Wystan and Amelia liked her, and she was certainly good with the children. Hatty, by contrast, was extremely sociable, though she complained early on about her appearance. 'Mary made me wear it,' she said, in reply to Amelia's compliment. 'I loathe and detest dresses, but she made it for me so I'm forced to wear it. But at least I've got proper tights,' and she lifted her skirt to show that this was indeed so. She was fascinated by the twins, and they in turn were thrilled by an older child's attention. Juan had put them together at one end of the table and waited on them with ferocious indulgence, pouring apple juice into grown-up wine glasses for them, and when one of the twins wept because of the bread sauce – 'Slimy white. I hate it' – he whipped away the plate and transferred the chicken and vegetables to a clean plate with the chicken cut up, while Hatty told them about ponies and tropical fish.

The chicken was followed by meringues and chocolate ice-cream, designed for the children, but he noticed with pleasure that the food and wine seemed to revive Mary, who was in animated discussion with Amelia about the relative merits of private as opposed to state education. The weekend had gone well. He had invited Rosalie, after all, and her father for the Saturday-night dinner party, so he felt he'd provided enough society for Wystan and Amelia, and they'd spent the day touring the gardens and visiting Stonehenge, which the twins had thought very boring, as – privately – did he. But it was an outing. For the rest, the twins had brought their tent with them, which Wystan had helped them to pitch, and they spent hours in it, fortified by snacks brought to them by the devoted Juan. As soon as lunch was over, they took Hatty with them to see it. 'You'll have to take it down,' Amelia warned. 'We have to leave very soon.'

And so, while she was packing the car and Wystan had gone to deal with the tent, he was alone with Mary.

'I will marry you,' she'd said, 'if you still want to.'

For a moment he was overwhelmed – exultant, awkward with triumph – at getting this last thing that he wanted, that had seemed so uncertain of success, and had therefore become steadily more desirable. He'd won. She'd accepted him and he was overcome by a relief so powerful, with an odd, hot stinging in his eyes – a sensation unknown to him until now – that he stood before her speechless, until he was finally able to say, 'Yes. I do want that, Mary. Mary,' he repeated, using her name as an endearment.

They were standing outside on the steps, in full view of the others dismantling the tent on the lawn, and as he moved towards her she put out her hands to hold him at arms' length. 'Only one thing. Please could we keep it a secret until Thomas is back? I want tell him myself, not have him hear of it.'

'Of course. Anything you like.'

'Only for a little while. Just till he comes back.' Her smile was a plea.

'You think of everyone before yourself, don't you?'

'It means I shall think a great deal about you.'

The tent crew on the lawn had finished, and they were tramping towards the cars in front of the house.

'I must say I think I ought to have a tent, Mary. I'm much, much older than them and I've never had one.'

'We'll see. Thank Jack for lunch. We've got to go now.'

One of the twins burst into tears when they discovered Hatty wasn't coming with them, and then, as usual, the other joined in. 'I'll see you again in a few years, I'm sure,' Hatty said, clearly delighted they liked her so much. Goodbyes were said and she and Mary left. He helped the others stow their luggage and waited with Wystan while the twins were taken to the lavatory. 'You've got lovely neighbours,' he said. He longed to tell Wystan about Mary, but he'd promised.

When they'd gone, he went back into the house, but not with the flat feeling he usually had when people left. The future was at last arranged, the house inhabited, and he would become husband to the most excellent and considerate wife. There would be children. He spent some time imagining them; two boys and two girls, he decided, would be the perfect number. But before that, after they were married, he would take her somewhere exotic and exciting where she'd never been – Rome, perhaps, or the Bahamas, anywhere she wanted. He'd spoil her, make her buy beautiful clothes and give her everything she seemed never to have had. It struck him then that the point of his struggle to be rich was simply to have more to give. And at that moment he felt he'd have given anyone anything, but now he needn't, since he could give it all to her.

THOMAS

I had to leave her in the end. I'd stayed far longer, really, than was fair to Mary, and Percy was going off to stay with her father for a bit, which is a good thing, I think. I'd done everything I could think of to help her with leaving the house, and Francis was there. It looked like he might've found a place to live and said, if there was a hiatus between leaving Maida Vale and her flight to Amman, she could always stay with him. I'd been pushing my luck, really, by hanging about. What she needed was time and, I thought, time without me so she could recover a bit more.

I could tell, also, I irritated her sometimes: my concern for her was clumsy and, worse, even a bit feeble and I provoked frustrated icy asides from her. Then she'd start to be heartbreakingly kind and polite, which upset me more than any flashes of temper. The gap between my love for her and the depth of her mourning seemed insurmountable. Shamefully I even got sort of resentful. I *really* cared for Floy. If she was alive now, I'm sure things would be very different – if only she hadn't died just then. Her sudden death, when I wasn't even there to help darling Zephie through that first awful night, was, well, unlucky, to say the least. I know it's a bit callous and selfish, but that's what I felt – feel.

So I had to go. She'd given me Floy's notebooks, her sketches and designs for gardens, with plant listings and several dozen reference books. 'I know she would've liked you to have them,' she said and, trying not to read too much into it, I'd said how much I'd treasure them. The night before I left, as Francis went out to fetch some fish and chips, she helped me pack the books and sketches into two boxes and we were alone together. I knew her father had sent her an open air ticket, but I didn't know when she was going – 'Very soon, I expect,' she said, when I asked her. She said it in a way that invited no further questioning and everything seemed too fragile for me to persist. We sealed the boxes with brown tape, and I lugged them into the hall. I knew Francis would be back any moment with the food. This would be my last chance to say anything private and I desperately needed to be sure she knew – really knew – I loved her. So I said so, said I'd wait; she should take all the time she needed, but I'd always be there for her. The words seemed so inadequate, so dull and weak compared to how I felt. All the time I spoke I was longing to touch her, to take her in my arms, to comfort and soothe and shelter her, to ease her sadness with my love. But it came out like a formal proposal, and a corny one at that.

She was leaning on the chest in the hall, propped up by her hands, the sleeves of her dark jersey pulled up so I could see the delicate slate-coloured veins that ran down to her wrists. She didn't look at me until I'd finished, then said, 'Did you tell Floy about this?' and I said yes, and she said, 'And what did she say?' and I told her she'd said it wasn't her affair, but that I'd felt she was in favour of it. She was looking at me now, and after a moment's silence, she said, 'Thomas, thanks. I'm truly sorry to be like this. I just – am.'

'I know. It doesn't matter how you are. It will all come right.'

And then Francis came barging through the front door with the fish and chips and that was that.

They both saw me off in the morning. I took a cab to the station because of the books, and they helped me get everything into the taxi. Then, just as I was about to get into the cab, she touched my arm, leaned towards me and kissed the side of my face. 'I do thank you so much for all your help. Please give my love to Mary.'

I sat all the way to the station touching the part of my face she'd kissed. If the immediate future was hard, leaving her for a while was nothing compared to the rest of our lives. She would surely never have kissed me if I meant nothing to her, and to mean anything at all was enough. All the way back in the train I thought of that.

MARY

The relief of having made the decision to marry Jack was extraordinary. It was— It must have been right because she felt so clear, so immediately released from the hopeless passion that had consumed her for so long. Such unreciprocated love had obviously made her feel wretched and worthless; the only scrap of self-respect was the fact she had never told him, he had never known. Whenever she reflected how nearly she'd done that, she imagined the humiliation of his embarrassment and kindness; not to be borne, but she would have had to bear it.

She'd escaped all that, could afford now to sweep it away. The future, with Jack, lay before her. She was wanted, needed. She'd seen the tears in his eyes when he'd repeated her name – had wanted then to throw herself into his arms, but she also thought of Thomas. He had to be told before anyone else and Jack seemed to understand that.

He'd called her the night after the lunch party, after Hatty had gone to bed. 'I suppose I can't give you the ring now?' he'd said, and she'd promised she'd wear it when she was with him. For a few days they'd met while Hatty was at school. Once he'd taken her all over the house, wanting to know which room she'd had as a child, and they'd stood in what had been the nurseries, now transformed into an elaborate guest suite. She remembered the chipped painted furniture, the cracked lino-leum, the holland blinds that would snap up when you tried to pull them down, the two ceiling lights with their milky glass shades and, at opposite corners, the two little iron bedsteads in which she and Thomas had lain at night listening to the mice, whose feet, Thomas said, sounded like loose bootlaces on the linoleum. She looked now at the luxuriously appointed uninhabited room and could think of nothing to say. 'You don't like it,' he said. 'We can make it just how it was if you want to.'

'Oh, no. It was pretty basic. I don't remember much about the rest of the house, but we spent a lot of time here. I mostly remember how cold it was.'

By now scraps of their past lives were being offered as tokens of intimacy. Twice he'd called for her and taken her out to lunch, and once, after the second, he'd kissed her, a tentative, nervous kiss that moved her more than his confidence could have done. She was beginning to feel how difficult he found the expression of any feeling, how lonely he must always have been, and to realize how the failure of his marriage had shocked him. 'It was my fault, really. I married her for the wrong reasons – had no idea what I was getting into.'

'She was a blonde, you know,' he said later, as though that explained one of the wrong reasons.

'And you?' he said, during the second lunch. 'Have there been people in your life?'

So she told him about Adrian and how that had come to an end after Celia had died. 'He was just somebody I went to concerts with, really. I lost touch with him when I came down here to look after Thomas – and Hatty.'

'And that's been your whole life? Looking after Thomas and Co?'

'Yes.' She didn't want to tell him about Francis. One day, perhaps, she would, but it was too soon. She wouldn't now, she felt, be able to tell him in the right way.

'I suppose he'll miss you a good deal, won't he?'

So she told him about Thomas being so much in love with

Percy, just as he had been with Celia. 'It's why he's been away for such a long time because, of course, poor Floy dying has made everything more complicated.'

'Well, I'm going to enjoy looking after you – and Harriet, if she wants to come.' He picked her hand up with the pretty ring he'd given her. She wore it when they were alone. He noticed she'd taken to putting cream on her hands and they were gradually looking less workworn by the day. 'I don't think I've met anyone as good as you,' he said, 'so gentle and kind and unselfish. You've changed my life.'

In those few days he talked about the future. He was going to cut down on work, he said. They would travel; he'd take her anywhere she wanted to go. They could have a flat in London, if she liked, so they could go to concerts and theatres, and when they had children, he'd buy a place in France or Italy where they could spend the summer holidays. He was experimenting with endearments; she'd become his dearest Mary.

Keeping their engagement secret, principally from Hatty, had become a delightful game. Their meetings and phone calls had all the more allure for being illicit. The second time he kissed her was different for both of them: there was nothing tentative on his part, no mere fondness on hers. Eventually he drew away from her and, holding her shoulders, looked intently into her face as if he was seeing it for the first time, and she, trembling, trying to smile as her eyes filled, felt she'd never seen him before.

'I love you,' she said, and for a moment, he closed his eyes as if receiving a blessing, but he was trying not to cry.

'I've never – nobody has ever said—'

She put her fingers on each side of his face to stroke him dry.

'I love you,' she said again and this brought forth a flood of endearments. He loved *her*, had been falling in love with her more and more, ever since she said she'd marry him; he'd never felt like this in his life – she was his darling, his love, his sweet,

sweet girl, his beloved Mary. 'When you told me that,' he said, minutes later, 'it was almost too much, but I believed you – at once.'

They'd been walking in the gardens, had reached the large glasshouse with the ancient vine – now pruned and once more producing quantities of grapes: it had been repaired and reglazed, and the staging contained neat rows of geranium cuttings. They went in to see if there were any grapes left, and she recalled sitting there while Thomas, on the rotting stepladder, hunted for some and ruminated on his possible career, and she had asked what would become of her. Marriage, he'd said, and she'd replied she wouldn't marry anyone if she didn't love them; he'd told her his secret plan that he would make his fortune and she could live with him at Melton. She remembered how she'd cried with delight. And now she was in love with Jack, and the house was his and she was going to live in it – but not with Thomas.

'I think we've had them all. Mary? Where have you gone to?'

'I was just remembering coming here with Thomas when we were children.' She said no more about it.

At lunch he asked if there was any news on how Thomas was getting on with Percy and she said she didn't know. 'But he's coming back the day after tomorrow.' He'd rung yesterday evening, and for some reason – she wasn't at all clear why – she'd put off telling him.

'That's good. Then you'll be able to tell him.'

'Not the moment he gets back. I need to know his plans first. About Percy and everything.'

'Well,' he said, after a moment's disappointment, 'I'm sure you'll know the best time for that.'

Later, after they'd had lunch and he was driving her home, he stopped the car and said, 'There's something I feel I ought to tell you. I don't know why I haven't before, but now there's nothing I want to keep secret from you. I once asked Percy to marry me, and she turned me down. I was rather depressed about it at the time, but I know now I didn't love her. I just thought I ought to get married.'

'Like you felt about me?'

He looked at her with an attempt at indignation, then laughed. 'Oh dear. Well – a bit like you at the beginning, but not really, even then. Anyway, thank God she rejected me. I might have gone through my whole life without understanding the point of it. I would have missed you.'

'And Thomas would have missed Percy.'

'Yes. We should all have lived unhappily ever after,' he finished jubilantly. 'What shall we do tomorrow then, our last secret day on our own?'

'Tomorrow's tricky. It's my day for teaching and then I have to do a huge shop, and there's Jimmy Peabody to oversee a bit. I've been rather bad at keeping up with the house and with Thomas coming back . . .'

'Perhaps I could help you with the shop.'

'No, because I've got to pick Hatty up and take her to a friend's birthday party.'

'I could meet you back at the farm, come to tea in a decorous manner – darling?'

'All right. About five.' She couldn't resist him.

And so the next day he helped her unload the car of a dozen carrier bags filled with household supplies.

'Do you do this all by yourself?' he asked, when the bags were in.

'Usually.' Francis used to help me sometimes; she was able to think of it without a pang. 'Not always.'

She made tea for them and it was then she managed to tell him he mustn't ring her once Thomas was back; she would ring him. He agreed: 'It won't be for long, will it?'

'It won't be for long.'

Before he left, he kissed her until she was faint with wanting him.

'Oh, Mary, could you come tonight for a while? I can't bear to leave you like this. I want you so, so much, my darling.'

She shook her head. 'There's Hatty coming back. I can't. You know I want to, but I can't.'

She went, with his arm round her, to his car. 'You do love me?' he said, as he got in.

'I do love you – with all my heart.'

She watched him drive away, out of sight, before she turned back to the house. How extraordinary, she thought, to be so happy and also to feel so sad.

★

'So, good old Lady Yoxford. If it hadn't been for her I wouldn't have known about the job, and even if I had the new Yoxfords might not have taken me anyway.'

'It's partly good old Hatty too, you know. Lady Yoxford has got very fond of her as she's such friends with Betsy.'

'Well, good old Hatty as well, then. But, Mary, think of it. It's on a par with what Floy did up at Melton, and Percy gave me her notebooks so I can use them for this. I've done some measuring already, but I'll have to take Jimmy up there to do it a bit more accurately, and then I can get down to drawing, which will have to be to scale, and then they want an estimate – that's the worst part. Young Lady Yoxford was quite beady about that.'

'And you'll have to find labour for it.'

'I know. But Floy found people, so it must be possible. I've taken Jimmy on full time, which is a start.'

'Oh, Thomas, can we afford to?'

'We'll be able to. This job's worth a fortune.'

Ever since his return he'd been full of energy and plans. She hadn't known him so animated for years. On the first evening she'd asked after Percy and he'd talked of her far into the night, until she had the whole story of Floy's death and Percy's grief. 'She lost everything so suddenly. She was – she still is in shock.' He described the funeral, ' . . . that man at Melton, Jack whatever-his-name-is, sent the most amazing wreath of freesias, which Percy said were one of Floy's favourite flowers.' He told her then that Percy's father had sent her money and invited her to the British Embassy in Amman and that he thought it was good she should go. 'She kissed me when I left this morning. She sent her love to you too. So, you see, I know, I absolutely know, it will be all right in the end. I've just got to be patient, and God knows, I'd do anything for her – and she knows too.'

His shining eyes, his energy and determination infected her. Of course it would be all right in the end. She almost told him then about Jack and herself, but it was very late and there would be plenty of other good moments to do that.

And there were, but for some reason she didn't take them. A week went by and she had no chance to see Jack. There were a few brief, snatched phone conversations that became increasingly tense. 'I can't see why you don't just tell him,' he said, and she heard the irritation in his voice. 'I've got to go out to Dubai for a few days. Maybe it's better I go now.' And she agreed, grateful for the respite.

He called her the next day as she was helping Thomas to pin his scale paper to a drawing-board on the kitchen table.

'I'm off tomorrow morning, probably for three days, but possibly a week. Are you alone?'

'No.'

'Well, you didn't call yesterday and I wanted you to know. Do you love me?'

'Yes.'

'Well, I shall break the rules and ring you from Dubai when I know about my return. OK?'

'Fine.'

'Please tell him by the time I get back, please, darling, do that.'

'All right.'

She rang off.

'Who was that?'

'Just someone from the school.'

He's not interested, she thought bitterly. He's only fretful about *his* love and *his* life. It doesn't occur to him I might have my own love, my own life. And she very nearly told him then and there, but she couldn't bear to when she was angry with him.

One evening Francis called. It was a shock to hear his voice again and it caught her completely off-guard. She didn't know what to say so she asked if there was any news from Percy in Jordan and Francis told her she hadn't gone after all and was staying with him. She felt uneasy, troubled, even cross – no, angry: angry for herself and angry for Thomas. Of course Percy should have all the time she needed, but she could at least tell Thomas where she was. Was she avoiding him? She'd rung off rather brusquely, as Thomas had come in just at that moment and she didn't know what to tell him. She decided to say nothing and suddenly realized she had no idea where Francis was living.

That week was one of the hardest of her life. Thomas roped her in as a kind of lieutenant to work on the rough estimate for the Easton Park gardens and when she wasn't cooking, ferrying Hatty about or teaching, she was fully occupied with looking up plants, costing them and, in the case of trees and hedging, helping him to incorporate them in his design. In the evenings, after supper and when Hatty had been urged to bed, he wanted to stay up and talk about Percy.

'Do you think I should tell Hatty?' he said, one evening. 'After all, it will be a huge change for her – a stepmother and all that.' But she said she thought he should wait. As she was going to bed, he called, 'Someone rang up from Dubai while you were out. I thought for a moment it was Percy, but it was the wrong country. Just a wrong number.' I'll tell him tomorrow evening, she thought. It's Hatty's night to stay with Agnes, so it'll be a good time.

She went to bed that night, thinking of Jack and their marriage, and had just reached the point where she was showing him their first child – a fantasy she had recently been indulging because every time it enveloped her in a mist of happiness, of safe and lovely joy she felt would be even more marvellous than she could imagine – when sleep overcame her.

She drove Hatty to school the next morning – 'I can't possibly take my games things and my pyjamas on my bicycle' – and afterwards went into Melton to the fishmonger where she bought half a dozen scallops – Thomas was particularly fond of them – and then to the supermarket, where she bought all the other dull things that were needed. The last time she'd done such a comprehensive shop Jack had helped her get the bags out of the car. And the next time she saw him, she would have told Thomas about them and she'd be free.

There had been a frost, and now there was a pale violet sky and a silvery yellow sun that shone without warmth, gilding the puddles on the road, turning the drops of water caught in the cobwebs in the hedgerows into glittering beads and behind them clusters of red hips and darker hawthorn berries. She drove slowly so that she could take note of all this.

She parked the car near the kitchen door and staggered in with as many bags as she could carry. She had to dump some to open the door and there was Thomas, slumped at the kitchen table, his head in his hands, shoulders heaving. He glanced up when she shut the door and at the sight of his white, anguished face her heart skipped a beat. She immediately thought he'd lost the job at Easton Park, but realized in a second it was something much worse. As she went to him, he held out a piece of paper clutched in his right hand. He was unable to speak.

Dear Thomas,

I should have written this before, or perhaps I should have known and been able to tell you. I didn't go to my father's, but stayed in London with Francis. I can't marry you, because I know now I don't love you in the way you'd want, and I shall never feel like that. I thought this was because I was too miserable about Floy to know what I felt about anything, but I know now it wasn't that. I'm so sorry to have taken so long to tell you this. I've got myself a job editing travel books for a new publishing house. It's quite small, but the people who run it are very nice, so I'm recovering some bits of my life. I do hope so much you'll do the same. Please believe me about this letter. I wouldn't have written it if there had been the slightest chance that I'd change my mind. And I'm sorry to cause you the slightest unhappiness.

Yours most sincerely,

Persephone

'You see? You see what she says? Oh, Mary, how can I bear it?'

As she put her arms round him, he was racked by an intolerable sobbing, and pity for him engulfed her. Celia, she thought. It's all to be gone through again.

FRANCIS AND PERCY

'So what do you think? I don't want to bind you in any way. It just seems silly for you to have a mortgage when I could pay for half the maisonette and then you needn't have one.'

She was kneeling on the floor putting a top coat on the skirting-board of the large kitchen-cum-sitting room and now sat back on her heels to see his reaction.

'It sounds like a good idea,' he said cautiously. 'But suppose it doesn't work and you want to move out?'

'Well, then, I suppose you *would* have to get a mortgage. But probably so would I. It's a wholly practical idea. Unless you want to live alone,' she added.

'No. I don't particularly want to do that.'

'And we do get on with each other, generally speaking.'

'We do.'

'We could have a contract. In fact, we *have* to.'

It was funny, he thought. Some days he made tentative moves towards a more permanent arrangement and she was noncommittal; now she was suggesting it. Best way, really. After all, it wasn't tying either of them down, which they'd both agreed was a bad idea.

It was a Saturday. Three days a week she now went to the publisher she was working for, and he, well, he did a whole load of different things: worked on the flat; enrolled himself for an evening life-drawing class; put ads in the local papers offering professional portraits of children or landscape-painting classes by an experienced artist, at weekends on Hampstead Heath or at the flat. He also went round small local galleries with his canvases, trying to get a show, and in between these forays he painted. None of his efforts had produced a result so far, but it didn't worry him much. He drew Percy a good deal – studies of her cooking, washing her hair, up a ladder as she picked out the paint from the egg-and-dart frieze round the main room, sitting at her worktable reading typescripts, and one of her asleep on the old sofa from Maida Vale, which he used to make a fully fledged painting.

Percy seemed much better. She could talk about Floy without crying. She seemed to enjoy decorating the flat with him, and there was no sign of her wanting to leave and find her own place. The last really sticky time had been about Thomas. A few days after they'd moved he had rung Mary one morning when Percy was out. In some vague way he felt he had left the farm rather too casually, left her without much thought. She was launching into a whole new future. Why hadn't she told him about Jack Curtis earlier – sought his advice, like the old days? He wanted to make it all right, would suggest coming back for a weekend if they'd like him to.

The conversation was uncomfortable, prickly in some way. She seemed at once agitated and reserved, but she asked at once if he had news of Percy and how long she was staying with her father, and when he told her Percy was fine, hadn't gone to Jordan but was staying with him and had got a job, she'd stammered something incoherent and stiff about Thomas and rung off. He thought about it all morning. Thomas had left Maida Vale, thinking Percy was off on a nice holiday and would then come back to him. He *would* think that, because it was clearly what he wanted so much. And Percy had left the whole matter open. That evening he tackled her.

'Have you thought any more about Thomas?'

She was chopping onions for a stew and didn't answer him at once.

'Have you?'

'Thomas? No. I haven't thought about him at all.'

'Don't you think you ought to?'

She put down her knife and turned to him. 'If you want me to go, I will – honestly. Just say so. Don't wriggle around about it.'

'Percy, I'm not talking about you staying here. I'm talking about Thomas. He's in love with you – remember? He thinks you're with your father. He thinks you're sorting out how you feel about him.'

'I know. I know he thinks that.'

'All I'm saying is, if you know you don't love him back, don't want to marry him, you ought to tell him.'

'I don't feel I'm going to love him. But he's had such a sad life. I can't bear to hurt his feelings.'

'Do you mean you might marry him simply because you're sorry for him?'

'Of course not. That would be terrible. He'd know and it would hurt him more than anything else.'

'Well, then, you have to tell him. Don't let him go on hoping – that will hurt him most of all.'

There was a silence and she said, 'Of course, you're boringly right. I just don't know how to face him.'

'You could send him a letter. It might be best, because then he'd be clear. No room for him to think you didn't really mean it. If that *is* what you mean,' he added.

'It is.' She said it sadly.

⋆

She spent the rest of the evening writing it. The first draft was about four pages and when she showed it to me I thought it was too long, and that, in trying to save his feelings, she hadn't been clear enough about her own. I drew her while she wrote.

The second attempt was more like a telegram and unduly brutal. She made me look at what she'd written, like a child producing homework. She's only four years younger than I, but sometimes she seems much younger. The third effort seemed to me just right, but she cried while she was writing it and blotted the paper. 'I feel so awful when I think of him reading it,' she said. I gave her a hug and told her she'd got it right and all she had to do was copy it. We had scrambled eggs for supper as we'd both forgotten about the stew.

She sent the letter and we heard no more. But, then, she hadn't put any address on it and I was disinclined to ring Mary again: cowardice, I suppose. I was afraid of what she might tell me, but I felt I'd done my share of picking up the pieces and, after all, Thomas is her brother, not mine, and the fact Percy's living with me would only complicate things. I decided to leave it for a bit . . . until things had settled down, anyway.

After we'd had the conversation about sharing the flat everything seemed much easier, except that I wasn't really earning a living and my money wasn't going to last for ever.

We finished the huge living-dining-kitchen room in the end. We painted the kitchen end, north-facing, a strong Chinese yellow, and the living end, south-facing, what Percy called duck-egg blue.

'Idiotic name for it. It's robins' eggs that are blue, ducks' are a sort of dirty greyish white.'

We started a new game in which one of us described a colour in interior decorators' terms and the other had to guess what it actually meant. Percy kept the score. I won with Dowager's Neck – 'a sort of suffused plum' – and she said crossly that she hadn't met any dowagers so how would she know?

We spent a whole weekend dragging bits of furniture and crates of books down from the third bedroom on the floor above where we'd dumped almost everything from Maida Vale except the beds and kitchen stuff. This room, which is eventually going to be my studio, is the largest and faces north, looking on to the small rectangle of our derelict garden. For the time being, I'm painting downstairs in a cramped sort of way. We had to shut Marvell in there for a fortnight because we had plumbers refurbishing the small and rather horrible bathroom and Percy said on no account must he be able to get out or he'd go back to Maida Vale. She used to bring him down in the evenings to have supper with us. To begin with he sulked, but in the end his enforced imprisonment made him value our society. He's getting old but has made it clear he's prepared to lower his standards for a bit more freedom. He took to sleeping on Percy's bed and when eventually we fitted a cat door for him in the french windows at the kitchen end of the big room he started using it at once.

'He's used to a much better garden,' Percy said, when he went on his first outing. She sounded sad. 'I think we ought to make it nicer for him.' So we went out and bought some apple and pear trees. We had Floy's gardening tools and planted them together. They're surrounded by weeds and the remains of a ragged lawn, but it's a start.

We'd settled into a kind of island life together. There was always plenty to do in the flat, and once a week we'd go to see a film and eat dinner out. Otherwise, we spent little, except on materials for decorating. It wasn't unlike the life I'd once had with Celia before she married. Percy seemed content to come home to me without making loads of new friends, and I, while I met gallery owners and such like, never felt the need to know them any better. I enjoyed her company; I loved watching her, her small darting movements when she cooked – seizing a knife, rubbing flour and fat together for pastry, decorating a tart with olives and anchovies – or lying barefoot on the old velvet sofa with a book. She always reads with an intense enjoyment that shows on her face and I love the way she wriggles her toes at certain moments. When she laughs, her eyes are like horizontal emeralds; they go round and cloudy when she cries. Often she absently twists a strand of her dark hair round and round one finger until it's taut against her head. They're mostly Floy's books she reads: Victorian and turn-of-the-century novels. Her bedroom, when we eventually papered it, is hung with Floy's pictures – her Brabazon watercolours, Edward Lear landscapes and, her most prized possession, a Gwen John drawing of a cat.

One day she came back from work to say she thought she had a commission for me from her publisher. 'Only they want to see your work. I thought if we asked them to dinner they could see things here. It's to draw the author of this book I've been editing. I suggested a drawing instead of a photograph, and said it was just your thing. They won't pay you much, but it's a start.'

So we did. They were partners; Percy didn't know if they were married because she used her own name. So Hubert and Jenny came into our lives. They arrived with a bottle of wine and a bunch of anemones. I guessed they were both in their forties, she was small, with a round face and short dark hair, cut with a fringe that barely kept out of her eyes; and he had the air of faded nobility that meant you could see what he'd look like when he was old. He'd inherited a large house in the West Country that he couldn't afford to live in, so he'd sold it and bought himself a narrow-boat moored somewhere on the Grand Union Canal where they now lived. He'd sunk the rest of his capital into launching their own imprint, Cockatoo Books. 'It's our first list,' Jenny said. 'We're after books of a more social and domestic nature. We think readers are always interested in how people lived – what they ate, what they wore, how much they travelled, how they dealt with disease and death, all that. Some novelists tell us a bit, others hardly anything. Sorry, I do go on about it – I expect Percy's told you anyway.'

She hadn't much; all I knew was that she was editing a book about food with lots of letters and excerpts from handwritten cookery books with marginal notes about the likes and dislikes of guests. The author, it turned out, was a retired doctor who'd spent eight years on his research, had submitted his work unsuccessfully to ten publishers, one of whom was known to them, and she had sent him to Cockatoo Books.

By now we were well into Percy's Moroccan lamb stew. 'So that will be our start. Alongside a marvellous novel called *A Book with Seven Seals* that has been out of print for ages, although Percy knew it, didn't you?'

'It was one of my aunt's favourites. That and *Lark Rise to Candleford*. She used to read it to me at bedtime.'

For a second nobody said anything, and then Hubert said, 'Lovely stew, Percy – never had it before.' So they knew something about her, I thought, and began to like them there and then.

After the pudding, a winter fruit salad, they asked to see some of my work. I had photographs of drawings I'd done of Hatty. And, of course, there were the studies I'd made of Percy. They were gratifyingly enthusiastic.

'The thing is,' Hubert said, 'we wouldn't be able to pay you much and we'd want you to design the whole jacket for us. It's Percy's idea to have a drawing instead of a photograph of the author, but we've also decided we need to make the jackets uniform, so people will hopefully recognize the imprint.'

'Yes, we're starting out a bit like Virginia and Leonard Woolf, mail order straight from the office, except for a few small bookshops that have expressed interest. And we'll be putting ads in as many of the literary magazines as we can afford.'

'Jenny does that part of it. I've never been very good with the money side.'

'You've never been the slightest use at money.' But she said it fondly.

By the end of the evening I'd agreed to do a jacket. Hubert was very taken with the painting of Percy on the sofa and said he wished he could buy it, but Jenny asked where he would put it in the boat. 'Anyway, we must be getting back. Enid will be wondering where we are.'

'It's his father's cockatoo,' Percy told me, when they'd left. 'He inherited her along with the house. He doesn't like her much, but he can't send her to a zoo, because she's used to company. She comes to the office sometimes – they've made a perch for her there because she so loves Hubert. She doesn't like women, though. She bites Jenny and me if we give her a chance.'

'Well, thank you for getting me the job, though if he'd bought the picture of you, it would have been more like buying a Mini than a Rolls.'

'They've got a Mini.'

'Well, selling one, then.'

'You were a great success,' she reported the next evening. 'They thought you were my brother.'

'I hope you disabused them.'

'I did. But you are, really, aren't you? In a way?'

'In a very small way.' For some reason I felt resistant to the idea.

'I feel so comfortable with you and that's how one feels about brothers.'

'Or friends,' I said. 'Serious friends.'

We were clearing the table and stacking stuff on the draining-board.

'That reminds me,' she said. 'We haven't drawn up our agreement.'

'I don't think we need bother with that, do you?'

'Not if you don't think so.'

'I don't.'

'You're sure? I don't want you to feel trapped.'

There was a pause while she lifted Marvell off the draining-board, where he was busy confirming that he intensely disliked apricots. Then – taking a risk – I said, 'I quite like feeling trapped.'

I could see her considering this, and saw a faint colour rise, the nearest she ever gets to a blush, and she said, 'Well, I suppose we're still choosing, aren't we? We can choose to be not trapped . . . or trapped.'

'We can both choose whatever we like.'

She gave a small sigh – of pleasure? Relief? 'Anyway, it's good we both feel the same.'

'Absolutely.' I wondered then, and for a while afterwards, if this was true.

MARY, THOMAS AND JACK

When his first paroxysm of misery had spent itself, he became frantically determined to go to London to find her – to reason with her, to beg her to give him the time he'd been happy to give to her. Mary pointed out there was no address on the letter and they had no idea where Francis was. He just said he'd have to go to the Maida Vale house where they must have left a forwarding address, and failing that, he'd somehow find the publishers she now worked for. 'Sorry to have caused me the slightest unhappiness,' he quoted bitterly. 'She just doesn't *understand*.' He wept like a child, like Austen's Marianne Dashwood after she'd received the offensive letter from Willoughby, she thought, endlessly rereading Percy's letter, stunned afresh each time and then dissolving into bursts of tempestuous misery. She tried to comfort him, but gently discouraged him from trying to find Percy, who, she was sure, meant what she had said in her letter. Inwardly she was shocked that a grown man could relapse to such a degree but, then, he wasn't any man: he was her brother whom she had protected and loved all her life. Thank goodness, she thought, that Hatty was away for the night. It gave her some time to help him over the worst of the shock. She made some coffee and got him to drink it while she fetched the rest of the shopping from the car. When she heated some soup for their lunch he sat with the bowl in front of him in dead silence and didn't touch it. She suggested they should do some work together on the Easton Park design, but he said his head ached and he wanted to lie down for a bit. She gave him a couple of aspirin and he went upstairs.

To be alone was a relief of sorts, but although she forced herself to carry on with household tasks, it meant she had her own anxieties to deal with. She couldn't tell him about Jack now. She'd have to see him through the worst of this calamity. There was Hatty to be considered, too. What should she tell her and when? And how would Jack take a postponement of their marriage? Why, oh, why couldn't Percy have loved him? Love brought out the best in Thomas. He would have been a devoted husband and become his old self, as in the days of Celia. It seemed so unfair that somebody who had suffered as much as he had, who'd only, she realized now, fully recovered from Celia's death when he met Percy, should now have a second blow, and this one almost worse. Percy had never been his, was alive but unattainable. Of course he was shattered by it. She had to put her own happiness on hold, be patient. She had loved him all her life and he would recover. Time and patience were what was needed.

Both were sorely tried that evening. He came down while she was cooking dinner and went immediately to his study from which he emerged with a bottle, three-quarters full, of whisky.

'Want one?'

'I'll just have a glass of wine.'

He poured it for her, then half filled a tumbler with whisky, which he topped up with water from the tap, then sat at the table to drink it.

'I've been thinking,' he said. 'If I write to her at the Maida Vale address, I'll have no way of knowing if she gets the letter or not – that's the trouble.'

'No, you won't.'

He drained his glass and poured himself another slug.

'But if I actually went there, then either they know her address or they don't. And if they don't I start on the publishers.'

'Thomas darling, I really don't think it's a good thing to do. Percy meant what she said. It can't have been an easy letter to write and she wouldn't have written it unless she truly meant it.'

She put the supper on the table and sat opposite him. The fragrance of rice and scallops steamed between them.

'You think I should just do nothing? Just lie down and give up?'

'I think you have to accept it. And now you've got to eat. Just do one thing at a time.' She put the food on a plate and handed it to him, then helped herself. 'You pour the wine.'

He finished his second whisky and poured the wine.

'I think I was wrong now to be so restrained with her. All those weeks I was longing to take her in my arms and kiss her – to sweep her off her feet – and I didn't because I thought she wasn't ready. The frustration! Mary, you can't imagine what it was like seeing her every day, so beautiful, so enchanting, and then, when Floy died, so desperate . . .'

All through the meal he talked about her and she listened and urged him to eat, with only minor success. He finished the wine, went back to the whisky and reread the letter, which he kept in his pocket. 'Do you suppose she'll stay with Francis?'

'I've no idea. Why? Do you think he's in love with her?'

'Good Lord, no. She treats him like a brother. Anyway, I don't think Francis has ever been in love with anyone. Celia once told me she thought he was queer, but unable to do anything about it. You know Francis. He's never shown the slightest interest in women, has he, in all these years?'

'No.'

'No, I don't have to worry about that. Anyway, I told him

how I loved her and he'd have said something then, wouldn't he?'

'I expect so.'

Round and round he went, mourning the loss of her, blaming himself, searching for any way to change the situation. It was like a bleak merry-go-round with no chance of getting off. He became steadily drunker and more repetitive, till he started accusing her of not understanding him. By ten o'clock she could take no more and announced they were both going to bed. He seemed compliant and she helped him upstairs to his room. He was unsteady on his feet and, at his request, she got him some more aspirin because his head was bad again, three this time as she wanted him to sleep. She offered to help him undress, but he said he could damn well do that, thank you very much. She waited until he had downed the pills, then left him on his bed fumbling with his shoes.

She was exhausted. Nothing is so tiring as unaccepted comfort. She had done what she could and it seemed of no avail. Her head ached and she was drained of all feeling, as dry and light as a dead leaf. She wanted nothing but oblivion and no sooner had she got into bed than it came.

She woke very suddenly. It was still dark, but there had been a sound from below in the house – a crash, a slam of a door? If it was windy, she might have thought a window had blown off its latch, but there was no wind. Someone breaking into the house? That had never happened before. She sat bolt upright in bed and listened, but there was nothing to hear. Her alarm clock said half past six. She could feel her heart thudding – why was she so frightened? It was very cold and the silence seemed menacing now. In the dark she put on her dressing-gown and opened her bedroom door. Her room was at the end of the passage, furthest from the stairs, but she could see at once that the lights were on below. Thomas's door was ajar, but the room was empty.

At the head of the stairs she could see the kitchen table, the empty whisky bottle and a glass anchoring a piece of paper.

Dearest Mary,

I'm truly sorry to do this to you but I can't go on without her. I've lain awake for three hours now trying to find some other solution, but there is none – at least none for me. I shan't 'get over it', 'find someone else' or any of the things you so kindly suggested. I know you'll look after Hatty, as you always have. You can't know what it is to love someone as I've loved, do love her, to do without somebody who's the whole meaning of life to me. I know people say that doing away with oneself is an act of aggression: not in this case – for me it's just an act of total despair.

Thomas

It took her seconds to read this and seconds more to understand the noise that had woken her. The back door past his study slammed shut automatically if you didn't stop it. She went to his study. The gun he kept for shooting pigeons and squirrels had been taken from its slot on the wall. She ran back to the kitchen to find the torch. She'd heard no sound of a shot – there was still time, though she had no idea how much. The cinder path led to a five-bar gate, which opened on to the nursery and its plantations of young trees.

'Keep away. Don't come any nearer.'

He was standing by the further gate that led to the back road where customers parked their cars.

'It's Mary.' She walked steadily towards him.

'I left you a note, Mary. For God's sake, leave me alone.' She shone the torch full on his face and continued to walk. 'Put that damn torch down.' He put up his arm to shield his eyes. 'Why are you making this even more difficult for me?'

'If you'll put the gun down, I'll tell you.'

'Stop where you are, then.' But he didn't put the gun down and she continued forward until they were a few yards from each other. 'I really don't want to do this in front of you.'

'I should hope not. You said it wasn't aggressive, but it is.'

They were a yard apart now. The gun was hitched under his right arm.

'I told you in the note, Mary. I can't go over it all again.' He sounded weary.

'You didn't tell me – you didn't tell me how to explain to Harriet, your daughter, *Celia*'s daughter, that her father has killed himself because he loved someone more than her. You didn't think what it would be like for me. Perhaps "selfish" is a better word than "aggressive". Don't you realize I love you? Hatty loves you? For God's sake, put that gun down and talk to me.'

Then, surprisingly, perhaps because she had produced the right note of pure exasperation, he laid the gun on the ground.

'If only you hadn't turned up like this, it would all be over.'

'You should be very glad I did. Have you even thought what it would've been like for Percy?'

'What do you mean?'

'How she would've felt when she discovered her letter had resulted in you killing yourself? I thought you said she'd had enough to bear as it is, without this to deal with for the rest of her life.'

'No . . .' he said slowly. 'I hadn't thought of that.'

There was silence between them and she was gradually aware that she was shaking with cold.

'No,' he repeated at last. 'I hadn't thought of that.' He sighed deeply, more moving to her than anything he'd said or done before, and bent down to pick up the gun. She held out her hand to him and led him back to the house.

They stopped in his study as he put the gun back in its rack on the wall, but it wasn't until they were in the kitchen that he exclaimed, 'Mary – your feet! You've no shoes. You've hurt yourself,' and she realized it hurt to walk and they were bleeding.

'I'm just very cold,' she said. Her teeth were chattering and she sank into a chair. What followed amazed her. He fetched a coat from the rack near the door and draped it over her shoulders. He filled the washing-up bowl with hot water and put her feet into it. He put on a kettle and made tea, then knelt by the bowl, examined each foot, and from one extracted a thorn. 'Better without that,' he said, holding it up for her to see. 'You shouldn't go out barefoot – you of all people should know that.'

She tried to smile at him. She didn't want to cry and certainly she couldn't say that if she'd stopped to find shoes she might have found him too late. 'I promise not to do it again,' she finally said. She was trying to remember when he had last been so solicitous, so gentle and outwardly affectionate, but memory failed her.

They agreed to try to get some more sleep. He had dried her feet on a tea-towel and then they went up together.

'At least I have you,' he said, as he bent to kiss her cheek, 'and I *do* thank you for reminding me about Percy. It would have been wicked to cause her such pain.'

'Undress before you go to bed,' she said, and he said he would.

In her bed in the dark, tears poured from her, ran between her breasts, and it occurred to her that in saving his life she might be losing her own, but she was too exhausted to consider it.

In the morning she rang Agnes's mother and said that she thought Thomas was coming down with flu and it would be most kind of her if she could keep Hatty for a couple more days until he was over the worst of it.

★

'You say he's been back a week now and you still haven't told him. Darling Mary, what on earth's going on?'

'I'd rather not tell you on the phone. It's just that . . . things are quite . . . rather difficult.'

'Fine. Let's meet. Shall you come to me or I to you?'

'I'll come to you.'

'Can you come now?'

'No, I—'

'Well, this evening, then.'

'No.' She was thinking desperately, trying to find some safe slot when she wouldn't be missed or needed. 'I'm teaching at the school tomorrow morning and I could skip lunch there.'

'Good. I'll take you out.'

'What I'd really like, Jack darling, is if you could just bring a sandwich and we could meet at that place where we often stop to look at the sunset, you know, our place . . .'

'If that's what you want. What time?' She told him.

'I've missed you. Going away has at least shown me that.' There was a pause and then he said, 'Have you missed me?'

'Oh – I *have*.' She could see Thomas getting out of his car in the yard. 'I've got to go. See you tomorrow – one fifteen.'

The week had been one of the most difficult in her life. While Thomas made a heroic effort to work, eat the food she put before him, avoid, by and large, drinking too much whisky and take an interest in his daughter, his heart wasn't in any of it. He alternated between apathetic obedience to what he called her 'rules' and a sullen, often self-pitying misery.

Hatty wasn't deceived. 'You know what I think is the matter with him?' she said. 'He doesn't have a best friend. Agnes's dad has one and they play games and kill things together and Agnes says it's a good thing because it means her mother can have a nicer, more interesting time. I think a best friend really has to be of the same sex so it's no good you being it for him. Poor Dad. He seems very gloomy and thin since he came back from

London. Do you think it would be a good idea if I suggested it to him?'

'I don't know, darling. You could try. Why don't you get him to teach you to play chess? He used to love it.'

The evenings, after Hatty had gone to bed, were the most difficult. All he wanted to do when they were alone together was talk about Percy, wonder where she was and if she'd find someone else to marry, and how he'd be able to bear it if that happened. Sometimes he simply wept and then she'd put her arms round him; there was nothing to say. On the worst evenings he simply got drunk, slumped in front of the television news, staring blindly at whatever it chose to present to him. She removed all the ammunition kept with his gun, but still, however tired she was, she didn't dare to go to bed before him.

Mornings were always better. He went off to the nursery and worked with Jimmy Peabody, and he accepted that she had to go to her school to teach. Those were the days she'd leave lunch for him and Jimmy, and he knew she wouldn't be back until she'd fetched Hatty from school. She'd chosen the best time to meet Jack.

He was waiting for her and the sight of him almost running towards her car filled her with an unexpected pleasure that submerged everything else that had so beset her. In a moment she was in his arms and they were kissing with hunger and delight, a mutual bliss followed by incoherent endearments, his hands on her hair. The scent of his skin made her almost faint with a delectable blend of love and desire, and the joyful certainty that he felt the same.

The sandwich she'd asked for was an unexpected full-blown picnic: 'We'll have to eat it in the car. It's too cold to sit out.'

He'd brought his Land Rover and they sat in the back with the food on the seats in front of them. Champagne, chestnut soup in a Thermos, slices of game pie, chocolate mousse in little white pots and a bowl of clementines were laid before her, all – she could tell from his face – designed to surprise and charm her. When he'd poured the champagne he lifted his glass and said, 'To you, my dear, dearest Mary. And may I never have to be so far from you for so long ever again.'

Looking at him, her heart was too full to respond. She touched her glass to his and they drank.

'Such a feast,' she said.

'You deserve a feast and, more, you look as though you need one. Tell me, what's been happening?'

So she told him. About the letter from Percy – 'I'd planned to tell him that evening and came back and found him with the letter.' She tried to describe Thomas's devastation, but even as she told him, the words seemed inadequate.

'Poor chap,' he said, in much the tone he might have used if she'd said Thomas had broken a leg.

'He's not like most people,' she said. 'He's only ever been in love once before and that was with Celia.'

'He got over it, though, eventually, didn't he?'

She said yes, but didn't point out that it had taken almost eight years and the appearance of Percy. Eight years sounded ominous, even to her then, and she desperately wanted his understanding, his sympathy. 'He's like a character in a Russian novel,' she said. 'You know – intense, almost violently romantic.'

'I haven't read any of them. Isn't there a chance she might change her mind?'

'I'm sure she won't. I saw the letter. So, you see, I just couldn't tell him about us then. He's heartbroken.'

'I can see you couldn't that night,' he said. 'But now, surely, I mean, you have to tell him some time.'

So then, although she'd not meant to, she told him about that first night and the gun, and how she had just prevented Thomas killing himself. She could see this shook him, but it was chiefly for her sake.

'My God. He might have turned it on you. He must've been out of his mind.'

'Yes. That's what he was – is. But he would never have turned the gun on me.'

'Oh, my darling, what an awful time you've been having.'

'It hasn't been easy.' Against her will, her eyes filled with tears. Instantly he put down his glass and put his arms round her. 'My poor, poor Mary. It must've been terrible. I'm so sorry. You mustn't cry. It must've been terrifying.'

He got his handkerchief and tenderly wiped her face. 'There. Blow your nose and have some soup.'

The soup was hot and comforting and she began to feel better.

'It sounds as if he should see a doctor,' he said. She paused before replying; the thought of trying to get Thomas to a doctor for anything was daunting. She said, 'I don't think doctors are much good at broken hearts.'

'Oh, I don't know. They might give him something to help him sleep at night – tranquillizers. You've got rid of the gun, haven't you?'

'I've got rid of the ammunition. But I don't think he'll do that again.' Not in that way, she thought, but there are others.

'Well, that's something.' He refilled their glasses. 'I've had an idea. How about I talk to him?'

'No.' That certainly wasn't the way. 'I don't think it would be a good idea at all,' she said. 'He'd feel I'd betrayed him.'

'But we can't go on like this. Secret meetings, as though we're doing something wrong. If he loves you surely he'd be pleased you're going to have me to care for you. Unless he's so wrapped up in himself, so selfish he doesn't care about you.'

'I think very unhappy people are selfish. They *do* get wrapped up in themselves.'

There was an uncomfortable silence. Then, he said, 'So, what *do* you propose?' The coldness in his voice hurt her.

'I've got to give him some time.'

'How much?'

'Jack, I don't know. I only know I've got to stand by him through this. I'll tell him the moment I think he's able to take it, to understand.'

'So until that happens, I can't even ring you. I can only see you when you've an odd moment to spare, and our life, our plans are all delayed.'

'You talk as if you think I want it to be like this. I don't. I hate it. I want to be with you. But we have everything and he has nothing.' She wanted to say 'except me' but desisted. She was aware that dangerous ground was opening between them – a kind of no man's land that couldn't be safely trodden.

'At least we both feel the same.' His tone was gentle again. By a mutual but unspoken consent they said no more about Thomas. He asked about Hatty, of whom he was fond, and she asked him about Dubai. She didn't really want any more lunch, but managed to eat enough of the pie and the chocolate mousse to mislead him. They finished the champagne and they kissed.

'We're like teenagers in the back of a car,' he said, as they gradually regained the love and desire with which they'd begun their reunion.

MARY AND JACK

'Thomas darling, there's something I have to tell you. I've fallen in love with Jack Curtis and he wants to marry me.' No, that wouldn't do – too sudden. 'Thomas. I know this will come as something of a shock, but I've actually found someone I want to marry and he wants to marry me, and luckily it's all very local so I shan't be far away.' No. That didn't sound right either.

For the last three weeks, she had stretched out her arm in the freezing dark to still the alarm clock and had lain full of frenzied determination to end the miserable stalemate where nothing she did or said seemed to be right. The strain was worse because the circumstances weren't static. Things oscillated as Thomas seemed, if not better, at least more reconciled and Jack became by turns more urgently demanding, more despairingly irritable.

Their meetings were curtailed by the weather: frosts had set in. It was too cold for picnics in the car and they'd taken to meeting in a gloomy little pub well outside Melton. But they'd fallen into a pattern she'd begun to dread. At first they'd be delighted to be together, but that would rapidly degenerate into his questions, his cross-examination of the situation with Thomas. Sometimes she was able to say she thought he was getting better; more often than not she couldn't. She was painfully truthful about this. But when she tried to explain how awful, how difficult he'd find it to be left alone when he was so unhappy, Jack exclaimed, 'But I'm all alone – now.' And she'd look at his incredulous, angry eyes and say he had her and she loved him; she truly loved him. In the end, when they were going to have to part anyway, he'd usually reconcile himself to more patience.

And so the weeks had gone by. Thomas alternated bouts of feverish activity on the Yoxford contract and despair. Sometimes he drank too much, though he was careful to wait until Hatty had gone to bed. The evenings were what she had come to dread most. If Francis were here, she thought, there would at least be someone else for Thomas. A perverse thought: not long ago she would've wanted him there purely for her sake; now it no longer mattered. He'd been so good with Thomas when Celia died; if he had been here now, the effortful strained suppers with the three of them round the table would be less edgy.

'I don't want to play chess with him,' Hatty had said to her yesterday. 'He lets me win like I'm a baby.'

'I don't think he does.'

'Well, in that case, he doesn't care whether he wins or not. You can't have a good game with someone who doesn't care about winning.' One evening she'd asked, 'Couldn't we ask Francis for Christmas?'

'It would be nice, but he's moved house and we're not sure where he is.'

'Why didn't he tell us? I suppose he just forgot.'

One day when she got to the usual pub where she was meeting Jack, she found he'd left a note for her.

Sweetheart,

Had to go to clear up some muddle about building permission for land in the Algarve. Darling, I'm sorry to tell you like this, but if I can't ring you up, it's the only way. See you same time next week.

Love, of course, and all of it,

Jack

Then, later that week, she found something that really shook her. The tweed jacket Thomas wore most days had worn through at the elbows and she had bought some leather patches to mend it. The pockets were bulging with bits of paper, used handkerchiefs, a pen that had lost its top and leaked into the lining. As she pulled this detritus out, she came across a bulging envelope, only lightly sealed. Something made her undo it and two small bottles of pills fell out. They were Anadin, and both unopened. For seconds she stared at them trying to find a reasonable cause for them being there, but she couldn't. For a moment she was overwhelmed by sheer rage, and worse. If he wanted to kill himself, who was she to stop him? He was betraying her and she'd been trying so hard to save him. If he killed himself, which he clearly wanted to, why struggle against it? If he succeeded, she'd take Hatty and they'd all live happily ever after. But this callous nonsense, the unlikelihood of it, immediately hit her: how could she possibly be happy if she allowed the brother she loved so much to die?

It was then that she realized fully she could no longer have it both ways. She could save Thomas or she could marry Jack, but not both. This horrible realization sank painfully from her mind into her heart and she was paralysed by its enormous simplicity.

JACK

He had sat at the small corner table they always had and watched her get up and walk out, push the swing door with 'Saloon' etched in the glass panel and go through it. She didn't look back. The door swung to and fro after she left, less and less, until it stopped. He heard her car start outside, but didn't look up to see it. From the moment she'd arrived, brushed her cold cheek against his, he'd known something was wrong. But it hadn't helped him deal with it.

'I can't marry you,' she'd said, with a steady finality that chilled him to the bone. He'd kept his head, he thought, at that point.

'Can you tell me, precisely, why not?'

'I'll try. I just can't abandon Thomas to live on his own. I can't see any way in which I could leave him to that.'

'But you've been telling me for weeks that all he needed was time.'

'I know. I was wrong. I'm truly sorry to be so wrong.'

'Mary, you've been telling me all this time that you loved me.'

There was a silence then as the waiter brought their sandwiches and two glasses of Guinness.

'Telling me you wanted to marry me, wanted our children, wanted to live – with me.'

'Yes.'

'You've been lying to me?'

He saw her flinch, but she answered steadily, 'No, I've never lied to you – about anything.'

'Then I don't understand. You say you love me, want marriage and children, but you have to give it up because your brother can't sort out his own life. Darling, can't you see, at least, this is a bit mad?'

'I can see it must appear rather like that. But I also love him, you see. I've loved him all of my life. I can't abandon him to despair.'

'You love him more than you love me. That's becoming particularly clear.'

'Oh, Jack, no. It's not like that. He's Hatty's father.'

'So, he wouldn't be alone, would he?'

'I can't leave a nine-year-old with a father who drinks too much and is liable to kill himself.'

'He does sound attractive, I must say.' He was angry now; fear he would lose this fight had ignited to rage.

'I've discovered you can't change someone to make them lovable. You just have to love them whatever they are.'

'Well, it's clear you can never have seriously loved me. I suppose it was the good life that attracted you. You *have* lied to me, really – strung me along, hoping, I presume, you could somehow have it both ways.'

'Oh, I'm afraid I did think that, the both-ways part, I mean. And I'm sorry. I don't know if it makes it easier for you to know that I do love you – it isn't at all not loving you—' She couldn't go on for a moment. She picked up her glass and swallowed some beer. 'I didn't know any decision could be as hard as this. But I've had to decide. Please believe that.'

She looked at him then and for a second he recognized, though it seemed strange, that she *did* love him. But how could she give him up for a drunken dependent brother, a life of domestic slavery, rubbing along with never enough money. If she really loved him surely she'd have had the courage to face this wretched brother – for God's sake, he'd never heard of any man going to pieces because he couldn't have the woman he wanted. She must just need to be a martyr. She didn't seem to realize she was ruining his life. Perhaps she wanted him to plead; for a second he entertained the idea.

'Mary, I can't believe you realize what you're doing. You look like you haven't slept for days. What you're telling me now is so bizarre. I just can't believe you mean it. I know you don't.' He reached across the table and took her hand. It was ice cold. 'I think you've made yourself ill with worry.' His ring was on her finger – a sign of hope. 'Look. You still have my ring. That tells me what you really want.'

But she withdrew her hand, took it off and laid it on the table. Her eyes were large and blurred, as if she could hardly see him.

'I have to give it back to you. I can't marry you. I'm so very, very sorry.'

He regarded her intently, the quiet way in which she spoke. The steadiness of it finally reached him – he'd thought a moment earlier she might cry – and he knew he'd lost her. He, who all his life had known how to get what he wanted, had lost what he wanted most of all. He was possessed by a cold bitterness, a desire to wound her, a hatred of this person who had exposed him to feelings he hadn't known existed – then betrayed him.

'You'd better keep the damn ring. It will remind you of the good life you've missed. I must say, for someone who talks about love, you don't seem to know much about it. The loyal spinster sister is what you've turned out to be. Good luck to you.'

At that, she made an inarticulate sound and got to her feet.

'You *will* find someone else,' she said – he could hardly hear her. 'You *will* find someone and you *will* be all right.' He looked up at her. 'Thank you. I'll keep the ring,' she said, and put it back on her finger. Her hands were shaking. And then she left and her absence rang in his ears like silence.

For a while he sat there, stunned, senseless, as though he'd been hurled into a terrible void, a changeless dark in which he became nothing, would very soon cease to exist.

He became conscious that he'd been staring at the two plates of untouched sandwiches, the two glasses of Guinness, his half drunk, hers nearly full. He finished his and, after a pause, he picked up hers. There was a small mark on its rim where her lips had been and, seeing it, he was seized by a pain so intense he felt giddy – had to shut his eyes. It died away and he looked once more at the glass before deliberately draining it. He stood up, went to the bar at the far end of the dark little saloon, paid for the meal and went outside. He need never come back to this place, he thought, as he unlocked his car.

Driving back to Melton, he realized he'd taken the road to the place where he and Mary had picnicked and changed his route, a longer way round, but that didn't matter now. She was something he had to get over.

The road he took, he discovered, went past Richard Connaught's cottage and, on impulse, he decided to stop and offer Rosalie the driving lessons she'd so wistfully told him she couldn't afford. It would put off going back to the house for an hour or two – and he'd nothing to lose. 'I've absolutely nothing to lose,' he repeated, trying to present this state as a triumph, a freedom, an exit from a position he would otherwise neither be able to deal with nor endure.

THOMAS

That last conversation with her had shaken him. 'You have to start living your own life again,' she'd said. It had made him see with an awful, shaming clarity what it must be like to live with someone who banged on about how miserable they were. Supposing it was the other way round. Supposing it was she who was unhappy and went on and on about it. How would he deal with her? The fact that nothing of the kind had happened to her was beside the point. He'd constantly accused her of not understanding him, but he knew, because she loved him, that she did. He could see now that these last weeks he'd worn her out with his desolate ruminations and self-pity, and had noticed how strained her face was – at times actually sad. It wasn't fair that he should make her suffer on his account.

He'd been shutting up the polythene tents for the night – there would be more frost. The sky was cloudless and dark and the moon, nearly full, was rising behind the black branches of the immense beech on the far side of the house. He watched until the ribs of spectral illumination changed as it rose above the tree and cast a general silvery light that sharpened all objects – the trees, the house, the gate leading to the car park – in return for an unearthly lack of colour. A fox barked, breaking the night silence, and the sky was beginning to be pricked with stars. Then, perhaps because he had been standing so still, an enormous bird swooped past his head, so close he could feel the air disturbed by the rush of its wings, and landed on the fence a few yards away where it stood, motionless. The barn owl, seldom seen, but identifiable by the surprising sounds it sometimes made, a screech, a wheeze or a gurgle, had arrived for a night's hunting. Seeing it gave him intense pleasure; there was something both rare and reliable about it. The owl, or its descendants, would be here always.

As he turned to go back to the house, he remembered how Mary had come, barefoot in the dark, to stop him killing himself, and how, when they got back to the house, he'd been overcome by her courage, the shock he'd caused her, and had tried to make amends. But I haven't done much of that, he thought, either before or after. He'd always known she loved him, but he wondered now if she had much reason to feel he loved her. Resolutions, both remorseful and extravagant, crowded in. At least, he thought, I can make a start with some of them.

MARY

'What's the difference between a weasel and a stoat?'

They were halfway through Christmas dinner and Hatty had suggested that as there were six crackers they should pull one each before the Christmas pudding and the other three afterwards. She was extremely deft at getting the business end, and now had two. She wore a yellow and red paper crown and was consulting the pieces of crumpled paper from within.

'Come on, Dad.'

Thomas, after apparently deep thought, said, 'A weasel is weaselly distinguished and a stoat is stoatally different.'

'You've heard it before. Well, what did the earwig say to the beetle as he fell off a cliff?' A satisfactory silence. 'Earwigo! That's a bit silly, isn't it? I bet earwigs can't talk to beetles – they wouldn't have the same language. Quite funny, though. *Quite* funny.' She clearly didn't think much of it. 'You should put your hats on, you two.'

They put them on. Thomas's head was too big for his dunce's cap, Mary noticed, as she pulled on her white chef's toque. Soon, it would be time to light the candles, heat some brandy in a big spoon and pour it over the Christmas pudding she'd made last year. Then they would retire to the sitting room where the small tree, weighed down by its glittering decorations, stood on a table with the presents. Once they'd been opened there would be some respite from the ritual. A piercing whistle interrupted her. Hatty had found one in a cracker.

'What can I use it for?'

'Useful if you had a dog.'

'Dad, I haven't got a dog.'

'I keep forgetting that.' His eye met Mary's with a conspiratorial gleam. He's enjoying his surprise, she thought. He's actually enjoying something. And felt a surge of affection – and hope.

'If that one had a whistle, there must be something in my other cracker. Oh. A ring. Oh, Mary, my first ring.' It had a silvery hoop set with a bright red stone. 'Not as nice as yours, Mary, but pretty nice for a cracker.' She put it on a finger and gazed at it lovingly.

Involuntarily, Mary glanced fleetingly at Jack's ring and began clearing the plates.

'I'll do that. And *you* can help me,' he said to Hatty. He's really trying, she thought, as she warmed the brandy.

When the pudding had been eaten – Hatty got a horseshoe and a threepenny bit – Thomas went to light the candles on the tree next door, and Hatty helped her with the washing-up.

'All ready,' he called, before they'd finished. She knew he was impatient to get to the next step.

There were seven presents under the tree and Hatty was frantic for them to open hers to them first, so she did. She'd bought her father a tie striped in purple and yellow 'because you don't seem to have any, Dad'. She searched his face for an expression of delight and gratitude.

'It's lovely,' he said.

'You really and truly love it?'

'It's perfect.' He never wore ties. He put it on now over his jersey.

She had knitted Mary a muffler in multicoloured wool. 'I did it all in secret at Agnes's. It isn't absolutely straight because I kept getting more stitches, but when it's on, I don't think it'll show.

I've been knitting it for ages.' It was indeed long and undulated like an exotic snake. Mary put it on at once with a suitable expression of pleasure. 'I thought the colours would make you happier,' Hatty said, as she received her hug.

Mary had made Thomas a Guernsey sweater of a beautiful Tuscan red. She remembered, when they were both far younger, how much he'd loved having good clothes. He was pleased, she could see. For Hatty she'd bought a locket on a chain, because Agnes had one that Hatty deeply admired and this, also, went down very well. There was also another more surprising present to come. The seventh present was from Francis, her godfather – a book token for five pounds and a card he'd made with Greeny Hopper on it. Last Christmas he'd been with them, she thought, glancing at Thomas for any sign of distress, but he had something else on his mind.

'What about your present for Mary?' Hatty said.

He felt in his pocket and produced a bulging brown envelope. 'Not much good at wrapping things up, I'm afraid.'

It contained a worn dark green leather box. Inside it, slung on a thin gold chain was a locket, turquoise enamel set with a single rose diamond.

'It opens, Mary. It was a secret, but I knew about it. It opens both sides.' The front opened to show a tiny photograph of a young, radiant Thomas. The back displayed a minute plait of golden hair.

'I gave it to Celia when Hatty was born.'

'It's my hair, Mary, but she cut it when I was much older and plaited it herself.'

'You do like it?'

Looking across the room at him, she could see that he really wanted to know – cared about pleasing her; she saw his anxious expression relax to complacency as she admired and thanked for such a lovely present.

'Dad? You haven't given me anything.'

'Nor have I. Must have forgotten. Hang on a minute. I'll see if I can find something.'

He went to his study and, after some delay, returned with a white shoebox. 'There.'

She opened it and inside was a small black-and-tan puppy, its bulging round eyes looking up at her with immediate devotion.

She was speechless for a moment; then, as the puppy tried to scramble out of the box, she took it in her arms and a great deal of mutual and enthusiastic kissing ensued. 'It's the best present I've ever had in my life. What kind of dog is it? Has it got a name? Can we take it for a walk? On a lead?'

Mary had decided they couldn't afford a pony for Hatty after all. She'd made a list with Thomas of the things the puppy would need and he'd hidden them in the old pigsty, in the playpen Hatty had had when she was a baby. She watched them bringing it to the house, lining its floor with newspaper and consulting a booklet *How to Train Your Puppy*.

'Oh Dad. It's so thoughtful of you,' she heard as she went upstairs, and as she turned back to look at them, Thomas winked at her. It had been her idea he should give Hatty the puppy and it was clearly bringing them together – a real success on all counts. 'Have a good rest,' he said, after the wink.

'Yes,' Hatty called. 'You deserve it; you must be tired after all that cooking.'

Mary thought back to the time a few years previously when Hatty was cast as one of the Wise Men in the school nativity play. 'You can wear your beard at home, if you really want to, but I'm not taking you Christmas shopping in it. That's flat.' She smiled to herself as she reached her room.

She was always tired. Her room was cold so she switched on the electric fire and drew the curtains to shut out the darkening winter sky. She *was* always tired, but sleep at night was difficult. In the first few days, she'd been haunted by him, by knowing her decision was both painful and incomprehensible to him. 'Darling, can't you see, at least, this is a bit mad?' And then, later, 'I must say, for someone who talks about love, you don't seem to know much about it.' Well, I'm finding out, she thought, as she climbed wearily under the bedclothes – her back had been aching lately.

After she left him, she had driven very slowly, almost as though she was drunk, to the place where they'd had their autumn picnics and stopped there because she was blinded by tears, besieged by a storm of grief and, in the anguish it brought, she'd heard herself crying aloud, 'Oh! Oh! No!' as she'd rocked to and fro, almost as if someone might hear and rescue her. If she'd had to die for this, there would have been an end to it, but it wasn't like that. She had to go on. Supposing I can't? she'd thought. Can't go through with it? Go back to him – tell him I was wrong – want him too much? She'd given herself a final chance to choose love and, as she had known she would, rejected it once more. She had wept herself dry, used up the box of Kleenex she'd brought and had then driven home. The house was empty when she returned – she had been lucky there. It gave her a chance to wash her face in cold water until it resumed more recognizable proportions.

Now, lying in bed, she thought of the last time she'd had to change her life: when Celia died, when Thomas was an inconsolable wreck and Hatty a much bereft child, and how, after a short while, Francis had come into their lives and together they'd forged a family life. She'd come to love Francis for the difference he had made, had – it seemed extraordinary now – imagined, fancied herself in love with him, but looking back on it she saw it was the consequence of affection, convenience, her desire to have something for herself and there'd been no one else in sight. Fantasies, alluring as they could be, were like a conversation conducted by only one person. She hadn't allowed it to occur to her that he didn't feel as she did. The pain she'd suffered had been self-inflicted – it all seemed distant now. She missed Francis, because he was so good with both Hatty and Thomas, and she could think of him with a fondness she knew was mutual – no fantasy there. It was sad he wouldn't be with them for a time, but he was doing what she knew he did best: helping yet another person over their loss.

She felt both tired and restless, wanted to sleep, but couldn't.

These last weeks – nearly five now – she'd struggled through the seesaw evenings with Thomas. Sometimes he'd play chess with her, or discuss ways in which they could make a little more money, watch the news on television, plan what bedding plants they were going to seed for next year, but more often he would relapse into endless, repetitive rumination about Percy. On one of those evenings she'd been unusually brisk.

'You have to give her up, Thomas. I know it seems awful, but that's what you have to do. You have to start living your own life again.'

This had provoked a stream of objections. She could have no idea what it was like to be in his place, to love someone and be hopeless. If she did she'd be sorry for him.

She'd hesitated before replying. 'It's difficult to be sorry for someone so sorry for themselves. Have you ever thought of that?'

That had startled – unnerved him.

'But, Mary, you love me – I only want you to understand.'

'I do understand. And I do love you, but sometimes you make it hard work.'

'Yes,' he said slowly, 'I can see that. I do try, you know.' Then, and she could see it was with the utmost effort and some incredulity, he said, 'And I expect I'll get over it . . . in the end.'

He'd walked over to the sink where she was drying the supper things and put his arms round her. 'After all, I have you. I've always had you – the next best thing.'

'To fall back on,' she said, after he'd kissed her. She didn't know whether to laugh or to cry.

With Hatty, she thought, it was easier, easy to show calm, cheerful interest and pay attention to her curiosity and play. One day when they'd got home from Hatty's Christmas shopping – the tie for Thomas, a small stuffed owl for Agnes as 'she's afraid of owls and I thought this might make her get used to them', Hatty suddenly said, 'Do you believe in God?' A question that surely required an honest answer.

'I'm not sure, darling. Why do you ask?'

'I just wondered.' She thought for a minute. 'I think it's safer to believe in Him. I mean if He's there, He'd notice if you didn't believe, and if He isn't, it wouldn't matter anyway.' Then she said, 'But I suppose He'd know if you just believed in Him to feel safe, and it wouldn't count then. Are we not going to see Jack any more?'

A shock. She'd shut her eyes for a moment. Her mouth went dry. 'No . . . not for a while. Maybe not at all.'

There was a short silence. She'd turned to look at Hatty and met a gaze full of anxiety and sweetness. 'That's sad for you,' Hatty said. 'It's why I mentioned God, because He's supposed to make people happy.'

No more was said, but she knew, somehow, that Hatty would never talk about Jack in front of Thomas again. That night, when she went to say goodnight to her, Hatty said, 'I *do* love you. Terrifically, enormously, gigantically, gargantuanly . . .' She ran out of words and fell back on a strangling hug, and as Mary was enveloped by a cloud of toothpaste and Vinolia soap, some of her misery, the secrecy and isolation of it, dissolved.

Children, she thought, as she lay there, are never one single age – never entirely five, or six or, as Hatty was now, ten. They leapfrogged over the years, both behind and ahead, with disconcerting ease; a talent lost at some point by adults.

It was when she was alone, as now – with no distraction of duty – that her heart ached, sometimes her whole body ached for him. It would have been their first Christmas together. Perhaps he'd had those nice friends she'd met to stay – he wouldn't be alone. She looked, for comfort, at her ring. She had taken it, held on to it, because it was the first thing he'd given her, the only possession she had except the note she'd been given at the pub. All pride, all notions of acceptable behaviour, had left her that last time. She'd simply wanted, desperately, to keep the ring. It was a comfort, a challenge, a kind of talisman, a reminder of what she must do. He – she knew this to be true – would find someone else to love and when he found them, she would, in some way, be forgiven.